ABDUCTED

WEAPON OF WAR

BOOK FOUR

ALETHEA STAURON

WEAPON OF WAR SERIES, BOOK FOUR
ABDUCTED

Printed in the United States of America

Written by Alethea Stauron

Edited by Adele Brinkley

Cover Design by Emily Crenshaw

ISBN 979-8-9895326-9-8 (Paperback)
ISBN 979-8-8556595-7-3 (trade hardcover Barnes & Noble)
ISBN 979-8-9895326-5-0 (Ebook)

1. Fantasy. 2. Supernatural—Fiction. 3. Suspense.
4. Humor. 5. New Adult / Romance.
6. Christian 7. Science Fiction.

Those who listened and believed knew that the unraveling of the thread would come at a price, a sacrifice, so they were caught in the tightening of the dimensions as the war raged on. Their own sacrifices could be their undoing if they were to faulter in their promises.

～～ Alethea Stauron ～～

For my thread master.

Pronunciation Guide

Lucius(lü-shŭs)
Dextorus(dĕks-tôr-ŭs)
Yaztarifenn(yăz-tĕr-ĭ-fĭn)
Yuleshua(yü-lĕsh-yü-wŭ)
Hoshtravay(hŏsh-trŭ-vā)
Baàlsarideem(bŏl-sĕr-ĭ-dĭm)
Deasja(dēz-jŭ)
Oobadoave(ü-bŭ-dōv)
Shuelltyson(shüĕl-tī-sŭn)
Apollyon(ŭ-pŏl-ē-ŭn)
Powtray(pow-trā)
Vincentine(vĭn-sĭn-tēn)
Artorus(är-tôr-ŭs)
Rueshta(rüsh-tŭ)

Akhtar(ăk-tär)
Gamerilaye(gŭm-ĕr-ĭ-lā)
Nicholson(nĭk-ŏl-sŭn)
Hatrueshian(hŏ-trü-shē-ĭn)
Samstarsey(săm-stär-sē)
Dugand(dü-gŭnd)
Buovouste(bü-vowst)
Moarscii(mȯr-sē-ī)
Arstoleci(är-stō-lē-sē)
Avledon(ăv-lŭ-dŏn)
Quiashay(kü-wī-ŭ-shā)
Jett Commdearadea(jĕt\kŏm-dēr-ŭ-dāy)
Constantinople(kŏn-stănt- ĭn- ō-pŭl)
Jazee Su Thrace(jā-zē\sü\thrās)

Pronunciation Symbols

ā....aid, made, tray
ē....feed, seed, meat
ĕ....elephant, egg, led
ă....apple, map, tram
ī....eye, thigh, rye
ŭ....umbrella, mud
ŏ....ball, ominous
ō....boat, slope
ĭ....it, hip, sister
ü....moon, tune
är....ark, star, mark
ȯr....shore, floor
ĕr....air, tare, where
wŭ....wall, what
b....baby, bark, tab
k....carrot, car, crack

f....far, whiff, full
g....gig, gone, gore
h....hollow, hum
j....jet, gelatin, jack
l....limbo, lull, loud
m....man, mambo
n....nice, non, naked
r....race, runt, reek
s....sauce, sass, say
sh....shadow, shush
thr....three, throw
tr....tree, trunk, troll
t....tut, mitt, tail
v....vow, vacate, stove
w....wane, water
y....you, yule, yolk

-....Hyphen divides syllables.
()....Pronunciation of item word
   is placed between parenthesis.
\....Usage of reverse virgule indicates
   transcription break for dual items.
,....Commas separate variant
   pronunciations.

One

(Purple) Mojave Turquoise

The sun rises across the San Antonio wilderness. Bluebonnets cake the fields surrounding the Gamerin cabin. April is bursting with wildlife, and Josephine lies cozy in her bed beneath blankets. A steady arm spreads warm fingers across her ribs from behind. "Mmmm," Josephine says and barely moves in her sleep.

Lucius tries again, this time pressing his awakened body from behind her. Reading her emotions, he whispers, "Good morning, baby. You're waking up now." He kisses her shoulder. "I can feel you waking up." Lucius rubs her abdomen and says, "I've been thinking of you for hours."

Smiling, Josephine covers her face with the edge of her pillow and mumbles, "Are you always this happy in the morning?"

"I am when we're trying to make a baby. Trying every morning for a baby was your idea," he says pulling her hips closer to him. "I know you're waking up, Josephine." He nibbles across her ear. "I know everything about my wife."

She moans and says, "Awake, barely." She rolls over to bury her nose in his chest hairs. They tickle her nose, and she says, "I need to wake up first, Lucius. I'm an early riser, but you're seriously…" and glances at him, "an early riser."

Lucius chuckles. "I can fix that. You're a part of me." He moves his hand gently to hold her hip where the crease of her bottom meets her thigh. He releases his desires through his bioempathic ability and draws her snug against him. He says, "How's that?"

She gasps. "I feel all your love over me. Everything. I don't know if that was fair or not, but I'm ready."

Lucius wastes no time in sharing their morning tradition of love. He raises his wife's shirt and kisses between her soft peaks. He says, "I cherish you." He slides over, and Josephine wraps her legs around him. Her thighs hug his entire body. Lucius tastes the sweet aroma of her skin by touching his tongue to her neck and savoring every moment. "You're my yoshawn yulee Josephine. My most precious blessing."

Clenching him tighter, she says, "Keep talking like that, and I might not leave this room all day."

"It's true." He gasps, holding back the urge slightly while they make love. "I'm not hurting you, am I?"

"No, you're gentle." She nibbles his shoulder.

Thunk.

Lucius's portal key flips off his shoulder and lands on her cheek.

"Sorry, baby." Lucius takes off his portal necklace, squeezes his eyes closed, and says, "I got excited. You do that to me." He's barely able to move away from her warmth. His right arm reaches over, and his mouth opens. Lucius haphazardly flicks his key across the bedside table, as he is fully concentrated on something else. With his key on the table, he moves back to what he was doing in giving his wife all his attention. The silver rope of his necklace hangs from the bedside table as they sing their love in each other's ear.

After making love, Lucius is lying almost on top of Josephine with little air between them. He grips her like a lost treasure that's finally found and strokes her cheeks. His fingers play with a small amount of sweat on her neck, and he says, "Seeing you in the morning next to me…You're an amazing creature. How can you be so wonderful every moment?"

Josephine wraps her arms around his ribs and looks at him, but her thoughts are the opposite of his as she says, "It's been three years." Her eyes hide in his upper body, and she says, "You want a large family."

"Don't think that way." Lucius cuddles her. "You haven't done anything wrong. We're still trying." He digs his nose down, seeking her out from her hiding spot. He immediately stops. "I sense everything you feel." Lucius clasps her fingers over his chest and says, "Baby. Baby, it breaks my heart to see you sad. You've given me everything. You have no idea how lost I would be without you. Don't be disappointed like this."

"Why though?" she asks. "I wanna know why." She looks into his eyes and says, "We've been trying. It's been over three years. I never turn you down, and I pray. I'm broken. I know it's not you. You can self-heal. I thought He said sons and daughters, but I'm broken. I'm not working anymore." She plops her head onto her pillow. "Cursed."

Speaking into her ear, Lucius says, "I don't know why you haven't gotten pregnant. I told you He's mystery. This is Yeshua's planet. I can't open your womb here because there's a purpose for everything. And believe me," he says making circles with his finger over to the area where they were bound together minutes earlier before continuing, "You're not broken. Everything's working just fine. I can testify."

Josephine asks, "What do you mean open my womb? Can you do that on your planet?"

Lucius gasps. "Um…actually…"

"Can you?"

"Yeeesss," Lucius stretches out his answer.

She says, "You never told me that."

"Baby." He exhales and says, "I can do many things, but it's different on this planet because there are more rules I must follow. This entire world is a test. A battlefield. A gambit of many things. I can't simply—"

"Then take me there. Only for a short while. We can leave the door open like last time. I can give you the family you desire. The family I desire. We can…can have a baby."

He shakes his head and answers, "I'm not allowed to go back without permission. You know this, my yoshawn. Don't tempt me into sin for you. I live to please you. But after my resurrection, I was told I couldn't go back to Gamerilaye without seeing Him first. I would be punished, baby. I'd be punished and not blessed. He's to be honored in all that we do. He commanded the order. I was punished for taking you there the time you're speaking of."

Josephine's expression sinks. "But this is important. Maybe we can talk to Him?"

"We do when we pray," Lucius says while stroking her belly button under her shirt. "He's very busy, and us wanting a baby probably isn't high on His list for setting up a meeting. Me dying in Jesus's arms four years ago…was important. I'm sorry, but I don't have that authority here." Lucius smiles and kisses her with tickling breath. "We're just gonna have to do this the old-fashioned way, baby," nudging her playfully, "Nothing wrong with that."

Josephine squirms.

Lucius stops and yanks his head up. He looks over her shoulder. His eyes shimmer with blue and silver, but a flicker of Mojave turquoise enters his irises.

"What is it?" Josephine asks. "Why are you activating your heat sensors? I see the purple hue in your eyes."

"Because they're talking." Lucius looks around the property and says, "There are different kinds of soldiers out there today, and I'm identifying some of them. Wow, very tall guys too, more than normal. There's a larger number out there showing up with shields and armor activated. And they're being quiet about it." Lucius deactivates his vision and smiles at Josephine. "I'll ask them when I go downstairs. Probably trying not to bother my private time with you, as we agreed." He shrugs. "Might be shift change, giving some of the guys leave, or running drills. Probably just report and nothing special."

Two

(Aquamarine) Turquoise

Adding his special Gamerin oils into the garden tub, Lucius changes the bathwater into a velvet, milky white that sends out aromatic perfume into the air. Josephine climbs into the bath and sits between his legs. He tells her, "I'm gonna hold you forever like this whether we have a large family or not. I'll always have you. I'm blessed," wrapping his arms around her breasts and holding her closer. "You're my everything."

Laying her head against his warm heartbeat, Josephine nestles in his arms and says, "I guess you're right. I can still give myself to you." She giggles. "I kind of like you, so I guess I'll keep you."

"I guess so, huh." He chuckles and plays along with her joke. "I guess you're stuck with me until the end of time."

The statement silences him. His actions with a washcloth are stuttered for a moment and tries to play his movement off.

She nudges her chin slightly, but keeps her thoughts to herself, almost identical to his actions.

As if a gong sounding between them, he says, "I know what you're thinking." The silence of the air after he acknowledges the tense sensation causes a sinister feeling of unrest. He continues cautiously. "I've been trying to avoid the sensation. I feel the same way that you do every time I mention eternity with you. As if something is hidden."

"Well, it obviously isn't me because I can't hide anything, can I? I haven't said anything. Why do we feel this way? Why is it so heavy every time we talk about being together? Why do I wanna cry?"

"Don't cry, my yoshawn." He exhales. "My fears are probably bothering you, and my emotions are bleeding over into you."

"What are you thinking?"

"Not so much as thinking, but it's a feeling we've both been experiencing. I've felt like we don't have forever, that's why. Like there's something else, and it's been bothering me, like it's hidden."

"Is the feeling because you found out about the abductions up north?" She peeks momentarily up at him before staring at her toes. She stretches her toes out and plays with the faucet as she continues. "Lucius, you still haven't told me why the abductions have been bothering you either. I wish you would talk to me. Maybe that's the reason why your emotions trouble you and feel like a weight on your shoulders."

Lucius exhales. "It's not that, baby. This is something else."

"Whatever feeling this is, the dread of it is disturbing me, even in my dreams." She looks at him. "The Father gave me your lifespan. He wouldn't do that without a reason. I think we're fine." She relaxes and nestles back into his arms. "We're probably just overthinking everything because I haven't been able to get pregnant again." She shrugs. "We're probably obsessed because you want that baby boy so bad."

Lucius lays his cheek against her wet hair. "Maybe so." He sighs deeply. "I've already mixed the blue paints together. Our hotheaded friend finished a mobile for a bed he's designing. He won't let me see it yet."

"Artie is so excited for nothing." She gazes at their wedding bands and compares them as she plays with the rings. "I guess I can rub on the stones of our rings because I can't open one of those portal doors."

He strokes her fingers and says, "Portals can be dangerous. And so is your ring. The ring still works, even if what it opens isn't as big as a doorway."

"How is my ring dangerous for me? I don't have psychic abilities. You told me—"

"Let me finish explaining, my yulee." He kisses her forehead. "I need to show you how to use your key because someday you might need to. We're connected. You have my DNA inside you because your first pregnancy spread who I was throughout your blood, and our baby girl bonded us deeper."

"My ring is small compared to yours."

"Our rings are different in size, but the true difference is what doors each one opens." He raises his hand up. "Mine has Jazee Su Thrace, but yours has Gamerilaye, the home of the Gamerin people."

She says, "There used to be twelve thousand of your kind on that world."

He says, "Correct. I've got to teach you several planets that are located within the portal stones on your ring."

She gazes at the encrusted stones. "I can't believe these represent different planets. You do your little psychic thingy, and zip, you're there."

"Psychic abilities, permission, or Gamerin bloodline can open them, but only if you know the cornerstones."

"So not only must I have psychic abilities, but I also need to know a cornerstone of each one?"

"Memorizing each world is not that difficult. Most of the time, it's easy because cornerstones are the king of whatever world you are wanting to go to or an icon of the area like a moon. You must know the right cornerstone to have a connection. You'll get the hang of it."

"I don't know any cornerstones, and I don't have abilities."

Lucius rolls his lips inward from the thought of him being the ordained cornerstone of Gamerilaye. He hears her thoughts, and remains silent about his identity.

Josephine studies each jewel that she has memorized over the last four years. "My eternal darling," she says and glances up. "What's the cornerstone of your world?"

"Baby," he says, as he fights giving in to her tone. He speaks softly, "I know. I know you want to please me," and strokes her cheek. "My yoshawn, I can't take you there without permission from the Father. Don't let your mind give birth to such ideas. Those ideas grieve you. You and I having a lot of babies will have to be in His timing."

"Sorry." She sinks down until bathwater is slightly under her nostrils, and then she blows bubbles as if giving up.

"Don't do that," he says sliding her up like a toddler against him. "No pouting." He pecks over her cheek and makes smooching sounds over her ears. "Not before church, my queen."

Because she does not know that she is a true queen, but only his wife, she asks, "Why do you call me that? I'm just a country girl. A daughter of God perhaps, but I'm no one special like a queen."

"You know not of what you speak. Besides, you're a queen to me, so don't talk like that. You'll always be my queen. Here," he says as he elevates her fingers into the center of his palm. "I'll show you which stone represents Gamerilaye, but I won't tell you the cornerstone, not yet." He turns the ring around on her finger until an aquamarine diamond with accents of lapis lazuli and Mojave turquoise flashes in view. The stone is slightly larger than the rest, but no larger than a few grains of sand bound together. "This is my world. You rub this stone as you think about the cornerstone. If you open a portal, you need to command the stone shut by the same thought which opened it." He hugs her with a subtle moan in her ear. "You see? No need to be upset this morning. I'm wrapped around your finger."

"Seems simple enough, but only if I had abilities to open one like you can."

He says, "Commanding stones this way is a safe technique to keep the portals secure. There are worlds that don't know about the war and can't simply open without preparation. That is one reason that there must be a relationship between the wielder and the destination of the portal."

"Really? You can't just do your zap thing to anywhere?"

"Correct, I can't." He raises his fingers to use them as a quotation. "I can't just do my 'zap thing.' Opening a portal from anywhere could kill people or cause blindness if say…I was to go to Oobadoave and then open a portal directly from Oobadoave to Earth. The flesh here comes from the cursed ground because it's the prison world and covered in sin. That's why y'all need new bodies here and can't look directly on God."

"So Earth is the only battlefield then?"

"I didn't say that, baby, but that's not what we're talking about. You're gonna confuse yourself."

"There's so much I don't know though," she says. "I wanna learn, but I'm afraid I might hurt someone after hearing that."

"Let me tell you an example then. There are civilizations that are so pure in thought and body, even if someone told them of the war, they still wouldn't understand what they were being told, like Adam and Eve in the garden or Nicodemus when he was chatting with Yeshua. You can't enter those worlds directly."

"Why not?"

"People have to be ready." He stops and stares at her. "Baby, it's dangerous in your current body because of the curse. The light from those planets would kill, blind, or completely freak out anybody witnessing that opened portal."

"Oh," she says. "Like when people used to bow down to angels because they were freaked out, and the angels had to tell them not to bow to them? Like that?"

"Yes. Some people are not ready or have the bodies that are required for such a visit."

She says, "I was trained about heaven. When you showed me Ooba-doave, you did so from far away so that I wouldn't become blind. Some other worlds and civilizations are like that?"

"Now you're getting it. Skin of a holy being glows with the Father's glory. Only certain warriors can enter without their skin glowing because their skin is designed to keep from freaking people out."

"Like when Moses had to wear a veil," she says as she looks over the edge of the garden tub. A fluffy tail catches her eye. "Their skin glows unless a specially designed warrior."

"Yeah." Lucius reaches over and strokes Leo's tail. "I think our lesson's over. Someone's jealous for his time now."

"Leo. Silly cat."

Leo stands on his hind legs and sniffs the tub.

She says, "Well, I need to start getting ready for church."

"About time, I guess." Lucius glances through the walls. "Must be a long report going on," he says eyeing the masses of guardians standing in various places. "Not one of the angels this morning has left yet. There's more now. Their minds are blocked."

"How come?"

He shrugs. "Not sure. Their minds are blocked with Trinitarian power, usually done for protection. The Father sometimes blocks the minds of certain people to keep information safe. I can't simply enter those minds."

"He's hungry," she says as she scratches behind Leo's ear. "I need to fix my hair."

"I know what that means. I'm not complaining about my chore, little momma," he says and points at Leo. "I just know what this guy's about to start doing, and his choir isn't the one I was wanting to hear this morning." Lucius kisses Josephine before he exits the tub. He says, "Leo," and winks at Josephine before looking back toward Leo. "Are you hungry? You wanna eat?"

Immediately, Leo meows for breakfast.

"We spoil him." Lucius smirks. "My chore, ladies and gentlemen," he says as he covers himself with a robe. "I love you, Leo. You're a cute cat. Food and attention are all you need." Lucius opens the bathroom door and asks, "How long?"

"I'm getting out now." She flips the drain and begins robing herself. "When you're dressed, it'll be okay. The guardians never come in here. They truly don't think that way, like they're nurses, and I'm a patient."

Lucius says, "Of course, I told you that our relationship is rare and doesn't happen," and thumbs back at himself. "Only me. I guess it's a Gamerin design to fall in love with women."

"All twelvish of them?"

He says, "I shouldn't have brought it up."

She says, "You still haven't told me everything of their story."

He exits the bathroom with a grin, says, "You should have been an investigator because you like to pry." He closes the door to the bathroom and grabs his church clothes from the bed.

From the other side of the door, she says, "It's not prying when you are my husband. I hope it makes you feel terrible keeping secrets from me."

"That's not very nice, Mrs. Gamerin. I said I would tell you someday. I don't know everything yet, so I can't go into speculations."

She asks, "You'll tell me everything?"

Plopping an undershirt back on the bed, he exhales and then says, "I need a little more time. Someday I will."

Deasja enters the room and says, "I can hear you two talking." He shrinks the distance between him and Lucius and whispers, "You still haven't told her yet?"

"I can't." Lucius unbundles his socks and speaks to Deasja psychically, *"She thinks I'm perfect. What if...what if she thinks I'm a failure? Right now, I'm someone with a perfect past when I'm with her, and not someone who's destroyed two worlds, lost his entire family, and we're trying to have our own. I'm the reason for the flood, Deasja. I'm the reason all her...our friends here on Earth will die of old age."* He frowns. *"One tear in her eyes from—"*

Meow.

Lucius glances at Leo who is tapping a furry paw on the door. Lucius continues with his mental transfer toward Deasja. *"I couldn't handle her crying. I'm trying to get over my losing them by not hating myself. She comforts me every day, like I've done nothing wrong. I feel like a new creature when I'm with her. Remembering my past, reminds me that I'm a failed king, and she doesn't need to know that about me. Here...at least here, I'm her husband, her desire. She looks up to me and thinks I have all of life's problems figured out. Her eyes stare at me in amazement, Deasja, and I admire her in my wonderment of how such a beautiful creature could love someone like me. I'm healed in her arms. She's my yoshawn, my yulee, my Josephine, and she adores me even with nothing to my name here. My life is simple and perfect."* Lucius opens his hands out, and says aloud, "Why would I mess that up?"

Meow.

Lucius lowers his shoulders. "I'm coming, buddy. You're not gonna starve."

After the cat meows, "Lucius," Josephine's voice carries through the bathroom door. "Leo is sounding an alarm."

"I'm talking to Deasja and still getting dressed." He smiles and says, "He'll be fine. He's not too loud right now, little momma. A couple of minutes and I'll be ready to go downstairs and feed him."

Deasja takes a few steps back and transfers the thought, *"Imagine her surprise on the day that you do tell her."* Deasja mimics what Lucius would look like as he plays out the scenario in his head. *"By the way, Josephine, dear, you're a queen. Oh, and your husband's the cornerstone you wear around your finger that I designed with the Almighty Father Himself. I'm a principality over nearly countless stars and planets…um…that we both rule over in case you're wondering. Just thought I should tell you."* Deasja raises his brows with several flicks and whispers, "I wouldn't wait too long, Lucius. Artie's itching to kneel before her as his queen and feels he's doing something wrong with his king missing from his kingdom. We're not allowed to bow before anyone here, but a quick visit in Gamerin jurisdiction would change all that. Life on Earth is not the same thing. The heavens are different." Deasja leaves the room to wait on the loft outside the door.

Three

(Cobalt Blue) Lapis Lazuli

Buttoning his dress shirt, Lucius exits the master bedroom. He lifts his leg from a furry bundle charging underneath him as Leo races toward the stairwell. Lucius's eyes bounce around and counts how many extra angels are in the house. He gazes back at Deasja on the loft, says, "She's in the bathroom. She'll let you know."

"Actually," Deasja begins answering as he gestures toward a handful of soldiers walking closer to them to stand guard outside the master bedroom, "I have to leave."

"What's going on today? Why are there so many of you on duty here?"

Meow.

Lucius walks a short distance behind the feline hunger serenade. He tells Leo, "Shush, I'm feeding you right now, buddy. Keep it down. Let me get breakfast done first." Lucius enters the kitchen and glances back toward the heavily guarded loft area up on the second floor. He continues, saying, "You're not the only one here, Leo. Keep it down. What have I told you about meowing so loud in the morning?"

Deasja follows Lucius around the kitchen and watches him gather a can and bowl with a mixture of dry food. Deasja says, "We've—"

Meow.

Deasja rolls his eyes, says, "We've—"

Meow.

"Sorry," Lucius says as he grimaces. He places a bowl down so Leo's crying will cease. "I should've done this first. He's spoiled in the morning and thinks he's gonna starve or something." Lucius points toward Deasja and says, "Continue. I'm listening." Lucius takes out a carton of eggs, a slab of bacon, and a large bowl of plump strawberries and prepares breakfast.

Deasja explains, "This weekend was just a short visit for me. I must meet with a couple of commanders. I'm leaving now."

"With who?" Lucius speaks psychically, *"Tell me this way, so they can't hear. I've noticed that everyone is blocked by Trinitarian power. I can't enter their minds to find out what is going on."*

"You're correct. I'm meeting with Commander Albercase from Alaska and also Dextorus." He continues verbally, "The Nephilim curse has gone missing up north."

"Shhh." Lucius waves his hands and presses his index against his lips. "Shush, Josephine doesn't know about all that. I can barely take the information myself. Just speak psychically." He continues psychically, *"You can say the names of the commanders this way without alerting them."*

Deasja nods and transfers, *"It's been quiet around the Arctic circle, and there's no trace of them. It's like all the activity has disappeared right as they were finding a hot trail to your brothers, and now…nothing. We must formulate a plan."*

"Have they abducted more women before disappearing? Do you think my brothers are on board that vessel?" Lucius looks around the house with activated vision and begins counting the hundreds of guardians outside, surrounding his home for protection. He immediately stops when he wonders in thought toward Deasja, and asks, "Why so many, Deasja? What are y'all thinking?"

Deasja shakes his head and answers telepathically, *"It's just a precaution. There's not enough gold and quartz in the ground here for Nephilim teleporters. They would have to enter the atmosphere above your house, and there would be sightings all over the Internet of their ship. I don't think they'll risk it, but you being here is a—"* Deasja is interrupted for a moment when a light flickers over his time band. He checks his time and shrugs before finishing what he was saying out loud, "You're a secret. I must meet them near Nome. They're calling me."

"That's unsettling," Lucius says and watches Deasja vanish through a portal.

Lucius stands in silence for a minute and says, "Not the report I wanted to hear today." He switches the griddle on and sizzles the bacon. He scrambles eggs and slathers them with cheese and sautéed onions. He's in the middle of cooking when a little being makes her way down the stairs.

He's completely unaware of the person walking down the steps as he sneaks a bite of bacon from a plate. "So good," he says and smells coffee brewing. "That coffee is calling my name."

Several guardians silence their discussion. They wear smiles as the little footsteps of someone with long blonde hair and bright blue eyes patters into the kitchen. She drags a blankie and a stuffed toy behind her. A little voice breaks through the crackle of breakfast, and says, "Morning, Daddy," and her little fingers reach up.

Lucius nearly squats completely down and wraps his warm arms around her. "Good morning, princess," he says as he lifts her up to rest on his shoulder. "How's my baby girl doing?" He removes everything from the burners to give his daughter his undivided attention. "Did Leo wake you up, pumpkin? I was about to go up there and get you out of bed, Claire."

She yawns and her nose scrunches with a teeny sigh. Her tired eyes glare into nothing. She says, "Love you, Daddy," as if she could see miles through walls like him.

He says, "Love you too," and pulls his head back so he can look at her. "What are you looking at?" he asks while rubbing her back. "You're half asleep, aren't you? Just staring into space?" he asks while rocking her in place by swiveling his hips. "Daddy has you. You're a daddy's girl."

She nods and barely bats an eye. "Leo didn't sleep. He's a super cat, Daddy."

"He did sleep, princess," he answers and smiles at her. "He was in Mommy and Daddy's room last night." He closes his eyes with his cheek against her ear, simply holding her. He takes a whiff of her hair. "You take after your momma. You always smell so good." He exhales a soft sound that blankets her ear. "Babies smell so good. You smell like a baby, Claire."

She answers over his shoulder, "I am your baby, Daddy." And continues mumbling into his shirt collar, saying, "Love you, Daddy."

He sighs before whispering, "My life is so wonderful," and closes his eyes as he rocks his little girl in his warm arms.

"Daddy," she says clutching a handsewn doll tighter beneath her arm, "where's Momma?" She drops her blanket after clutching her doll, and Lucius catches the corner of her blanket in midair. She asks, "We go to Jesus's house today?"

"We go in a bit," he says, sliding her soft locks away from her cheeks with his pinky, and kissing her flushed morning glow. "Momma'll be down in a minute for breakfast. After we eat, then we'll go to Jesus's house and see your friends." He waves at a few soldiers passing through the kitchen. They are a few feet taller than Lucius and duck down away from the ceiling.

He continues speaking to Claire. "Aunt Carissa has the nursery today. That means that Evan will be there with her." Carrying her to the table, he kisses her a few more times. "Maybe, Evan won't hit you today…with a toy." He huffs. "Aw, boys. He'll behave with her there. He listens to his momma pretty good."

He continues swaying her in his arms beside the chair, as if reserving her spot. "Claire, you wanna eat? I made some bacon and eggs. You like the cheese and veggies I put in the eggs." He points toward a heaping bowl and says, "I got some strawberries from a hothead last night."

Her head shakes a definitive no that sends her curled ends moving across her lower back with each swivel.

"What do you mean, no?" he asks. Lucius looks over and notices the nervous smiles of two guardians chatting in the foyer. Reconnecting his gaze at her, he tells Claire, "You've gotta eat. I just made our morning meal, pumpkin."

"Momma said," she begins as her voice takes a hyper sounding breath and continues as if she has big news. "She said that I could have cereal today, Daddy." Her voice squeaks as she adds, "Aunt Amber said so too!"

Lucius's ears are ringing, "What?" He sets her down in the chair and asks, "Cereal? That's not breakfast." He's nearly offended and points at the platter as he places strawberries in the center of the table. Lucius reaches toward the bar and grabs the meaty breakfast assortment.

He pauses when he sees the uneasy faces of several armed guards clasping their weapons closer to their bodies and staring at everything that moves around them. Lucius shakes his head, says, "Y'all must calm down. I can hear all of what y'all are doing. I can't tell you psychically to settle down." He waves his hand peacefully and says, "Your minds have been blocked. Your apprehension is flooding the atmosphere of the house. Peace be upon you. This is breakfast before church with my family. These memories stick to children," he says and points at Claire. "She can sense what you feel whether she sees you or not. She's a Gamerin."

"Who you talk'n, Daddy?"

"Not sure, pumpkin. Daddy sometimes talks to himself."

"Sorry, Lucius." The soldiers nod. They lower the discussion with one another. The guard in the study who apologized says, "I'll keep it down." Other guardians nod with their confirmation as well, and the volume of the house decreases to some measure below what it was.

Lucius brushes off the constant rumble of background noises, discussion, and heavy breathing. He places a tray in front of Claire and him and grunts before grabbing a chair. He points at the food he has prepared and says, "This is breakfast, Claire. This'll put hair on your chest." He heaps a pile onto his plate. "Don't you wanna be big and strong like Daddy?"

Claire's brows frown together. She wipes her sleepy eyes. "But, Daddy, I don't want hair on my chest."

Silently chuckling, Lucius squints as his body shakes from holding in his laughter. "I don't want you to either, baby." His face turns red behind his hands.

Josephine crosses the kitchen tiles with a fresh fragrance trailing behind her. "What's so funny?" she asks while studying her husband. She glances at Claire's concerned expression, and asks, "What happened?"

Lucius swallows and moves his hands. He says, "She doesn't want hair on her chest," laughing even harder. "I can't help it."

Josephine steps over and asks, "What? What hair?"

He looks up with watery eyes and tries to explain, "She believes everything I say. I was only talking." He points toward the platter. "I told her about the bacon and eggs. I said that you can grow hair on your chest from it…and she believed me."

Josephine opens her mouth wide in shock. Her hands go directly to her hips, and glances back at Claire, who is more concerned seeing her mother's expression. Josephine turns back toward Lucius with a teeny tap on his arm. "You can't leave her hanging, Daddy. She believes everything at this age." Josephine hunches beside Claire. "Baby," she starts to say as she can hear the laughter of her husband crescendo behind her. Josephine fights smiling and says, "Claire, don't worry about stuff like that. That's not what your daddy meant. He's just teasing you, angel." She rubs over the sleeve of Claire's gown. "Girls don't grow hair on their chest, only men do. That's why Daddy's laughing. He didn't think you'd…" she stops and turns to look back at him, "Daddy, explain what you meant to her."

With an ulterior motive behind his words, "Okay," he begins to say, and leans forward and makes a jab at those who eat cereal. "Processed food will put hair on your chest, and it doesn't matter if you are a boy or girl."

Josephine enters the main part of the kitchen. She reaches into the cupboard and shakes her head. "Good grief."

Claire asks, "What's proscesk food, Mommy?"

She answers, "Don't worry about it, angel."

"Hey." Lucius folds his arms and begins to say, "Claire told me that you said..." and he gasps. "What is that?" he asks, gesturing with his entire hand. "What are you giving my baby?"

Josephine opens a new box of cereal with the word *HONEY* written across it. "You overreact," Josephine pauses to call him, "Honey." She winks.

"You dare give me that pet name?" Lucius asks as he wrestles with smiling. "This is mutiny. Absolute mutiny." He watches as a small bowl is filled by Josephine with processed oats in the shape of little rings. "You're gonna give my baby honey." He grabs some strawberries and slices little pieces for Claire's cereal. He lays them on top. "We're gonna have a talk about this."

"Hardly something to have marriage counseling over." She pours her daughter's milk. "She likes this cereal, and it's good for her."

"Neil says it's good for her, but he's a doctor, not Jesus." Lucius takes his seat as he grabs two more slices of bacon. "I'd rather her have hair on her chest."

"Nonsense." Josephine sets the bowl in front of Claire. "I told her she could have cereal today."

"Why is there honey in this house?"

"David got it for her. He feeds this to Emily every morning, and she's healthy and never gets sick. Amber sends her to daycare with an extra bag as a snack."

His shoulders drop. "David is breaking our team," he says and gets up to reach for Claire's sippy cup. He fills the tiny cup with orange juice. "Traitors, all of you," he says while he chokes on his chuckling.

Josephine kisses Claire's cheek. "Daddy's silly, isn't he?"

"The people are scared, Mommy," Claire interrupts the conversation.

Josephine asks, "What people, baby?"

Lucius doesn't realize what Claire has said. He continues slicing a few more strawberries for her and says, "Well, at least, my baby knows that strawberries are good, and they heal her too. I'm not..."

Abruptly, Lucius pauses from Claires previous comment, and asks, "What people, pumpkin?"

"What is it?" Josephine stands up and turns toward the bar to grab Claire's juice cup. "What are you asking her, Lucius?"

"It's gone quiet," he says as he stands to his feet. "Claire senses what they're feeling." He realizes the conversations of the house have gone flat with only the grandfather clock ticking. He gazes across the house. No more guardians are huddling in clusters or walking freely.

No chatter.

No indoor troops.

"I don't feel so well all of the sudden," Josephine says. She turns toward Lucius with deep eyes, the color of her cheeks have faded, and she's patting her chest. "That feeling like earlier is pressing at me, thick and not right."

Lucius accesses his vision to investigate. "I feel it too," he says and soon his color fades as well.

Four

(Pure) White

Lucius witnesses hundreds of angels surrounding the house and they are all gazing up. A deep feeling of dread floods over him as the sky darkens above the countryside.

A shadow dims the windows of the kitchen like a storm brewing outside. Josephine studies Lucius's expression and asks, "Why do you look like that?" She glances at the window behind Claire. "Is it getting dark? Is that a storm?" Her worried eyes flicker back over toward Lucius. "Are you doing this?" she asks but anxiety increases when seeing her husband's shocked expression.

"I'm not doing this," he says as he looks up with activated eyes. He points and says, "They are, and they're not camouflaged either." He sidesteps from beside the kitchen bar and moves closer to his family.

An enormous craft hovers closer over Medina Lake, and Lucius swiftly walks toward the dinner table. "Don't panic," he whispers. "Josephine, grab Claire. I don't know this craft."

"What craft?" Josephine takes Claire into her arms. "You're scaring me, Lucius."

Unexpectedly, screaming surrounds the area as Nephilim transporters, from out of nowhere, snatch several guardians from the property. Large angels pull out their swords for instant battle. Lucius screams, "Nephilim!"

"Transporters!" A guardian runs in through the walls. He points at Claire and screams, "They can't get her! Run!" In a blink of an eye, a Nephilim appears behind the guardian by latching an arm around his waist. "Activate your—" they both disappear.

Reaching for his portal cross, Lucius's eyes enlarge. His necklace is gone.

"I left it upstairs!" he hollers. Lucius activates his wedding band. A small portal opens, and Lucius pulls Claire from Josephine's arms. He pushes Claire through the small opening as Artie is standing in his kitchen with a cup of coffee. Lucius yells, "Artie, Nephilim! They're here," and shoves Claire into Artie's arms. "Here, take her. We're under attack." Artie drops his coffee and grabs Claire. The portal closes.

Josephine asks, "What are we—"

Lucius clasps onto his wife and yanks her from the table area. "We don't have time to talk." Running through their living room, Lucius triggers a shield on his arm. A cloud of Mangoram laced daggers swarm through the house. "Infused metal," he says blocking several of them and deflecting the rest. "These can penetrate me." Blue ripples shine across his shield with each hit. "Hold on," he says with Josephine held tightly in his arms. As he jumps up to the loft, he supports his wife's head. "I've got you, baby."

Two Nephilim enter the cabin and lock eyes with Lucius as he and Josephine race into the master bedroom. Lucius activates his shielded wings and wraps them around his wife. He blocks a barrage of daggers and spears speeding like bullets across the house. Furniture and walls are turned to pulp within a matter of seconds from the arsenal. Lucius leaps with Josephine over the bed. He grabs his portal cross as five Nephilim enter the room through the door.

"Don't let them get away," a Nephilim says as he dives across the bed toward them, needing only one touch to transport his victims.

Lucius activates a portal beneath him and Josephine as daggers and a hand fling through the air. Metal of the weapons wedge into Lucius's shielded wings, and he holds Josephine under him as they fall several feet onto a different floor. Pinging and pelting sounds stop as the portal closes above them.

The portal deactivated, Lucius only hears heavy breathing. He looks over his shoulder and sees two Nephilim daggers wedged inches from his nose. He studies over where the portal had closed above them. "None got through," he says and exhales.

Hyperventilating builds in his chest. Josephine clenches his shirt, burying her nose into his chest. She's gasping.

"Baby," he says and examines her body for abrasions or injuries. "Did they get you?" She's not quite looking at him, so he says, "You're in shock," and holds her close. Her heart thunders, as he strokes her back, still wrapped in shielded wings. "Calm down. I've got you. Shhh." He breathes into her ear. "You're okay. We're okay." Her breathing slows with each stroke. "Peace, peace," he says, but he himself struggling to calm down. "None got through," he whispers, almost as if counseling himself. "We're safe. They can't get you here." His wings disband into an interdimensional pocket. He and Josephine are both lying on the floor in a completely different living space.

When she's calmed enough, Josephine studies the area. There's a massive roaring fireplace, a pure white bearskin rug three times bigger than any bear she's ever seen. "Who's..." she can't seem to finish asking. The rug is stretched out over granite and ruby flooring. Red glistens like glitter with each fiery sparkle causing the granite to emanate from its embedded crystals. "What is..." The walls are covered in mahogany and spruce. A woodsy smell, fresh, pristine, and warm, floods her nostrils. She is in a quite comfortable home with cedar beams holding the living area's vaulted structure in place. The beams are several feet thick in some places and easily four times bigger than her Texan cabin. "Massive," the word falls from her tongue. White orbs of sun rays catch her attention, steering her vision toward one side of the living area where there are colossal windows from floor to ceiling. The ceiling is easily sixteen feet tall. Clouds cover the sun's rays, and she can see beyond the windows. "It's snowing."

Snowfall covers the landscape and is barely visible beyond the terrace area. Moments later, the snow blankets everything outside from further study. This morning it was spring outside, but now she sits in a strange house with a wintry snow pounding the windows. There are flickers of light from large bowls that she sees through each wave of white on the terrace balcony beyond the wall-sized windows. "Fires," she says. "Bowls of fire out there. Big ones." The fire continues to flicker and doesn't die down with the growing storm.

Soon, the white snow becomes so thick that she can no longer make out anything beyond the windows.

Lucius says, "They're about to go out from the storm. Those fires are from his landing bay urns." He strokes her cheeks. "It's a snowstorm, and it's my fault. I'm sorry." Lucius breathes in as he closes his eyes. "I got upset, but I'm getting better."

"We're not on Earth. How can you effect the...Where's Claire?" she asks with a gasp. Her eyes water as she climbs over her husband like scaling a mountain. She grabs his shoulders. "Lucius, where is she?"

"Calm down, baby. Artie wasn't on Earth." Lucius touches both her cheeks. "She's..."

He pauses as a cabinet closes beyond a vaulted river-rock wall. A small voice giggles as the sounds of stirring from inside of a mug follows Claire's laughing. Lucius and Josephine lie on the floor and stare over with stretched necks toward the wall opening in the nearby dining area. A warm voice answers Claire's giggling with, "Your momma probably makes it better, but you'll have to decide."

Lucius smiles. "She's fine," he says. "She's safe." He covers his face and feels as though he can breathe. "Everybody's good." Lucius bumps his head back onto the flooring, enjoying the heartbeat of his wife directly over him and the laughter of his daughter in the next room. "We're safe."

Artie walks around the opening with a blond-haired bundle over his hip. Josephine releases Lucius's shoulders as she exhales with relief. Claire rests on top of Artie's right arm. She holds a large mug of cocoa in her hands and is wrapped in a blanket. Artie says, "I wasn't expecting visitors today. I would've made sippy cups." He glances out at the new snowstorm and back down at his guests currently occupying his floor space. "This is a pleasant surprise. You're always welcome. I'm glad everyone's okay." Artie places Claire down with a partial kneel as far as he can go without spilling her mug. He says, "Princess, you're okay."

"Artie!" Lucius snaps. His eyes open wide, and he shakes his head. "Not yet," he says.

"Really?" Artie nods while remaining at a lower level than his princess. He appears as though he's merely placing a three-year-old down instead of bowing to royalty. "This is going to be tough for me, Lucius."

Claire walks close to her mom and dad. Josephine reaches her arms out and says, "My baby," and embracing Claire, cocoa and all, in one motion. She moves over from Lucius. "You okay, Claire?"

"I have cocoa. He gave me some," Claire answers. "He spilled his coffee."

Lucius lifts himself up from the floor with a grunt and helps his wife and daughter to stand alongside him. "We'll be safe here." Lucius leans forward until almost touching his knees for a moment to take in one more deep breath before standing straight again. "Artie doesn't mind visitors."

Artie fights stuttering, "I...I..." and manages to press out, "I should say not. Never with you," he pauses as he is unable to take his eyes from Lucius. "This is odd, Lucius." He swallows with a deep breath, and says, "This might be a new experience, but I do know I could say—"

"Artie," Lucius says to warn Artie again.

Artie raises a palm. "I was just going to say that while you're here, I will treat you like royalty. You are family to me, and there's nothing I wouldn't do for you. You have my word."

"Thank you," Josephine says. "This is your house?"

"My house," Artie says with a pause as he winks before continuing, "is your house."

Lucius smirks. "Artie, that's quite enough."

Artie can't wipe his smile away and shakes his head in pure delight. "Welcome home." Artie inhales while fighting tears of joy. "Finally, welcome. Would the Gamerin family like to eat?"

Five

Humble Silver

Artie is busy in the kitchen while Lucius and Josephine carry on a discussion in the living room. Artie and Claire stick close together. "I'm just going to hold you," Artie says, keeping her away from parental dialogue. He prepares breakfast while hugging her close and cooking with one hand as he sets a table in between stirring.

As they walk to the table between one of Artie's trips to the dining area, Claire peeks in the living room and says, "I like my mommy." Claire points at her mother while Artie balances her on his hip as he finishes placing forks down. Claire watches her father running his fingers through his hair because of the discussion. Claire says, "And my daddy's silly."

"Sometimes, he is," Artie answers with a nod. "Do you like cheese on your grilled vegetables?"

"Daddy made me some," she says. Her eyes squint to a thin line as her voice squeaks. "but not in bread…eggs." The squeaking bongs directly into his ear.

Artie smiles with his ears ringing. "You'll like these veggies. I guarantee it," he says stuffing pita bread with warm vegetables smothered in cheese. "I can put eggs in it if you'd like. It's close to noon here, so this is more of a brunch."

Claire says, "I was gonna have cereal." She raises her crumb filled fingers that are still sticky from honey coated pieces. "I only got a little."

"Aw," he says washing her little fingers with a wet linen. "Maybe sometime I can make some for you. I don't have any honey coated cereal here. Your daddy doesn't like honey." He places her down into a chair and says a small prayer over her food. He lays a lesser amount of seasoned flatbread in the center of her plate. Cheese oozes from the warm bread. Artie takes a seat beside her. "Did your daddy ever tell you about me? I know you couldn't see me on Earth." He holds a hand out and shakes her entire hand with only two of his fingers. "My name's Artie."

She nods and takes a bite with a tiny hum. She swallows a partial amount and smacks. "Yes. I saw you. Daddy said you're a hothead."

"You saw me?" he asks and glances over at Josephine and Lucius who are still deep in conversation. "I didn't know that." He looks at Claire and says, "That's a new one to me. I didn't know that you could see me."

Claire says, "Sometimes, but you're a hothead, and that's what my daddy said. That's how I knew you was not a stranger."

"Were not. It's pronounced were not a stranger, princess." Artie looks over and studies the discussion and body language coming from the living area.

Lucius tries calming Josephine, but she raises her voice again, "What do you mean never going back? We're gonna be late for church."

Artie gazes at the little Gamerin girl and decides to stay out of the heavy conversation taking place in front of the fireplace. He asks Claire, "Did your daddy tell you why I'm a hothead?"

Her big blue eyes latch onto his gaze with a teeny shake of her head. She says, "No. He said you're a hothead, and you get fired up."

He has a crooked smile and stoops down toward Claire, saying, "Do you want me to show you?"

⊸⪧⊷

Meanwhile, Josephine weeps. Lucius holds her and speaks softly in her ear. "Please don't cry. I didn't choose this situation. I had no idea. There is no way that I could've prepared for an attack today. We can't go back. I've already seen many angels abducted. The Nephilim...I can't defeat them there, not on Earth and not with their abilities. Earth is not my world, and the Nephilim have my DNA. They are powerful, and there are too many of them. I'm must report to Oobadoave and let them know we got out safely."

"I didn't know that the Nephilim existed anymore. You didn't tell me. Let's do what I'm about to say. Maybe, in a few days we can hide somewhere else. Hawaii even. My dad's old cabin is there. Carissa has an extra room at her house."

"They'll know. Besides, we can't put our friends at risk. Scouts are everywhere, and the enemy armies work together for that information.

Leaking information is why I had to die, so they wouldn't find us. They thought I was infertile and that I had died. With a large army protecting you at the cabin, the enemy attacks died down."

She buries her head into his chest. "Everything my father worked for, all our friends. David, Amber, their daughter Emily, Carissa, Neil, and little Evan. It's all gone."

"Living with them would place them in danger if we were to go back."

"But people are gonna think we're all kidnapped or murdered. Bishop Jones is gonna freak out without the piano player today," she says gesturing toward Lucius, "and part of his choir is missing now. I didn't even get to tell anyone goodbye. I have nothing. Can I not leave a note, a letter…e-mail?"

"No," Lucius says with a shake of his head. "We can't."

"What was it all for? I don't understand. We had all those ministries we were doing. We were helping the community."

"We can't risk going back." He strokes her hair, says, "Baby, I know you don't understand, but you can't hide our attack and hidden lives, not us, especially if the Nephilim were willing to retrieve us themselves and in the open. The abduction was taking place in broad daylight. That was a gutsy move because they knew we had an army protecting us."

"How do you know that? How do you know it was planned?"

"I'm a commander, baby. I saw how the Nephilim were attacking us this morning. They were strategic when they started to move and started attacking from outside of our defenses first. The Nephilim grabbed what they could in private and were dwindling down our number of troops before going inside to grab us. There were too many of them, and they were trying to get us by ourselves before alerting me. The attack was less than thirty seconds."

"We have nothing."

Lucius pats her shoulder and says, "Hey, we do have everything. You still have me, and we still have Claire. We got out unscathed, barely, but unscathed nonetheless." He speaks over her head. "Baby, this morning could've been a lot worse. We're alive, and I don't know how many angels…" He gasps. "Oh man, I must report to Oobadoave. I have to find out what happened on the battlefield today." His eyes tear up. "I'm not worth losing my troops." He rubs over her hair. "You are. My girls are. We're still alive. My little family is not hurt. I know you don't understand, but the war isn't your fight; it's God's, and that's why you're secured before anyone. I'm sorry to bring my burdens upon you."

Lucius and Josephine hold each other silently in front of a seven-foot fireplace. The fire crackles and roars from the updraft of the storm blowing with harsh winds outside.

Abruptly, at about twenty feet, Claire begins to giggle at first, followed by outbursts of strong childlike laughter every few moments.

Josephine and Lucius look at each other as they listen. Curiosity. What could be making Claire laugh so hard? Artie speaks up with his laughter that follows every strong laugh of Claire. "Pull my finger," Artie says.

Lucius and Josephine glance over and watch as a blaze of fire nearly exits the kitchen. They swing their hands up and rush toward the kitchen. Lucius enters first and picks Claire up into his arms, saying, "No, Artie. You're gonna get me in trouble," pointing over toward Josephine, and begging with his eyes at Artie. "This is a girl, and that's her mother. Did you wanna talk to her mother about why gaseous humor isn't appropriate to do?"

Artie is quiet. He stares at Josephine with her arms folded over each other and showing her piercing eyes. He looks at Lucius for help. "Do I have to? She looks scary right now. Is she going to kill me?"

"Of course not," Josephine answers him while dropping her arms. She shakes her head and closes her eyes in disbelief. "Can this day get any worse? Now, I must teach an angel proper etiquette for children."

"Kids love me," Artie says. "I was only playing with her." He points at Claire. "She thought it was hilarious."

Lucius knows that any peace he had placed over his wife has quickly evaporated. He exhales and says, "Baby, this is petty in comparison to what we've been through today. She needs to laugh." As Lucius holds onto Claire, he wraps his other arm around Josephine and places more peace over her. "Calm down, Momma. How about this idea? After I report to Oobadoave, we find something better to do since we can't go back to Earth. There's no reason why we can't enjoy what's around us. What do you say? Our momentary grief shouldn't bring Claire down. She doesn't understand because she's happy if she has her momma and daddy. She's just a baby, innocent, like you. A three-year-old should never worry about war."

Josephine exhales with the euphoric feeling calming her nerves. "Thank you for making me feel better."

Artie points with his chin toward his bay windows. He nearly speaks too much as he says. "It's snowing outside. There should be a decent accumulation of powder on the mountains by the time his maje…umm…by the time Lucius calms down. Maybe I can open these doors. We can go sledding and build a snowman together."

"Doors?" Josephine glances over. "Those are doors?"

Lucius' says, "They are. Big doors. That's a great idea, Artie. And therapeutic for all of us, and it will be good to get out. We'll stay away from the villages today and simply spend time together." He playfully pulls Josephine closer to himself. "Come on, yulee. We're on a different planet. You need to experience this new part of life."

Artie says, "That's true. I miss having vacations. I've been waiting for this day."

"Vacation!" Lucius exclaims. "That's true. This is like a vacation. We've gotta go have fun when I get back from my final report of Earth. I haven't gone sledding in decades. Claire has never been in the snow before. What do you say, Momma? We can make this situation a legitimate vacation."

But Josephine lowers her shoulders and asks. "Lucius, what are you thinking? Vacation? We have nothing to wear for cold-weather. We didn't prepare for winter this morning."

"Baby, be instant in season and out of season," Lucius says. "We'll make the most of our situation. You can be spontaneous, like when we went to Gamerilaye or that time Carissa and Neil tried kidnapping us to Houston."

She points at her outfit and says, "I'm in my church clothes. This is springtime attire." She points out Lucius's outfit and says, "You're wearing your jeans and a short-sleeved dress shirt. You're the only one with an extra layer because of your undershirt." Josephine looks at Claire and says, "Claire is still in her bedtime gown, and she's barefoot. That baby can still catch a cold. I don't know how it is on other planets, but to me, snow is still freezing cold anywhere you go. I don't think there's a supercenter around here where I can get her something, and a blanket isn't gonna cut it with a blizzard out there." Her arms fall as she exhales a huff. "Even if there were a clothing store that I could go to, I don't think they'd take American cash or credit."

Lucius nods and says, "The conversation is difficult when you don't understand our ways. Yoshawn, my love, most planets don't take cash anyways in the heavens. Those are pieces of paper. They're just notes representing forms of payment. We don't do that out here. We can make our own garments or we make trades for goods. There's never a need for a supercenter out here. This isn't Earth. I told you I'm a builder." He pops his nose in the air toward Artie and says, "He's extremely talented. Artie can make anything."

"You think so? Thanks, Lucius." Artie blushes. "You just made my day even better."

"Of course, you're welcome." Lucius winks, glancing back at his wife, he says. "Come on, little warden, serving you would be his greatest pleasure. Let Artie make something for you."

"Yes, my lor...I mean...Lucius," Artie says successfully stopping himself. "I don't mind making anything."

Lucius gives him a cautious nod. "You see?"

"I hate that nickname, Yuleshua Lucius Gamerin. Don't call me warden. It's trickery to make me feel bad." Josephine drops her hands to her sides. "I don't know."

"I hate when you call me, honey. We're even from this morning," Lucius says. "Come on. Don't be a curmudgeon, yulee." Lucius looks around until realizing how he can get away with their circumstance to encourage a playday. He places his fingers on Claire's cheeks. Their noses almost touch as he gives his little girl a glistening smile. "Do you want Daddy to make you something? You can go outside and play with Mommy, Daddy, and Artie. Maybe, play in the snow for the first time?"

"Oh, you're not fair...honey," Josephine says. "You never play fair."

"I'm always fair...warden," he answers.

"Please don't go where you two are going with the name calling. Her getting angry scares the dickens out of me," Artie says.

"Yes," Claire says, her blues eyes twinkling and her voice squeaking excitedly. "Daddy, I want a princess dress."

"Now, that's what I'm talking about," Artie says.

"We never go beyond funny name-calling." Lucius snickers, and gazes at Claire. "I can make you one later, princess, but it's too cold for a dress to go and play in the snow. Artie and I can make you a furry outfit with some, cute, furry boots to go with it. We can make you look like a little, fuzzy bear cub. Would you like to go outside and play with us today?"

"Okay," Claire says reaching her arms over her daddy's neck. "Can I have my princess dress later, Daddy?" Her bottom lip puckers out.

"With all that is good in me," Artie says. "That's cute. How can you ever say no to her?"

"I can't." Lucius nods. "I can't say no to her." He continues talking to Claire. "I can make you anything you want as long as your momma is okay with it."

"Cheaters. All of you." Josephine grumbles. "Mutiny. Absolute mutiny."

Lucius says, "Ironic, isn't it?"

Claire gazes at her momma and asks, "Can Daddy make me look like a teddy bear and go play snow?"

Lucius fails in hiding his laughter behind blubbering lips. He asks, "Yeah. Momma, what do you say?"

"You're reading my mind," Josephine says as her right brow goes up. She thinks, *Don't make me out to be a bad guy, Lucius.*

I'm not, he transfers to her. He speaks aloud, "Momma, it's up to you. We could just," he pauses in between nearly every word while exhaling a lengthy breath as he continues saying, "mope around…indoors…pouting …all day long with nothing to do."

She nods before looking at Claire. "Yes, sweetie. Momma's not a spoilsport. If Daddy says he'll make something warm for you, then that's fine. We trust your daddy in everything. He only has our best interests at heart."

"There you go, my yoshawn. I'm not ambushing you. I'm merely stating facts."

"Yay," Claire says and points at the thick snowflakes with a gasp as she misspeaks, "We'll drowned though."

Lucius silently chuckles and says, "You can't drown in snow, pumpkin. It'll clear up when I get back. Promise. I know the weather here."

Josephine smiles and says, "Of course, you do." She whispers over Claire's ear, "I'm still learning how your daddy knows so much. He knows something we don't if he's making promises about it."

Stretching his back, "Okay, let's not go into trailing conversations," Lucius says.

"Yay." Artie claps his hands together. "I love playing in the snow, Claire, and you're going to have so much fun here. I'll take care of you."

Josephine shakes her head, says, "What am I gonna do with two playful angels?"

"Angels?" Claire asks. "It's just Daddy."

Lucius says, "That's right, pumpkin. I'm your daddy." He kisses her cheek. "I'm gonna let you in on a little secret we never told anyone at church. Something that no one ever knew." He gets close to Claire's ear and says, "I'm an angel with wings. I work for God."

She gasps and slaps at a wide mouth. She looks at her momma for the confirmation. When Josephine nods to let her know that he is telling the truth, she asks, "Daddy has wings?" She glances behind him. "Where?"

Josephine says, "He sure does. They're hiding. Daddy keeps them protected."

Artie says, "Claire said she could see me sometimes when I visited."

Lucius nods, and answers, "Occasionally, but not all the time. She could sense them a lot. I realized it was because she is a Gamerin. Her knowing that they were there was getting tougher to hide from people."

Josephine asks, "When were you gonna tell me that she could see them?"

Lucius shrugs and says, "Honestly, I was just hoping that she wouldn't say anything to anyone in public because we were trying to stay a secret." His arms squeeze his family closer together into a huddle. He says, "I've got my girls, and that's all that matters now. No more hiding." He kisses Josephine. "I love you, little momma."

"I love you more," Josephine says.

"That's impossible." Lucius looks over toward the bay windows that are collecting snow. He says, "After Daddy comes back from work, we'll get warmed up and play in the snow together."

"Daddy, you go to heaven were angels go?"

Lucius nods. "That's right, precious."

Claire's face grows concerned, and she says, "Daddy, if you go to heaven, you come back."

"I am coming back, baby doll. I'll only be gone for a short while."

Artie says, "I can make the outfits while you're gone."

Lucius says, "Josephine isn't used to the cold, Artie. I need you to get extra material together. I want jaustrawl lining for them both. They might have Gamerin DNA, but they're human, and I can testify that they get cold." He points at Josephine's feet and says, "Trust me. Freezing cold, to the point of utter shock when you're touched by them."

"Hey," Josephine says, but soon pauses. She asks, "Lucius, what's jaustrawl? Is that what you're gonna make for us to wear?"

"Yes, baby. Artie will make most of your outfits today. I love when I'm able to teach you this stuff. You have a great memory." He smiles back at Artie and hands Claire over into Artie's hands. "Hold her for me, will you?" Lucius smiles at Josephine and says, "Jaustrawl is like wool, but warmer. When the material touches your skin, it imitates body heat. The material never gets too hot because of cellular memory embedded in it. Even though the fur is not alive, there is intelligent enzymes within its fibers. Jaustrawl comes from keratin of a woolly creature living near the cavernous poles on Artie's planet, both the northern and southern mountain regions."

Artie says, "Don't forget our moon too."

Lucius nods. "And also on the seventh moon orbiting around this planet."

"You have moons?" Claire asks. "Do they hit each other?"

Artie says, "No, the guy who put them there—"

Lucius coughs and interrupts Artie from speaking.

Artie continues but stays away from mentioning how Lucius had built and placed the moons that are currently orbiting around the planet that they are on. "They don't hit each other. Many planets have multiple moons."

"Like Gamerilaye?" Josephine asks. She turns toward Lucius and asks, "Darling, can you please tell me where we are at the moment? I guess I'm funny like that, but I usually like to know what part of the universe I'm in."

Artie begins to say, "Oh, we're on—"

Lucius covers Artie's mouth. "No. Don't tell her!"

"Why not?" Josephine asks.

Lucius drops his hand and answers her, "Josephine, we can't let that information get out." He glances back at Artie. "We were under attack today. They might track us somehow because she can't block her mind. I don't know if Josephine will forget when leaving."

She asks, "What do you mean forget?"

Lucius says, "No one is allowed to know where this planet is. The atmosphere is made to cause any visitor to forget where they have been. It's protected by the Trinity in that way. I don't know how the atmosphere will work on you. You can't have the location, name, moons, or any identifiers of this world in your memory."

"That'll lower our defenses here." Artie nods. "You're right, we can't tell her."

Lucius continues, "Only I have that information when I leave because the information is blocked by the Father himself." Lucius glances at Artie. "She hasn't gone to see Him, and she has my DNA in her because we're eternally bonded. She might remember where this place is if we tell her with her having a Gamerin memory. With that information in her, somebody might have access to this location with a simple thought running through her head."

Josephine asks, "Can you explain a little better? Why is this place such a secret when everyone in the universe knows the location of Earth?"

Lucius takes in a deep breath and says, "The same reason I never say Artie's true name and why my real name was to remain a secret on Earth. There are secrets in the heavens because of the ongoing war. The war doesn't happen on Earth only. Every realm must protect their borders from the war; however, this world is different. It was foretold that this world would be safe throughout the history of the war, and none would ever invade its horizon. I can't let anyone know it's location, not even my wife because you're a human, and your mind is read easily by others. You don't have the ability to block your mind to guard your thoughts."

Artie says, "I thought you blocked her mind already. I couldn't read her thoughts on Earth."

Josephine gasps. "What does Artie mean by you blocking my mind?"

Lucius explains, "The Gamerin, many angelic beings, and other celestials can block people's minds from being read. I would block your mind, but I couldn't block your speech. Like Claire, you're innocent of heart and might say something that unintentionally hurts others." He turns to look at Artie and says, "I never told my wife about the different things of our worlds because Earth definitely isn't a safe place for this realm's secrets."

"Why's this place so secret?" Josephine asks. "I wouldn't even know how to find this place on one of those jurisdiction map thingies you talk about."

Lucius says, "Realm map of quadrant zones and jurisdiction laws. Artorus is his real name because it was given to him by the Father. Artie is the only person from this entire world who is fighting in the army as a soldier. There are no other harvesters who are angels or who travel to any other world beyond this one. For that reason, Artie is the only guardian who has ever lived here. His mind has also been blocked, and no one can gain the information from him."

Josephine asks again, "How can this place be hidden if you know where it is?"

Lucius says, "My mind was blocked by the Trinity. Only when I am here do I remember, but my ability to explain where this world is after I leave this atmosphere has been erased in a way where I cannot utter its location."

Artie nods. "This place is hidden by something, but we can't even remember what is hiding it. Some sort of deflective shield."

"But why is this place so special?"

Lucius answers, "Because this planet provides food for many worlds during certain periods of famine and war. The harvesters that reside here will provide the wedding feast for the mighty banquet that Earth will have during its massive harvest. Harvesters are chosen specifically by the Lord."

Josephine asks, "If people don't know where this world is, and Artie is the only angel from here, and it's such a big secret, then how come you know about this place? This isn't Gamerilaye."

Lucius stands straight as he reads all their minds. "Oh, that's what you're asking?" Artie nearly answers her, but Lucius quickly snaps his finger for Artie to remain quiet. "Artie, stop. I'm reading your mind. I don't give you permission. I must protect her and Claire. This is not the time. Just give me a minute."

"Sorry, Lucius," Artie says.

Lucius looks into Josephine's eyes and says, "My love, I know I must tell you something, but I'm not ready right now. Please, don't be angry when I do tell you because it hurts to think of what you'll see me as. I love you, Josephine. All that I am and all that I wanna be is your husband, father to our children." He places her hand upon his heart. "You know me inside and out. I took a vow and made a covenant with you before the Almighty. I'm gonna protect you. I'll always be your husband. I'll fight to protect you and our family. I'm true to my word. You know this of me."

She nods. "I trust you, Lucius."

He releases her and nods, "Okay, Artie and I need to get the jaustrawl material together. He's going to start on your outfits. I must report to Oobadoave. Let's get you situated in the craft room before I leave."

Six

Craft Room

As Lucius helps Artie bring materials that he has requested into his warm craft area, Josephine follows closely behind. She says, "Y'all are talented if you plan on making us outfits." She watches them carrying large bundles above their heads.

"And we do so with a grateful heart," Artie says as he opens his craft room.

Josephine gasps as she enters the craft room. "Whoa." Claire holds onto her mother's neck and imitates her response. Claire sighs behind her fingers. When Josephine lowers Claire down so she can stand, Claire follows her mother around the room with a study of each handcrafted surface.

Josephine studies the creative artwork interlaid across the walls. "You did all this?" Josephine asks. Three-dimensional paintings and mosaics are interlined with textile work throughout each piece that drapes the walls and tapestries. Everything is made with natural bits from what look like elements from all over the universe. Josephine says, "Breathtaking." She points at a painting with water that appears to be moving by a bioluminescent ripple effect.

Artie shrugs. "This artwork is nothing in comparison to some others in this galaxy."

Lucius chimes in. "You do have a striking gallery, Artie." He points at the antler braided chandelier with its roaring candle fixtures that are held overhead. "Not everybody has wax that doesn't burn with a fire that never dies."

Artie half smiles and says, "I wonder who it was that gave those to me."

"That's enough." Lucius chuckles. "You're dancing all over an explanation."

Josephine stands beneath the eternal flame that flickers with fiery brimstone that is centered in the chandelier. "Did you do this?" she asks.

"I'm a brimstone angel. I can make an eternal flame," Artie answers. "Few in existence can make an eternal flame."

As Claire walks over toward another fireplace, Josephine says, "Don't get too close. Fire still burns here." She follows her daughter and stands beside the fireplace stones next to his work area. "You have," she says as she counts with fingers, "one, two, three fireplaces in here. It's cozy but still bright in here."

Artie replies, "Two of them are fireplaces, but one is an incinerator."

"What's the difference?" Josephine asks.

"Incinerators are for my trash, like when I have leftover scraps. I use the ashes for gardening in the fields. There is a chute beyond a panel in there that flows to a cave system."

"It's the lime and potassium and trace nutrients he uses for mushrooms," Lucius adds into the conversation while he finishes straightening the jaustrawl material on the worktable.

"I use the ashes in my compost as well," Artie says.

Josephine says, "It's so comfy in here." Her fingers follow along a leather chair with silvery brads woven throughout the framework. She glances up at wild animal trophies. "There are a few massive species that you have on the wall." She smiles with a swift turn. "A bachelor's dream. Definitely not a Mrs. Harvester who lives here."

"Artie doesn't think that way, little momma," Lucius says.

Artie says, "That would be bizarre. Better not birth those ideas."

"Well, this is a wonderful home you have," Josephine says. "Amazing craftsmanship, Artie. I had no idea. The design reminds me of Alaska."

Lucius and Artie splutter. Artie answers, "Yeah. I made this, but it's nothing like Alaska. It's safe here."

"Artie," Lucius says. "Stop talking so much."

Curiosity strikes Josephine and she asks, "What? Y'all don't have bears here? What about the rug out there? Is that what you're referring to?"

Artie asks Lucius, "Can I not tell her about Alaska? It's difficult to know what she knows."

Lucius sorts through material with a special wool comb, as he does, he psychically speaks to Artie, *"You can tell her about Alaska, but don't let her know I had anything to do with it. I just found out recently myself."* Lucius nods and says,

"Be careful because they're kind doesn't accept the information well. She's not a soldier, and her mind is innocent like a child. I want to allow her to keep her innocence for her protection, Artie."

"I can take it," Josephine says.

Placing down the comb and stepping over toward the nearest light, Lucius stands quiet for a moment and turns toward a fireplace. He raises his hand to his mouth like he is thinking to hide his reaction of grief. He says, "Just..." he pauses briefly before continuing, "be careful about telling her." He braces himself while he gazes into the fire.

"I'll be careful," Artie says. "Alaska is a beautiful, one of a kind, gold and quartz rich land. The only bad thing about gold and quartz is that its elements can power many of the enemy's weapons. Earlier today, you were visited by an army with transporters. The Nephilim."

Lucius clears his throat to let Artie know that he is telling her too much. "That's...um," Lucius says. "Keep it basic by not relating things together, if you know what I mean?"

Artie backtracks his thoughts. Clasping his hands together, he continues. "Let me see what I can say. Okay, so, the big bad guys in the big bad army, some of them have transporters. They zap in and zap out." Artie opens his fingers of his hands like a firecracker and says, "Whoosh. Disappeared."

"How does this have anything to do with gold and quartz? You're going to have to relate something together for me to understand a few things, right?" Josephine asks.

"Yes, tis true," Artie says. "Transporters can pick up people and take them back to their craft in a flash." He raises a pointed finger and says, "Because of the relationship they have with gold and quartz, these elements that are found within stones and metal increases certain abilities, acting as conductors, linking them to the ground. It's like an antenna."

"I had no idea," Josephine says.

Artie continues. "Our lesson gets better. You know how soothsayers carry quartz stones around their necks, thinking they're safe. The tradition is a tactic of our enemy, telling spiritualists to wear the amulets, thereby making them easier conductors for work."

"Those liars," Josephine says.

"No way," Artie jokes. "You don't say. The devil is a liar?"

Lucius speaks beneath his fingers. "Don't make fun of her. She's just learning. Enemies hide this stuff on Earth well with the pawns they use."

"I wasn't making fun. Sorry," Artie says. "The liars, our enemies, are very crafty, and like Lucius said, they hide behind pawns using the façade of good spirits to manipulate and trick the Father's children into their world. Incantations, tarot cards, stones…you name it, anything to mislead them. The Bible is very strict on never speaking to the spirits, or consorting with the dead. Those who have passed on don't answer anymore, and any answer that someone receives is not what they think."

Lucius half turns. "My love, angels work for our Father, not His children. Angels won't answer a human child, but the devil and his minion will. They'll do anything to mislead them into his con."

Josephine says, "I spoke to you, Lucius. I didn't know."

Lucius answers her, "Baby, I couldn't hide from you. I tried, remember? I fell in love with you. Us being together was God ordained. You weren't entering into witchcraft of any sort. However, the enemy would've taken, and did take the opened door as such. They knew you'd be able to contact them, and they could lie openly to you. It's why I hid who I was so you wouldn't be found guilty, and I protected you in any way that I could. They would've viewed you as a soothsayer, an enchantress of the dark arts like a witch, and they would've taken you after getting rid of me. They tried."

Josephine slowly turns toward Artie and says, "Gold and quartz. Go on."

Artie winks at Lucius. "They like my lesson so far." He glances back with a bounce in his shoulders. "Texas isn't rich in gold and quartz, so transport-ters must be closer to the ground in order to abduct the General's children."

"That's why the sky grew dark," she says. "That was their Nephilim vessel covering the sky."

Lucius tries to stop the conversation from connecting him, but Artie continues with, "And it's shaped like a city too." Artie smiles.

Lucius says, "Artie, stick to the lesson. You'll confuse her. You're nowhere near Alaska at this moment."

Artie raises a palm. "I'm getting to it." He hunches down near Claire and continues. "In Alaska, the enemy's crafts don't have to be directly above the land because of the rich resources. They can be out of the atmosphere. Ground angels are unaware of what's going on until the General's children and even sometimes the angels are abducted. The Nephilim are sneaky. In Alaska, we have specially trained angels guarding the children to reduce the abductions taking place by Gamerin technology."

Lucius squeezes his eyes. "Oh, that was too much, Artie."

"Abductions?" Josephine looks over toward Lucius's back. She gasps and repeats, "The recent abductions of all those women," and realizes that the story is all making sense. "Up north. Nephilim. Alien abductions. Lucius, you're reading my mind, aren't you?"

Artie stands up as stiff as a beam. "I think I said too much."

Lucius groans.

Josephine swallows but manages a small smile. "Thank you, Artie, for the lesson." She turns away from the group and stares into a different fireplace away from Lucius.

"Alien abductions," Claire bursts out. "No such thing as aliens."

"That's right," Artie says. "I'm not an alien. That's not a nice thing to say about family."

Josephine rubs her thumb over her nose. "Alien abductions are the same as the Nephilim abductions? Is that what you're trying to tell me?" She turns toward Lucius. "The thing that bothered you so much that you didn't wanna tell me? I was almost abducted today by our own family? Your nephews?" The silence is palpable between her and Lucius. She says, "Yep, evidently, this day can get worse." Josephine gazes only at Lucius and tries to remain quiet.

Artie picks Claire up and sets her on the desk. "Let's give them a few minutes," he says and allows her to pick what color jaustrawl fur she wants.

Josephine steps closer and whispers against Lucius's arm, "Can you read my mind?"

Saying nothing, he nods.

She transfers her thought. *Is this why you were so upset when you found out about the abductions…because it's your nephews who are abducting women? The abductions have been going on for a long time, haven't they?*

He nods.

Do you wanna talk about it?

He shakes his head quietly.

Artie pulls a pair of scissors from the hands of an inquisitive child and says, "Maybe not those. I have some crayons around here that are much safer." Glancing at Lucius, he says, "Sorry, Lucius. It's hard knowing what she knows, and what she doesn't."

"It's not your fault," Lucius answers. He then turns to face Josephine and holds her for comfort. "Baby, I'm sorry for keeping this information from you. It's been difficult knowing. Shameful even."

She shrugs. "What would telling me have fixed? Honestly, I know that you protect me, but you need to feel that you can speak to me so then I can protect you."

He nods. "I do. I want to," he says and kisses her. "I must leave. I'll be back in a little while. We can all spend time together for a family vacation when I return."

Lucius hugs Claire one last time and says, "Daddy will be back soon. You'll be safe here with Artie and Momma." Lucius hands Claire the pair of scissors and winks at Artie. "He'll teach you how to use them."

"Lucius," Artie says with a shake of his head. "Those are diamond bladed scissors and very sharp."

Josephine takes the scissors from Claire and says, "You'd better let me." She points the scissor handles toward her husband. "You let her get away with everything."

"My baby's talented," Lucius says as he hands Claire measuring tape instead. "How do you learn, pumpkin?"

"When someone teaches you," Claire answers.

"That's right, princess." Lucius points over toward Artie and says, "You gotta teach her in order for her to learn." Lucius kisses his wife one last time. "I have to open a portal to Jett Commdearadea before I can go to Ooba-doave."

Josephine asks, "Why?"

"I can't open a portal straight to Oobadoave because the light will blind you and burn your skin."

Josephine gasps. "Oh, that's right. You taught me that this morning."

Lucius says, "When I come back, my skin will be glowing. I'm telling you now so then you don't get scared. Claire most likely won't be bothered because of her age."

Josephine asks, "Like Moses?"

Lucius smiles. "Yes, similar to what happened to Moses."

"I thought Dex was from there, so why doesn't he glow?" Josephine asks.

Artie makes a funny sound through his lips, like gathering a laugh and a cough at the same time. "She catches everything."

Lucius says, "Now, you know what I've had to live with, Artie." He turns toward her. "This is what I was explaining this morning without telling you everything. Only onyx-skinned Jett angels can enter Oobadoave and not glow from exposure. Jett Commdearadea is the next planet over, full of warriors, and Jett commanders were specially engineered for easy transition from the Crystal city. It's why their skin's dark. They absorb light, instead of it bouncing from them. They are truly holy beings in perfect camouflage. Their skin is remarkable."

She says, "I love hearing you talk about the heavens. I get a chance to know you more, and it makes me feel like you trust me." She kisses his cheek. "It means a lot to me when you trust me," she says patting his chest. "And I'm gonna enjoy today with you, on this no-name planet."

Rubbing his chest from the heaviness of her compliment, Lucius huffs as he says, "You might not wield a weapon but...baby..."

Artie says, "Yeah, I caught that one as well."

"What?" she asks.

"Baby, your manipulation for information can really cut deep."

"What manipulation?" she asks. "I'm not manipulating you."

"Oooh," Artie says.

Lucius nods toward him. "Yeah, and she doesn't even know that she's doing it."

Artie says, "I'd better not say anything anymore. I'm closing my mouth now."

Josephine lifts a hand up. "What are y'all talking about? I was only sharing my thoughts. I'm not prying."

Lucius exhales and says, "I know I must tell you, but I need a little more time. I love you, Josephine. I'll be back soon." He kisses her one last time.

Lucius leaves the crafting room and enters the cavernous springs beneath several main floors of Artie's home. He walks a memorized path by bioluminescent mushrooms and fluorescent cavernous flowers. Rushing waterfalls flood into lakes with glowing fish, helping to light his path. He enters a darkened portion of the cave that is only lit by glowworms. The area is covered in glowworms that make their webs appearing more like stars and galaxies in the sky as if floating in space. Lucius braces himself and says, "To my old barracks." He gathers his strength. "Come on, Lucius. Find your strength. You're not the same guy anymore," he says and enters a portal into the dense forests of Jett Commdearadea.

Seven

Jett Commdearadea

The portal closes behind Lucius and he breathes a deep breath filled with humidity from the dense air of Jett Commdearadea. A feeling of heaviness covers him as he sees an overgrown trail. The humid air reminds him of his years of training. He remembers the constant excessive work he had to undergo to be considered a good enough soldier. Or the humbling of himself to even work as a soldier in the army and learning how to take commands from a commander that he could've easily ripped in half if provoked enough.

Lucius remembers how he had given up in those dark days and how enlisting was his last silent cry for help. His power had dwindled, his heart was asleep, and his motivation to continue had all but gone completely out. He was alone, abandoned, and dried up on the inside.

The air is thick with his first step. The slightest breeze chimes through thick leaves like a mellow howl. *This day is a bumpy ride*, he thinks. He walks a thin trail through the overgrowth of bushwhacked areas, and tunes a keen ear toward loud hollers in the distance. They're the training calls from warrior angels. They send tremors throughout Lucius's body. *Come on*, he tells himself. *You're not training today. Calm down, Lucius. You're just passing through and following the code of ethics to let them know that your command was lost today.*

Walking over a ridge lined area, his heart thunders. His lips grow taut as he sees the training army below.

Heavy-duty battalions are performing drills with an enormous species of Seraphim. *There they are. Seraphim, a step below archangels.* He nods. *Armageddon and the white throne judgment*—their calls interrupt his thoughts—*training for the final battle.*

Lucius flies down a high cliffside toward the clearing were the Seraphim and Jett warriors are training. He lands close to a handful of armed commanders who are giving orders to the troops.

A commander briefly speaks in Jett Commdearadea, saying, *"Shireefa kloken,"* and repeats what he was going to say in English. "We were wondering who had entered our world." The commander's eyes look off in a different direction. He barely bothers to look at Lucius as he continues. "Then, I saw you." The commander glances over at Lucius. "I almost sent a battalion up there. We didn't have any scheduled arrivals."

"I know what shireefa kloken means, for I understand Jett. I am no 'unwanted invader,' but I apologize for the abrupt entrance," Lucius says with a nervous wave of his hand. "I didn't mean to come unannounced. I'm a commander, and my passage has been preordered as such. My situation is extremely complicated, but I'm giving report through the chain of command to follow the law in accordance with the code of ethics."

"That happens only under certain circumstances, and I don't recall scheduling this report." The Jett commander eyeballs Lucius's Earthly attire. "Only principalities and certain celestials can block their minds. You're not in uniform." He nearly sneers, causing a twitch in his upper lip as he continues. "You're blocking your mind, shireefa kloken. Shielding your mind is why we almost sent a battalion. We could hear your steps, but we couldn't make out your thoughts."

"I was letting you know I was here by walking through the forest. It's why I allowed you to hear my steps." Lucius stands strong only a few feet from staring eyes of intimidating commanders. He tries to keep a semblance of authority before speaking. First, he nods and then says, "You're right, I am a principality. I trained here."

"How quaint," another austere commander speaks up with mild sarcasm. "A principality is gracing us with his presence." With almost enough contempt to mock Lucius, the Jett commanders all bow their heads with reservation in their respect.

"I'm not hear for your praise or prejudice. Bowing is not necessary," Lucius says. "I'm an equal on the battlefield. I usually answer to Commander Dextorus. I took over his command in his absence from my station."

A commander says, "No need to explain." His eyes shift in a different area as if tired of the conversation already. "I know exactly who you are.

You're the only principality who ever trained with us." The commander meets Lucius's gaze before saying, "A Gamerin."

At this revelation, the battalions of Jett warriors and Seraphim quit training and gawk at Lucius.

"Quite a surprise," a kind faced commander says in response. He introduces himself with a handshake. "A surprise, if you don't mind my saying. I'm Commander Philip. I know Commander Dextorus. Not many knew that you were Gamerin. I always wondered why those involved kept quiet."

Lucius greets him with a handshake. "I remember all of you. I'm Lucius."

One of the other commanders finally smiles and says, "Yuleshua Gamerin, my apologies for sounding cold. You are one of us, Lucius. I'm Terrence." He gestures toward his large army. "Everybody, this is Lucius, a Gamerin principality who became a member of the Jett warrior family. He battled beside Dextorus. He is known for his durability in battle and loyalty to our General." Terrence nubs the air with his nose and says, "As you see, he's been fighting on the forefront and is undercover."

"That's right, those are civilian clothes," another commander with massive dreadlocks says as he grins. "I'm Boaz, and I remember your story. You're most welcome here, Mangoram slayer. Commander Dextorus speaks highly of you."

"That's me." Lucius nods.

"A mighty warrior, huh?" The fourth commander takes a step back and says, "I suppose you want me to introduce myself." And snaps with his words. "What's your bidding here, Gamerin? We have battalions to train and don't have time for pleasantries."

Lucius gulps. "I have to pass through here for an emergency meeting on Oobadoave."

Boaz asks, "Why not appear there?" gesturing toward the cliffside. "Arriving here isn't necessary. You shouldn't check in at your old barracks if you're already a commander. Besides, Dextorus isn't here this cycle of training. You can simply enter the chambers and check-in if summoned."

Lucius's expression falls and says, "It's one of the rare occurrences…My emergency meeting." He meets their gaze and says, "I was attacked by a Nephilim army today. I am reporting to the chambers of the Hagia Sophia and providing my testimony. I was told to come here first."

The fourth commander spits on the ground. "Nephilim curse. Every one of you Gamerin have become a thorn in our sides. No greater than the Shadow Cluster."

Philip nods at Lucius, says, "Continue," and glances back toward the speaker of the harsh remarks. "Please continue, fellow soldier and son of God. Please finish your report, so you may be on your way for the emergency testimony."

Blinking momentarily, Lucius swallows. "I must speak with my brother, Yeshua. He must know I'm safe, but that I lost my commanding unit. Those I guarded were attacked after the invasion of my home today."

Terrence shouts, "What? The Nephilim made it to Gamerilaye? I thought they were stuck on Earth. You come here dressed in civilian clothes. Have they figured out how to get back without your key?"

Lucius braces himself and says, "No. They don't have my key."

"Spit it out, Gamerin," the fourth commander says as he scowls. "What's your purpose?"

Lucius takes another deep breath before saying, "I was on Earth, and they tried abducting me, my wife, and our child from our home in Texas. I must pass through here first to protect them and to follow the code of ethics because I am the acting commander over the unit that was attacked."

Each Jett warrior grabs a sword.

"Seize him," a commander orders.

The fourth commander steps forward with his blade pressing over Lucius's neck. "Have you taken one of the General's daughters, you Gamerin scum?" Lucius's chin arches up as the fourth commander continues. "Are you making a Nephilim army for yourself?"

Trying not to make any movements. "Awesome," Lucius says. "No. I haven't broken any laws."

Philip says, "Explain yourself, principality."

Realizing his discussion has turned into a negotiation, Lucius calmly raises his hands submissively. "I bid you not harm. I come openly and speaking the truth as I was instructed by Commander Dextorus and my Father. I must guard my family by this preordained passage. Lower your weapons. This is an act of treason against a fellow commander."

But they don't lower their weapons.

"Don't twist our minds, Gamerin," the fourth commander says. "Prisoners will say anything to avoid capture."

"All right. I want you to remember that you chose to greet me this way." Lucius telekinetically bends every blade away from him. As he does, he straightens his head and back so he can look at them. The commanders each take a step back. Lucius says, "I was given the queen of Gamerilaye by the General himself. My marriage while on Earth was kept a secret for her own safety." He wipes the bloody scratches from his neck and stares down at his fingers. "My child is a daughter. She's a testimony of my purity. I'm the only blessed Gamerin among my people that did not fall. I'm in holy matrimony with my wife, Josephine. I serve the Trinity as his Gamerin son and principality warrior. I can't simply open a portal into Oobadoave. The light will hurt my family because of the human bloodline."

"How are you doing this if you come from Earth?" Terrence eyeballs a blade that is currently pointing inches from his face.

"I'm not fallen, and I could've done worse."

Boaz asks, "What are you planning, Gamerin? One whistle and I could call these Seraphim over to destroy you."

Lucius exhales and repeats, "I must report to my brother Yeshua because I have been summoned due to this attack. It is your duty to give me fair passage after reporting with you."

Every weapon is lowered, including every Seraphim's blade that was split in two and bent around each pair of Seraphim's hands to keep them bound.

Lucius says, "Please take my response as a form of self-defense and not an attack. I will release the Seraphim from their temporary bonds momentarily. I told you my rare circumstance for why I had to be here." He nods. "I will exonerate you of any treason against a fellow commander. I already told you, I'm a son of God and obeying strict orders." Lucius raises his hands for them all to see. "I'm unarmed," he says before dropping his shoulders. "Let's think this through, guys. If I were going to fall and invade any planet at all, I would have to be a complete and utter moron to choose one of the strongest planets to invade first and by myself. I wouldn't have announced I was here."

Philip nods, says, "I heard it took archangels and a whole legion of our own to train you, Lucius." His eyes glimmer as he grins. "Between us, you always gave our guys quite a scare. Only Dextorus was crazy enough to work alongside archangels to train you fulltime. He's braver than anyone I've ever met. The guy has nothing left to lose."

Lucius exhales with his well-hidden anxiety level leaving. He says, "Thank you." He rubs his chest. "That makes me feel better."

The fourth commander tries bending his sword back. "I'm sorry, Gamerin king. My name's Nolan," he says meeting Lucius's gaze. "Can you fix my weapon?"

Lucius winks. "Think of the bent blade as a memento of my forgiveness. A reminder of our encounter and how you were exonerated of treason." He rubs a portion of his neck and heals the area before saying, "Consider us even."

Nolan nods. "Fair enough, principality. We can't be too careful with the threat of the Gamerin and Nephilim armies plaguing Yeshua's system. They have long taken and tortured our soldiers. I apologize for my preconception of you. Many have fallen, and not all of those that we have fought against are as powerful as your kind, especially a principality. Please forgive me. I shouldn't have called you scum."

"You are forgiven, Nolan. Truth be told, I knew this conversation would not be as easy as just passing through, but I tried keeping an optimistic mind. Besides, I bent every single dagger you have on you the moment you said that."

Philip gives up on bending his sword and tosses the blade aside. "Lucius, your life on Earth must've been kept an incredible secret. I heard Dextorus was working on a sensitive mission. Mouths were ordered to remain silenced under punishment of banishment. This makes sense with your testimony to protect you and your family."

"This has taken me off guard," Terrence says as he studies the curved metal of his blade. "I know on Earth, or even outside of their jurisdiction, principalities can't hold their power if they must do battle all the time. You must've been well protected."

Lucius answers, "Yes, an entire army protected us. I wasn't allowed to leave Earth with my family, until just today when the attack happened."

Boaz's brows frown as he asks, "To better serve this report, why do you believe you were attacked?"

"I can't be certain, Boaz. I know that I can't let them get their hands on a Nephilim female."

"You speak of your daughter," Boaz says.

Lucius gives a slight nod. "She's Gamerin. If they know that I have an ageless daughter then they know that they can breed. I was ordered to leave if invaded and to not enter Gamerilaye without speaking to Him first." Lucius glances over toward a silent sea of eyes. "That's why I must check in at the High Council Chambers and give my report. I was ordered to pass through here first because of the soldiers I commanded."

"Your family's safe," Nolan says before asking, "What of our soldiers?"

Lucius swallows his grief. Philip swiftly catches a slight gloss from the corner of Lucius's eye. "Take your time," Philip says.

Lucius respectfully looks at each one of the commanders and says, "Our soldiers were taken from the field today while protecting my family. I don't know if they've made it home or not, but they were taken."

Sorrow spreads like wildfire over the field as they mourn the loss of the fallen soldiers from battle. The chiming breeze of the dense forest is drowned out by the wheezes behind covered faces. Lucius watches as the Seraphim rip their garments in grief.

"Their sacrifice saved us," Lucius says.

The commanders keep their faces as stoic as possible, but Terrence turns away and is unable to swallow his heartache.

Before the mourning can escalate any further, Lucius, hyperventilating inwardly says, "I must leave. I'm sorry to bring such horrible news."

"You're alive, and your family's safe. The threat has been reduced, and they will be remembered for their services while enslaved. We will visit them after they return home." Philip pats Lucius's arm. "Thank you for your service, Lucius. The Father must be proud of you to trust you with such a task as guarding his children."

Not saying a word, Lucius nods his heavy head and turns back. Before he leaves, Nolan says, "I don't exactly know how you examine yourself, young principality, but the General must have a purpose for you. Don't doubt your calling. Their suffering should not be in vain."

"You sound like, Dex." Lucius rubs a clear golden crystal over his trinket.

Sending an intense light over the sobbing observers, the Oobadoave portal opens. Lucius inhales deeply as he leaves.

Eight

Oobadoave

With his head down, Lucius focuses on hiding his shame and the terrible news he brings today. His eyes gradually look upward to take in his Father's home. "The epicenter of all existence," he says to himself. A large mountainous building is embedded with many mighty roaring waterfalls that cascade down multiple layers of terraced garden areas.

The mountain itself is a city within a city, a place where diverse children enjoy their Father's home. The metal of each structure is pure and shining as flawless as crystal glass. Clear mineral waters surround each building. Between the buildings, gargantuan trees cover the landscape as the light from the orbiting moons brush against the skyline. A churning river separates the capital from the surrounding cities.

Lucius stares at the capital, says, "I don't belong here," and scoots a step back. Magnifying his surroundings in vivacious colors, the holy brilliance beams across his face. Even with the beauty around him, Lucius is sorrowed in his heart. "I'll never be who I once was."

He remembers the last time that he stood this close to the capital city. It was the day that he had received his winged stallions as a gift for his army. Lucius exhales. "I never deserved anything."

He walks by a bustling street, beyond a local garden, and over sparkling clear waters, reflecting a glorious color of gold. Every native Oobadoave angel refers to the sight as home. Lucius closes his eyes. "You have to be here," he reminds himself. Lucius forces his steps to the dividing bridge of where Oobadoave meets the Holies of heaven.

The high bridge arches over the roaring river and leads to the outer gardens of the capital. Lucius hides a grimace as he orders, "Just," forcing his leg, "move," but his legs are heavy and knees wobbly. With each step, they become heavier and heavier with his fear of the unknown. Lucius is nearly sweating as he walks with his head down toward steps of the massive mountain center. Lucius thinks to himself, *He told you to come here.* He glances at the Hagia Sophia, *the Hall of knowledge. You will be known, as you were known,* he recites in his mind. *I can never hide who I am here.*

His expression deepens.

Purposefully keeping to himself and trying not to make eye contact, Lucius passes other galactic kings and renowned celestial principalities known for holiness and good fortune. These kings and principalities have blessed the Father with many volunteered warriors and have spotless reputations. Worlds have been won by their good deeds, instead of loss.

Spoken with a low volume at first, a stunned king stands and says, "Gamerin," as Lucius scurries by. "Gamerin."

Out of respect, Lucius shyly waves and shrinks deeper between his own shoulders. His steps are quickened so not to bathe in the humiliation of his being a Gamerin among so many righteous rulers.

The moment worsens.

"What Gamerin?" Another angelic king speaks up, saying, "Here? In the heavens? In the holy city?"

The voice echoes through Lucius's soul and makes his steps falter. Stumbling over the side of his heavy foot, he nearly trips as he tries to get away from the feeling of suffocating humiliation.

"But he's there," a celestial says as he follows the walkway a little and points a finger toward Lucius's vying steps. "Do you not see him? It's a Gamerin coming to visit."

"What's a Gamerin?" another asks as her nose bounces in the air. "Is it a muted race?"

"It can't be a Gamerin. They all fell, and their principality died on the bridegroom's world. There are no Gamerin left in existence."

"But he's there," a loud king says as he follows a dozen or so yards behind Lucius.

Lucius speeds up, gradually widening in the distance between him and the king trying to be closer to him.

Another king comes out from under a fig tree and stares curiously. He says, "No fallen Gamerin would be allowed here without purchase."

At this point, Lucius is sprinting up the steps. His nose dives into his collar as he plugs his ears to keep from hearing anymore of how awful of a king he must be. If his tongue weren't attached, he could swear that he was choking on it from the lump in his throat. Embarrassment, humility, and shame is written in a flushing red color all over his face as he races as fast as he can over the steps that he used to take leisurely. He remembers how he was like the other kings that make eternal acquaintances on those very steps that he runs from.

Now, shame floods his heart and flushes his face. He wishes that he would have just stayed in Josephine's arms so he could hide from his failure because all the pain leaves when he's in her arms.

He passes by the doorways toward the Hall of Knowledge. Immediately, someone exits the doorway. Realizing who he is, her eyes latch on to him. She says with a stutter, "You're a…a…a Gamerin." She covers her mouth and accidently says, "Fallen sons of God from Gamerilaye." She quickly bites her lips together. "I didn't mean…"

His painful expression silences her, and he enters an unnaturally quick speed to get away from the area. Lucius pants while guarding his thoughts and his expression and shielding anything he can with a plaid shirt collar from those who gawk. *Get through this meeting,* he encourages himself as a tear bounces along his cheek. *Then you can go home to Josephine. She adores you, Lucius. She'll comfort you. She thinks you're perfect.*

Finally, Lucius reaches the top layers of the capital. His steps relax into a well-mannered walk. He enters a governed hallway with many chambers that are only accessible by a summon for any celestial, no matter how mighty the principality may be. Red-eyed and trembling, he crosses over the threshold of the first chamber. "I'm Yuleshua Lucius Gam— "

"We know very well who you are, Yuleshua Gamerin," a magistrate with striking yellow eyes says as he leaves his seat to stand only a few feet from Lucius. The magistrate says, "He's expecting you," and points toward a doorway. "You may enter on this day through the far-left door, His banquet hall. He's requested an audience with you upon your arrival."

Lucius nods. "Yes, sir."

"You may not enter the great hall, holy courts, or throne room today."

"Yes, sir."

"And," the magistrate says. "wipe your eyes, principality. Many of His children are mourning along this walkway, and beyond those doors and they are being comforted by the true King of kings and Prince of peace. Only His blood-bought children have the right to come and go as they please. They are His bride. You have already received your birthright and inheritance."

Lucius sniffles with a cowering expression.

The official presses his shoulders back and continues with a point of his chin, and says, "Remember, young principality, wiping every tear from every eye has not yet come to pass. We are still in the war of the heavens. The time of the great culling has not yet come, so be cognizant of your woes. There are children nearby just learning of those who are lost and praying for their return home. Be thoughtful of their young minds."

Lucius does as he's told and wipes his eyes. He had no idea he had been crying quite so much. "Thank you," Lucius says as he passes the threshold toward the mighty doors of the banquet hall. He keeps his sniffling to a minimum and nods with a smile when passing the other chambers with angelic beings directing children to temporary homes. Lucius tries, but can't manage to raise his chin above his slouched shoulders.

Suddenly, twelve feet from the granite door, his steps are so heavy that his knees slightly buckle in fear. *No,* he thinks as he starts grunting. *Not now. Not again. You can do this.*

A growing number of eyes peek around the columns and surrounding banisters of the great entryway. Mumbling increases with an echo from those who speak to the different magistrates within the chambers. "What's he doing?" a mousy voice whimpers beneath her tissue. "Is he being judged?"

The question paralyzes Lucius even more.

Help me, he thinks and closes his eyes. *They're watching. Move already, Lucius,* but his legs are frozen stiff. He's scared to death of judgement, and today he had lost an entire battalion.

But suddenly, a warm hand brushes his shoulder.

Peace, a soothing voice enters his heart.

Lucius exhales with a composed step forward as if a calming and supernatural wave has swept him onto a shoreline. Anxiety washes from his shaken legs as he crosses the left entrance. As he turns back to close the granite barrier behind him, his eyes search for the hand but no one stands anywhere close enough to have touched him. Lucius nods as the door is finally closed. He rests his head over the seal of the stone doorway. "I praise you, Spirit," he whispers. "Thank you, Father, for hearing me."

Lucius walks across jewel-encrusted tiles and enters a portion of the High Council of the Hagia Sophia. The visit to this area is his first time in ten thousand years. "I forgot what it looked like in here."

His voice echoes after speaking. His echo travels down a grand opening toward the innocent eyes looking back from a distance away.

He walks through the grand chamber with ornately decorated banquet tables bursting with the finest furnishings. Each place setting is complete with a name tag handwritten by an eager groom and each in the guest's own language. Napkins lay folded in simple shapes. Goblets of several sizes line the table spread and wait to be turned right side up for a feast.

Lucius arrives from behind a small grouping of individuals. His head hangs low, and his eyes are closed. The carefree laughter and joyous conversation that was taking place before Lucius arrived has decreased. Lucius kneels immediately. His face is flat, until he is fully prostrate in front of all who are there. "Yeshua," Lucius barely utters. "I'm not disobeying by being here. Please forgive me, my brother, and my king. I don't mean to interrupt. Can I be welcomed in your presence?"

"Of course, you are welcome," Jesus answers.

Several heads turn at the strange sight of the visitor's manners.

Jesus smiles as He stands from His chair. He says to the group that was speaking with Him before Lucius's arrival, "Come, my beautiful children." He reaches an arm over them like a mother directing little babes. "This is a treat," He says and squats down where Lucius lies on the floor. "You might not see his face, but this is my servant. I consider him a brother of mine. I'm very pleased with him." Jesus stands, smiles, and says, "Please, everybody, excuse us while we speak to each other. I thought he was abducted during an attack today. I'm glad he's safe. Many lives depend on his success."

The Lord nods and His smiling children exit the banquet hall. Lucius can't seem to raise his head. "I'm sorry for the intrusion."

"Yuleshua," the Lord says. "Why are you so downcast? I watched you, and from the moment you entered this world, you have been troubled. Be blessed. You and your family are alive today, unmolested by evil."

"I'm not worthy of this meeting," Lucius says. "Please forgive my sins."

Jesus's eyes open wide with the request. "And why do you say this? You keep your oaths and are an honorable king and father." He points at the doorway. "You were forgiven of anything you thought you did wrong before you even walked through that door. No unclean being can enter My house. It's considered holy for a reason."

Lucius rises from a prostrate position and into a hunched fetal one. He's unable to lift his eyes because of his humbleness.

Jesus exhales and says, "Please don't continue with a depressed attitude. People sense this emotion in you, and it suits no purpose." He rests on the edge of a table. "Let me explain something, Yuleshua. There's a difference between humbleness and humility. To practice humility is to acknowledge that you always make mistakes…and you always will. This is mainly for those who struggle on Earth."

"Yes, my Lord." Lucius nods.

Jesus continues. "Yuleshua, the difference of those practicing humbleness, as opposed to humility, is knowing you have great power through me. Those who choose to use this power wisely from what they have learned, they are the ones to serve a greater purpose, despite their imperfections."

"But I make mistakes."

"All my children make mistakes, Yuleshua. You're imperfect and humble by your imperfections, but you were never to be known as a mistake and covered in humility."

Lucius lowers his head and nods against the flooring. "Yes, my Lord."

"Arise, Yuleshua." Jesus pats the back of a chair and says, "Sit down and fellowship with me for a while. It's rare for me to see you in the capital. Usually, we meet outside the city or somewhere secluded."

Lucius crawls up from his spot and stays lower than the Lord's head as he takes a seat. When his eyes glance over, he reads the name setting that is beside him and gasps.

Josephine's true name is written on a one-of-a-kind setting, and shown before him as if he's always known, but never remembered. Lucius looks up toward Jesus. "Is this…?"

Jesus winks. "This is truly a treat for me."

"It's beautiful," Lucius says. "She'll love it."

"You won't remember her name after leaving, until her true name is revealed at my marriage supper." He snaps a couple of fingers together, and a bowl of strawberries appears beside an empty place setting. "I wanted to show My love for you, and you'll remember how much I love you because I showed you her name." Jesus scoops a silver chalice that is filled with strawberries up into his grip and takes a strawberry for Himself. He waves the chalice of strawberries in front of Lucius playfully. Jesus takes a bite. His eyes glimmer, and Lucius cracks a silent laugh. "There's that smile," Jesus says. "I've missed your smile so much."

Lucius says, "I'm here to give my testimony, Yeshua."

"We have time," Jesus says as He swallows His bite. "I want to visit with you first." He holds the dish toward Lucius. "Have some."

"Thank you," Lucius says and takes a strawberry.

Jesus finishes his strawberry and flicks the green stem into the air. Immediately, the green stem changes form before landing. Green floats upward, and a tiny jade and turquoise hummingbird with a stem-like beak hovers in the air. Jesus smiles as he lifts His pinky. The hummingbird perches on His nail, and He examines it. "I need you to deliver him for Me. I want you to give him to My daughter, your wife."

Lucius asks, "You want me to take him back with me?"

"No." Jesus waves his hands. The hummingbird disappears. "He's waiting on your beach for when you return home." The Lord gazes down at Lucius. "Think of him as a royal pet, like your birds that you love so much."

"My Lord," Lucius says and swallows. "I can't tell my wife who I am yet. I'm afraid she'll…"

"She'll what, Yuleshua? What are you afraid of?"

"My Lord, right now she adores me, and I need her to. Her love for me encourages me. I'd be lost without her."

The Lord nods and says, "I know very well how she loves you and why I united you two together."

Lucius raises his palms and says, "Her love is soothing to me. She comforts me. I feel complete because of her. I know that it's because she doesn't know who she's fallen in love with." Lucius gestures at the place setting beside him. "She'll lose faith in me if I tell her of my failures."

Jesus says, "Don't worry about her faith in you, Yuleshua. Worry about your lack of faith in her. It's a real problem with you examining everything with negative eyes. You must trust your wife if you're to be complete with her. How could she be whole with you if you're not willing to share all of yourself…your entire story?"

"But I never wanted it. I was made that way."

"So was she. You're who I made you to be, and you can't escape it. That's something that the fallen do. They run from me, but not you." Jesus takes a strawberry and pops it in the center of his palm a few times. "I know you've built a mental barrier in your head, but you're going to have to tear it down. Tell her before you take her home to Gamerilaye."

"You're giving me permission?" Lucius asks.

Jesus nods. "I give you permission," He says as He leans closer to Lucius's face before emphasizing, "to take your queen to her new home world, yes." He straightens his posture. "When you're there, open her womb and continue your line." His teeth glisten through his smile. "She will nurse your son by this time next year."

Lucius silently chuckles and says, "Thank you." He soon remembers something and says, "Oh, I wanna…I mean, want to show you something." Lucius reaches into one of his back hidden holsters, and pulls out a Nephilim dagger. "It's from this morning's attack." He points at the Mangoram tungsten that has been forged within Gamerin metal. "This is poisonous." He directs his index over an area of blade. "Do you see the fly insignia? I thought this was a myth, that the two of them couldn't have been related."

Lucius gazes into Jesus's eyes. "This is one of Baàl's, my brother, Baàlsarideem." His eyes immediately tear up and asks, "What treachery has become of him? He was my second-in-command. I never knew what happened to him, but now I know for certain what rumors were true." Placing the dagger back into his hidden pocket, he lowers his head into his palms. "Had I of known this about him, the information would've destroyed me a long time ago. All of what he's done, all those children, women, and soldiers. He was my closest Gamerin brother. He knew everything about me. I loved him." Lucius weeps.

"They were all close to you. I saw what was in his heart long before his exile. He didn't like to share you, and even more, he didn't like sharing the power that he had through you." Jesus points at Lucius. "I chose not to tell you this information for a reason." He then massages Lucius's shoulder. "You're so tender and still so sensitive about their betrayal. What would that information have done other than hurt you? I never want to see you like this again, crying and blaming yourself."

"It's all my fault," Lucius says and sobs into his wet hands. "I should've seen the fault in my brothers before, but I sent them. I destroyed two worlds in the process." He pounds his chest. "It's all my fault."

Jesus says, "Yuleshua," and places his hand over Lucius's crown. "Their sins are not yours, and they never were. I saw their betrayal before you could ever fathom it, but that doesn't make you or me guilty by no means." Jesus pats Lucius's upper arm. "Please don't cry."

Jesus helps Lucius to wipe his tearful eyes.

The Lord says, "Don't forget where your heart was when you sent your people as a gift for our Father, who protected His children, and your brothers all willingly went on their own. Their own, Yuleshua, pay attention. Your brothers made their own decisions." He raises a brow. "We sent you to the same planet and watched you succeed. The Gamerin sins are not yours, and they never were."

Lucius looks up and dabs his cheeks with his shirt collar.

"You are strong in obedience, and you need to remain strong if you are ever going to free your brothers who still serve the Almighty, those brothers who remain trapped in captivity. They call out to me. That's why your blood was shed."

"What?" Lucius's gaze fluctuates between Jesus's eyes. "I was a blood sacrifice for them? I thought I was a sacrifice for Josephine to keep her safe."

"That was my job. I shed my blood for her." Jesus chuckles. "A clever Gamerin like you...Truly, I thought you would've figured the reason of your sacrifice out by now."

Lucius gasps. "Lord, when can I save them?" He hugs Jesus's thigh and asks, "Where are they? How many have fallen? If my blood was shed for them, where are they? I'll get them now."

Jesus pats Lucius's shoulder and says, "It's not time for that. All in due time." He raises his hand and says, "Look at you. Your house, your realm, dominion...You haven't even told your wife who you are, and you need an heir to be your second-in-command before gallivanting as a savior for your people. Josephine is not to be your second-in-command. She is you, a part of you. You seek her for counsel as an equal."

"This is big news." Lucius runs his fingers through his hair. "Some of my brothers aren't lost to me. They're redeemed, and I could bring them home."

"If they survive Baàlsarideem's wrath, yes." Jesus nods. "Listen, you want an heir first. The moment your son is born, it'll be easier for you to overthrow Baàlsarideem. Right now, he is powerful, but he will diminish a little when your son is born, for your son will be a great leader of your people as your true and loyal second-in-command. He will do great things for the Father."

"Why?"

"It is always such. Your son will be begotten of you." Jesus continues with a half-smile. "The rightful power will leave Baàlsarideem's body and spirit. The power of the second-in-command will then enter your son through his lungs during his first breath on Gamerilaye within his rightful world, holy and true, as it should be. Baàlsarideem's evil reign will be limited when he's purged of that power. He'll be equal to your Gamerin subjects, still strong, but not as strong as you or your son."

Lucius stands to his feet. "That's why we couldn't have another baby."

"The Father loves you."

"We barely got out. You saved us." Lucius smiles and says, "If I had a son, they would've known I was alive immediately and captured us. I would've never been able to end Baàl's reign."

Jesus stands beside Lucius. "Now, you're thinking like a principality. Sometimes, you must take a step back to see the entire picture of the tapestry. Everything is for a purpose."

Lucius hugs Jesus's neck. "Thank you. You bless us without us even knowing we're being blessed. You know all things and love with a true love. You're good to us. I love you."

Jesus chuckles and pats Lucius's back. "I'm glad you're safe." When Jesus releases himself from Lucius's hug, He says, "Yuleshua, I want you to enjoy your family, truly I do. However, the only way you truly will is if you tell my daughter who you are. Secrets like the one that you keep from her is not fair for a queen. It isn't good for her to be kept in the dark when her subjects know who she is, and she doesn't. Is she no better than your subjects? She's your wife, Yuleshua, and it is her right to know you fully. She completes you. Allow my design of your union to grow between the two of you. She brings you strength, and I have a purpose for her as well. Not telling her is holding her back."

Lucius nods and says, "I'll tell her." He hugs Jesus again briskly. "Thank you for all your mighty blessings upon me in my life. It's always good to meet with you, my Lord."

"If this is true, you'll visit more. I love you, Yuleshua." He walks with Lucius along the unfilled plate settings. "After you've planted your seed, I'll disperse guardians to protect your family when I feel that she has conceived my newest blessing over Gamerilaye. Dextorus, Deasja, and many others will want to celebrate with you." Jesus pats Lucius's shoulder. "And do come and see me some time. It saddens me to see you paralyzed outside my doors and needing healing in your body so you can move. You are a celestial and belong in my presence. We used to fellowship all the time before you had brothers, so why shun yourself from me now? You're who I designed you to be."

"You're right. I shouldn't doubt what you have made me to be. You love me, and I love you, Yeshua." Lucius nods and says, "I will visit with you more often. You are also always welcome in my home whenever you so desire."

Nine

Snow

Lucius enters his realm in the hidden location of the harvester's planet. His skin glows as he walks through Artie's mushroom caverns. Every crevice is revealed by the light that emanates from his skin, as if a window had been opened to let in sunlight. He takes a long stairwell until he goes through a hidden pantry passageway. He steps carefully through Artie's house and listens to the conversations of his innocent wife and child as they are being fitted with warm outfits.

Josephine stands at the door of the craft room so that she can listen for when Lucius returns. She smiles at her daughter who plays with fuzz on the floor, and fluffy boots covering her little toddler feet. Josephine's back is to the doorway. "Claire, Daddy's gonna snuggle you all day as soon as he sees you dressed like that." Suddenly, the room's brightness increases. Josephine squints and glances at the chandelier. "Why is it so bright in here?"

Then, two hands brush her shoulder. "Baby," Lucius's soft voice whispers behind her ears, "don't turn around yet. Close your eyes for me."

"Is that you? The light?" she asks.

"Yes." Lucius places his palm over her eyes so she won't be scared. "I want you to keep your eyes closed, but I want you to turn toward me in a second."

Claire's eyes are wide as she steps closer. "You look like a Christmas tree, Daddy."

Lucius nods with a smile. "Thank you, pumpkin. You look like a teddy bear."

Claire looks down at her boots and steps in place. "Thank you, Daddy. The hothead made them for me." She snuggles with a new handmade toy that Artie had given her.

Artie snickers. "I've learned I have a new nickname."

"Call him Artie, Claire. His name's Artie." Lucius whispers, "Josephine, I want you to touch my skin when I turn you around. Touch my skin the entire time your eyes are closed so that you know you're safe." He turns her gradually with guided hands. "It's me. It's only me."

"Of course, it's you, Daddy." Claire tugs on her daddy's blue jeans.

"I know, baby, but Daddy doesn't want Momma frightened." He looks at Artie and asks, "Artie, will you hold Claire for me, so I can tend to my wife?"

"Sure." Artie sweeps Claire up with a tickle beneath her arm until she giggles.

Artie stands near a fireplace, and Claire watches from over Artie's shoulder. She says, "You're pretty, Daddy."

Artie chuckles. "The things that children say."

"Thank you, pumpkin, but Daddy's handsome, not pretty." He rests his forehead over Josephine's forehead. Her eyes remain shut as he has asked. His breath brushes her nose as he says, "I want you to slowly open your eyes, but only a little at a time." He takes a deep breath. "It's me, baby. Once you feel safe, I want you to open them a little more and continue to open them gradually with small breaks in between, until, your eyes are completely adjusted, and you know it's only me."

She nods and asks, "Will the light hurt my eyes?"

"No, my love. I will never hurt you. The light on my skin will fade in the next few days. But the light will also make sleeping a little tougher for you at night."

She smiles and says, "You can remedy that."

He laughs with her and says, "True, I could place you into a sleep." He removes his hand and asks, "Are you ready? Slowly, baby."

"I trust you," she says, and as her lids separate barely. A bright glare takes her breath away. "I can almost see you perfectly, and my eyes are technically closed."

He nods.

She says, "You're nodding."

"I know, yoshawn. Take your time. You need to acclimate yourself."

"Why do you look so worried?"

"I can't handle you pushing me away, not even in the smallest measure. It crushes me to think you don't want me."

She releases a little more tension. Her brows furrow and she says, "I couldn't push you away."

He rubs her upper arm and asks, "How are you feeling?"

"Are you not reading my mind?"

He frowns. "I told you that I can't handle you rejecting me. Are you okay?"

"Don't disconnect from me. You're beautiful. That's what I'm thinking." Her lashes shield the crease of her eyes.

Lucius caresses her cheeks with both hands. "You know it's me. Are you scared?"

She shakes her head. "I feel your love. The love of my husband. I can smell you. The smell of my husband."

His eyes shut in relief. "I love hearing you call me that. I will always be your husband."

Her fingers brush across his cheeks, and he's unable to open his eyes when he feels her love for him. She says, "My eyes aren't fully open, and I can see you perfectly. It's you, my Lucius, my snuggle bug."

He says, "You're like medicine to me with your words right now," and gazes at her. "You complete me, my yoshawn, and you don't even know how much."

She smiles, as her eyes fully open. "Now, you look like an angel."

A wholehearted grin stretches across his face. "You're not scared?"

"How could I be?" She strokes his cheek and says, "I know you, and there is nothing scary about you."

Artie's eyes open wide at her comment as he remains silent on the other side of the room. Lucius glances over at him and winks. Lucius gazes back down at Josephine. "You think I look like an angel, huh?" He takes a step back and asks, "How about this?" Lucius opens his wings and poses in a pronounced masculine stance.

Josephine bites her bottom lip on one side and slowly nods. "Yes, definitely like that. You look hot."

"Augh, man," Artie replies. "Not here."

Lucius braces his abdomen from guttural laughing at his wife's thoughts. "Artie," Lucius says as he glances over. "Don't enter the living room tonight when everyone goes to bed because Josephine and I need to talk."

Artie rolls his eyes and places Claire down. "No, you're not going to talk. You're going to wrestle. And I guess you're doing that on my rug." His head blazes with fire as he says, "That's just great," and continues with his final touchups with the jaustrawl lining of Josephine's suit.

Claire giggles and says, "I like Artie, Daddy."

Lucius winks and jokes with Artie. "The way I feel, Josephine and I aren't gonna wrestle, we're gonna gently spar."

"I knew it was going to happen," Artie says while emitting a higher blaze.

Lucius picks Claire up with one arm and places his shining fingers upon her cheek. "You think your daddy looks like a Christmas tree?"

"Daddy, you lose hide and seek." She gasps. "I can look for you."

"We're not playing hide and seek today, remember? We're playing in the snow." He looks over at Artie. "Are we just about ready, or do you need me to do something?"

Artie answers his king, "I'm almost finished, sire," and jerks his head up, swallowing, "sure...I mean, sure. But I'll be done in just a minute, Lucius."

Lucius tries recovering from the blunder of words, saying, "I could help you, Mr. Tongue-tied."

Immediately, Josephine examines their nervousness and tilts her head.

"Uh, if you want to...I mean, wanna," Artie says while nervously laughing. "See? This new language is getting to me. All these new words are making me mess up my own." His head shakes toward Lucius. "I'm terrible at this, Lucius. This isn't Earth. I must retrain my brain to keep from what I was taught."

Lucius raises his hand up. Speaking without moving his lips, he says, "You're doing fine. You'll get the hang of it. Just give it time. It's only because you're excited today."

"Why are y'all acting so funny?" Josephine asks. "What are y'all talking about?"

Stunned silence is her answer.

Her eyes squint and she says, "I know that you two are hiding something. You've been doing this for a while," and gestures at Lucius. "I know I haven't figured it out yet." She points sternly over at Artie. "But I will."

Artie's face grows long. "She is so scary, Lucius. Why are you getting me in trouble?"

She leans forward and says, "I've been through a lot today. I was almost abducted by aliens, who turned out to be related to me somehow. I lost my home, my lifelong friends who are going to be worried sick about me, and a car I just paid off." She points toward the mounted creatures of a species she can't identify on Artie's wall. "I'm on a distant planet without a name, and I'm not allowed to know where it's located. I have nothing but the clothes on my back, and only your word to go on. Everybody else seems to be really excited about my being here, but I'm trying to be optimistic; however, the only treasures that I have are in this room, and one of them is keeping secrets."

Lucius's expression sinks as he stares through the floor. He nods depressingly and says, "I'm sorry."

She exhales. "Ugh, that's not what I was trying to say. I need to catch my tongue." She pinches the bridge of her nose and lifts her eyes to look between two quieted angels. "I'm saying I trust you, and I only wanna enjoy my day, vacation, or whatever you wanna call our refugee time. But, Lucius, I do trust you. It is your silence," she says with a short pause so that she can breathe out. She steps forward before finishing her words. "I'm not gonna lie. You hiding things scares me."

Lucius says, "Please don't be scared. Why would you be scared?"

"Because on Earth, you hid what was very scary from me. When I found out how much danger was lurking around me—"

"Please," Lucius interrupts her. "You're in no danger here."

She nods and says, "That's what alarms me."

"Why?" Lucius asks.

"If I'm in no danger here, then why are you hiding something from me, when on Earth, Hell was knocking at my door every day?"

Lucius closes his eyes and nods. "You're a wise woman."

She says, "I have a few questions, no matter how dumb you might think they are. First, am I gonna lose you?"

He holds her arms and rests his forehead against hers. "No. No, you're not gonna lose me. I don't know why we felt that way before, but we are safe here. I wanna hold you for eternity."

She lets out a sigh of relief and places her hand upon her breast. "Good. Thank you." Josephine looks over toward her daughter's blonde hair, as Claire uses her little fingers to tickle a button nose on a handsewn doll. Locking her watering eyes up at him, Josephine asks. "Does Claire have our lifespan? I can't lose her."

He strokes her cheek. "She's ageless. Just like you and me. We're not losing her, Momma. I see where your worries are stemming from."

"One last thing, and I'll be done with all that worries me."

"What is it, my yulee?"

She inhales deeply and releases her question quickly. "Am I competing for attention like Leah and Rachel in the Bible? Do you have a hidden wife somewhere out here, betrothed, or engaged?"

Lucius and Artie gasp simultaneously.

"No," Lucius answers with a roar and a step back. His glow from his body diminishes from the insult. "Absolutely not," he says as the pictures on the walls rattle overhead.

Josephine glances at the portions of the clicking and chattering room. "Is that an earthquake?" She points at Lucius's skin and says, "Your light is going away."

But Lucius continues. "That question is absurd, Josephine, and not of God. We are bound as one flesh and that must not be born of anyone's mouth or mind." The rumbling increases with the chandelier chattering.

"Um, Lucius?" Artie asks as his eyes anxiously skip around the room at articles starting to drop from shelves. "It was just a question that she made. Please calm down. She gave you a heads up with the stupid question comment."

His glow diminishes even more, Lucius turns to look at Artie. "Well, it was a horrible question." His nostrils flare as he asks, "How could she ask such a question? I would rather be dichotomized with a small, dull blade." Lucius turns toward his now worried wife and grabs her hands, placing them upon his chest so he can calm down. He is nearly crying over her nose. "I'm bonded with you, my yoshawn, my yulee, my Josephine, don't you understand? In the heavens, we live by our bonds. We keep our words when we say no and honor our yeses. Our words are law here. These are heavenly laws and the word of God. I would rather die than anyone ever lay a finger on you in the way that I touch you or in the way that you touch me. That traitor's life would be forfeit for dishonoring you, dishonoring me, and dishonoring God. I would kill the offender myself."

Lucius glances back, and Artie's hands fling upward. Artie says, "I didn't touch her. I don't think like that. Please don't hurt me?" He gulps and says, "You can keep the rug."

Exhaling, Lucius shakes his head and says, "Of course not, Artie."

Josephine says, "Your glow has diminished much."

Taking several moments, Lucius exhales and holds her so that he can calm down. He raises her hands to stroke his face for comfort. "You never have to worry about my faithfulness."

She wipes beneath his eyes as his arms wrap around her back. She says, "My goodness. Calm down. I didn't want to upset you. I was erasing my concern from your silence."

He nods and says, "I know that I need to speak with you about my secrets." He gestures at the beams and paneling along Artie's walls that were shaking so bad that sawdust was loosened from the wood. He says, "Please stop asking these questions. By this evening, I won't have a glow at all if we keep this up."

She smiles and says, "I'm no longer worried."

Artie blows out a long-held breath and says, "I'm glad that's over with because I really didn't want to die today."

Josephine stands on her tippy toes and kisses Lucius's nose tip. "Baby, fix your temper. I liked how bright you were." She points toward Artie. "Also, you were scaring him, and he didn't realize the earthquake just then. He was more worried for you. Remember, he's a host, and we're guests in his home."

"A host?" Lucius glances at Artie.

Artie swallows his laughter from her temporarily placing Lucius's title on him.

"Don't let it get to your head." Lucius nods and says, "I think we need to go outside for a while. Maybe, preoccupy our minds with other things, instead of backward conversations."

Artie nods with a following shake of his head. "That's the truth. I think I need a beer after that."

"You know what?" Lucius's eyes light up. "That's a great idea, Artie."

"How so? I was only teasing about the beer. If you don't mind my saying, please don't start drinking again?"

Lucius drops his shoulders and says, "No. That's not what I meant. And I'm comforted by my wife." He smiles at Josephine and begins to ask, "How about," he pauses while tapping his bottom lip for a moment, "tomorrow? Yeah, tomorrow. Tomorrow, I will take you to several planets before going home to Gamerilaye."

Ten

Moment Filer

The craft room door swings open, and Josephine poses in her new fur coat that is lined with extra jaustrawl. Claire imitates her momma's pose.

Lucius says, "You two look adorable."

"I did a good job," Artie says.

"Can we get a picture with your moment filer?" Lucius gestures toward his girls and says, "I never wanna forget this moment."

Josephine asks, "What's a moment filer? I thought you said get a picture."

Lucius nods. "A moment filer is a camera, but it's immediately filed in your eternal file on Oobadoave through the Oobadoave network. Our Father can look at it whenever He wants and experience the moment all over again as if in this moment."

"How is that?" she asks.

"A moment filer provides several multidimensional specs of everyone captured as it's uploaded."

Artie says, "She doesn't know what that means, Lucius."

Lucius continues. "Baby, a moment filer records what you're feeling, thinking, the day, year, your location, and every molecule around you, even the number of hairs on your head. A moment filer truly records the moment and files it." He raises his palms and says, "The device is called a moment filer and every angel of the guard has one."

"No way," she says. "Did you have one on Earth?"

"I did but it was fried when I got struck by lightning."

Artie faces Lucius, who wears a large grin, Claire, who snuggles in her daddy's arms over his chest, and Josephine, who is wide eyed to the amazing device that seems to know everything. "Say cheese," Artie says as he snaps a shot. "That was a good one."

"I can't believe what just happened," Josephine says.

Lucius kisses her cheek. "Moment filing has been happening your whole life, but you never knew it. His love runs deep for you."

Artie opens the giant glass bay walls and walks outside. He passes a couple of ice-covered tapestries that are currently hidden by the snow. The tapestries would normally signify that an honored servant of the house of Gamerin lives on that mountain, but icicles and a blanket of white from the earlier storm helps to hide the Gamerin insignia.

Artie walks toward the huge bowl urns on the terrace. The urns are made of slate stone and are four feet in diameter nearer to the glass walls and six feet in diameter nearer to the white marble banister at the edge of the terrace. He sets the urns ablaze once again with the weather now cleared of any storm like earlier. Artie says, "Only when you visit, Lucius, do these flames ever go out here."

"Sorry," Lucius says.

Artie looks over with a smile and says, "That'll keep the terrace area warm while the doors are open."

Lucius places Claire down, and as he does, he tightens the straps on her gloves so they won't fall off her tiny fingers. Seeing her staring at the powder that has accumulated on the terrace, Lucius says to his daughter, "This white stuff is snow, Claire. It's frozen water, so don't get it on your skin."

"Like a snow cone?" Claire asks.

Lucius nods. "Close, pumpkin, but there is no syrup in the snow. Snow tastes like cold water but don't eat it because it's on the ground. We don't eat from the ground unless it's vegetables that have been washed."

Claire takes little steps, and the snow sticks to the furry ends of her boots. Her steps pick up speed as she attempts to knock off the clumps. She says, "Snow likes me, Daddy. Snow is climbing my shoes."

He chuckles. "Daddy sees you, pumpkin." He says to Artie, "Activate your living photo, brother. Get her walking around in those so I have the moment for later."

"Is that a video recorder?" Josephine asks. "Like the moment filer?"

Artie starts recording as a multidimensional square activates a few inches in height on his forearm. The actions of Claire are picked up as if she is walking on his arm.

Lucius nods and smiles at Josephine who is astonished at the technology. He says, "Pretty much a home movie. The Father can watch that too if uploaded to the Oobadoave network."

Josephine smiles as she nestles within her husband's embrace. "I love you, little momma," he tells her. "This is all I ever wanted."

She sighs deeply. "Me too."

Lucius smiles over at Artie and asks, "You want to show them what we do when it snows?"

"You mean show off our natural talents?"

Lucius winks and then leans down to eye height with Claire. He asks her, "Pumpkin, do you want to see real snow angels?"

Josephine lifts Claire into her arms. "You two are silly."

At the same time, Lucius and Artie stretch out their wings with a flare of their back muscles. Artie's wings are stunning and colorful. Brown feathers cover his wings from the top to midway down and are separated by a bright, red stripe before long, black feathers take over. Artie's harvester design is his own special watermark.

Lucius's wings are three times as big as Artie's and are pure white. Because of Lucius's wings' size, they have three joints, making them tri-fold wings. The first joint is located at his scapular bones. They are so enormous at eighteen and a half feet long each, that they must be kept slightly bent at the joints to keep them from knocking into something.

Claire shrills with a gasp. She has never seen her daddy's wings and has never seen dark wings on an angel. She says, "Ooh, pretty. Artie is like a birdie, Momma,"

"Ready when you are." Artie smiles.

Lucius nods, and they both lie on the ground to make imprints in the newly laid snow. The movement of brushing their feathers against the black slate of the landing bay, gives the artwork the impression of shadows as if the imprints of wings are moving through the air. When finished, they shake their wings off and stand beside Josephine and Claire to marvel at the differences in their artwork.

Because Lucius must pull his wings in some when in close surroundings, he looks down with his lip raising on one side. "My wings make me look like a big ball," he says.

Artie points and says, "Look at mine. I look like I'm wearing a dress because you took up all the room." He laughs. "I couldn't even reach them above my head because you were slapping me in the face with your feathers."

They both laugh.

"Here," Josephine says as she hands Claire to Lucius. She finds a small area and lies down. The fur of her coat kisses the snow with every movement and sticks to her arms as she makes a snow angel in her little corner.

"This is gonna be good," Lucius says. He takes a step away from the hanging icicles as Claire reaches toward a Gamerin colored tapestry.

Caressing her tiny features over white flakes like a ballet between two enormous works of art, Josephine moves gracefully as she finishes in the snow. She smiles when she stands to her feet and feels the need to hide her blushing cheeks after playing in the snow like a child. Josephine joins the group and Lucius dusts her back off when she turns around to see what she's done.

Artie says, "She's not even an angel. How come she can make one so good? It looks like she has wings."

Lucius says, "She's an angel to me."

After exploring and disturbing every inch of the landing bay around Artie's cabin estate, Lucius says, "Let's go sledding." He points toward a mountain range in the distance. "Our sleds are there."

"That's quite a hike," Josephine says. "Lucius, you're not wearing a coat. Aren't you cold?"

Lucius hands Claire to Artie and tells him, "Be easy with her. She's not like us. She's just a baby." He whispers to Claire, "Hang on, pumpkin."

Josephine raises her voice, "What are you suggesting?"

Lucius raises his hand to calm her. "It's okay, baby."

"Humans don't fly, Lucius," she says.

"You're safe, little momma. I won't let anything happen to any of you in this world," he says.

Artie holds Claire tightly. He says, "I've done this before, your maj…I mean, Josephine. Trust me," and Artie takes off toward the mountain, flying with Claire giggling in his arms.

Josephine immediately holds her hands up like a stop sign as Lucius steps close to her. She says, "But I'm wearing a heavy jacket." Josephine quivers. "What if you drop me? We've never done this before."

"My everlasting love, don't be scared of me." Lucius gently wraps his arms around her and whispers into her ear, "Baby, this is safer than an aircraft. I've done this before, multiple times. I won't drop you. Do you trust me?"

Her gaze fluctuates between his eyes in study as her facial tension relaxes. She nods and says, "With all my heart, Yuleshua."

Hearing her use his real name makes him smile. She meant her words, and she trusts him. Lucius says, "That's all I needed to hear." He wraps her snug in his embrace.

"Aren't you gonna get cold on the mountain without a jacket?"

"I'm too hot with you in my arms," he jokes with her. "I'll be fine because my body heals quicker when I'm here. Are you ready?"

She grips tightly to him and says, "Til death do us part."

Lucius's wings open. He says, "I've got you safe in my arms forever," and they fly off.

From above, Josephine sees a mountainous, snow-covered landscape and heavily forested mountain trails with white boughs passing beneath her. "Stunning," she says. Josephine becomes relaxed and kisses his neck.

They arrive at the peak, and Lucius floats down until the balls of his feet hover over powdery snow.

Josephine says, "That was weird. It was almost like you were levitating just then."

Hearing her comment, Artie peeks over. Lucius nods at Josephine and says, "It did seem like I was levitating, didn't it?" He looks at Artie and speaks with telepathy, *"She doesn't know that I can levitate anything because that information was dangerous while on Earth. Only principalities and the Gamerin levitate objects from the ground."*

Josephine gasps out of nowhere.

Lucius stares over at her. "What?" he asks.

Her fingers wave as she points at a small detail beyond the base of the mountain, toward a valley. She says, "There's a little town down there. Look, can you see it?" She squats beside Claire, so she can point out the area and direct her attention. "You see the little structures, Claire? There are different kinds. And that…that," she glances at Lucius and finishes what she was trying to say, "What is that down there? I see fires burning. Use your special vision gizmos in your eyes. Can you tell me what it is?"

"I don't need to, little momma. I know the structures well." He squats down near the girls and points a finger as he describes what they are looking at. "That's a greenhouse. They harvest all year-round here," he says. Using a light voice, he says to Claire, "See the little homes where Daddy points?"

Claire answers, "Upside down bowls, Daddy, with smoke on top."

"From here, that is what it looks like, pumpkin. But they're big homes with chimneys in the middle, and people live in them." He points to another area and says, "And those are shops."

"What's that big one in the middle of those squares?" Josephine uses her reddened nose and nubs the air. She says, "The one in the center that is shaped like a round cross."

Lucius says, "I'll let Artie explain everything down there."

"Me?" Artie asks while he is readjusting his gloves from some snow that had gotten stuffed inside of them. "Really?"

Lucius stands and says, "Why not?"

"Okay." Artie places his gloves into a pants pocket and squats beside Claire. He points with a warm finger that is covered in vibrant freckles across the ends of his hands. Claire is staring at his multicolored hand as he says, "Those squares are seasonal farms that are covered with snow, and that there in the middle, that's the cathedral. They've lit large fires down there to protect the area. The fires have melted the snow over the cathedral. Those are flames you see. At the cathedral, people gather daily there for fellowship, prayer, and food. They're all family, my harvester family, and they share everything that they harvest. Many towns fill this world, and every one of them share what they harvest like a family at a generous banquet table. The table at mealtimes is overflowing with food and laughter several times a day. Sometimes the meals last for hours at a time." Artie smiles at Claire and lifts his fingers that are naturally ornamented so she can memorize them. "Those are harvesters."

"Wow," Claire says. She holds his hands and turns his palm a few times. She rubs an area where the red freckles turn into larger orange speckles near the base of his fingers. When she does, microscopic sparks light his skin from underneath. He smiles as she asks, "They have hot cheetah spots like you?"

Artie nods as he answers, "Yes, ma'am. It's in our design, and every day we gather and eat."

She asks, "A lot of food?"

Lucius says, "Sure is, princess, with big tables too."

"How lovely." Josephine sighs. "I wish people everywhere did this."

Lucius nods as he embraces her. "Likewise, our Father wants this for all his children."

Artie walks toward a boulder under a tree that has grown in a strange shape around the indentations of the boulder. He picks up two bowl shaped sleds from a tree trunk. He bangs the sleds against the stone to remove the caked-on snow. When the sleds are free of snow, he asks Claire, "Ready?"

"Okay, Artie," Lucius says with a stern finger point toward Claire. "Go slow. Keep your wings open for the steep areas and stay clear of the drop offs. She must learn to trust you."

"I'll have her the entire time," Artie answers. "I've memorized this trail for over thirty-four thousand years."

"Artie," Lucius says and then stands silent.

When Artie hears nothing, he turns to face Lucius. "Yes, Lucius. What's wrong?" Artie becomes curious by Lucius's expression. He looks serious but also pleased. *"What is it?"* Artie asks by using telepathy.

Lucius nods and speaks out loud, "I want to profess openly what I am about to say because what I am about to say is a highly trusted privilege."

"As you wish, Lucius," Artie says.

Lucius says, "I want it to be you. I trust you."

"You want what to be me?" Artie asks.

"I want you to guard my daughter."

Artie's jaw drops, and he immediately covers his eyes. He becomes emotional and begins swallowing so he won't blubber in front of Josephine.

Josephine studies his response. She feels she can almost grab whatever importance is happening in front of her. There is silence until Artie can no longer bottle the pressure of his joy. He wails as he says, "With my very life!" Lucius hugs Artie, and Artie says. "Thank you for this. You honor me."

"Peace." Lucius calms him and uses telepathy, *"Shhh, my dearest friend. You had to have known the honor would be yours someday. And that day has come."*

Artie nods and is unable to speak.

Lucius says, "This means that you won't be called away for duty because your home needs you." And transfers the rest of his words, *"Your place is in my family. You're at home now with me because you have always been a part of my family."*

When Artie controls himself enough where he can stand straight, he wipes his mottled cheeks and wet eyes. He nods as he smiles down at Claire. "You ready, princess? I'm going to…I mean, gonna take care of you for now on." He chuckles and looks over at Josephine and Lucius. Artie speaks to Lucius psychically, *"Thank you for honoring me, my lord. This restores everything as it was for me. I have longed to serve again as a servant in the Royal House of Gamerin, a great honor."*

Lucius gestures silently for Artie to go on down the trail with Claire.

Before he walks away, Josephine steps forward. "Are y'all talking with your minds right now?"

"Okay, Artie," Lucius says. "Y'all go ahead, and we'll catch up."

Artie nudges the sled forward. He and Claire take off down the mountain with his wings acting as a steering wheel.

"You're not answering me," she says.

Lucius positions the other sled. He says, "Baby, you saw what happened, and his reaction. He's her guardian angel now. Artie was only psychically thanking me."

"Oh," she says. "Because he would've started crying again? That was intense."

"Yeah, he definitely would've." Lucius stands beside her and caresses her cheek and neck so that she is looking at the trail. "Do you see them? I wanna show you something." As Josephine watches a winged sled going down the trail, Lucius opens a psychic bond that she has never experienced before.

She breathes in deeply before saying, "I can feel her," and she closes her eyes. "I see what she sees." Josephine laughs and begins guarding her stomach. "She's having fun. It's tickling me." She looks up at Lucius. "She trusts him. How wonderful."

"This is how I see people."

"You knew she would trust him already."

He smiles and says, "This is also how I knew you trusted me when I fell in love with you." The thought reminds him of what discussion is yet to come, and he detaches his bioempathic connection from her, so that she doesn't find out before he has a chance to tell her.

"What was that?" she asks. "I felt something, and then you disconnected from me."

"Don't worry about it." He turns and re-situates the sled. "All in due time. I don't think I'm ready yet." He pauses and says, "I thought I was, but I need more time."

Josephine steps away from him. "Is it so bad that we can't enjoy linking together anymore?" she says and continues stepping back. "Is it so terrifying that you feel that you have to hide it from me?"

Lucius turns from her and closes his eyes. The snow starts again and he says, "Please, not now. Give me time."

"Are you causing the storms all the way out here?" She looks up but continues to step back without looking. "What is it about this place, Yuleshua Lucius Gamerin." She is unaware of the drop off behind her. "You're terrifying me."

"Please," he says as he finally faces her.

One last step is taken by her, and she drops into a screaming freefall.

Eleven

Freefalling

Josephine covers her eyes with her arms. Shielding her from seeing to rocks on the bottom. The bitter wind whistles past her.

Immediately, the rushing wind goes silent, and everything stops.

Josephine opens her eyes and looks at the rocky boulders a hundred feet below her. She's confused because Lucius is nowhere near her, and she hasn't landed. Lucius is still on the mountain top and hasn't swooped down and grabbed onto her.

"I'm floating." She looks around and is levitating at eye level to a frozen waterfall. Slowly, her trembling body levitates upward for what feels like a thousand feet.

Lucius is on top of the mountain, but he stands quivering with his arms outstretched for her.

Josephine is gracefully levitating through the air to him. Her brows frown, and she asks, "Was that you? Did you stop me in midair?"

He holds onto her and says, "I'm sorry I never told you."

Held close against him, her voice is muzzled as she says, "You le-le-levitated me." She's trying to catch her breath from the adrenaline. "How come you never told me?"

"I shouldn't have detached from you," he says.

"Let me breathe a second," she says. Lucius lets go of her a little so she can recover from her shock. She stares at the snow beside their boots and takes several deep breaths before saying, "I can't believe that I almost died, and then I floated. I felt weightless." She looks at him as though she might be dreaming, and asks, "Did I almost die?"

"It's possible," he says as his eyes soon stare toward the ground. "I have let my guard down too many times because of my secrets. You're the one that always suffers for my insecurity. My silence can no longer linger where danger is possible." He looks into her eyes. "Are you okay?"

She holds his hands. "I'm f-f-fine."

Delicately this time, he embraces her. "Baby, you're still shaking really bad."

Her voice wheezes for breath, and says, "You too."

"I've got you now," he says a handful of times, repeatedly echoing the words for peace and calm, as he holds her. His glow is nearly gone. As her heartbeat slows down, his heartbeat is thunderous and he starts sobbing over her head.

She realizes he's crying when she hears his sniffle. "Calm down. Your light has faded, Lucius. Do that peace thing you do. I wasn't watching where I was going, and it was just a stupid mistake. You caught or floated or levitated me. Whatever, but I'm fine now." She rubs his cheeks.

He agrees with a nod. "I've got you."

"That was amazing."

Shaking his head, his brows furrow and he says, "It was horrible, Josephine."

"I mean, it was stupid of me, yes, but amazing." She points to the drop off and says, "Somebody should put a sign there that reads, watch out, dangerous drop off." She shrugs and has a sideways smile.

"Josephine," he says with another sniffle. "This isn't a time for joking. People can die in the heavens." He looks her over and asks, "Are you sure you're okay? You're not looking at me."

"Yeah, I'm calm now. I'm alive," she says while sheepishly looking down at her boots. "I'm embarrassed. That was completely my fault, not yours. I was the one who decided to fall off the side of a mountain top."

"I wouldn't have forgiven myself for disconnecting my presence from you."

"My fault, not yours." She shrugs. "I might have lived," she says and thinks of the scene in her head. "Eww, but you could've healed me. If…I lived. You're right, that was a horrifying experience."

He closes his eyes and says, "You getting hurt would've been my fault more than you know. It's why I've hidden certain things from you."

"Why?"

"I have a bit of a past and I have made mistakes."

"Everybody does." She points at the area she has just floated from and says, "Did you not see what I just did?"

"Yoshawn, folding different socks together, leaving a toilet seat up, or not thawing meat are mistakes we can live with. But my mistakes are what terrify me. The ones I can't live with." He straightens her furry hood and stares at her until she makes eye contact. "I never would have recovered, even if you did."

"If it wasn't for you, I would've died. I believe in you, even more now."

Artie flies up while holding Claire and a bowl-shaped sled. "Hey you two. Good news. Your daughter evidently likes sledding as slow as snot in winter down this trail."

"Wait a second," Josephine says. "I know what's going on now."

"What?" Artie asks and steps closer. "You told her about—"

"Stop! Artie, no. I didn't." Lucius exhales and finishes saying, "Let her talk."

"Yes, sir," Artie says.

Lucius interlocks his own fingers behind his neck as his head falls back. His eyes stare into the sky and his afterglow is completely vanished. "I haven't felt this stressed since we were dating." He squeezes his eyes shut. "Please, continue. What were you gonna say, baby?"

"A couple things," she says and studies his skin. "You're not glowing anymore." She fakes a smile. "Never mind. You're stressed, and I don't wanna be the cause."

"No, please," he says. "You need to speak freely because I'm gonna need to speak freely with you later today."

"There is something that I've noticed," she answers. "You want me to trust you, right?"

"That's right." Lucius cringes by the weight of her statement sounding as though there is a clause. "I don't like hearing where this is going already."

"It's a frame of mind I'm leading you to understand, and I need you to follow what I say."

"I'm listening," he says.

"I don't know how much you trust me."

As soon as she makes the statement, Lucius rubs his chest as if hit by heartburn. "This day has been a brutal mess for me."

"I take it you've noticed," she says. After he nods, she says, "There's something else bothering me. It's bothered me for years, and I've tried not to pressure you, hoping, praying you'd notice and grow. I keep from thinking of it when I'm connected to you, but I have prayed about it."

"What? Have I been so awful to you, my love?"

She inhales deeply before saying, "Lucius, you don't believe in yourself."

"What?" Lucius asks.

"You don't trust yourself in the slightest measure with things even I know that you can handle."

Artie gasps. Lucius looks over at him. Artie says, "I'm just standing here. I didn't say it, she did."

Josephine touches Lucius's cheeks, redirecting him to look at her. Her voice is delicate when she says, "How can you trust me when you don't know how to trust yourself? By y'all's reaction, even Artie knows more about your issues than I do. That is what I mean. He knows your secrets."

"But, baby, he's been my accountability partner for many ages."

"Long before I was born," she says.

"Yes," Lucius answers. "Before I knew you and before we were married."

"Before," she says.

"Yeah," Lucius says. "Before we were married, that's what I said."

She says, "I'm gonna say what you just said and change out the word before with the word until." She straightens her back and says, "Until we were married, you confided in Artie."

After she says this, Lucius realizes what she was trying to explain to him.

"You must know how that makes me feel. I'm your wife. I do trust you, but only as far as you will allow me to trust you. Does being your wife not count for anything that you hide? Can I be closer than those who were there before me? Can you allow me to truly be one with you?"

Lucius closes his eyes. "That burns."

"Wow, I feel awkward." Artie folds his fingers together and takes a step to the side. "This is one of those marital discussions, and I accidentally walked right into it. Can Claire and I go sledding now?" Artie waits a moment. "Please."

Josephine nods and tells him, "I'm not trying to make you feel uncomfortable, Artie."

Lucius says, "You may go," and watches Artie hold Claire for another ride down the mountain. Looking over at Josephine, Lucius says, "I don't deserve you. Your words counsel me even when they hurt. I've also realized something on this day."

"What?" she asks.

"You've had to live with the burden that I have secrets, and you haven't felt free to speak with me about what troubles you either."

"I guess we're both guilty of secrets."

"You hold no guilt. You've been as open as you can be while I was withholding myself from you." He nods and says, "I promise you that before sunrise you'll know what troubles me."

"I hope I didn't ruin our family day."

Lucius kisses her and says, "Nah, we've got snowmen making to do, and we're gonna eat that pot roast Artie's cooking. I'm gonna sing a little song when putting Claire down for the night. Then, we will enjoy our quiet time together in front of the fire. I couldn't ask for a more perfect life."

"Are you gonna sing her that lullaby tonight?"

Lucius guides Josephine over to the sled as he says, "Yes. It'll be a perfect end to a crazy day."

She smiles and says, "Then, you're gonna tell me campfire stories in your sexy voice?"

"Yes." He chuckles. Josephine climbs onto the sled and sits between his legs. "Whatever you desire, my queen."

Sitting between his legs, she looks back and asks again, "Then, you'll tell me?"

"Before dawn, no secrets. I promise this truth to you, and nothing that can be spoken will be hidden between us ever again." He wraps his arms around her as she resituates. Lucius speaks against her ear from behind her coat hood. "We are weaved together, Mrs. Gamerin, and bound by the Holy Spirit. You have the right to know me."

"Can you tell me where I am?"

"No," he says while shaking his head. "Nice try."

She snickers. "Hey, you have not because you've asked not. Isn't that in the Bible?"

"Don't throw Bible verses at me, Mrs. Gamerin. I know His word. Women. Do all y'all connive to get what you want?"

"I wanna know how you levitated my entire body. It was incredible. I felt weightless. I've never seen you do that with anything other than your weapons. My whole body was caught in midair, and you weren't even looking at me. You said something about visiting other worlds tomorrow?"

"I sure did," he answers her.

"Tell me a good story about that. I love science fiction."

"It's not fiction out here. I got some good stories to tell." Lucius pushes off with his hands, and they sled down the mountain.

Twelve

Shadow Cluster

They build snowmen on the terrace. The black slate floor is nearly swept clean as the snow is transformed into lumpy creations with twigs and left over jaustrawl. Lucius holds Claire up as she dresses a cap over his and her snowman. "Good job," he says, as the material slides to one side.

Josephine centers the furry cap on the snowman for her. "Her nose is red, Daddy. We probably need to get her fed and washed up for bed. She's had an adventurous day. I don't know how the time difference might affect her."

He taps Claire's nose and says, "I guess you're right."

Claire lays her head over his shoulder and begins yawning with a sigh. Blowing fire until a stick burns at the end, Artie stands a few feet away with his snowman. Claire says, "He's a dragon, Daddy."

Artie chuckles, and he partially comments, "Dragon…as if," and situates the branch that is now smoldering on the end. The snowman looks as though it has a cigar in its mouth.

Lucius says, "Artie isn't a dragon, princess. A highly skilled brimstone angel is what he is." Lucius smiles at Artie and says, "That's a nice replica of Dex. The sun is setting, and we should eat so Josephine and I can get Claire ready for bed."

"The roast should be done by now," Artie says. "And thanks for the compliment."

After dinner, Lucius and Josephine bathe their little girl. She is in her gown once again as Lucius tucks her snugly into bed with fluffy down blankets. "This bed is different, Daddy," she tells him. "Can you turn your Christmas light on?" she asks, patting his skin.

"Sorry, pumpkin. That light was only temporary."

Josephine points toward the fireplace and asks, "You want me to see if Artie has extra firewood?"

"He's getting it," Lucius answers. "He's bringing a whole cartload for her. He'll keep the fire burning all night to keep her warm."

"Oh," she says and glances back with wonder in her eyes. "I didn't see him." Artie is not there. No cart. No firewood and not a sound. "How do you know? Are you speaking psychically or something?"

Lucius answers, "I just know because I can see him in my mind's eye. The ability is as if I'm standing beside him and watching what he is doing, and I also know why he is doing it. I know everything about his movement because I am a bioempath and can sense those around me, along with their intentions."

"I thought that you could only do that to people you were guarding over or when doing report. I didn't know that…" she stops saying.

"I will explain when we go into the living area." Lucius looks down at Claire to help her feel safe. He taps the wicker bed and says, "Pumpkin, this bed has been used by your daddy a long time. Before I met your momma. This is where I stayed when I was trying to relax from work. Daddy used to feel unwell, and Artie would let me stay in this room without distractions so I could feel rested." He brushes Claire's hair behind her ears. "Close your eyes, princess," he says and prays over her, as he strokes her cheeks and memorizes her features. Just as she's drifting off to sleep, he sings,

"A little rest, a little song,
A little tired from all day long,
A little girl, a little dream,
A little water in a little spring,
The light of a new day in the song of the wind,
And a loving daddy holds you like a friend.
A precious child as sweet as a dove,
Is bathed within her father's love,
A trusting child and a loving king,
Can come together with words and sing,
A little child in a great big world,
Is loved by a big God who made this little girl."

"I love that song," Josephine whispers.

"Sleep, Claire," he says, and he blesses her with sleep. "I do too."

"Time for our campout on the floor," she says.

Exhaling nervously, he nods and says, "I know. I'm coming." He stands and looks into her eyes. "I'm ready. Let's go." He leads Josephine into the living area as Artie passes by them with a rather large load of firewood. "You could've made more than one trip, Artie."

Artie trundles by and says, "I know," and looks around logs. "The cart's too noisy. I didn't want to go searching through one of my pockets for logs either. I'd get bark on my weapons, and I can't levitate things like you can to clean my stuff that would be dirty in an interdimensional space. See you after sunrise."

"Good night, Artie," they tell him.

In front of the fire, Lucius unbuttons his dress shirt. He slips off his undershirt, a white, cotton top, and hands it to Josephine. He says, "Baby, wear this as a gown."

She takes the shirt and begins to change. As she starts to take off her shirt, she pauses, and says, "Thank you. Where am I gonna—"

"He won't disturb us. You can change in here. I told him after sunrise, and that's what he'll wait for. I'll make sure you're dressed long before then. Changing your clothes in here is modest for you. Don't worry." He puts his dress shirt back on while Josephine covers herself with a long undershirt that fits her like a gown.

As soon as she is covered, Josephine snuggles between a mound of pillows. "It's so regal," she says stroking fine linens under her fingertips. "I know it's a pallet on the floor, but these are the nicest materials I've ever slept on."

"Artie's good about giving the best for me when I visit."

She stretches her back on top of the bedding and says, "This doesn't feel like a pallet. The material feels like butter. It must've been expensive. I think Artie went through too much trouble for us. We're gonna overstay our welcome if he keeps this up."

"That's impossible."

She raises her brows and says, "Remember the Bedouins I told you about? I've seen overstaying a welcome happen with all kinds of people. They accept you with open arms and treat you like royalty—"

Interrupting her, Lucius snorts while pressing down his laughter. "I'm sorry."

"I'm serious," she says with wide eyes as her smile increases. "The stress of over-caring for someone makes them stop caring, and before you know it, you've become a headache to them. They overexert themselves." Her head tilts sideways as she continues. "I don't wanna lose his friendship after losing my home."

"You know not of what you say." Lucius moves the pillows and props himself up with pauses in between his statements. "Artie and I," he says with a pause, re-situating a sliding mound from the slick materials. "We go way back." He pounds the pillows again, bending, slanting, and flexing his material dune. He leans back slowly, but the mound of pillows slips again. "We...uh." Lucius does nothing, gradually letting gravity take him down while simply staring at the ceiling as he winds up on the floor and halfway off the pallet.

Josephine giggles and playfully reaches for him as if he's slipping away into oblivion. "You're falling away."

"I've given up trying with these things," he says, half off the pallet and not moving.

"Come back to me, Lucius," she says while laughing, hardly catching her breath and continuing to titter sideways.

He's quiet, completely still in his position, but a serene smile grows while listening to her. "I love hearing you laugh." He glances over. "I could hear you laugh all day and never get tired of it."

"You make me laugh. You always do." She pats on the pallet beside her, and says, "Climb back over here instead of being sprawled out over there. Come to me. Tell me a story."

Lucius gets up and moves to a spot catty-cornered from her. Together, they tangle their legs, and she rubs her shins against his blue jeans. He says, "I'm sitting this way so you can lie down and get comfortable while I watch the fire."

"Are you gonna sleep in those jeans. You're making me feel nervous about my bare legs."

"I'll take them off before sleeping," he says and pauses in mid-thought, thinking to himself out loud. "Sleep. If I sleep tonight."

"Why wouldn't you be able to sleep? You're not on duty." Her hand rests over his thigh.

"I'm always on duty." A fiery glow brushes over his face as he gazes at her. "I can't sleep when I'm troubled. There's something in me—gnawing at me. My presence is ongoing in this area of the universe to get work done and to fix things that need to be fixed." His thumb strokes her backhand as he continues saying, "I become obsessed. Only when pure exhaustion, or doing things making me forget, can I finally find rest and turn my mind off. It's like an illness. A curse." He smiles at her. "But not with you. You comfort me. I've never had the feeling of comfort like the way you give it to me."

"Then, you should sleep like we did in Texas. I'm here with you."

"Maybe." Lucius inches closer, until the bottom of his hip touches her hip. "Let me tell you a story instead of discussing sleep."

She adjusts a pillow and looks up at him. "I'm ready."

"Let me think. What's a good one?" he asks himself with an exhale. "I'll tell you about the heavens before telling you of my troubles."

She wiggles her hips in place with excitement and says, "This is gonna be good."

"Depends on how you see what I'm about to say. The Father saw this occurrence that I am about to mention as good, and it was at first." He strokes her thigh that is laid over his. "Okay. From a time long before time was counted, a time that only our Father can remember, there was peace. There were galaxies, planets, civilizations, and they were all His children, and He knew all their hearts. Nothing was hidden."

"You can't hide anything from God anyway. Nobody can."

He raises a finger and says, "Except those that He purposely hides."

Her lips formed the letter O while cooing. "This is getting good."

"It's not fiction and depends on how you look at what I explain." He strokes her cheek. "But, yeah, it's an intriguing story." He leans back on his hands, and continues. "There are galaxies so old that not many people know when they started."

"How do people get around? Do they all have your keys, and vessels?"

"That's a good point. Let me start somewhere else." He raises his key and says, "Only angels of the guard, and very few people have ownership of these keys."

"What people? Other than the guards, who would be allowed to have a key?"

He answers her, "First, you need to know about the galaxies to understand which people would have permission to use a key. That permission rests within each galaxy. In each galaxy, there are billions of planets. Some planets are habitable, and others are stations, moons, or gas giants. On habitable planets like this one, they are usually run by a king, or a form of government that was placed on that planet. But no matter which one is used as accountability, they must answer to someone else that rules over that galaxy. A dominion."

"God. They answer to God," she guesses.

"Although true because He rules over the heavens and the Earth, that's not what I am trying to tell you. Each galaxy answers to someone called a principality. A principality is a celestial leader that only answers to the Trinity. Principalities bow their heads only to the Trinity because they are the celestial leaders who were placed over an inheritance."

"What's a principality? I don't recognize it."

"You don't understand the role of a celestial because the Trinity is your principality. Yeshua, or Jesus, himself is the King of kings and the Lord of lords. He is over His children on your world. It is why you are the most loved, and you belong to Him. He was willing to die for you. That is how much a principality is supposed to love and protect a realm." He pats her hand. "Let me explain a principality a little better. I said there were civilizations, worlds, and they are within a galaxy, billions upon billions of stars swirling around in a massive display of light. This is the dominion or inheritance of one principality. A principality governs over an entire galaxy."

"Wait," she says and slightly sits up. "One person?"

He nods and says, "One galaxy, one principality. It's how the govern of a principality was designed."

"How exhausting. Aren't there a whole lot of galaxies?"

He nods again. "Yes, and that is the reason why principalities speak with only the kings or world chiefs that they govern rather than to each person. That kind of leadership would be exhausting. The Father knows this, so He blessed His principality children with special gifts, so they could serve in their kingdoms and protect the Father's children completely."

"Like what?" she asks.

"Let's go back to where I was starting. There are galaxies that are very old and have become well-known. Usually, galaxies near one another are made around the same time and neighboring each other."

"How come?"

He tells her with a pause so she will understand the significance. "So the principalities won't become…lonely," he says.

"How can they become lonely? They have all those people."

He shakes his head as he explains. "Think of it, my yoshawn. Do the leaders of your world go to your house, sit on your couch, and tell you all their woes?"

"No," she says as her expression sinks. "I understand what you're saying. They would lose respect from their people."

Lucius nods. "And with losing respect, they would lose honor among their people and the love of their people as well. A principality must maintain an image, so he can govern his people so they will not fall away from God. Principalities are to represent God inside their jurisdiction."

"That makes sense," she says.

"Now, for the story. Once, there were six galaxies, older than even I would know. Each galaxy was rich in resources and run by a talented principality. They are well known, and other principalities would show up to see them."

"Why would other principalities show up?"

He smiles as he says, "Because of their gifts."

She shrugs. "What gifts?"

"That's what I'm about to tell you. All principalities have a specific gift encoded in their DNA, and not many principalities are exactly like the other. Each gift that is encoded in a principality is almost like a fingerprint. There have been principalities who can wield fire."

She gasps. "Like Artie?"

He nods and says, "Yes, but many other angels and beings have similar gifts. But, in the example of Artie, he's nowhere near a principality with his small ability. The power I'm speaking of, is the kind an entire world could be burned by."

"Intense."

"They are, which is why fire wielding is rare. But I'll talk more about that in a minute. Some control water and anywhere water can be found within his realm including the atmosphere and even in the soil. Other principalities can move entire planets, rearranging time for the inhabitants. But you get the picture. They're powerful beings, and no one understands them but the Trinity. Principalities must remain reserved with their emotions."

"I guess that would be lonely." She raises up some and asks, "Baby, where do they live? Is it in heaven?"

"Oobadoave? No," he says. "They have a special planet within their realms, their inheritance, with their own people.

"What do you mean by 'their own people?'"

"Principalities usually have tribes in their likeness, those who are closest and share a lot of the same traits. Those people have a portion of the principality's gifts, a small measure of what that principality has for the principality to feel loved and relate to others. The tribesmen aid in keeping the principality from feeling abandoned and having no counsel. Principalities need comfort like everyone else." Lucius turns his head, holds his breath to keep from becoming emotional, and rubs around his eyes.

"Is it an eyelash?" she asks.

He re-situates while glancing at her momentarily. "It's good. I'm fine."

"Please continue," she says and pats his thigh. "I'm enjoying this story."

Lucius continues. "Anyway, those six galaxies that I had mentioned, over time the galaxies started to converge into one giant cluster, of which there could be only one supreme leader."

"Who would the supreme principality be in that case? That seems like a real problem."

He answers, "It was. And this was the first convergence in history. The largest inheritance, which was the oldest of the group, would have more reign. His power would be increased with extra portions in his DNA to enable him to control his inheritance. Each converging galaxy would make him more powerful. He would inevitably be over all his neighboring principalities as well, and they would all serve under his reign, making him the supreme principality. Those principalities, who once kneeled before no one while ruling over their own realms, would have to bow to a new leader, honoring him publicly for the people to accept. The only problem was that the principalities bowed only to the Trinity. Principalities were, and are, considered equals, no matter how powerful one is over the other."

She asks, "What did they do?"

"The supreme principality gave his brothers ordinance, making them as equal as he could. He separated the converged galaxies into minor jurisdictions and called the joined realm the *Cluster*."

"He solved it."

"Many thought that he did," Lucius says. He nods, and his eyes instruct her with a look of seriousness. "But he didn't ask what the Father wanted because he felt sorry for his brothers. The giving of such power from his inheritance caused issues, instead of repairing them."

She asks, "How so?"

"Well, the Cluster's supreme principality couldn't go back on his word once given. A principality's word is law. Taking back his word would be breaking his own laws, making his word worthless, and losing the trust of his people. The Cluster was the first of its kind with many principalities running it. Because of this situation, other principalities visited because the preexisting principalities became equally stronger, second to the supreme principality's abilities."

"What's so wrong with that? It's less lonely."

"Yes, they thought that too." He kisses the back of her hand and says, "I love your innocence, and that's why I'm telling you this story. Not all solutions are true solutions."

"What happened?"

"The principalities started to change a little at a time in their hearts. Because they were once over a realm, and they were tangled into someone else's, they began pressing their power a little more in public, strutting their stuff, and proving themselves in a way. You know what I mean?"

She nods and says, "They were showing off."

"Exactly," he answers. "The behavior became a show of power, and the other visiting principalities would join in for fun. In doing so, raising themselves up in front of others like a spectacle, and that's what the show of power became, a spectacle." He gazes down at her with seriousness in his eyes and says, "The Father did not approve. The new normal for that realm had shifted power in the minds of His children, making them disregard the honor that God had placed in front of them that had once kept them accountable. Some of the inhabitants stopped fearing God, and others disregarded authority as only playing with power and not worth their time since they had none of their own. The shift of power in the Cluster had changed many hearts."

"Oh, no." she pants. "That's terrible, Lucius."

He nods and says, "You're right in your response. The disrespect of power troubled the Father, so He sent an entire world of commanders and guardians to the Cluster. Jett Commdearadea was released for the first time to restore order and functionality into a failing realm. Many royal kings and their families had their own personal Jett Commdearadea guardians to keep the peace and protect the royals of each world. People enjoyed the attention, the care of God…but…"

"Uh, oh, that pause doesn't sound good," she says.

"You're right. The royal leaders, and celestial principalities didn't like answering to any power of a commander or a mere soldier, even if the soldier had the authority as a representative of God to enforce laws. The Lord saw this for the first time. There were scuffles on several worlds within the Cluster. Many soldiers were publicly punished and put down by force on the streets for telling a celestial leader what he should be doing."

Josephine pops up and yaps, "Oh, my goodness. That's evil."

Lucius looks at her. His voice heightens, says, "That's what I thought. The way they treated people made my blood boil when hearing about it. No one should ever get away for disrespecting the word of God. It angered me until I was shaking with such news."

"That must be when you joined the army."

He shakes his head. "Not at that time."

She asks, "What did the Father do? How did He fix it?"

Lucius's expression saddens as he takes his time in saying, "Some things…can't be fixed, baby."

She gasps.

He continues with a slight nod. "Those who will not listen or obey the word of God are the very ones who offend the Holy Spirit. He turns His back on them."

"Is this Earth?"

"Very similar," he answers.

"What happened to the Cluster?"

"I don't know everything, but I do know that He removed his Jett commanders and guardians from that realm with strict orders. They were ordered to relocate those who faithfully served God somewhere safe, away from abominations."

"Aw, because He loves His children who love Him," she says.

Lucius nods. "That's correct. He loves all His children, but before God's army could travel back for those that were left behind, the realm was barred from reentry. God's children were imprisoned or executed. Every border of every world was closed off. The soldiers could not get back into the heliosphere of the galaxy with their vessels. Many Jett warriors were destroyed as they passed the barrier." He breathes deeply and continues. "The Father called His soldiers away before more of His sons could be taken from His army."

She gets up and arches her shoulders back as if ready for battle. "Did He go in there and kick some butt?"

Lucius's head shakes and he answers, "He punished them, but not in a way you're thinking. He has plans within plans, and those plans are the mysteries of God. This is the first time a great falling away had been done. There was no one to make purchase for their deeds any longer."

"How so? Are you saying, a sacrifice like Jesus?"

"Every principality, who was once a holy representation for their people, had fallen in that realm. God will not enter an unholy area, and there was no one to pay ransom for their unholiness. There was no principality to die for them as a sacrifice. The Cluster became cursed." His nose nudges the air while gesturing at her. "For this reason and because you are special to Him, He chose to protect your kind in the Milky Way from such destruction. He sent His Son, your world's King and Principality, so then you could have a bridge back to Him, and see the Father someday. It is through the Lamb of God that you can enter the courts of heaven and stand before His Throne. This is not so for other realms. Their principalities keep them accountable, and the Father can visit them."

"Someone would have to die for them?" she asks.

"Not so simple. I've heard that many principalities have gone in, but no one leaves. We no longer turn toward the Cluster because it is closed and seen as death."

She asks, "How come?"

He says, "They were powerful. The Father used their own authority against them to punish them. He does the same for many who have turned. He gave the principalities in the Cluster authority to begin with, and He never goes back on His word. By their own sin, He finds judgment within that authority that was given."

"What did He do?" she asks. "How did He correct the sin?"

"Because they closed their borders, He had decided He would make it permanent. I don't know much of how He cursed that place, but I do know that He cannot look upon it because of how dark it is there. None can leave. The Cluster has become the bowels of Hell for our universe in a way. Also, why it has been renamed the *Shadow Cluster* and it was the day the war began."

Thirteen

The Good Principality

"I love hearing your stories," she says with a smile as she caresses his large fingers that tangle into hers.

"More like a history lesson," he says as he plays with her wedding band. "A story nonetheless."

"Tell me more. What did the people of the heavens do when the war began?"

"Well." He inhales deeply and says, "Other principalities were appalled at the deeds of those who had caused the fall of people." He raises a finger and includes, "But the closing of the Shadow Cluster and the beginning of the war created more problems."

"How so?"

He wiggles his fingers in circles chaotically as he says, "The news of war created fear, and a great meeting was called for all the principalities. The unfallen principalities voiced their concerns and learned many truths about what had happened."

She asks, "Like what?"

"They learned that principalities who govern over more than one galaxy receive an extra portion of power." He looks at her. "And that was their biggest fear. If they were to battle a principality stronger than them, they could lose their inheritance, and their people would fall. The Father consoled them, but some allowed fear to guide them, instead of His words."

She nods. "He is not the author of fear."

He nods as well. "That's right."

She rolls her wrist and says, "Please continue."

"I'm going to give an example of a story I know." He re-situates again and leans forward slightly. "In the universe at this time, a newer portion was teaming with young realms, civilizations, and young principalities. In the heart of this new portion, there was a good principality. The good principality was a shepherd to his people, and he listened carefully to the guidance of his Father, and he trusted in his Father's word with all that he was. The good principality was a true shepherd to his people and was powerful, but he had only one realm and cherished every person within it. They were like little lambs to him.

Now, I know you don't quite understand the ways of the heavens, but in this case, it was rare because he knew all of them by name and was one with his people because of how he was made. He joined them for meals, festivals, and harvests."

She smiles and says, "Aw, I love that part. They were precious little lambs to the good principality. He must've been a good shepherd."

"He was," he says nodding, "and he hid much of the war from his realm and protected his borders, so they wouldn't be worried about war or invasion. They were so innocent. This tactic of remaining silent about what scared many increased their faith in God, and in the good principality, so they would never fall. It was a peaceful realm, and he vowed to guard his inheritance with his very life. It's who the good principality was."

"Was?" she asks and tilts her body while sitting up. "You said 'was.'"

He breathes in for what feels like minutes. "Yes...until war entered his section of the universe." He gazes at her. "Remember when I said many galaxies are formed around the same time so principalities will not become lonely?"

She gestures yes.

"There was another principality in a neighboring galaxy to the good principality. The good principality could see the neighboring galaxy in his night's sky. The neighboring galaxy's principality was named Moarscii, and the good principality was close to him. Moarscii and the good principality played games together, using their talents and gifts to train, thereby increasing their protection over their kingdoms."

"What was," she pauses briefly as she tries pronouncing the name slowly. "More...sea...I? Anyway, what is his power?"

"He could hide—invisibility. He could vanish completely in front of you, and throw his voice. Moarscii could even make apparitions of himself in different forms. He was able to watch his people, keeping them accountable without their knowing, and take them in for judgment if he was unable to help them. He protected his people by his special gifts. He had perfected his ability with the good principality because they were equals."

"What was the good principality's gift, could he vanish or shape shift?"

Lucius answers, "He could read the future in a way. He was able to link his mind, body, and spirit to those around him, even if he was weak, and he was good at it. He could predict what anyone was going to do before doing it. The good principality could shepherd his people before making mistakes and would counsel them so they wouldn't fall. And…he never had to send any of those he loved from his realm to judgment because of it. They all bowed to him as an honorable king, and he treated them like brothers and sisters—his family."

She says, "I see a difference between the two. He sounds more like Jesus."

Lucius pauses for a moment and says, "Moarscii loved his inheritance. Don't get me wrong, but he had a different way about him when it came to shepherding his flock. He was more forceful than most when the war started corrupting things, and the good principality counseled Moarscii a lot when trying to ease his mind." Lucius gestures as he continues. "During one of their games, Moarscii's secrets of winning were found out. His mind was elsewhere while worried about his kingdom. The good principality started winning games every time."

"Because the good principality could read Moarscii's mind," she answers. "I thought all angels could do that."

"There's one thing I haven't mentioned. It's important for you to know. Principalities can block their minds from other principalities and all those beneath them. Only the Trinity knows everything, and principalities cannot block their minds from God."

Her brows crease, and she asks, "How did the good principality know what Moarscii was thinking?"

"The good principality might not have been able to read Moarscii's mind completely before that day, but he was a spiritual empath and could predict his reactions and then later his intentions. It was only on that day, when Moarscii's mind was preoccupied that the good principality could see clearly how each tactic worked, making Moarscii's secrets for defense vulnerable."

"Uh, oh," she says.

"Yeah. Moarscii feared what could happen if the good principality were to turn because he knew how powerful the empath was compared to him after that day. The good principality counseled Moarscii with his whole heart, promising that he would never break the law and forcefully take over Moarscii's jurisdiction. But—"

"Oh, no. You said, 'but.'"

Lucius nods. "Yes. What you understand became Moarscii's worse fear nonetheless."

"What did Moarscii do?"

Lucius continues. "Moarscii became secluded within his realm and wouldn't leave his borders. He was obsessed with protecting the Buovouste galaxy. It wasn't until a few years later, when a neighboring principality named Dugand, in the Arstoleci galaxy, was invited by Moarscii to a feast."

She perks up and says, "That's nice. Moarscii invited Dugand for dinner."

Lucius hangs his head and scowls. "That's not how I would define the invite. Let me explain. When a principality leaves his jurisdiction, he becomes weak if exerting too much ability in someone else's govern. Even though Dugand was close to the Arstoleci galaxy and could absorb small amounts of his ability, he was still within Moarscii's jurisdiction. The closer a principality is to his realm, the stronger he is. And Moarscii had unlimited access to his strength in his own kingdom."

"It was a trap," she says.

Lucius nods. "It was a trap. And the good principality warned Dugand."

"What did Dugand say? Do you know?"

He nods again and says, "A little. Dugand was aware of Moarscii's objectives, and Dugand believed his galaxy was close enough to protect him."

"What happened?"

"During the good principality's warning, Dugand blocked his mind and assured the good principality that all was well with his reasoning." Lucius smirks and says, "It wasn't until later that the good principality realized that Dugand and Moarscii had shared similar intentions."

Her brows come together and she asks, "What were they planning?"

"They were going into battle with each other under the guise of a friendly meeting. By the end of their meal, one would be a supreme principality over two galaxies instead of one, extending that principality's border, and increasing the power for just one of them. And the good principality's kingdom was smack dab in the middle of both galaxies."

Nibbling on her nails, Josephine asks. "What happened?"

He lowers her fingers from her lips and tells her, "Moarscii defeated Dugand. He had become a principality with a double portion. Stronger than before, and Dugand had lost his inheritance."

"Did Moarscii kill him?"

Lucius's head shakes. "No. Dugand ran for his life with what little power he had left, but he had lost his inheritance by entering into battle." He gazes at Josephine, studies her confused expression, and explains, "I told you we keep to our word in the heavens. If we say yes or no, it is law. Dugand knew the penalties, and because his mind was as corrupt as Moarscii's, he did not rely on God and lost his inheritance. He was therefore judged without birthright."

She gasps. "Moarscii must be judged for his actions."

"You don't understand," he says and exhales. "An agreement was legally made between the two of them, and they fulfilled it. No law was broken, and Moarscii did not abandon what God had given him. He was trying to increase his ability to protect his people."

"But he can't rule over people with that mentality."

Lucius agrees, saying, "The good principality understood this and mourned the loss of his brother, Dugand. Moarscii became quiet again, never leaving his realm...until—"

"Oh no," she says and exhales sadly.

"Yep. Moarscii sent an invitation for the good principality to meet with him."

Josephine springs up and says, "He did not fall for it. Please, tell me he did not fall for that."

Lucius speaks without an expression, saying, "He met with him."

Josephine slaps her forehead. "Now, I'm just sad. I don't think I can hear anymore."

He chuckles. "Let me finish," he says stroking her arm.

She nods. "Okay."

"Anyway." Lucius stretches his back as he says, "He met with Moarscii, but this meeting was different than he had expected. Moarscii had a way with his words and tried confusing the good principality. But the good principality was very close to the Holy Spirit and would not allow Moarscii's twisted understanding to govern him."

"What happened? Did the good principality beat him up?"

Lucius smiles and says, "Remember when I said that principalities have people on their own worlds? Tribesman with similar DNA like them with only a smaller portion of power?"

She nods.

He continues. "The good principality took his own army with him. Just like the good principality, they were powerful, more than Moarscii's people."

"How big was the good principality's army?"

"Not as many as Moarscii's, but definitely more powerful. This is where Moarscii showed his pompous ignorance. He had allowed his new formed power over him and his people to shroud his wisdom."

"What do you mean, 'power over his people?' I don't understand."

He glances off momentarily before saying, "When a principality is increased, those of his blood are increased as well, making his direct tribe stronger on his home world. This is even more so for a principality's second-in-command."

"Second-in-command?"

He gives a single nod and says, "Every principality has a confidant, a second-in-command, someone who attends the principality's people while he's away and shares in his burden. The second-in-command must be powerful to govern those people. Almost as powerful as the principality, but still a loyal subject to him."

"So Moarscii had a powerful second-in-command?"

He says, "Absolutely. His second-in-command had also received a double portion."

Her palms flare up as she asks, "So what happened?"

"The good principality bluntly confronted Moarscii, and in front of both armies."

She winces. "Embarrassing."

Lucius agrees, saying, "It was."

"What did Moarscii do after being called out in front of everyone like that?"

He continues. "Moarscii became indignant from the accusations, and bowed up, telling his men to arm themselves. The good principality advised Moarscii to stop, but Moarscii was dedicated to what he had planned. He acted in anger. The word of God says to be angry, but sin not." Lucius nods and says, "And it came to pass. Against holy laws and against the good principality's wishes, Moarscii attacked."

Josephine wheezes and asks, "In whose realm? Where were they?" She latches onto his arm. "Lucius, who's jurisdiction?"

Lucius gazes silently at her.

She covers her mouth and whispers, "Moarscii's." She plummets back in her spot. "Oh, no."

"Yes," he answers. "The good principality was in Moarscii's jurisdiction, and the good principality's army was forced to defend themselves in an unlawful attack. One army was left slaughtered and the other completely victorious."

Her shoulders sink and she says, "Oh no, the good principality lost all his people?"

At this, Lucius's eyes shut, and he swallows for a moment. He raises his gaze toward her before saying, "No, baby. The good principality had to destroy Moarscii's army, but not one of his subjects was lost to him that day."

"Well, Moarscii deserved it," she says.

His head shakes. "Maybe so, baby, but not Moarscii's people. Moarscii's subjects were following the authority of their principality. Their shepherd. They entrusted him with their lives. It was a terrible day, and the good principality had imprisoned Moarscii. The Buovouste galaxy and the Arstoleci galaxy had lost their shepherd that day. The Arstoleci galaxy had lost two shepherds in a matter of just a few years."

"I didn't think of it that way," she says. "How did the good principality imprison Moarscii?"

"He trapped Moarscii with a special trans-dimensional device he had made. The good principality was known for craftmanship, and he came up with many designs and technologies. He had made an orb of Oobadoave shielding so he could trap unholiness inside. In this case—Moarscii."

"What's Oobadoave shielding?" she asks. "How could it trap Moarscii?"

"Oobadoave shields are holy barriers. No evil of body, spirit, or the mind can pass through."

She asks, "Moarscii was stuck because he had bad intentions and had broken the law?"

"Correct," he says. "He had sinned against the good principality."

"What did he do, the good principality? Is Moarscii still trapped?"

Lucius continues, saying, "The good principality was heartbroken. He had already lost, Dugand, a celestial brother, and felt because the offense of

Moarscii was against him, he could seek the Father in absolving Moarscii's wrongs." Lucius pats her backhand and curls his lip for a moment. "He went to the Father, presenting Moarscii in his prison and his testimony of the occurrence. The good principality asked if there was any way he could have his brother back…" Lucius stops. He blinks several times and waits a moment.

He succeeds in keeping from crying in front of her, and Josephine says, "This is a sad story." She strokes his arm. "You must've been sad when you found out what these guys did."

"I was. But let me finish." He breathes deeply, and continues. "The good principality was instructed to leave without an answer. An archangel took the orb from the good principality, and the good principality went home. He had no word, and two realms were left without a shepherd. He was troubled. His army tried comforting him while gathering around him in prayer."

She smiles and says, "They must've been very close."

He strokes her cheek and says, "Oh, baby, they really were. They were an army of brothers who could not be defeated because they worked as one."

Her eyes open wide and she says, "Because they could feel each other. They were like one person, weren't they?"

He nods. "Yes." He struggles momentarily and leans back, pretending to stretch while hiding his tears. When he is controlled, he raises up and continues. "They were one people unlike any other."

"What about the other realms?"

Lucius says, "Sometime later, an archangel and a Jett Commdearadea commander visited the good principality. He could not read their minds because they had been blocked by Trinitarian power. The good principality was summoned for a meeting at the high Council of the Hagia Sophia on Oobadoave. They left immediately."

"Oh," she says. "I'm getting nervous."

Lucius nods. "He was too…very nervous. Anyway, when he entered the courts, his eyes scanned the area." Lucius pauses for a moment before continuing. "But Moarscii was nowhere to be found. The Almighty caught the good principality's attention by asking what he was looking for. The good principality said, 'Where have you taken him? Can my brother not come back home?'"

"The Father answered, 'Are you one to judge what happens?' At these words, the good principality knew he would never see Moarscii again. The good principality answered, 'You are the judge, and I am your servant,' but his tears poured out anyway."

Stroking her hand, he says, "The Almighty asked, 'He would've destroyed you if he could. Why do you cry?'

"The good principality explained, 'Because, my Lord, two galaxies are left without a shepherd, and I loved my brother.'"

"How sad," Josephine says.

Lucius says, "It was. The Almighty said to him, 'I know you loved him. If you could go back, knowing what you know of him, what would you have done with that knowledge?'

"Immediately, the good principality fell to his knees and sobbed bitterly in front of all who watched. He finally answered, 'Father, if you know a way, please tell me of how I can help those who will listen, so this will not happen to them?'"

"Oh, wow," she whispers.

He continues. "The Almighty told the good principality to rise, and when he did, he was bestowed with all three realms. His own, the Buovouste, and the Arstoleci."

"Oh, wow," her voice increases.

"The Almighty trusted the good principality, but He also warned him."

She gasps. "Warned?"

Lucius explains. "He said, 'There are many around your jurisdiction that have been tainted by Dugand's and Moarscii's understanding. You will counsel My principality servants, and those who won't listen, you will take over and steward for Me.'"

She asks, "He inherited them?"

Lucius shakes his head and answers, "Inheritance isn't the same thing as stewarding. To inherit something, means it's yours. But to steward something, means you're a caretaker until the master comes home. His galaxy was his birthright, but he had inherited the Buovouste and the Arstoleci galaxy. He would be a steward only to those he would take over."

"That makes sense. That keeps him accountable."

"Correct. But the good principality still had three times more than any other principality which meant he was stronger than most. He was strong to begin with, but when he had inherited two other galaxies, he became three times more powerful than the principalities had in the beginning."

Josephine raises a finger and says, "And his second-in-command was very strong."

"I'm glad that you are paying attention because the second-in-command had power equal to any principality. The good principality had an unstoppable army."

She asks, "Did he counsel the other celestials? Was he able to help them?"

Lucius nods and says, "He was good at counseling them, and he had successfully eased the thoughts of hundreds of his brethren around him."

"But..." she says, rolling her finger for the rest.

He points and answers, "But you're correct. Over the course of a thousand years, the principality became the ruler over seventy-two galaxies, making him one of the strongest principalities in existence."

"It must've been hard for him to rule over such a large area," she says.

"It was," he says. "That's when the keys were created with the Almighty." Lucius elevates his portal cross and says, "Because of the keys, the good principality could visit these worlds in a twinkle of an eye, allowing him to act faster."

"So that's why soldiers have them now."

"Yes," he says, nodding. "The technology aided in the war, and is the reason only the angels of the guard, and certain principalities have access to them."

"People must've really loved him then," she says and smiles.

"Not really, baby. Many people feared him because of his great power and knowledge of technology. He counseled them in any way he could. When the good principality realized that his existence was scaring people, he shed his celestial clothing and changed his image, making him as normal as possible."

She clasps over her breasts and exclaims, "Aw, poor guy! It's not his fault."

"Well, the good principality's actions were in vain and didn't work because many in his jurisdiction knew so much about him. He wanted a new image. He wanted to make it the way it was and show people he meant no harm when serving the Almighty. He was just a servant, but he couldn't erase the thoughts of others once the thought was born in someone's mind."

"What did he do?"

He gazes at her and says, "He saw a new prized world, and he came up with an idea. He would help this new world as he had helped many realms before. Usually, a planet isn't quite so famous on its own, but this world was a world everyone in every realm knew about. The news of this world spread as far as the universe stretches. The good principality thought, finally, they would stop fearing him if he were to lend aid because the war had struck the planet so harshly."

She raises up again and asks, "Earth?"

He says, "Yes. Earth had many problems, and because the good principality couldn't leave his vast jurisdiction, he sent an entire world of his along with his technology to help the Lord's children in his place. He gave that army as a gift to the Lord."

"Wait," she says. "When was this? I don't remember this happening in scripture."

His eyes squeeze shut and he nods. "Yes...you do."

She gulps and asks, "Your brothers? He sent Gamerilaye." Josephine strokes his leg. "He sent all your brothers. Is that what you're saying?"

His eyes slowly climb up and fights tears. "Yes. My brothers agreed to help their principality. When they fell, their portal crosses were taken, and they never returned."

Josephine covers her mouth when thinking she knows what he's been hiding. She says, "That's why you never told me." She comforts him by rubbing his chest. "All your brothers went missing, and you were left alone."

He nods silently, wanting to wrap his arms around her and apologize for what he'd done.

She says, "You two must not get along."

His expression melts away and he asks, "What?"

She explains, "Well, you've been troubled for a long time after losing your brothers, and you've been trying to find them. You and the good principality must not get along because you've never mentioned him."

Lucius burst out laughing as he falls back.

"What's so funny?" she asks.

"Baby," he says as he continues chuckling into his hands. His face is covered as he says, "You're right. I definitely don't get along with the guy. I can't stand him."

"Well, that's not nice to say," she says. "He was only trying to help with abilities just like yours," and she gasps, "Wait...he's..."

Lucius sits up.

She continues with several pauses in between her words. "he's your...but...that would mean." She stares at him for a long time, until finally she says, "Baby," and closes distance between her and Lucius, until her breath brushes his cheeks. "What's his name?"

Lucius takes his wife's hand and places it upon his beating chest. His eyes gloss over, and he exhales before saying, "Those closest to him, call him...They call him, baby," gazing deep in her eyes, "or Daddy." He caresses her cheek. "I am he."

Fourteen

Comfort

Feeling as though several minutes have passed with a silent stare and not a sound, Lucius becomes more terrified than ever with Josephine taking in the information. He strokes her skin and begs, "Say something, baby. It's just me, little momma. It's your husband." He tries to restrain his emotion after receiving no reply or even a wince.

Finally, her eyes shut, her head shakes, and she raises a hand. Although silent as she places his information into her mind, at least she still responds with something before he can fall apart.

"Okay, okay, I'll wait." His voice shudders.

Josephine rubs the bridge of her nose, breathing quietly for a time of several minutes. "I'm just…" she pauses another full minute before saying, "I'm trying to wrap my brain around…" her exhale plays a tune like a long sigh. "Are you not reading my mind?"

"My yoshawn," he says and shakes his head. "I can't."

Her eyes meet his and she says, "I thought a principality could. This whole situation is confusing."

"I mean, I can't read your mind because I can't handle you pushing me away. Everybody pushes me away, but it would destroy me if you did."

She gasps. "How dare you?"

Frozen in place, Lucius is unable to reach for her. He watches her stand to her feet and begin pacing the floor.

Before he can react, she stops him with a palm. "Don't cry and don't overreact, Yuleshua Lucius Gamerin. I meant, how dare you disconnect from me, after what we went through today, and even now, making this discussion more difficult for me. I can hardly think clearly. How could I respond with my mind so jumbled?"

Lucius says nothing, and his shoulders sink.

She slouches and says, "I'm not mad at you, Lucius. I'm surprised. Shocked."

Terrified to stand and appear bigger than her, Lucius stays seated. "How do you mean?" he asks and clasps his hands together. "My queen, my love, my all, my yoshawn—"

"That," she says preventing him from continuing. "You act like I'm some brute, like you don't know me." She gestures at his spot on the floor. "You're even scared to stand up, and I don't have to read your mind to see what you're doing. I know exactly who you are," she says, bumping her chest with soft fingers. "I know who you really are. I know your heart."

Lucius finally stands, but slants his head just below hers, partially hunching forward. "I'll give you anything, my love."

"Now, you're just irritating me," she says and holds onto him as he melts into her arms. "You're making me feel sorry for you. Why do you do this? You hurt my feelings by your fear of not trusting me."

Lucius exhales. "I never wanted any of what I was given as my inheritance. I would've given everything away in a moment if the Lord had desired."

"I know, Lucius." She huffs. "Please, connect with me. I hate explaining what has been obvious about me for the past six years of my life." Lucius connects his thoughts as she continues, saying, "Have I not given myself freely to you, as your wife? Have I not carried your child?"

His eyes close as he says, "I feel your emotions." He releases her some and gazes into her eyes. "I was terrified."

"Of me?" Her brows furrow. "Why?"

"I told you. Many people are frightened of me, and other principalities are disgusted with me. Even today my celestial brothers were gawking at me, making me...Anyway, I did as I was ordered and met with my brother Yeshua."

"What did they say?"

"They said no Gamerin would be allowed here without purchase." He rubs the back of his neck and says, "Some of them chased after me, making sure I was Gamerin. One said that all the Gamerin fell, and I couldn't be one if I were there." His lip quivers. "You should've seen the shock in their eyes. I felt like I didn't belong, and all I wanted was you holding me. I needed your comfort."

"*Shhh*," she tells him. "This doesn't make sense. What did you tell them? What did they say when you explained your situation to them?"

He rubs his nose against her cheek. "I didn't. I ran and was hoping they didn't remember me. I've hidden my face for ten thousand years."

She pulls away and asks, "You haven't been to the Father's house for ten thousand years? How would they even recognize you?"

"I went today, and at the Father's house, you are known as you were known."

She stares off at nothing and asks, "Wait. You didn't stop to answer them?" She shrugs and continues. "You just avoided them? I don't understand. I thought you were summoned. I thought that you were a principality. I thought that you were a soldier, and it was your duty in all three counts."

Sheepishly, he nods. "Yes. I had a right to be there, but as I told you, I can't handle people pushing me away. Everyone has pushed me away for so long. They spoke so loudly, and it was raising attention. I didn't want my faults advertised, so I ran."

Her shoulders dip and she says, "That doesn't sound like you...Not understanding what's going on."

Lucius frowns. "I saw how they acted."

"You saw what you feared and weren't connected to their thoughts. You were driven by fear and didn't counsel them with your words."

His mouth opens. "I didn't. A couple of them chased after me."

She says, "Lucius, what do we do when Claire is hurt?"

"We comfort her." His eyes raise, and his tension releases. "We run to her aid...because we love her."

"And don't I raise my voice the more concerned I am for her, nearly racing to her when seeing her cry?"

His eyes close and he says, "That's exactly what they did." He embraces her. "Little momma, your counsel and love restore me," he says as he sways in place with her.

"It's about time you've noticed."

With a tiny giggle between them, they dance slowly in place, letting their love for each other calm them. Lucius kisses along her neck. After a few minutes, she feels his breath against the lobe of her ear and across her soft hairs of her neck. "Are you pouring those principality gifts over me, or one of those kissy-kissy ones you do?"

"No."

She flicks a brow and says, "Oh."

"Mrs. Gamerin," he says and gazes into her eyes. "Are you getting turned on by me?" Josephine tries subduing her smile. He nods for them both, and says, "You are. I can feel it. You can't hide those emotions. You have pheromone fogging out from your nostrils." He dresses his chest with her hands and says, "And I need to feel your comfort over me." He soon smiles, and raises a brow. "You want to make love to a principality?"

"For the first time, I want to make love with my husband for all he is, bound to me by the Holy Spirit, and what appears to be his kingdom."

He lifts her body up, she wraps her legs around his waist, and he carries her onto the center of the pallet. Nibbling on her neck, he strokes her thighs, and then pauses. "I can't," he says.

Unzipping his pants, she's panting. "Why not? You said Artie wouldn't bother us."

He groans from where her hands caress his skin. "It's not that, and, baby, you're tempting me." He sighs and says, "I want this."

"What is it?" she asks while stretching her body for more.

"I was ordered. I must wait until we're on Gamerilaye." She stops moving and his head falls between her neck and shoulder, as he starts grunting.

"That's a bummer," she says.

Lucius's head pops up and he grins deviously at her, as his brow arches. "I know what we can do."

"What?"

"We might not be able to ride the horses, but that doesn't mean that we can't visit the petting zoo." Josephine laughs, and Lucius pulls the blankets over his head to savor the comforting love of his wife.

Fifteen

Sunrise

Lucius wakes up early in the morning before the sun rises. He holds Josephine. She is robed only in a cotton shirt. "I'm unconditionally in love with you," he says and kisses Josephine's ear. "Stay asleep, my queen." He supports her head and pulls his arm away from the pillow. Lucius gazes toward a dimly lit sky through the bay area before turning to look at his wife. "I'm covering you now. I don't want anyone to look upon you the way I see you, and you need your rest." He kisses her again. "We have a busy day ahead."

Carefully, Lucius modestly dresses her with her dress pants and covers her in a blanket. "I'm going to make some coffee before Artie wakes up." He strokes her cheek and says, "You've restored me to who I was. You've made me whole again."

In the kitchen, he prepares breakfast and sips coffee with an occasional smile. Every few minutes, Lucius peeks around the rock wall at Josephine while she sleeps, and the sight of her makes him smile all over again.

Sunrise dawns, and Artie walks through the living area. He remains respectful, keeping his eyes away from the pallet that his king and queen were sleeping on. He enters the kitchen and pauses in place. Lucius is leaning against the countertop, silent, sipping coffee, and thinking to himself. Artie studies him until Lucius glances over. Artie's eyes open wide as if awaiting an answer. His chin points out a little before bobbing his head in suspense.

Slowly, Lucius smiles and nods.

Artie exhales and says, "Really? I mean, really, really?"

"Yeah," Lucius answers.

Artie falls to his knees, bowing before his king. "How long I've waited. This feels right and is an honor for me."

Lucius says, "I see that now. Arise, my old friend. I'd rather give you a hug."

Artie sprints and embraces him. "I love you, sire. If you don't mind my asking, what all was said? I want to know where my boundaries are."

Lucius brushes his thumb over Artie's forehead—a form of transmitting instant knowledge, and immediately Artie understands. Lucius says, "She has completely accepted me. As you know now, she has restored me."

Artie steps back and paces in place. He says, "We must tell everybody. We must celebrate. There will be festivals and banquets all over. The galaxies will worship the Father because of your healing. They've been praying for you." He pauses and stares at Lucius, says, "The king has returned."

"We have time for that later," Lucius says. "She's only beginning, and introducing her to my…our govern, it would be best not to overwhelm her." He places his crystal coffee mug onto the marble slab. "She's a queen, and I'm a principality. Without a principality's ability, she would be mentally exhausted. I need to take her training one step at a time with her before I show her what we govern together." Lucius's nose nubs the air as he says, "I have breakfast cooking in your brick oven. I'm glad you have bacon here. I would've missed bacon."

Artie pours himself coffee and glances up. "What are you planning today? If I know you, you have a whole itinerary scheduled."

"First things first." Lucius asks, "When does your housekeeper get here?"

"Powtray?" Artie pulls a breakfast cake stuffed with maple and bacon from the oven. He sniffs the aroma and says, "Breakfast smells amazing. I forgot that Powtray would be here. He usually comes in the late morning. I could dismiss him. While we're here, I won't need him to keep my house for me, and my queen could sleep in."

"No. I'll make sure she's ready. I don't want someone witnessing my wife sleeping on the floor and dressed in baggy clothes, appearing as if I take care of her less than one of my subjects. She's worth more to me. Powtray needs to continue tending to your home."

Artie collects butter from the cooler and lays it toward the edge of his kitchen. "Are we going home this evening?"

"We're going home." Lucius finishes his coffee and continues. "But not too late. We have a few stops to make before I show her the Gamerin palace."

"What do you have planned?"

Lucius smiles and says, "I want to show her Avledon. She's only seen such creatures in movies, and movie creatures are nowhere near as beautiful as they really are."

"Oh, yeah, Avledon." He winks at Lucius. "It might take her breath away."

Lucius nods. "She can take it. She's seen the Mangoram, sleepers, two-headed viper's, hounds of hell, and so much more. The woman can take it."

"Are you taking her and Claire to the observatory? It would be the safest place. I don't know how those creatures will respond to her. You know how they can be after you taking over the Arstoleci."

"They'll be obedient, or they'll be punished. They're my inheritance and no longer an Arstoleci birthright. Arstoleci has been renamed as part of the Gamerin galaxies. I'm their king. They'll honor Josephine as their queen, or I'll place them on Forawvi with the others who betrayed me. I would let them sit there and think about their trespasses for a while."

"I almost forgot about the Forawvine. Is their sentence almost up?"

"I never forget my govern, but they're there until the Father believes they should be pardoned." Lucius gazes at Artie and says, "Or I take them for judgment. Their punishment is better than death, and their banishment should serve as a reminder of what I could've done. They're the ones who revolted because of Moarscii." Lucius shrugs. "Anyway, I'm taking Josephine and Claire to Avledon." Lucius says, "We must wait though, it's still too dark for my family to see the forest from the observatory right now. We need to eat lunch here first."

Artie pauses in place and slowly asks, "When you say…here," pointing a finger toward the floor, "you mean…."

Lucius nods, "I mean with the harvesters, yes."

Artie is overwhelmed with joy and covers his eyes.

Lucius hugs him and says, "It's okay. I know."

"You honor us. They're going to be so happy." They release each other, and Artie says, "We'll fellowship with them, visit Avledon, and then go home?"

Lucius smiles and answers, "No, my friend. One more stop, and then we'll go home."

"Where?"

"I need a second-in-command that is of my blood. I spoke with our Lord, and he's given me permission to open my wife's womb and continue my line. We're gonna need handmaids and someone to help me deliver my son."

Artie's eyes broaden as he asks, "Bengaldoes. We're going to Bengal, aren't we?"

Lucius nods. "I know just the ones I'll ordain as royal attendants."

"A second-in-command," Artie thinks aloud, "He'll be powerful."

Lucius says, "As soon as my son breathes his first breath, he will gain Baàl's power, and Baàl will be therewith stripped of his second-in-command control, leaving him no stronger than any of my Gamerin brothers."

"This is good news. I can't wait to get started."

Lucius lifts a brow and says, "When thinking about adding to my line, I can hardly wait myself."

"Ugh, and there you went," Artie says. "Some things are better kept to yourself."

Lucius chuckles as he leaves the kitchen, saying, "Time for me to wake my wife, my queen."

Lucius crawls under the blankets to cradle Josephine. "It's time to wake up, my yoshawn. I don't want anyone seeing you on a pallet in a servant's home." Her lids slowly lift, and he says, "And Artie doesn't want that image of people thinking he treats royalty as refugees in their own kingdom."

She stretches towards him and grunts in his ear. "I slept like a rock." She inhales. "It smells delicious in here."

Clang, ting.

"Is that Artie in the kitchen?" she asks.

"Yeah, he can hear you," Lucius says and gestures with his eyes. He connects to Josephine through telepathy, saying, *"So keep your words G-rated about our talk last night. Nobody needs to know that last bit."*

She snickers and says, "I wish I could enter your mind at any time and say what I think."

"I always hear you, and from now on, I won't disconnect unless I have to."

"You know what I mean."

"Maybe someday you will, and we'll be as one with our thoughts, as I was with my brothers. But until that day," and tells her with telepathy, *"we should keep certain things to ourselves."*

Lucius cuddles her, kissing on her neck and shoulders. In the middle of their personal time, a little Gamerin girl climbs in between them. They make room between them for her. "I love you too, Mommy and Daddy."

Josephine says, "It's a lovefest over here," as she and Lucius take turns kissing Claire on her cheeks.

Claire acts embarrassed and says, "Oh, goodness," but angles her cheeks toward each kiss to take all the attention that she can in.

Lucius chuckles. "We have a lot to do today." He helps his family up. "First, we need to have breakfast, and I need to get you ladies fitted with new attire." He gestures at Josephine's slouchy clothes, worn two days in a row and highly wrinkled. "You can't go around dressed like this."

Josephine defends herself by covering her chest. "What's wrong with my outfit?"

"Don't be embarrassed," he says and strokes her shoulder. "It isn't fitting for a queen's debut. You don't see a celebrity walking on red carpet dressed in their second-best."

She covers her mouth and says, "I didn't think of that. Now, I'm nervous." She gasps, and Lucius holds her. "Lucius, I've never done this stuff before."

He says, "You have and never realized. My love, you've been guarded and watched your whole life, a daughter of God, loved beyond all creation. It's only clothes and ornaments and my chance to finally robe you in honor because you are to be honored as my wife. Allow me this privilege to finally give to you what I've dreamed. I want a blessed first impression, so our subjects will follow my leading, and treat you as royalty. If I do not place boundaries and bring forth my highest regard in front of them, they will learn to disregard which should never be disregarded. As the queen…I know it's different, but as their queen, it is your duty to help their minds to honor the authority that God has put before them."

She nods silently.

"I feel you, and I'm glad that you understand. Maybe you're not comfortable with the change," he says as he picks up Claire, "but you understand."

—◦◦◦—

Lucius escorts his family to the breakfast table, and Artie excuses himself momentarily, saying, "Give me a minute, your majesties."

Josephine quickly turns toward Lucius. He tells her, "He honors you, but it's still Artie. Allow him the pleasure of doing what he's longed for. He loves you the same as he always has, and he is like family to us." Lucius points toward his family and says, "You are his royal family, and serving is nothing new to him. Remember, this is new only to you."

Artie folds materials and gathers items from the pallet, placing them in storage areas hidden in the walls. Artie agrees while stuffing an extra-large pillow into a cushioned seat. "Absolutely, your majesty. I've dreamed of this day, and now I have permission given to me by my king to act accordingly how I was designed."

Lucius pulls a chair out for Josephine, and she says, "This is very different," as she lowers herself into the chair. "I always knew you were chivalrous, but is this to be expected all the time?"

"Our subjects will tend to you in this manner, but I do it because it is my privilege as your husband." He signals over as Artie joins them. Lucius says, "He would have gathered your chair for you, but I instructed him not to so he could clean the floor."

"You spoke with your mind just then?"

"I can do many things at one time in this realm," Lucius answers.

She says, "Because this is your jurisdiction, your principality realm?"

"Exactly," he says. "I am reading many minds right now and have already instructed some of my subjects to prepare for later. I'm watching them like how I could watch Artie gathering firewood last night."

"Where the people, Daddy?" Claire asks.

"They're in the towns, sweetheart. Daddy is their king, and you are the princess."

"I get my princess dress today, Daddy?"

Lucius nods and says, "Yes, pumpkin. Daddy will robe you in honor so you can meet the people who love you. They already know who you are."

Josephine sits silently while processing the information.

Artie asks, "How many? Did you tell all of them?"

"Lucius," Josephine says sitting stunned.

Lucius continues while partially smiling at his wife. "I told a handful, but currently," he says as he glances between Artie and Josephine. "The whole world is buzzing about the news. Expect a large banquet." He guards his face in laughter, "So many banners, desserts, Obang's special apple pie, even Terrydines legendary potato, bacon, and cheese quiche." His mouth starts watering. "I can hardly wait for that one."

Josephine asks, "Right now? You're talking to them right now?"

Lucius gazes at her. "Wait until Powtray gets here," he says and glances at Artie. "Powtray has been busy all morning with his chores and shoeing a horse, but he doesn't know we're here. He's going to be surprised. He's not planning on going into town until lunchtime, so he'll drop by here first."

"All those people." She rubs her chest and nearly stares through the table. "At one time."

Lucius squats beside her and caresses her back. "Peace be upon you, my yoshawn." He nods at Artie. "Give us a minute." As soon as Artie leaves, Lucius speaks gently against her. "This is nothing. I know every one of them. You will simply enjoy the company—"

She interrupts him with a gasp. "Lucius, I don't know how to act. What if I say, or do something and embarrass myself?"

"*Shhh*, have no fear. There is no shame in your presence. And you have a clear knowledge on how to present yourself." He raises up and leans over to embrace her. "My love, you have empathy, which is a form of my abilities, and can apply it almost as if you were equal to me. You counsel me. Honestly, I want you to be yourself, and I will be reading your mind the entire time. If at any point you are scared or confused on what to do next or need guidance in anything, you will be linked to me entirely. If I move left or right, you will know before it happens. By this direction, you will act as one with me in front of our people without any shame or fear. This is the power of the Holy Spirit through me and you."

She exhales. "I understand where these gifts come from now, and I feel your guidance. Thank you." She kisses his cheek. "I'm at ease. I trust you entirely."

He smiles and says, "I sense your trust, and it strengthens me." He stands up and winks at Claire. "Pumpkin, you have nothing to worry about. They're gonna love you because toddlers are not something that they see every day."

Artie enters the kitchen and takes a seat. Josephine says, "Oh, wait." They all stare at her, and Lucius smiles. She says, "I felt you. You spoke to him, telling him to come back in here. That was cool."

Lucius nods. "Yes, like that. You'll feel me, and be directed by our connection. You will know all my conversations."

At this moment, Josephine's mind is opened. "I feel them, all of them." She smiles up at Lucius and says, "They're talking to you, asking all kinds of questions, and you're easing their minds, so you can surprise them." She brushes her cheek to her shoulder. "Aw, they're gonna be so happy."

Artie says, "I love my king's gifts. He's been able to link to his people in such a way that not many principalities have access to. From the beginning of the Gamerin galaxy and now known as the Gamerin galaxies, he's been one with the people."

She smiles at Lucius and says, "That's why you didn't tell me the good principality's galaxy name. I would have immediately known who you were talking about."

Lucius says, "Yes."

As they eat their morning meal, Josephine glances at Artie through conversation, and says, "Yesterday was a long day. Can I use your bathroom to wash up, since I'm gonna meet a bunch of people today?"

Artie immediately bows his head. "As you wish, my queen." He glances at her with a smile. "My home," he says pointing at everything nearby, "is yours. I would be delighted and honored if you used my bathing lounge to prepare yourself." He points an index finger toward Lucius. "My lord helped me to build this place in my first years of life. He prepared my healing waters, and that's the pool area you'll find within the bathing lounge. He's good to me. Everything I have is yours."

"Even your bearskin rug?" Lucius winks.

Artie raises his brows and starts smiling as he says, "Don't go there, Lucius. You might be my king, but you know I hunted that thing with my bare hands, and saved an entire town."

Lucius says, "I want it."

Artie looks at Lucius. Josephine stares with concerned eyes, and Claire continues nibbling on her bread. Artie says, "As you wish, my king," and manages a smile.

Lucius says, "Of course, I want your room to be as comfortable as you can make it. You'll be in Claire's room." He smiles, watching Artie's expression lift. "The room you used to stay in when you lived at the palace. I want you relaxed in your new home."

Josephine asks, "Palace?"

Artie rubs his forehead and says, "Thank you, my lord." He nods. "I can always trust you."

"Wait," Josephine interrupts. "Palace?"

Claire's feet swing back and forth from under her chair. "We live in a castle, Daddy," continuing to nibble on her food, and speaking with her mouth open. "Pretty."

"A palace?" Josephine asks again.

"All in due time, my yulee." Lucius gestures toward her plate and then down the hall. "We still need to get you ready before presenting you before your people. It'll be better if we take this one step at a time and allow the peace of the Lord and His Holy Spirit to guide you."

Josephine takes a bite of her food. "It's no wonder you weren't bothered yesterday about never going back to a beat-up old cabin in Texas ever again."

"Not completely true. I enjoyed every moment there," Lucius says and rubs her hand. "I wouldn't take any of it back." His eyes stare off at nothing. "Augh, I just remembered. I left my blue paint."

Immediately, Josephine catches his thought. She stands to her feet as she says, "This means…" but she can't finish speaking.

Lucius stands to his feet and embraces her. He hushes her and says, "Oh, little momma."

"Finally," she says as she pushes back her tears. "That's why you said you could open my womb on your planet. You have that ability here."

Gazing at her, Lucius nods and brushes her hair back with his fingers. "He'll be my second-in-command and a mighty Gamerin commander." He strokes her cheek, and tears fall from his eyes. "By this time next year, you'll be nursing him."

"Who, Daddy?" Claire asks.

Josephine and Lucius look at Claire. Josephine answers, "Your new baby brother."

Lucius includes, "But not yet. We still need to get home, and before doing that, we need to appoint our royal attendants to help me deliver him."

Josephine says, "This is the best day."

"Wait until you get a load of Avledon," Artie says.

Lucius smiles and says, "It's true. I'm taking you to see some of the creatures we govern after celebrating here—behemoths and leviathans."

Josephine asks, "Dinosaurs?"

"Yay!" Claire hoots. "I like that."

Lucius corrects their understanding by telling them, "Not quite dinosaurs, but we'll talk more about them later."

Artie says, "Every galaxy has something similar to what you're thinking." He gestures toward Lucius. "Our king had experience defeating kingdoms led by these creatures. The Gamerin were always victorious."

Lucius nods, adding, "He's right, and that is why I came up with the idea for my brothers to help Earth. Mankind once was in war with these creatures, but they won't hurt you. I'll be sure of it."

"Sounds scary," Josephine says.

He hugs her and says, "I have an observatory. You and Claire will be safe inside." He lets go of her and smiles. "Then we will go to Bengal and pick up some swimsuits."

"Those sweet little people?" Josephine asks. "The ones who helped you recover? Wait, swimsuits?"

He answers, "The females are called Bengaldoes, usually nurses and governesses for royal families. I'll ordain two female attendants today, and then we'll go home." He rubs her shoulder. "We'll go swimming on our beach, and Artie will grill us some dinner. When our day is done, we'll make our son."

"Ugh, I was all happy about the grilling part, and then you went there again," Artie says.

Sixteen

Garments

Lucius finishes penning Josephine's corkscrewed hair into dolloped ends. He dresses her royal braids in silver and purple flowers. "All you're missing now are Gamerin tattoos. We'll pick some up on Bengal," Lucius says.

"Tattoos?" Josephine asks while glancing over at Claire playing with her doll.

Claire stares at her flashy reflection through a mirror. She holds her dolly up and talks to herself about the vibrant colors of blue, turquoise, white, silver, and purple splashed throughout her princess dress. Claire twirls several times while pulling on her outer robe like a ballerina skirt instead of a cape.

Lucius says, "The tattoos aren't permanent, baby. They're just a tradition for royal families out here. On Bengal, they've perfected the art. Gamerin tattoos would be stunning on you." Her concerned face encourages him to explain further. "They're like henna, but they're in the Gamerin royal colors on your skin. The most beautiful thing about them is they're bioluminescent. They glow, and our maidservants can place flowers or hummingbirds on you. Whatever your heart's desire."

"I love hummingbirds and flowers." She kisses him.

"You just reminded me of a gift," Lucius says as he hears a knock at the door. He opens the door, and Artie is standing quietly while holding up a garment, which is folded in a perfect square and nearly shining with royal colors. Lucius stares at the fabric as if history has taken his words, and he stands frozen in place.

Artie shrugs and says, "I figured since you're—"

"Please, Artie," Lucius says as he slightly shakes his head, "not today. I'm wearing my Gamerin warrior covering."

"My lord." Artie stares solemnly at the garment and says, "It would only be fitting on a day like this." He points slightly toward Claire's and Josephine's tunics. "You will all match. It would please your people."

Josephine steps forward. She stands on her tippytoes to try and see around Lucius's shoulders. "What is it?" she asks.

Lucius answers Artie, saying, "I shed that garment a long time ago. It only brings fear to the hearts of people."

Claire skips closely. "A pretty dress," she says.

Lucius hides a smile. "It's not a dress."

Artie's full mouth smiles, and he says, "You're going to wear it, aren't you? I can already tell." He hands Lucius the garment. "You and I know that your family being there will bring the image that you've always desired."

Artie has caught Lucius's attention, and he stares at his friend.

Artie continues. "You're family to everyone in your realm, a loving king, and a true principality."

Lucius takes the garment. "Where did you find this? I thought I tossed this thing. The way that I disposed of it…It was ruined."

Artie shakes his head. "No, not ruined, but I did have to swim pretty deep to fetch it. I spoke to a rather large fish halfway down and asked him to retrieve the garment. The pressure was getting to me, and I can only hold my breath for so long."

Lucius chuckles. "Artie, you are one crazy and determined individual. Okay, but only until we get home. I don't walk around in a tunic during wartime."

Artie nods and replies, "Anything you say, but right now, we're in peace here. The people will be encouraged by your presence while robed in this."

Josephine gasps. "Is that your—"

Lucius nods and answers before she can finish her question. "You know what I'm thinking, and it's true." He unfolds the material out and places the tunic over his soldier attire. His eyes slightly dampen when he says, "It's my celestial covering."

"Daddy's a superhero, mommy," Claire says.

Lucius hesitantly poses in front of his reflection. The centuries of trying to forget haven't washed away how well the garment truly fits him. He says, "Well, it's been a while, but I guess it's time. I'll only wear it for today or on special occasions."

Josephine pulls her gloves on and the material covers her arms well over her elbows. She says "Lucius, if I have to dress up in this get up, so do you."

Lucius says, "Fair enough. You look gorgeous." He breathes out nervously as he turns to look at his reflection again, and says, "Artie, will you take Claire into the living area until we're done." He exhales.

Artie closes the door behind him, and immediately Josephine senses Lucius's emotions like a mountain of hurricane debris. She caresses his back shoulder for a moment and says, "You're going to make me nervous. I sense everything you're feeling." She hops onto the top of the crafting table and leans forward into Lucius. Her lips touch his ear. "I don't need to read minds when watching you. I know you."

"I'm trying," he says. He takes her hands and kisses the backs of them. The soft material of her silver gloves rests against his lips. He closes his eyes and continues to smell the natural fragrance of his wife. It brings him comfort, and he relaxes by her scent.

She rests her forehead on him. "There you are. I was wondering when you'd show up today. Be nervous if you want but don't doubt yourself anymore."

"Baby, I'm barely holding together. I can do this only because you're here," he says. "It's been so long since acknowledging who I am here. I almost forgot how to be a principality." He opens his eyes, and they become glossy as he looks at her. "I don't know how I can face them. I go to our people without an army. I'm just a family man." He raises one side of his cloak and stares at the long fabric. "Claire's right. It does look like a superhero cape after living on Earth."

She slaps his hand and says, "Don't make fun. Leave your outfit alone. If this is what is worn here, then this is what is worn by us living here."

He chuckles.

Josephine squeezes his cheeks between her hands. She puckers her lips and kisses him in between every word. "They...see...their...king." She gazes at him. "I see my precious husband who is as sweet as always."

He nods studies her eyes and says, "I know why He ordained us together."

She flutters her peacock feathers and says, "Of course, because of my good looks and charming sense of humor."

They laugh.

"I guess we're ready," he says.

She strokes his jawline. "We're ready."

Seventeen

Harvesters

Lucius and Josephine enter the living area, and Lucius bows before his daughter. "My fair princess," he says and sweeps her up in his arms.

"I like my princess dress, Daddy." She points at the design. Her voice squeaks, saying, "I like this and this part." She finds another embedded jewel. "This too."

He wiggles his finger over a shiny stone and then tickles her under the arm.

As they are laughing, Artie's bay doors open. Powtray enters, carrying a bag of cleaning supplies and rags. He looks at the magnificently dressed royal family and becomes paralyzed. Powtray wants to bow but his arms lower instead. He says, "It's been ten thousand years since you've allowed me, but you're clothed in honor. I don't know how to act, Yuleshua."

Lucius nods and says, "I'm here as your king. I give you permission to honor me as such." Lucius opens his palm toward his wife and daughter and says, "Your queen and princess must be respected. She is a daughter of God, bought by the blood of the Lamb, and my wife, the mother of Gamerilaye."

Powtray kneels. "A wonderful honor to see you again, my lord. I have longed to see Josephine our queen. The woman who has comforted our Lord," Powtray looks over at Claire and says, "and our royal princess? A daughter?"

"You may rise, Powtray." Lucius introduces them appropriately. "Yes, Josephine is my wife. Our daughter Claire is a testimony of my righteousness. She is the first female Gamerin in all existence.

Powtray raises up. "I saw a gathering in the town as I was walking the trail over here and wondered what all the commotion was. There are banners and artwork strung everywhere."

Lucius says, "I wanted to surprise you, Powtray. I knew you were shoeing a horse today. There is no need to tend to Artie's house this afternoon. Wait until after the festival. This evening you should have time. I want you to walk into town with us. We're fellowshipping today. There's a banquet, and you'll sit beside Artie, as one of our guests."

Lucius asks Artie, "Did you get everything?"

"There's no more space in my trans-dimensional spaces," Artie says and snickers. "I even packed some banana rum for later. I'm ready for the barbecue this evening on the beach."

Lucius kisses Josephine on the cheek as he proudly holds his daughter in his arms. "Let's meet our people." He opens a portal on the outskirts of town, and the group walks through.

<hr />

As soon as they walk through the portal, music is playing across the harvester town. There are cheers of all sorts, accompanied by chants sung with love into each chorus. Rose petals douse the snowy walkway in front of them. Many of the harvesters line the walkway with banners on rods as they dance like swans with colorful cloaks on.

"This is exciting," Josephine says. "They're graceful." She realizes that they are all male and act and play as though they are like young children, fun and as innocent as Artie is, exactly the way that Lucius had explained how the Gamerin were at one time.

The harvesters dance, sing, play musical instruments, and fly high in the air with fire trailing behind them as they drop flower petals. Josephine then glances around at the enormous, bowled urns with a blaring fire in each one. She can feel the warmth from the fire, smell the flowers falling from the air, see the colors of the banners that swirl around them, and listen to the sounds of music and the harmonious voices singing with the Gamerin arrival. "Wow," she speaks softly.

Lucius speaks psychically, *"They love you already, my yoshawn."*

"I can feel their love. These people are magnificent."

Claire tries catching the flower petals that are dropped from high in the air with every harvester in the town that takes to the sky. A line of harvesters bearing gifts line the walkway. Many have just arrived to attend the festival from the other side of the planet. Several harvesters in the line on the walkway cover Claire with gifts. With each step the Gamerin family takes, Claire is given another gift. After a gift is given, the harvesters either fly while singing, dances with their song, or begin playing an instrument while singing a harmonious song toward the new princess.

Lucius opens a couple of his interdimensional spaces when they are several yards onto the walkway. He places the extra gifts of fabric, blankets, dresses, sewn dolls, big toys, small toys, flowers, jewelry, precious cut stones, ribbons, treats, and much more into his pockets, so Claire won't be overloaded. Lucius is opening his third pocket when he says, "I'll keep these for later, Claire."

"A pretty song, Momma," Claire says. "They have Artie's hands."

"It's for you. The song they sing is for you, Claire," Lucius says. "I told some of them who you were this morning. They made this song for you. That's why some are joining in and learning the simple song so they too can celebrate with their instruments."

A long time has come,
A long time has passed.
Our king now joins us,
Our king's here at last.
What gifts he has brought us,
What love he's bestowed.
In his arms is wrapped a princess,
Her cheeks all aglow.
Her hair shines of cornsilk,
Her eyes of Gamerin blue.
She is of royal blood,
From true blood, she is true.

Josephine memorizes the different instruments that are laced with colorful ribbons. Lucius smiles at her because of what she thinks. He speaks out loud, but also uses a psychic connection so that Josephine hears his words clearly. He says, "Those aren't tambourines. They call them catikas. The name is based on the sounds that they make." He points to another instrument that has a pleasant rattling sound, like a rainstorm from soft wood rolling against each other. He says, "The instrument is made from beetle infested trees. After clearing out the infestation, the harvesters celebrate by making these unique rattles that make the sound of a rainstorm because of the compartments. Some of the compartments have wooden balls in them, and others have sand or even rice." Lucius points toward one of the instruments being carried over to him. He tells Josephine, "That's not a rattle. It's a barsooma."

A harvester hands Claire her very own barsooma, and she plays to the sound of the harvesters. Her barsooma ribbons dance like a purple and turquoise ballerina as she twirls her new instrument.

⊷⊶

The parade of celebration, which again collects more followers, leads through a giant greenhouse, but this time the aroma of a savory barbeque coats the air, mixing with the sweet smell of flowers. The harvesters inside the greenhouse town all join in with singing, dancing, and celebrating. The large greenhouse is a city in its own right, with a main street that leads toward a town center where extra tables have been set up beside the massive cathedral.

Josephine stares at the area as they come close enough. She realizes that the greenery that she has been looking at and thought were vine covered walls are, in fact, the open cathedral itself. "It's outside." She had never expected the inside of the cathedral to be a garden, boulders, and logged benches for chairs, waterfalls trickling over carved out rocks for washing basins, and tables resting on grass.

Lucius enters her mind, *"My beloved, every culture is diverse, and all His children have a different way in how they worship. This is a greenhouse, cathedral, and a place of fellowship."* He then speaks aloud, "The Father started His children on Earth in a garden. His children here are no different."

"It's beautiful," she says.

Harvesters begin pouring wine and beer. They pass the carafes across the tables to set up dishes. The singing has stopped, but the crowd is loud with excitement and greetings of each harvester brother meeting up with one another to arrange the meal that they have brought for the banquet. The harvesters become quiet as they watch the royal family take their seats.

As soon as Lucius escorts his queen and princess to their seats, he himself sits.

Smiling, the harvesters immediately work together to place the rolls and drinks into set areas to be passed along the table. In no time at all, every harvester has joined the royal family in sitting.

There is not one sound.

Wondering what has happened to the sounds of the cathedral, Josephine looks around. Thousands have joined them and line the streets, but not one word is spoken. They all smile and are looking in her direction.

Before she can become nervous, Lucius raises a hand and he says, "My people," he stands. His voice then enters a special harmonic octave as he repeats his greeting. The vibration is unlike any Josephine has ever witnessed before. She can sense his voice like a bass down into her bones. His vocals reverberate off the greenhouse walls. The bird baths in the distance make ripples with those few words. The voice coming from her husband is surreal and takes over every sound that could be made. The waterfall becomes distant back noise with his words. Her heart races, but she can't hear herself. His voice is powerful in a way she could never describe, and she wants to hear more.

He links psychically to her and explains, *I'm speaking to the entire world right now, Josephine. This is for those who couldn't join us in person, I'm with them in spirit. They hear my voice, and they celebrate with us. This is only one of the many powers of a principality.*

He continues speaking to the harvester planet. "Harvesters, celebrate with us today. Enjoy this banquet now, but a day is soon coming when a larger feast will be celebrated. The King of kings, and the Lord of lords will return to His children on Earth, but until that time we will celebrate together in waiting." He raises his glass, and all the harvester do the same. He says, "I celebrate with you today as a principality. I bring your queen and your princess. Be blessed harvesters, it is my family and I who are honored by your presence, your gifts, your talents, and your love. I, along with my wife and daughter, join you all as one family."

Lucius bows his head and prays the Lord's prayer. "Our Father, who art in heaven, hallowed be thy name. Thy kingdom come thy will be done, on the planet as it is throughout the heavens. Give us this day our daily bread, and forgive us our trespasses, as we forgive those who trespass against us. Lead us not into temptation, but deliver us from evil. For yours is the kingdom, and the glory, and the honor, forever and ever. Amen."

Every glass raises with him. Lucius looks around at the people to his left and then to his right. Josephine studies the people and realizes that they are not looking at him, but are doing the exact same thing as he does. Lucius senses her wonderment and psychically explains to his family, with his ability of instant knowledge, why he looks in both directions as the people do. Josephine realizes within a matter of a split second that the act is a tradition of the harvester world to look to the left and then to the right, making sure that the harvest has not started without anyone.

When harvesters first learned that they would be supplying the feast for the mighty banquet, they had become so excited that they would count heads directly after praying to make sure that they hadn't missed the big event. To ease them, harvesters now look to the left and then to the right all at the same time while at the dinner table.

With Lucius's glass in the air, he says, "Today we feast and celebrate a new age for Gamerin people everywhere. My wife is a part of me and has inherited the Gamerin realm with me."

As soon as he speaks the words into existence, Lucius senses an ability shift, like when a new law is presented by a principality. However, this shift is different and more personal. The change feels deep within, painless but strange, as if his whole body, starting with his abdominal muscles, moves and is standing beside him.

Josephine inhales and completely experiences the new sensation flooding into her body. The shift was placed upon her with his words. She feels stronger, awake, and alive like she hasn't felt in years. She still feels like a human, but she knows that she is more Gamerin than human and that she is in control of her mind.

Lucius glances down at Josephine and says, "You can read my thoughts. You can enter my mind and speak your thoughts to me on your own now. You have the psychic ability in your blood now and are connected to this realm."

Lucius smiles toward the crowd. "The Gamerin queen is blessed. She is gaining more power every day on my authority given just then before all of you. Praise be to God."

———◆———

Sometime into the beginning of the feast, fresh food is passed along the table. Claire picks a little of everything. With every choice that Claire desires on her piling plate, Artie dips up another spoonful and says, "You know, princess, I believe your eyes are bigger than your stomach."

Lucius chuckles and leans over to Claire before she can ask for anything else. He says, "Let's see if you can finish this plate." He waves at the harvesters passing around the platters to take them away from her. "Claire, finish what you have before getting any more," he whispers into her ear.

Josephine points at many foods and says, "I don't recognize some of these but they look familiar. I taste of them, and they taste familiar too."

Lucius wraps his arm around Josephine. He nudges her shoulder and says, "That's because on Earth, they've engineered food to look differently over time. These are original, and what they used to look like. They're healthier for you."

She picks up a red fruit and asks, "What is this one?"

From around the table, several smiles arise, followed by snickers. Lucius grimaces as if caught about something. He finally says, "I know, I know everybody." He motions toward the fruit and says, "The fruit that you hold in your hand…" he pauses before adding, "is a real strawberry."

"What?" she asks.

He continues. "Everything that is eaten here is original and pure to its design. Only harvesters are trusted to keep the food untainted and completely free of mutation of any sort."

"Yep," Artie says to himself. He is thinking a certain thought, but doesn't say a word.

However, Lucius hears Artie's thought and defends himself, saying, "I like the way mine are. They might have been recoded, but they're cram packed with antioxidants, vitamin C, and you name it. I like big strawberries." He lifts his hands and continues. "I have the authority to alter things within my realm. It's my own personal preference. I still enjoy how they are prepared here, and I can plant my garden however I so choose."

Artie says, "Nobody's saying anything."

"You're thinking it though."

"But I didn't say it," Artie replies as he starts to laugh at how passionate Lucius is about the strawberries he grows in his garden.

Lucius includes, "To let y'all in on a little history, Josephine and I had our first meal together with strawberries that are almost identical to the way that they grow in my garden."

Powtray says, "A connection between the two of you."

Lucius nods. "My favorite food became a bridge that brought my yoshawn closer to me."

Josephine studies her husband's smile as he fellowships casually with those at the table. They are clearly a different race of people with their fingers and markings on them. They all have freckles across their hands, and all their eyes are golden or yellowish in color. But Lucius gets along and feasts with them as she would when she was growing up with friends and family. He is one with his people as he had described the night before.

As she sits feasting with her new family that she never knew that she had, she is reminded of a song that she learned in children's church when growing up. The little jingle plays in her mind to herself,

I've been feasting at his banquet table, and his banner over me is love.

Lucius stops what he's doing. He turns to her and asks, "Did I hear your mind correctly?" He enters her thoughts. *"The song you sing, doesn't represent what you think it does."*

"What does it mean, baby?"

"Remember what we did last night?" His brows lift high before he continues. *"The banquet table that is mentioned in the Song of Solomon is a buffet going on between King Solomon and his new wife."*

Josephine blushes.

———— ❦ ————

With his forearms over the table, Powtray makes eye contact with Lucius. He asks, "My lord, are you planning on more children?"

Lucius answers, "We are."

The crowd roars with excitement like thunder. Claire holds her ears and scrunches her face into her daddy's chest. Once the multitudes have calmed, Lucius continues, saying, "The Lord, our Father, has given me permission to continue my Gamerin line with your queen. By this time next year, our son will be nursing, and I'll bring him for you to see." Again, the crowds roar with excitement at the news.

After many jugs of wine are drunk, platters of food are emptied and refilled again, the time has come for Lucius to give his farewells and blessings.

Lucius stands with his family and says, "I'm enjoying this festival and believe that the festivities and fellowshipping should continue for several days. The hearts of my people are repaired by this gathering in celebration of my return. My family and I must leave now for several planets before returning to Gamerilaye. My people, you have blessed me, and we will return someday soon and sit among you."

Lucius gathers his group to prepare before a new portal opens. Lucius has his hand upon the stone to where they are going as he leans toward Josephine and says, "I have a treat for you, my queen. Get ready for Avledon."

Eighteen

Avledon

Lucius escorts his family through the portal gate and into a spacious room with rows of windows, paned with thick glass, in the wild world of Avledon. Josephine's eyes light up as she stares through the windows. Dragging her husband by a hand, she grabs the yards of skirt that make up her dress in front of her and runs to a window in the observatory. Her mouth drops, and she nearly sheds a tear. She manages to point as she wrestles with her body from the shock. She asks, "Are those, those…"

Lucius nods and answers, "Yes, dragons."

From the floating observatory, they see flocks of dragons in the air like large birds traveling in formation. Her eyes water as she says, "I've never seen something so breathtaking." She drags Lucius to another location. Lucius laughs silently with a slight hop in his step behind her to keep up. She points at a large oceanic lake near a clearing and asks, "What are those?"

A section of water begins to bubble and rumble as a large creature with enormous teeth and reptilian skin emerges from the water and reaches high into the air, as if playing like a whale. Her face presses against the glass, and in a high-pitched voice, she asks, "Are those massive crocodiles?"

From behind, Lucius whispers into her ear, "Those are Leviathans." He points toward the creatures that her mind refers to as dragons and tells her, "Those are behemoths, but we'll call them dragons since that's what you know them as." He's dragged again and jokes with her saying, "Okay, so we're going here now."

Dragons fly near the windows, and she places her palms against the glass. Lucius takes her hands from the glass and lowers them to her abdomen. He wants her to act dignified in her actions.

She's so excited that she can't hear his reasons or even remember why he had lowered her hands. She says, "Dragons. You have dragons here. I didn't know they existed. I'm really seeing dragons."

"I guess you like Avledon. You're enjoying what you see," he says. "Earth had similar creatures at one time. They were harshly tainted by the war on your world." He glances at Artie and smiles.

Claire is carried by Artie to several windows so she can see over the railing. Claire gasps, and Artie teaches her not to make a show of her enthusiasm.

Lucius tells Josephine, "These are in your govern."

Josephine holds Lucius. "This is incredible. I wanna know more about them," she says and calms with his peace.

Lucius says, "Avledon beings are wise beyond belief in many ways because they learn without borders. They are crafty, but they must answer to me. There are several different kinds." He points toward the beasts of the air, and then over toward the water. "There are two main governments—behemoths and leviathans."

"Governments?" she asked.

He nods and answers, "Yes. One rules over the waters. Those are the leviathans. The others that reign over the air are known as behemoths. Together, they both inhabit the ground, so they needed a government because the ground is the undeniable connection between the two species. The ground is an area of peace between them. To provide accountability between them in front of witnesses, I set up my observatory." He points toward the water. "Those enormous crocodile creatures are much simpler in color than the behemoths you see swarming around us. Leviathans are usually yellow, blue, and green. However, the older they are, the yellow fades into white, and leviathans never stop growing, depending on where they migrate to."

"They're like giant alligators and whales."

He shrugs and says, "I guess. But don't let the truce between them deceive you."

"How do you mean?"

He explains, "This war in the heavens has changed them, and the two species won't completely have peace until the white throne judgment. Before the truce between them, many of their kind have perished." He looks deep in her eyes. "They don't forget, and they loved their families. The ones who died were the warriors that defended their territories during their ancient battles. The creatures have fought in many battles on Avledon before I was their principality."

"So they're ageless?" she asks.

Lucius nods. "They are to a certain point, depending on their sins against each other. As long as they keep the peace, they should live on. However, if they turn on each other, they will age and be judged." He strokes her cheeks. "This used to be Arstoleci inheritance."

She gasps. "Dugand used to rule over the Arstoleci."

He says, "That's correct, but no more since losing his birthright. They are in my govern, my inheritance, and they must obey both you and me as one. It's why I'm visiting them today, so they know they must bow before you, and honor you as their queen."

Josephine glances over and notices a bay door leading outside the building. Lucius swiftly catches her thoughts, and speaks out loud, "I don't want y'all out there. They must answer to me because I have much power over them, but you're just now able to tap into my mind. That's not going to help you around them if they turn. These creatures constantly test boundaries in a relationship, and respect isn't given in this culture; it's earned. They have a primitive mindset. You must be able to prove that you're an alpha to govern them." He strokes her cheeks and says, "Yoshawn, they'd immediately test you, and this would not be a good meeting for them if I witness that."

"So sad," she says. "I really wanna know them." She looks around at the land. In the distance, the trees are as skyscrapers with vines so thick that they have a mist around them. "It's glorious here."

"I have an idea," he says. Lucius takes a few steps and turns back as soon as he is at the door. Before exiting, he says, "Stay here." He points toward an area outside the closed observation hall. There is a multi-tiered, outer deck that is large enough for large groups to land on. Lucius says, "They'll land on the bay landing. If you go to the windows, you can look at them. Up close. I want you to notice their colors and the different flags on their skin. It's their tribe insignias. Although they're creatures, they're still a civilization. I won't force them to do anything." He winks. "But for you, they might show off if I word it right."

He exits the building and releases his wings from hiding. His celestial cloak flows in the wind and shines like silver and sapphires glinting in the light. He levitates onto the landing bay and is directly greeted by four dragons.

The dragons are three times bigger than Lucius. The dragon, who is the king of the beasts, stretches his wingspan with a wild call to his officers around him. The dragon buffs his chest out in a display of power in front of his subjects still flying low to the ground. The dragon's nose twitches, and his eyes shrink into thin lines.

Because Lucius does not have the ability to speak in the wild guttural tongue of the Avledonians, he connects psychically. As he does, he speaks out loud for all to hear the voice of their principality. He makes whatever voice that is shared between them balanced so that the beasts understand his language as it is spoken, and those in the observatory can hear theirs openly.

Lucius says, "Jakarr, king of the behemoths. How do you welcome me?"

Jakarr's wings fold back as he leans forward. Lucius did not sound pleased, so Jakarr bows in submission. His monstrous grumble vibrates along the landing bay. Josephine is shocked when she understands his words because of Lucius transmitting the understanding to all who are within listening distance toward the meeting.

Jakarr grumbles as he speaks, *"Yuleshua Lucius Gamerin, mighty warrior, you honor us with this visit."* Jakarr's eyes meet Josephine's gaze as he continues. *"I see that you bring a new creature dressed in royal attire."* The king of the dragons studies Claire and then says, *"Two of them. One is held by your fire warrior, Artorus. She's a small species, is she not?"*

Lucius answers with a straight face that shows displeasure. He answers, "That is my wife and my daughter; flesh of my flesh, and bone of my bone."

Jakarr bows lower. He says, *"My lord, forgive me for my tongue. Rid me not of this land, for I have flesh and bone of my own. No ill intentions were thought by me. Again, forgive my tongue. I am delighted to hear this news of blessing upon you."*

"I realize that you are in earnest after your words just now given in front of all who are a witness to our meeting, including my wife. I will explain my blessing, for I have been blessed personally by the Almighty. This meeting is more than just a casual visit, for you are among the first in my inheritance to witness my family. I have come to grant you this great honor." He keeps his movements well directed as he points toward his family. He places his hand back to his sword handle and says, "I am here granting the honor to you because your queen has heard of your kind before, yet she has never witnessed your kind with her own eyes."

Jakarr's eyes light up as he asks, *"Has she now?"*

Lucius half smiles and offers a gentlemanly nod. "Jakarr, your queen, Josephine, is impressed by your abilities in the sky. My daughter is learning of your species for the first time and is fascinated by your flying as well. We will not stay long, for we have a grand inheritance to govern over."

Lucius then lowers his arms and slightly turns. He says, "I will leave you to your clan. I am proud of you." Lucius points at the large groups of dragons perched on trees and lining the deck. He continues. "Many tribes have joined you in peace. By your righteousness, they honor you. You will be rewarded due to your righteousness."

Jakarr asks, *"If you are rewarding me, I ask that you bless us with the fruits that are not in season. We have had a dry summer due to the blight over the southern marshlands, and our trees will not bring forth much fruit this year. Many river systems have been depleted, and, therefore the stock of fish, which is in our territory, cannot be hunted, or they will not replenish later on. The riches of the fruits would sustain our tribes and keep us from being tempted into the leviathan territory for food."*

Lucius nods, says, "An honorable request by a wise leader," and stretches out his hands toward the forested area.

Immediately, trees sprout and grow into extensive heights with heavy fruits until the branches bend.

"Would this be enough to sustain your tribe?" Lucius asks.

Jakarr bows. *"Thank you, my lord."* When Jakarr raises, he asks, *"Does your wife not want to come out?"*

"As I have said," Lucius tells Jakarr, while keeping his next statement diplomatic and inoffensive, "this is one of many stops. Your queen is delighted to have met you. We must leave to keep our schedule. Again, you have delighted my wife and daughter in your amazing abilities of flight." Lucius leaves the observation deck and enters the observatory. As soon as he does, he disconnects the psychic transference so that the language of the Avledonians is heard in its raw form.

Jakarr is still on the outer deck when he sprawls his wings out like a peacock to display his majestic appearance for the queen to witness. Josephine's eyes open wide.

Lucius embraces her from behind and says, "He won't be able to resist. Watch him. He's calling all of them."

Jakarr roars a ferocious howl and hundreds of behemoths join him in showing off. He takes flight toward the sky to perform tricks and stunts with fiery breath. Hundreds of dragons follow in formation around the observatory. They dive down and up again. Each time they are high in the air, they fan their wings out like a parachute. Josephine gasps.

Claire says, "Wow, pretty dragons, Daddy."

"They are…and they know it," Lucius says.

"How did you get them to fly like this? You just asked him?" Josephine asks.

Lucius says, "You can't ask a king to show off for you in front of his people. His name is Jakarr. I merely insinuated how much you enjoy his talents. I left the rest up to him."

Bright colors of vibrant wings spread throughout the sky. A flock of dragons send a spiraling rainbow for her eyes. She says, "You are sly, Gamerin. Just like Dextorus said."

Lucius opens a portal from behind them and says, "Which reminds me." He escorts his family to the opening. Before he takes a step, he says, "Dextorus and many others will meet us at the palace later this evening to guard my family. We should get moving, so we can greet them after I've had my time with you."

Josephine wraps her arm around his elbow and says, "Thank you, my love. I'll never forget these moments."

He kisses her cheek and escorts her. "We can continue our family and begin the rest of our lives after this stop."

Nineteen

Bengal

They enter through a portal and step onto a cobblestone bridge. The bridge is one of many among the waterways. The landscape is clean and manicured with several house boats lining the water ways.

"This is Bengal," Lucius says.

Suddenly after hearing his voice, inhabitants stop what they're doing. Some were in the water, and the lines and colorful markings that are still wet on their skin catches Josephine's eyes. They hurry to crowd around the royal family. Josephine tries keeping her jaw from dropping, but they are amazing to look at. Their faces with little fawn noses are the sweetest that she has ever seen. The males are much taller with towering antlers, but their eyes are innocent, and their smiles are adorable.

Josephine says, "They are the most attractive looking people. I didn't know this trip could get any better."

Lucius speaks psychically, *"They are like children to me, but do not accept any food from here."*

"I'm stuffed, I don't think I could," she tells him. *"Why?"*

"Just believe me." He transfers a thought of the globular glands located on their necks.

Josephine winces. *"Oh."* She hides her expression with a smile and greets her subjects.

A few giddy Bengaldoe females introduce themselves first, and Bengalbucks follow suit. The tiny females stand less than five feet tall, but the males are a staggering six feet, with antlers stretching beyond that. Their small muzzles raise up with growing smiles. Lucius and Josephine can feel that they are greeting their principality and wholeheartedly accepting any royal family with him. Josephine admires the colors and comments, "What beautiful shades you have over your skin."

Deciding to teach her who they are, one Bengaldoe points out her markings and says, "I have great gifts in music. I'm training to be a governess for a royal family within the galaxy." She points out her dreadlocked-weaved antlers and says, "This is what my banner stands for."

Josephine keeps her words to herself as she thinks that the innocent, nearly nude creature, must still be training. Josephine soon realizes that they're all underdressed. *"Lucius, you said that we would have maidservants and nurses from here. Where are their clothes? They're all wearing bathing suits."*

Lucius tries hiding his reaction, but chuckles loudly. He then transfers, *"I told you they are childlike in manners. They see nothing wrong with how they live. You are right in thinking she is being trained. When she has finished her training, she will take on the attire and complete culture of where she will instruct royal children. These people change everything about themselves, including their aroma."*

"They smell divine to me. It's natural and fresh." she tells him. *"They won't need to change this."*

"Not all cultures prefer water lilies, but you do. You've always enjoyed natural smells. I love that about you."

"You smell like rain." She smiles at him. *"I've always loved the rain."*

Through the crowd of colors and sackcloth covered bikinis, comes one fully dressed, fair skinned Bengaldoe with a familiar face and smile.

Lucius says, "Charony." He hugs her. "I wish to speak to you."

The crowd gives the royal family and Charony room to speak.

Charony says, "My lord, our Father foretold that our meeting today would happen."

"He did?" Lucius asks with a smile across his face. "He always knows. Why would I be surprised?"

Charony says, "I told my sister, Thimbette, that you would be here. We have both been training in your royal ways of Gamerilaye. Are you here today for your nurses and governesses?"

Lucius nods. "I am ordaining two nurses today. I will come later for the royal governesses."

The multitude cheers around them. Trained governesses speak among themselves. The exuberance of the crowd shines into Josephine's heart, and she instantly loves them. She says, "We only have one child right now, but in the next years to come we might require more attendants. Our children will be blessed by those your king ordains."

Lucius says, "In the next few years, we will also ordain musicians and those in the different arts to help lead our children in their talents. But until then, we are acquiring only two handmaids for my wife and to act as nurses for my daughter." He introduces Charony, "I am honoring Charony and her sister Thimbette if they accept their offer into the royal Gamerin home. We will leave shortly."

Charony curtsies and says, "I accept."

Rejoicing reverberates across the bridges, waterways, and footpaths leading to town. The celebration continues as Lucius escorts his family to the main Bengal capitol city.

As they walk, Lucius speaks with Charony, "I will need someone to help me deliver my son and someone to tend to Josephine's royal appearance. I would like her donned in Gamerin tattoos before our angelic army arrives tonight. I know you are a gifted nurse, and if our Father has foretold this, I know you have been trained on how to deliver children."

Charony says, "I have, my lord. I've learned many things about how to deliver human babies. I've never seen one in person. Your daughter is an amazing creature," and then she signals by nodding her nose toward Josephine before saying, "My sister and I are very talented in Gamerin tattoos. I have learned the arts of royal glamour in your realm and that of Earth."

He rests his arm across Charony's shoulder and blesses her. "I would like you to be the head maidservant. I need you to direct my nurses and governesses as they increase in our home. Gather any belongings you will need to feel comfortable. We will need a proper birthing stool for her to push from, along with all the supplies that you have attained in your training. I will meet you in the town center outside of Quiashay's bathing shop. We will swim later today on my beach. Artie will make us a barbecue this evening."

As soon as these words are finished being spoken, Charony leaves quickly, gathering her sister and her medical belongings for their new honored life among the celestial's home.

Walking the streets, Josephine's eyes jump from vendor to vendor. She says, "It looks like the River walk." She points at the waterways and adds, "Except, they're swimming in this water as part of their path. You can't do that at the Riverwalk. It's illegal."

Lucius says, "There are many similarities and differences." He winks at her and speaks psychically, *"Don't except any edible gifts."*

"I remember," she answers.

"Let me do the talking, my yoshawn. I don't want their feelings hurt."

Several vendors reach out their arms to present their bowls of medicine. Lucius raises a gracious hand and says, "We have already eaten. We do not need healing today. Thank you, this is much appreciated. What love you bestow upon us with your gifts. We are only here to fellowship with you. You honor us with your presence."

"Nicely done," Josephine tells him psychically.

Lucius smiles as he kindly passes on their offers of medicinal ointments and elixirs. He is careful every time he does not accept and then places peace upon each of them. He never offends one of them by doing so. He psychically tells Josephine, *"They truly are the sweetest race."*

They finally arrive at a three-tiered building that is stacked like an enormous pyramid. As they walk into the open lobby, Josephine sees a two-story chandelier that hangs twenty feet above them in the middle.

Lucius explains the name of the city using the Bengal language. "The name of this capital city is called *Alethea Tresterdy*. It means truth of the healers. This building is the main gathering place for Bengals on this planet. Every year, there is a festival, and the main events are held here like a fair. That is why this building is so massive and with many levels."

"It looks like a mall. I didn't expect a shopping center here."

Artie answers, "Bengals are talented, but it's not a mall."

Lucius nods and continues. "It's a hospital."

Josephine studies the different shops. "How can it be a hospital? There are no beds. I see no sick Bengals walking around in here."

Lucius says, "The understanding of a hospital is to be hospitable and to provide for one's needs." He points at various shops before saying, "This is the world of healers. They rarely get sick. When they need something, they enter the building of needs where they find what they need here. Many serve their community in this way, and the building is always an open door for those of this world."

A large crowd follows behind them, and Lucius continues teaching his wife. "We're meeting with Quiashay. I designed a swimming outfit for myself with him many ages ago. When I need a new pair of swimming trunks, I go to see him. That is usually when I meet with my people here. I will need to pick up swimsuits for you." Lucius points at Claire. "He will need to tailor a onesie for Claire. She is too young and her skin is too fair for Gamerilaye's star, I mean sun."

Lucius crosses the threshold of Quiashay's shop and glances back at the multitude. "We will need privacy during my wife's fitting." He pulls the curtain closed behind him as soon as Josephine, Artie, and Claire are completely within the personal privacy of the shop.

Quiashay greets him, "My lord, I am blessed. You visit me."

Lucius smiles. "I'm swimming today with my family," he says and points toward Claire. "My daughter will need a swimming jumpsuit. I would like her skin covered, so she is not burned by sunlight with her fair skin." Lucius eyeballs a beautiful blue bikini. "I would however," he pauses saying and smiles before continuing, "prefer something like that for my queen."

Quiashay gathers the blue bikini for them and says, "As you desire, and no trade is necessary."

Lucius shakes his head and dons a smile. "You know me, Quiashay. I never take things for nothing." He strokes his chin and asks, "Tell me, how is your houseboat?"

Quiashay returns a similar smile and says, "The roof leaks over the top platform during the windy season."

Lucius taps Quiashay's forehead and bestows a blessing of instant knowledge for building and repairing the issue. He says, "That should fix the problem."

"Thank you, my lord. What you have showed me will most definitely increase my comfort." Quiashay shakes Lucius's hand. "I'm always blessed by your presence."

"And I'm blessed by your talent. Maybe someday, I can have you tailor some things for me as my family grows," Lucius says.

"You're always welcome," Quiashay says and hands over the bikini and the reserved bathing outfit that he had made for his king. Quiashay unravels a measuring tape from his neck and squats down toward Claire. "Let me get your measurements." He stretches the tape out along Claire's face and says, "That's what I thought."

"What?" Claire asks.

"It says you're perfect," Quiashay says and wiggles her nose for her. "How about, I take your measurements while you try and count my antlers." Claire smiles, and Quiashay continues taking her measurements. As he measures Claire, her fingers play with his antlers so she won't wiggle too much as he gathers her sizes.

After they receive the final piece to their new life and have visited all the venues on Lucius's itinerary, the royal family meets with Charony, Thimbette, and gather all their necessities from Bengal. As they stand in a large portal opening, Lucius says, "Next stop…Gamerilaye."

Twenty

Welcome Home

As soon as Lucius gives his permission for the group to enter the portal, Charony and Thimbette cross safely through the opening with his family.

Lucius walks in front of the crowd with a smile that he hasn't been able to tame most of the day. "I wanna show all of you around first. We are taking the long way, so that my bride can see her home. It is a bit of a hike from here."

Josephine stays close behind Lucius, but she slows in her step as they approach crooked trees with braided trunks that are interlocked with one another in front of the trail. Beyond the trees, she can make out a cliffside mountain with what seems like walkways throughout manicured greenery and trails.

"I thought we were home," she says. "How long is this hike we're going on? You brought us to a forest. A tangled one."

"I brought you to our front gate. Beyond here is the winding path."

"Front gate? Baby," she says pointing at the tangled branches that look like an impenetrable wall. "I can't fit through here. They're knotted together and completely overgrown."

Lucius asks, "Remember what I did on Avledon with the tree? Our home is beyond what you see." His hand brushes against the bark, and the crooked woods unfold their knotted branches, respiring as if taking a deep breath with their boughs upright to embrace a vibrant sky. As they all watch, the spiraling mountain paths that outline the hanging gardens are revealed. The upward winding trail leads to a grand palace, built to double as a stronghold.

On the palace in the distance, sunlight glistens as it bounces from the windows and archways. Enormous sequoia trees on top of the mountain support the terraces in place as if they float from the side of a mountain.

Lucius says, "The Gamerin palace is hidden to outsiders. The palace has multiple levels, including some that are located underground." Lucius smiles at his wife. "Welcome home, my queen."

She says, "I knew that you weren't just a beach bum."

"I was tickled every time you wondered where I lived."

Josephine looks around at every detail. The palace grounds are breathtakingly pristine and majestic with carvings set in the finest Gamerin colored stones, handcrafted sculptures, and structures holding either greenery, or nurturing life in some way.

Josephine turns and says, "You were gonna give your home all up for me and live on the prison world with a short lifespan in a rundown cabin?"

"Before I answer that," he says as he stares deeply into her hazel green eyes with a reflection of blue flowers making her eyes so brilliant to look at that he could swim in them. "Yoshawn, I wanna remember this moment." He takes her hands and inhales her aroma. He kisses her gloved fingers and smells her scent mixed perfectly with Gamerilayean air, as if she were always supposed to be a part of him. He closes his eyes and exhales a silent sigh, saying, "Thank you, Father. For ten thousand years I lived alone, longing to feel loved again by someone of my blood. Because of your blessing, I'm about to walk this trail as a new creature, one so different from the one I was when I left six years ago." Lucius stares at Josephine who is now tearing up as he continues. "I walk this trail with Gamerilaye's future beside me. Willingly, she loves me. My yoshawn. My yulee. She lets me hold her hand, as if nothing had ever happened that could've tarnished her love for me. You've brought me life and a family when I had none."

───※❦❖──

They walk along the sweet-smelling trail of late summer flowers and bubbling brooks under bridges. Josephine snuggles against his upper arm as the rays of sun brush against her cheek from an opening of a fern filled forest to her right. She says, "I don't think I could compare to such splendor. This must have taking years to make."

"Hold your tongue, sweet woman. You know not of what you speak. I didn't love what reminded me of what I had once lost." Lucius brings her closer against him as they walk and says, "In all the majesty of the universe, celestial kings who bow before His glory, the epicenter of all creation in the flesh, the countless galaxies, unimaginable creatures with such beauty that they would make you cry at the sight of them, and much more, the Father and His true love that is unmeasurable, chose to live and to die on a primitive world in order to be with the family that He loved."

Lucius points at a decaying tree in the distance and says, "He died and resurrected." Around the softened bark on the ground are new blossoms and growth budding through the mulch. When he knows that Josephine sees what his heart was showing her, he continues. "He died so others would live. He did all that so He could have His family back. If all the splendor of the universe weren't enough to fulfill that void in His heart, why would you think I would be any different?"

Guiding them on the trail, Lucius strokes his wife's hand on his upper arm. He says, "All I wanted was to be your husband. If it meant living in a small portion of Texas, then so be it. I had my greatest treasure in my arms, someone who loves me for who I am." He glances back at Claire in Artie's hands. "I have everything. And I'm going to be blessed with a son soon. I am completed by his gift of trusting me enough to love his daughter."

"I love you too." Josephine pauses when she sees something darting around the corner of her eye. A creature that sounds like a bumble bee shoots by with green and blue feathers. Just as her eyes catch on to what flutters by her, the creature lands on her finger. "How cute! The bird landed on me. It's a little hummingbird."

Lucius says, "That's the present I was talking about earlier. Our Lord gave you this hummingbird." The bird flies from his perch and hovers a small distance from them.

Josephine asks, "Can I name it? Is that something you do here?"

Lucius says, "He's a male," opening his palm for the bird to land. "You can name him whatever you want. He was made from the stem of a strawberry."

"Flutter," she says and smiles, as it flies off to do a couple of loops around the small group. "His name is Flutter."

Lucius nods. "Simple, but fitting. Flutter it is then."

As they walk, Lucius turns with a delighted expression toward Josephine.

"What are you looking at?" she asks, trying to read his thoughts, but they're blocked. "You have a slight gleam in your eye all of a sudden. And I can't hear your thoughts."

Lucius speaks in the privacy of his mind toward her, saying, *"Your body is doing something. Your body did this the last time you were here too. I kept my thoughts to myself. It's why I was careful around you during our date with us not being married yet."*

"What is my body doing?"

He stares at her as they enter through the front walkway and answers, *"You're ovulating. Your body started changing when we walked through to prepare for when I open your womb. Last time, it took a few minutes, but it's like the atmosphere is picking up where it started off."*

"Wow. There are no secrets for you," she replies.

"No, and I don't think your body's response is a coincidence either." He leads everyone to the front of the grand entryway of the palace through the inner courtyard and continues his thought as he is walking up the steps. *"Your body has always responded differently around me, but on this land, I feel a connection between you and the soil with my DNA inside you. And now the reaction is stronger than before."*

"Maybe because I'm home," she says, as she stops in front of an oversized double door.

Lucius turns and says, "I welcome everyone. This is your home now, and it is my great pleasure to have you here. Charony and Thimbette, Artie knows his way around the palace because he always has a room here. He can answer any questions you may have. He's been a part of my family for over thirty-four thousand years. I trust him."

"Lucius," Artie speaks up. "When will the troops arrive?" He clears his throat and asks, "Do I need to put on another brisket?"

"We're not talking about a small number when the army arrives. And no. They will not be here for our meal."

Lucius waves a finger, and the large entrance opens by his thought. He continues. "There should be several hundred warriors later this evening, brother. They'll have their own rations for tonight." He swings his arm for his party to enter, says, "My queen, enter your palace," and bows slightly before her.

Josephine, Claire, Charony, and Thimbette enter. They take in the smell of rain and the rustic charm of redwood trees with vines weaved around marble. Lucius smiles behind Josephine with his forearm around her waist.

"It smells like you," Josephine says.

Benches and furnishings are interlaid with roots that act as wicker furniture covered in overstuffed pillows.

"This is extravagant," she says and points at the furnishings. "Did you make those?"

"I did," he answers.

Josephine's steps are slow around the mighty tree that is nearly forty feet wide. The tree is the focal point of the main room as it stands center of the grand entryway with branches stretched out, holding walls in place and big enough to hold a treehouse the size of her cabin on each limb. Blossoms sit near the leaves of the trees. The blossoms express a variety of royal colors. Beyond the first mighty tree are two separate trees that are slightly thinner. They stand nearly eighty feet back from the main pillar. Each of the two trees beyond the main tree governs a spiraling staircase for each floor of the palace.

"Those stairways go into different wings of the Gamerin palace," Lucius says.

The branches of the trees stand tall and go beyond several stories and arched solarium windows that take in the light below the first boughs. They are so tall that she cannot see the canopy because of the low hanging cloud. Lucius shows her through his mind what the solarium canopy looks like.

"We're in the sky," she says.

"The palace is built throughout a small mountain. We're not that high." He points toward the cloud. "The cloudy mist that is in those branches up there is here because of the weather changing. Fall is just around the corner, and it's why we're going to the beach today before fall gets here."

Josephine studies the largest tree with the different blossoms. "I don't recognize this middle one with all the colors," Josephine says. The Gamerin colors of silver, white, purple, turquoise, and blue decorate the branches. "I didn't know redwood trees bloomed in different colors like this."

"It's not redwood. This is the Gamerin tree. I designed it with the Almighty," Lucius says. "This tree is a symbol of my royal bloodline. There's only one in existence, and you're looking at it. Where this tree stands, was the very spot I was created."

Josephine walks up to the trunk. "So, basically, where my life began, for you are truly my yoshawn."

Placing his hand upon his heart after her words, Lucius closes his eyes from the tingles in his stomach. "I feel so much love for you with your words, yoshawn."

Without looking back at him, she stares at the trunk until her head leans back all the way. "I feel dizzy just looking at it. And it's still not as tall as the others." She snickers. "I bet you've climbed this thing a few times."

"A few times," Lucius answers.

Claire tries climbing.

"Whoa." Josephine latches onto her daughter, and smirks back at Lucius. "I shouldn't have said that. We can't give her any ideas, my love. She doesn't fly."

Lucius answers, "Someday she might." Josephine turns her gaze back at him. "She's Gamerin, my yoshawn. It's one thing that I was terrified about on Earth. She might have wings in there. The Gamerin bloodline can be passed on. I found out that Nephilim carry a lot of traits…not all…but many of them do. When she's able to access her gifts, she might have some beautiful wings stashed away like her daddy."

Claire gasps a high-pitched squeal. "I have wings like you, Daddy?"

He shrugs. "Maybe you do. Your baby brother will. I know he will because he will be in my image. He'll have everything that I have to be my second-in-command."

Lucius steps under the Gamerin tree and looks up. With a deep breath, he closes his eyes. He opens his arms and then opens his bond to the world of Gamerilaye. He feels the planet embracing him with all his attention open to hear the atmosphere, like in the way that it used to be when his world was whole. He nearly gasps from the feeling of healing upon the planet. He turns toward Josephine and says, "I can feel that the trees and every living thing rejoices because Gamerilaye has longed for you to be here."

The petals from the boughs of the Gamerin tree rain down over them. Claire tries catching some of the colors like flickering glitter as they shine from the rays of light breaching through the branches below the solarium glass. Light also shines in from over the bay windows beside a colossal fireplace in another area of the palace.

Josephine snickers toward the colors floating down. She catches a few Gamerin petals like a child catching fireflies.

Lucius stands back to be at Artie's side, and they watch as his wife and daughter, with the two Bangel nurses, play in the falling petals.

Artie starts to say, "Lucius—"

"Brother," Lucius interrupts while holding up two fingers, "give me a minute. I wanna watch Claire and the mother of Gamerilaye playing in the palace. Isn't the queen breathtaking? It's like she's always belonged here."

Artie takes a deep breath and waits. When Josephine has stopped chasing the petals so that she can study them up close, she starts walking toward Lucius. As she is walking over, Artie clears his throat and asks, "Why are there going to be so many guardians later? I thought we were safe here. Few people have a key to this place, and it's not like Baàl can get his hands on one without your principality permission or even your blood. He can't design one like you can because he's not a principality like you."

With a content expression, Lucius watches Josephine as she stops to look at a large root of the tree that has been formed into a bench. He answers Artie, "My children will have guardians until they are strong enough and have been trained in the ways of a Gamerin. My children will be and are part human, my brother; therefore, they take part under the law of the Father. Although my blood will run through their veins, Josephine is from the human bloodline, and she will be the mother of this world. Humans are His most loved children, and as such will be protected above all. The protection of law includes Josephine along with all my babies I'll have through her."

"But I thought we were safe. I understand that they need guardians, but there are only a few on this planet. Again, why so many guardians all the way out here?"

Lucius exhales and shrugs as he says, "We're still in a war. You're right, the enemy Gamerin wouldn't be able to get here without my stone."

Artie sees how close Josephine is, so he quickly asks before she can hear. "I hope she doesn't try to visit her friends. You said she could read your mind now. You don't think she'll try and open a portal with her new psychic ability, do you?"

"I spoke with her, letting her know the danger," Lucius finishes saying as Josephine stands beside them. "I'll talk to her again," he says.

"About what?" Josephine asks.

Through his smile, Lucius says, "In a little bit. Right now, I'm enjoying my family on a safe world, a world that celebrates a rebirth."

Artie says, "I should probably show them around to their new home. I'll have to set up a place to sleep on the couch in my old room where Claire will be. I can keep the fireplace going for her when the cool season arrives."

Lucius pats Artie on the back. "True. Let's think of good things today. Like you living at my house once again in the second largest room in the palace. Don't forget to open the window drapes to let in the sunlight in the morning. You might need to sweep off the terrace. It's probably covered in pine needles and old blooms from the hanging gardens of the top terraces."

Artie nods. "I remember my old quarters. I've been cleaning this place every week while you've been away. I've also been cleaning the terraces. Not to mention, I been tending to the garden so that I can supply the Gamerin principality and his family while they resided on another planet with proper Gamerin nutrition. I know the room well. And I know you. The room is across the hall and a little down from your quarters. Claire's room will be the first room on the right when entering your wing, and it is the closest room to the healing waters of the royal bathing lounge. That's not a coincidence."

Lucius says, "You know me well. It's a safety measure. Just in case she needs to take a dip in healing waters from a tumble. This palace isn't as easy to get around like your place, and it isn't kid friendly. You'll have to keep an eye on her." He gestures toward the spiraling staircase. "She's not used to such heights."

"None of them are," Artie says. "Besides your bedroom, you're giving Claire the best room. The room closest to that one is perfect for the nurses."

Lucius smiles. "I know. Charony and Thimbette will need your help to get acquainted. But there is a bonus. Claire's room has the nicest bathing lounge in it, about a thousand square feet and complete with a natural waterfall, and it is the closest quarters to the kitchen preparation area. You know all my favorite foods."

"You're going to spoil Claire, giving her the best of everything."

"You were never spoiled," Lucius says.

"I think it's what made several of your brothers jealous of me. I'm not Gamerin, yet you gave me the best of everything in your own home."

"They all had their own homes." He nods and thinks for a moment before saying, "I'm sorry. I never saw the treatment you spoke of before. I never investigated my brothers' hearts for such thoughts. You never deserved foul behavior." He nods toward Claire. "Besides, Claire is my first born. She is my testimony of righteousness, and you deserve the best because you never left me like my brothers did. You both deserve my love. I know my son will be my second-in-command, but he'll live in my room his first year. Claire is bound to be powerful someday. She needs to remember she was always my first. There's nothing I wouldn't do for her," he says and gazes at Artie, "or you. I would do anything for you."

"Thank you, lord," Artie says. He changes the subject and says, "Well, I've been cooking a rather large brisket in an interdimensional space for the past eight hours with heating stones." He gestures over. "I have to show the royal nurses where they will be staying so they can get settled before our barbecue."

"Remember, I need Charony to be closest to Josephine as my wife enters her third trimester of pregnancy. Show Charony where that room is that is directly across the hall from the master's quarters. I need her to be the closest attendant where she can call Thimbette for help."

"Help?" Artie asks.

Lucius explains, "Josephine became exhausted when delivering Claire. She delivered Claire in less than two hours before the midwife had arrived. I wouldn't let the midwife examine Josephine and used her late arrival as an excuse for what I had already done."

"You already healed her?"

Lucius nods and says, "Yeah, she was passing out from the loss of blood. I healed Josephine to stop the bleeding and to keep her womb from scarring."

Artie asks, "Why didn't you wait until after her checkup to heal her completely?"

"Because I am not human, and her body is. She was suffering because of me, and I felt bad. Throughout her pregnancy, I healed her a lot, Artie, sometimes without her realizing it."

She asks, "You did?"

"Yes, I did," Lucius says. "The worst part was the final trimester. It wore you out and wore me out because I was on Earth. The pregnancy was very stressful for you. I guess Gamerin babies are taxing on a human female." Lucius shrugs. "Anyway, I couldn't let the midwife see that I had shrunk your uterus immediately after delivery to repair the tissue's injuries. The way that I healed you was like you had never delivered. But I remember how tired you were afterward. I remember how you lay there nursing Claire until falling asleep from exhaustion."

She says, "I remember that you made a lot of the pain go away for me, but I could feel the muscles still cramping and pushing."

Lucius says, "I'm planning on absolving your pain, but I can't make promises. I want to, but I feel wrong about promising you something like that for some reason."

Artie says, "You're making me feel uneasy with your statement. I know that you can take her pain away completely here. What are you not telling me? There's something bothering you. I can see it."

Lucius answers, "Deasja helped last time. I couldn't remove Josephine's pain as much as I wanted to, but…"

Artie says, "But, what? What is it? You're blocking your mind and doing a poor job of hiding something."

"Josephine and I…" Lucius becomes quiet and stares into nothing. When he sees Artie becoming scared, he answers, "Josephine and I have been feeling strange lately. And that feeling returns when I wanna make the promise of absolving her pain."

"What? How do you mean strange? Lucius, you can tell me what's going on," Artie says.

Lucius shakes his head and says, "Probably nothing. It's probably just left-over anxiety of what happened yesterday. The Holy Spirit warns us. Josephine and I can't place a finger on what we're sensing." He looks at Artie and continues. "Something feels out of sight. Hidden." He exhales. "Never mind. It's probably just me. I've gone without my full abilities for so long and have been second guessing everything that I might take some time to learn new habits like relaxing. Everything's happening so fast and so perfectly. I'm not used to perfect or having everything I ever dreamed of at my fingertips. I'm used to everything taken from me. This is all new. Josephine is a blessed woman, and she and I are madly in love with each other. I've taken her home to be with me, and I have witnessed her dancing in my royal hall with my daughter as if they were in the living room of her house in Texas. I have a real family. It's more than I could've ever imagined. It's perfect."

"I guess so." Artie pivots sideways and says, "Probably nothing to worry about."

Josephine asks, "Are we living in the foyer?" She points toward an overstuffed sofa which could easily sit twenty people, "If we are, that one's mine. I love that shade of purple."

Lucius chuckles as he gets Charony's and Thimbette's attention. "My dear Bengaldoes, please come here. Artie will show you to your new chambers beside Claire's room. We'll meet you on the beach in an hour so we can enjoy our picnic together."

Twenty-One

Marriage Chamber

Lucius leads Josephine into their master's chamber and closes the doors behind him. Josephine stands quietly, still, studying every corner. He walks over and caresses her back, he himself looking around like she is. "I haven't been in here for six years."

Her mouth makes a noise, not quite a gasp, but not a word either.

He continues. "Artie has been keeping this place up for me. He and Powtray both on occasion. I'm glad. Otherwise, your first impression in here would've been embarrassing." He points toward the branches with glowing speckles holding the white marbled walls in place. "Those are natural nightlights for us. They are bioluminescent twigs chiseled into the walls. Claire's bedroom has some. It'll keep her from getting scared when the fireplace isn't going at night."

"Are those the same trees like on Jett Commdearadea?"

"Yes. I needed only one seed to replicate them here. You have a great memory." He helps direct her eyes toward an enormous opening of two doors that are slightly cracked open. The doors lead to a wide landing bay, big enough for someone with a vast wingspan.

"What's over there?" she asks.

He answers, "That's our terrace. We'll exit through there when you get changed. Because I'm the king and principality, I need a large landing bay to fit my wings." He shrugs. "There are a lot of terraces I could land safely on, but I need to levitate into a few of them because of tree branches."

Her vision climbs around to different points of the room. Her throat gawks with a sound, mimicking what her eyes would say, if they had a voice.

He smiles at her. "Are you okay? You're making a few funny sounds."

Josephine glances over her far left. About twenty-five feet away, hangs a smooth curtain that is pulled back along bed posts, revealing a white linen covered oval-shaped bed with a splash of color thrown in from decorative pillows that Artie had placed. The bed is wider than a normal sized king bed and much longer. Cherry blossom branches with baby blue flowers, instead of pink, decorated along the wall of their bed and act as a headrest. Even the white curtains hanging from the drapery of the bed posts have a shine on the outside with flickers of light, as if turquoise and blue glow worms were stitched into the fabric naturally.

He says, "Don't worry about the curtains having light on the outside of them. When they're closed, the glow won't bother you. It's seen only from the outside." He looks down at her with a quick movement that has a tad of nervousness when he says, "But I could flip them if you want. The curtains would look like fireflies while we sleep. It's no trouble, Josephine."

She shakes her head to disagree as she continues studying the marriage quarters.

The ceiling is over twenty-feet-tall. He says, "It's high, so I can have tall visitors like archangels. They have visited before."

Directly in front of her, on the far side of the room, a stunning turquoise and periwinkle bureau and vanity with an oblong mirror, nearly ten-feet-wide and eight feet tall dresses a long wall. The framing designed around the mirror is hand carved with an extravagant pattern and covered in silver. Some of the details carved into the dresser she can't make out from where she stands because of how small each carving is.

Josephine turns her head slowly to look at low hanging branches kissing the floor. Even the branches have been chiseled out with designs and formed into a loveseat. The loveseats of the room are soaked in silver and purple, overstuffed padding. Everywhere her eyes gaze along the walls, there are chalices, paintings, or designs carved into the formation of the room.

Lucius shrugs and says, "It's okay. I've seen prettier, but maybe I'm just used to it."

She gradually makes eye contact with him. "It's okay? Really?" She points at structures and statues. A natural flowing waterfall that trickles off branches and into a small pond that is surrounded by a flower garden. She says, "Lucius, it's breathtaking in here. It's literally the most beautiful room that I have ever seen."

He shakes his head and says, "None of this stuff can love me back, my yulee."

"But—"

"Baby," he interrupts her. "The truth is that my brothers made most of this stuff for me. I helped because I was training them to be builders. I remember every moment and every laugh while they were learning to craft with their abilities. I remember every joke we made about the flaws in their work. I remember every detail of our conversations in their training when each came up with a new design. Over time, when the design needed to be updated to grow with the trees, they fixed the issue with what they had learned, and I would silently watch them. When they were done, some saw the flaws, and others didn't. I told my brothers, the ones who realized what they had done, to leave the flaws, so I could admire how much they tried while perfecting their abilities."

"So many beautiful memories. Why would this make you say that it couldn't love you back?"

"Because staying in here always reminded me of what I had lost. I couldn't sleep in here anymore. After they left, I couldn't bring myself to repair the flaws either. My principality curse is to recognize every detail around my govern. In a moment, I could've changed the designs and rid myself of the reminders, but even with that ability, I had no power to bring back those who I loved." He gazes down at her. "I couldn't sleep in here. If I slept at all, it was never in here. Just like you were when your parents died, I couldn't enter certain rooms."

She says, "They were like my family was to me. You must've loved them."

"Yes. I needed you and your love. I had given up and was wasting away, slowly, and painfully agonizing. You brought me back to life." He points toward the door beyond the left side of the bed. "I only came in here to get washed up and to go on missions. If I wasn't working, I rarely ever came in here."

She points where he does. "There's a bathroom over there?"

He escorts her to where she pointed and tells her, "Yeah, a bathing lounge." He opens the door.

Immediately, the sounds of bubbling water from the natural springs fill the air. "You have a hot springs waterfall in here?" she asks.

Alongside a waterfall, sits a chair-shaped boulder surrounded by steaming water raining over it. In the far corner is a runoff area below the waterline where the used water drops off outside of his palace. The stone pebbles in the pool of water helps in cleaning the waters in the bathing lounge. Statues built with outstretched arms for holding towels and coverings. The most impressive feature in the bathing lounge is by far the pool shaped tub.

It's a couple of feet deep with dark pebbles covering the bottom like smooth river rocks. Carved out areas along the tub make for comfortable seating locations while soaking in a bath. Lucius says, "I can close the filter," and points up, "and block the waterways for you. I don't have nozzles like we did in Texas. This water always runs, so I must redirect the flow so that the water runs off through the pipes in the ceiling area."

He picks up a large, frosted, crystal bottle with tiny blossoms over it, and she recognizes the Gamerin soap. "Oh, those are Gamerin oils."

He nods, pouring much of the healing oils in their bath. "We can soak in this after tonight." He raises a hand and levitates a small boulder that redirects the waterfall so that it flows toward an outer window and keep the pool still. The filtration system quits flowing immediately, and the healing oils disperse into velvety white water. "It should cool down some before we come back in here. I know you like your bath hot, but the stones won't let it get cold. The bathing lounge holds heat for days at a time."

Josephine points toward the natural light below the waterline. "Where does the water go?" she asks.

He says, "It's a filtration system. The water pushes out through here," he points, "and waters my lower gardens." He gestures toward the milky bath. "Gamerin oils are natural, and won't hurt my plants."

"Everything has a design," she says. "It's flawless."

Shrugging, he says, "Everything is reusable, as our Father has made it."

"I can't believe how easy creating and engineering is for you."

"I'm a builder. Principalities build things, and the Gamerin are among the creative beings."

She half smiles. "I didn't see any flaws in your bedroom furnishings earlier."

"Our marriage chamber," he says and nods. "You wouldn't right now. Not many would." He meets her gaze. "But it's our room, yours and mine." Lucius embraces her and says, "I give all of myself to you. I'll pour all my love over you every moment I have you throughout eternity. Everything you see is yours through me." He slowly sways her body against him, dancing to the sound of running water.

Josephine rests her ear against his chest and says, "I might not know how everything works here, but I know the sound of your heartbeat. You're music to my ears."

"It's you. You make this old heart beat out of control, my yoshawn." He raises his head to look around at his bathing lounge and marriage chambers through the open doorway. "And it's beating out of control, thinking about later with you, and how long I've been alone here. We probably need to get dressed so we can go down to the beach. If we stay in here too much longer, I might skip a few of my plans and just lay your comfort over me a little early."

"Well, let's not skip our family time. Where do I get dressed?" She points to the open door. "That room is too big for changing. Is there a closet where I won't feel so exposed?"

He starts walking out of the room and says, "You can change in our bathing lounge. It's what I usually do." He stands in the doorway and gestures toward a column around the shower area. "There's a closet where I store robes over there, beyond that water fountain. I'll meet you out here, and then I'll fly you down so we can play on the beach."

Lucius opens the outer doors to the terrace and allows a breeze to enter their quarters. He waits for Josephine to exit the bathing lounge. He feels her body, and hears the doors open. He walks back into his quarters and is stunned in place, jaw-dropping with a gawk.

She tugs at her outer garment and looks nervously at him. "What's wrong?" she asks brushing her fingers along her see-through shirt. "I'm wearing that sackcloth thingamajig. Is it okay?"

Starting with a humming sound, he says, "You're so hot. I can see your bikini, and I have every part of you memorized. Am I drooling? We should go before I change my mind."

She smiles. "You're such a dude, Lucius." She walks over to him and kisses him. "I love that my husband admires my body."

"Adores," he says caressing her thighs, "cherishes," kissing her neck, "and yearns for."

She swats his hands and sends him into a slight chuckle. She says, "That's enough of that. Don't make me tell you no. They're probably waiting down there now."

He escorts her to the terrace. "Pretty soon. Artie's still unloading toys and clothes from his interdimensional spaces. He's almost done. We'll probably beat them down there."

She looks over the banister of the landing bay and says, "That's a far drop. I thought there'd be a walkway or something," as she glimpses the beach in the distance. "You're flying from here."

"We are." He grabs onto her. "I'm carrying you down."

Josephine wraps her arms over his shoulders, and he lifts her up. She says, "You know I'm worried about heights, so I need you to pay attention."

He pinches her bottom.

She laughs. "Pay attention. I don't wanna fall, Yuleshua Lucius Gamerin."

"I'm not gonna drop you. No need to get mad."

"What about yesterday? I remember my little tumble into no man's land. I wasn't paying attention, and I'm still freaked out over it."

He nods with a positive grin. "Okay, my yoshawn. I'll pay attention as you request."

Suddenly, their bodies become weightless. Levitating several feet above the ground, Josephine holds on tighter. He whispers, "I've got you. You're in our world now. I could move mountains out of the way to save you."

She exhales and hides in his neck. "Just tell me when it's over."

"Baby," he says and caresses her back. "I want you to look."

Steadily, she opens her eyes.

He stretches his wings outward, and the trees bend slightly back to clear a path for him to dive. "With all my being, I'll protect you." Lucius raises across several trees, and as the clearing is complete, he takes off with a calm decline that gracefully caresses the wind. "I'm being easy. I want you always safe in my arms."

Josephine releases her grip a little to look around. Her nerves relax. "It's not so scary when you're holding me like this. I feel pressure all over my body." She smiles. "You're levitating me against you."

"I am. Every part of you is held to me by the atmosphere itself. The wind, trees, soil, everything here wants you safe. We're bound together. This planet knows that we are one flesh. Please experience all the good about me and not worry yourself on things that won't happen."

She nods. "I never thought of a planet truly caring about something," she says and kisses his cheek.

"The word of God tells you something like this, 'If his people will not call out to Him, then even the rocks will praise His name.' Earth has longed for its cornerstone to be happy and has suffered a long time for Him, and so has this planet for a different reason. You bring the cornerstone happiness, and our planet here knows it. This world will not let anything happen to you. Gamerilaye knows I would be broken without you." They glide through the canopy, and he continues. "If you say, let this grow here or clear this path, our world will do it for you."

"That's beautiful when you put it that way," she says and squeezes him tighter. "I trust you even more now. You are the cornerstone."

"I am. I'm the cornerstone of this world. I am the thought that opens the gate to our world. Thank you for your trust. That means more than you'll ever know." His chin rests on her shoulder. "I feel your true trust, and you comfort me deeply."

Shortly, they land softly on warm sand, quickly followed by Flutter.

Twenty-Two

Beach

The soles of Josephine's feet touch the sandy ground. She glances around. "Flutter's down here with us."

"He doesn't wanna be far from you." Lucius gestures his nose up toward trees. "You wanna visit with my turquoise friends up there, little buddy?"

Flutter flies off and meets with the other birds in the trees.

"I guess he does," Lucius says.

Josephine realizes where she is and says, "This is where you proposed." Josephine's singing mountains stand amid the water and the shoreline. "Will they play a different tune this evening?" She glances up toward the palace beyond the canopy and says, "We weren't far that night. I can see the terrace from here now that the tree limbs have moved back."

"They will stay like that until we turn in for bed. Also, the song will be the same song because this is the same time of year that I brought you." He raises a brow toward the palace. "I had hidden my palace from anyone looking. I just now opened the pathways for sight and flight. A principality doesn't leave without securing his home's borders somehow."

He leads her to the picnic table and places down towels. Josephine gasps and says, "Oh!" She squats down, gathering old shoes, torn and aged four years with caked on sand. "I knew I had left them here." She lifts them up by a faded strap where silver once shined over leather. "They're nothing but scraps now."

"Let me see those, baby." Lucius holds them.

Before her eyes, the material rebinds. Sand sheets from the leather, and faded color becomes vibrant once again. They look as new as they were the day that she had lost them.

He gives the silver dress shoes back to her, saying, "Here you go."

"How did you do that?" she asks. "They're perfect. Like the day I got them. You didn't usually do this on Earth."

He shrugs. "I had to reserve my abilities, but here I'm all builder."

"You're a everything. I guess I have new shoes. That's a blessing."

"I'll make you anything you need." He winks and says, "After our bath, I'll make you a royal gown to sleep in. One you can walk around the palace in during evening. Many will be here, and you have an image you need to keep as a principality's wife. You're a queen. I'll make the nightgown to match these shoes for you."

She raises her hands and asks, "With pretty gloves like earlier?"

He nods. "As you desire. I knew you'd like those gloves."

"Can you make them white?" she asks. "Please, with pretty purple straps like a fantasy land?"

He snickers and embraces her, saying, "Not only that, but I'll make you a matching long cloak to walk around in, so no one will see your nightgown. I'll make it to where it drags several feet behind you. And when you're tired of the color, you'll be able to flip the cloak so that it is silver and shines as much as you do." He sways with her. "Charony and Thimbette will do your hair tonight and place Gamerin tattoos on you before we have company. You'll be all dressed up when our army arrives."

"Army?"

"I need an army to help me govern." He nibbles on her neck and says, "I already have a wife that looks amazing. I'll have to match her in something."

"Quit flattering me," she says and swings her neck back with a breathy laugh. "I'm gonna look like a diva. You're already spoiling me."

"You're gonna look like a queen for now on."

"Okay." She swallows her laughter and picks at his bottom lip as he continues nibbling on her neck and cheek. She says, "Not all the time, please say only a short time. I'd like a pair of blue jeans."

He shakes his head, and his mouth wrestles with her fingers that are still pinching his bottom lip in place as he tries to say, "You can't wear -lue jeans while -egnant. S-op doing dat." He psychically tells her again, *"You can't wear blue jeans while pregnant, Josephine. It reduces amniotic fluid and isn't good for the baby's circulation. We've already discussed this when you were pregnant with Claire."*

He pretends to chomp her fingertips, and she yanks back. "Oh, don't bite me. I just knew you were gonna say that. I like my old clothes. I'm not used to dresses all the time."

His brows raise high. "What you want and what you need are two totally different things. You're still a queen here, and our subjects need to identify you as such. You're not a soldier, so you can't walk around in pants like me." Caressing the small of her back, he says, "Don't make yourself unhappy. Give it a while. I'll create maternity clothes later for you." He lets go of her and points at her collarbone. "And I wasn't gonna bite you...hard." He chuckles. "Only a nibble for stealing my lip while I was talking."

He kisses her hands, and she says, "I love how playful you are. I just didn't want you to say that I can't wear blue jeans because I knew it was coming."

"I know," Lucius says. "I had to hide your tight clothes on Earth when you carried Claire too."

She pokes a finger in the air. "I knew you did that. Are they still hidden in your interdimensional pockets somewhere, maybe?"

He laughs. "No."

They both turn around as Artie places Claire onto the sand after flying down. Artie puts his red, striped wings back into a hidden pocket and says, "She loves flying and talked about it the whole way down here." Artie opens his hand and points toward her. "She's still talking about flying. Someone got her all hopeful for wings someday."

Claire says, "and I'll do this too," as she twirls her hands, as if making donuts in the sky. Her lips vibrate, sounding like a car engine rather than someone flying.

Lucius jokes, saying, "Evidently, she's imitating you, Artie. She's doing all but the fire from behind."

Josephine laughs out loud.

Artie slants an expression. "Har, har. One time, and I'll never hear the end of blowing fire out my back end now. She liked it. I didn't think of it being improper for that joke to a toddler. She'll probably forget."

Claire says, "He toots fire, Momma."

Josephine nods. "Yep. You just don't forget those kinds of things as a kid."

Lucius picks Claire up and walks toward the delicate waves. He says, "Let daddy show you something I don't want you to forget." He stops and looks back at Josephine. "I wanna show you too."

"Show me what?" Josephine stands beside him and lets the water brush against her toes.

He smiles as he takes one large step, and then another one over water, until he's walking on the water. Josephine's mouth drops.

Lucius walks toward the Yoshawn Mountains. "What?" Josephine asks. "You're walking on water? I thought only Jesus did that."

"Not true. Peter did as well, together with Yeshua. With a little faith, you can move mountains as His child." He points down as a school of fish swarm beneath him. "I could walk like this on Earth too, but I didn't wanna explain who I was."

Artie sets up the picnic table and hauls driftwood into a pile.

Lucius says, "Put rocks around it, Artie."

"I wanna walk too," Josephine says.

Artie answers Lucius, "That's what I'm gonna do, so Claire doesn't get burned."

Lucius says, "You're getting good at your Texan slang."

"I wanna walk out there," Josephine says.

Artie says, "Thank you, my lord."

Josephine folds her arms after being ignored. She puckers her lips and places one foot in front onto the water and continues with another. One step after the other, the surface of the water holds her up.

"How are you doing that?" Artie asks.

Stunned, Lucius's eyes speak louder than his words as he says, "Because this world obeys her."

She takes a stance beside Lucius with her hands on her hips. "I told you I wanna come out here."

Lucius is smiling. "You're an amazing creature."

She stretches her neck. "So are you."

Claire says, "I wanna walk."

Lucius nods. "Okay, pumpkin." He places Claire down and lets her take her footing. "I'll make sure you're held up."

The water becomes nearly solid like a stage under their feet, causing a flat surface. Several yards away from them, the water resumes its normal function as it claps against the rocks of mountains.

Lucius points out several monkey-looking creatures and tells Josephine and Claire, "Those creatures are called shawshean. I harvest their web-like materials for my shawshea war shirts."

"Those are the cute things you told me about," Josephine says.

"Yeah, it's a teflon fabric." Looking at Claire he says, "Your momma describes the material as warm butter against her skin." He winks at Josephine. "My shirts look better on momma than they do on me."

Blushing, Josephine says, "Stop that," and taps his shoulder.

Lucius chuckles and escorts them above an area of underwater caves. Through the crystal-clear water, Josephine sees lobster-like creatures. Lucius says, "This is breeding season for them. They're usually found in deep water, but inhabit shallow caves during the cool season. They're just now gathering for breeding."

With every movement of the creature's paddles, bioluminescent lines and spots flicker on their bodies.

She says, "They glow as well?"

"At night," he tells her. "The waters shine like the aurora borealis with these creatures this time a year. But only at sunset and when it's cold enough."

"I remember seeing them when you proposed," Josephine says. "I guess they'll get brighter later."

"They will." He nods. "Now you've seen them up close." He gestures at several plants, animals, and natural elements around them. "Many things on this planet give off certain colors. That's why the Gamerin colors are vibrant blue, turquoise, silver, white, and purple. These lobster things, as you call them, they're really called richens."

Claire asks, "Is it a spider, Daddy?"

"No, pumpkin. It's only a sea creature. They won't hurt you."

Just then, a richen moves from its cave shelf and swims quickly, close to where Claire is standing. She squeals and grabs her daddy's leg.

Lucius says, "You have to trust me, Claire." He lightly snickers. "They won't hurt you." He picks her up. "They don't even have big claws."

Artie clears his throat from the beach. Josephine turns her gaze toward Artie and says, "I can hear him from here."

Lucius raises his brows. "You must be attaching to this world every time we're near each other."

"It doesn't happen automatically?"

He shakes his head and says, "Your cells draw memory from mine with every experience you go through with me. The longer we work together, the stronger you should get. It took me a while after I was formed."

"How where you formed?" she asks. "Were you like a boy?"

Artie clears his throat a second time and says, "The brisket's done." He rearranges the seating for Charony and Thimbette as they arrive from the trail. "You ladies can sit over here with me."

Lucius answers Josephine as he walks back with her and Claire. "I guess we should head back to the beach. Over sixty-eight thousand years ago, this world was dirt and water. From both, I was formed. The Almighty and I together, along with my brother Yeshua designed this world and galaxy. They stayed with me a while, but knew I would be lonely. I wasn't a boy." He gazes at Josephine. "He gave me brothers, someone to command over and love me."

Waves kiss the bottom of her feet, and she asks, "But he never made Gamerin females?"

"We didn't think that way. We had everything we needed. We had each other." He signals toward the beach and says, "We would play games, joke, and run races. Children don't think this way about their brothers and sisters. They only love them and play in innocence. My brothers listened to the oldest. That's how we were because we were a family." Lucius places Claire down onto the beach sand, and she quickly runs toward Artie as he dips up the food.

"So," Josephine says. "Principalities don't get married?"

He explains, "Some do. But they're not bred to be soldiers like the Gamerin. Every creature is made differently." He gestures toward the richens. "Some of the Father's creation must have a mate," he says and then points toward the trees, "and others can make their own from their own body."

"You made your brothers from your body?"

He says, "No, the Lord did, so I wouldn't be alone. It isn't good to be alone. I woke up, and my brothers were there. They were all in order, and they knew that I loved them. I knew all of them immediately, like I had always known them. The Father told me they were a part of me, my brothers, and I named them with the Father."

Her face falls downcast, and she becomes quiet.

"Please don't be sad," he tells her, standing on the beach to themselves. "I have you now, and you're a part of me."

She looks at him. "You lost a part of who you were. Pieces of your own body. I never thought of your loss that way."

"The Father has lost a lot more than I have, and He loves deeper than anyone could ever understand. You carry His breath of life in you, and you are special. It's true. A part of me had gone missing, and I was broken in twelve thousand pieces because of it." He looks toward the beach as he continues, saying, "I lived on this beach in a way you never would've thought when you met me. I wouldn't eat. I drowned myself in sleep—alcohol—because I hated remembering every time that I was awake what was once in my hands. I drank until my body was too tired to stay alert. Not as an alcoholic, but sleeping through my sorrow, dreaming of a time they were here."

"Why make yourself go to sleep? Couldn't Artie place you into a sleep?"

"If I'm tired, yes." He points into several areas. "While I was awake, I punished myself. I tore things up—"

"You have such a temper," she says.

"I know. I thought I could hide my misery, so I didn't tell Artie or anyone I needed help. I consoled myself. I talked to myself and soothed myself as best I could."

"Why didn't you talk to our Father?"

"That's the thing. I was ashamed and dodged Him. I couldn't show my face, and I allowed my mistakes to play in my mind, over, and over again. I made Him cry. I made my Father cry." His eyes close. "I believed I was the cause of all human life dying in the time of Noah. I almost couldn't forgive myself. Everyone either forgot about me, or I was some loner who was an alcoholic, but Gamerin blood doesn't respond like others. There were very few times I got drunk, and if I did, I swiftly drifted off to sleep. Sometimes it didn't matter where I was. To forget became the only thing I wanted to do. My heart's intention was only to sleep. I never got drunk on purpose. I knew those closest to me had figured it out, especially, when it started happening in public places, making me drink more when not on duty."

She gasps.

"They didn't know who I was, or so I thought. It was right before I met you." He says, "Dex was very blunt about what I had become. And Deasja was a good counselor, but it made it worse when I saw Artie's reaction. His heart was broken over my new image, what I became in my loneliness."

She whispers, "That's why Deasja and Dex would look at you funny when you'd have only one cup with dinner? I remember how Deasja smiled every time you rinsed out your cup, and Dex would give you that eyebrow. They were monitoring you."

"Yes, Dex has always monitored me closely for some reason, but they all worried for me, knowing I didn't wanna live anymore. Living had become a curse in my inheritance. But the Gamerin sins weren't my own, and I was never made to be alone. I hadn't sinned against the Father."

Artie clears his throat a third time, coughing lightly beneath his hand. "Starving...*umm*."

Josephine and Lucius flash a flat expression toward him.

Lucius says, "We're coming, buddy." He gazes at Josephine. "We should eat, or apparently he's gonna starve to death."

Josephine snickers. "That angel can eat."

"My queen," Artie says. "I can hear you perfectly outside the palace. I love family time almost as much as I love eating time." He flips his palms outward in innocence. "I like good home cooking, and the food smells delicious over here." He eyeballs the savory meat. "My mouth is watering."

Lucius says, "You're always hungry."

Artie's mouth drops for a moment and his finger flicks up. He pauses, thinking his thoughts through, and resolves, "You know what? You're right. I am always hungry."

Josephine and Lucius chuckle as they join the group. After saying a quick prayer over dinner, Lucius delights in fellowship during their first supper as a family on Gamerilaye.

⁂

Lucius stands alongside Artie, watching Josephine and Claire play in the shoreline waves. Lucius says, "I saw the overgrown ferns in the bathing lounge. It's difficult for me to think that you simply forgot that they were there. I know you left them to show me how long I was away. I read your mind just to be sure."

"It was only a small hint," Artie says. "I actually trimmed those ferns for a while." Artie tries hiding a smile. "When you two got married, I left it for you." He stops and asks, "Oh, wait, she didn't—"

"I told her through a psychic bond, but we didn't talk about it."

"She's going to think I'm a disrespectful servant." He points at himself. "I meant no offense by leaving the plants unattended."

"You're good, Artie," Josephine says from a distance.

"You can hear me from way over there?" Artie asks.

She nods. "Barely, but just enough to make out what you're mumbling about."

"He's not mumbling," Lucius says. "Your ears will get stronger with time. But that's impressive since yesterday."

She restates what she heard, "He's not fumbling?" She grimaces. "Your tears will get longer with rhyme, and impressions tents yesterday?" She says, "That makes no sense, Lucius. Why are you speaking so low? I heard everything when he got upset."

Artie and Lucius laugh loudly.

"Don't laugh at me," she says playfully sticking a bottom lip out. "I'm trying my best."

"Don't pout, you faker," Lucius answers with raising his voice a little more. "That's not what I said."

She tells him telepathically, *"Just use your mind, I can hear everything that way, and I don't have to struggle."*

He nods. *"I'm sorry I laughed at you. You're just adorable."*

"My feelings aren't hurt. I would have probably laughed too."

"Are you two speaking to each other?" Artie asks.

Lucius glances over at Artie while still nodding. "I'm apologizing for laughing—"

Artie blurts out, "I'm sorry, your majesty. I meant no offense. I—"

"Let me finish, Artie. She's not upset. She even said she would've laughed. We're all family here. Don't make yourself uneasy around me. You know how I feel about that," Lucius says.

Artie exhales. "You're right. People already fear you enough. Some with good reason too."

Lucius deeply breathes in the Gamerilaye air. "But not here, not on my world. This is home. This is family." He smiles, watching Josephine and

Claire playing with the waves as if water is trying to catch them. "Everything is beautiful now, and I can give her anything she desires here. I wanna give her a gift for carrying my son."

Artie asks, "Like what? She has a whole world. She has you."

"I don't know," Lucius says and strokes his chin. "I wanna give her something because I know pregnancy can be difficult, and she willingly goes through carrying my children to please me." His eyes seal shut. "I wanna give her something good."

Artie shakes his head. Dumbfounded, he says, "I have no idea. Maybe, a bushel of apples. They have good nutritional value."

"Apples!"

"I don't know." Artie shrugs. "She might get hungry."

Lucius wipes his laughing tears from his eyes. "My goodness, Artie, you're always hungry." Wondering where the idea came from, Lucius raises his hands and says, "I said I wanna give my wife a present for carrying a baby," and stares at Artie, "and you say…apples."

"What are you two talking about?" Josephine asks and hops over a wave before water touches her feet.

"I wanna give you a gift for carrying my baby."

"I'm not pregnant yet," Josephine says.

"You will be," Lucius says and points beside him, "and he said apples."

Josephine studies Artie's expression and says, "That sounds wonderful. I love apples, and I could make an apple pie. You could make those cinnamon apple pancakes you always make so well." She points toward Artie. "He makes the best apple strudel, and I could have delicious apples the entire time I carry our son. That's such a sweet offer."

Artie's face beams. "She knew where I was going with the suggestion. She likes homemade food too. She's a Southern girl."

Lucius realizes that Josephine is trying to make Artie feel good about the offer, so he changes the subject, saying, "What would you want as a gift, my yoshawn?"

"Blue jeans," she quickly answers.

"Apples it is then." Lucius smirks.

Josephine giggles and continues playing with Claire. Lucius joins in, running alongside the water as waves reach across the light sand. "This is actually quite fun." Lucius passes Josephine as he runs toward Claire. "I'm gonna get you something better than apples."

Claire turns back and starts running from her daddy as if he's giving chase toward her. He immediately takes on the new game and says, "Daddy's gonna get you."

Claire squeals and screams with laughter. He sweeps her up into his arms as she's screaming while he tickles her. Josephine says, "Why don't you pick on someone your own size."

Nearly everything on the beach pauses. Lucius turns and stares at Josephine. Josephine takes a small step back as soon as she feels the atmosphere change. He slowly places Claire back down and says to her, "Play with Artie, Claire." He takes a step toward Josephine.

Realizing the challenge she had just given him, Josephine takes a few steps back and says, "I was only playing."

Artie says, "I know that expression." He picks Claire up and gathers sandcastle supplies. "I'm sorry, my queen, but you just got roped into a new game. You'd better run."

Josephine holds out a hand to Lucius and takes subtle steps back. "Lucius, I'm not that fast. Please, you know that I'm ticklish."

With a growing smile, Lucius raises a brow and steps toward her.

Her strides quicken as she turns to run. "No, Lucius. I was playing. No...*nooo!*"

He gives chase, saying, "Can't take it back. I won't let you."

Screaming, Josephine takes off toward the forest, "I can't outrun you!" She screams even more when she hears his long legs galloping behind her.

Artie's head shakes. "I knew that one was coming." He watches Clair as she fills a bucket with sand. "Now, he's just messing around. I've never seen him run so slowly before."

Josephine takes two steps beyond a large forest. The mist of the forest swallows her silhouette. Lucius enters milliseconds behind her, saying, "Like you could outrun me," and picks her up in his arms.

She squeals in his embrace. "You're too fast."

"You have no idea," he says and jogs several more steps toward a small clearing of moss-covered stones and fern filled forest.

"You're not even out a breath."

"I can outrun lightning, but that would've scared you." He places her down.

"You never told me how fast you are."

"I didn't enter a quick speed all the time. To tell you the truth, sometimes I forget that I have that ability. It would drain me quickly on Earth, so I get out of practice there." Josephine is fanning herself for air. Lucius waves his hand and sends a cool breeze over her body. "You like that?"

"*Mmmm*, are you doing this?" She leans her head back, closes her eyes, and takes the cool breeze all in. "You're wonderful."

Lucius shortens distance between her and him and whispers against her neck hairs. "You're beautiful." He kisses her skin. "And soft. And smell good," he says and nibbles, "and taste good."

She guards her neck. "Not outside, Lucius." Meeting his gaze, she continues. "They can hear us when you get started."

"I was quiet on Earth, for the most part."

She lifts a brow. "I remember our honeymoon before the guards were there."

He says, "You're right. They can't hear us inside the Gamerin palace. I designed the walls for privacy. But they could hear us out here."

"I'm glad you secured the walls, but how come it's different here? On Earth, many guardians could see through my walls if they wanted to."

"This is a principality's home. I couldn't very well let anyone listen when I would counsel with another principality, or even with my brothers. They trusted me. I couldn't break that trust. Only I can hear or see through the palace walls, me and the Trinity." He takes her hand. "I think it's time for us to go in."

"And make a baby?"

Lucius stops from walking toward the beach and turns toward her. He places his hand below her navel. "Do you feel?"

She inhales. "Yes. Wow," she says locking eyes with him before continuing. "My body feels relaxed."

"I opened your womb just now." His forehead rests on her hair. "Let's bring our son to life. I miss him already."

She points in the direction of the beach and says, "Let's say goodnight first. Claire will be in bed shortly, and we won't see her until tomorrow."

They meet Artie while he's in the middle of building a lumpy structure with a giddy three-year-old. Lucius says, "Let her play a little while longer, but she needs Thimbette to give her a bath. I'd like you to place her into a sleep when they're done tending to her. Just a light sleep though, so her body can naturally adjust to the atmosphere." He glances at Charony and Thimbette and says, "When you're done washing her up, the queen and I will have need of you. We'll call for your assistance after we check on Claire. Prepare any Gamerin tattooing supplies for the artwork on her arms, and one of you can do her hair, if you don't mind."

Smiling, Charony and Thimbette kneel before Lucius. Charony says, "She'll be radiant for when the army arrives, my lord. I've studied for years how to do royal glamour."

Josephine folds her arms and blushes. "I'm not used to the royal treatment. I'm grateful. I've never had Gamerin tattoos before. Does it hurt?"

Thimbette says, "Your majesty, they're like drawings painted on your skin. When the ink dries, it stays on for several days and shines like Oobadoave shielding on your skin. It's a symbol of royalty for principalities. Usually, only the wives are dressed with such design because their husbands adorn them to show their care."

Charony says, "We would never purposely hurt you. I hope you're not tender-headed. I love curls and braids in royal hair, and your hair is very long and gorgeous. I'm gentle."

Josephine shakes her head. "I'm not tender-headed. I often did my hair on Earth."

Charony's and Thimbette's eyes broaden. Thimbette says, "You have this talent? What a wonderful queen you are." She curtsies. "Beautiful and talented."

Josephine covers her face and says, "Oh, goodness. I don't know what to say."

"Okay, the queen is tongue-tied by your gifts and praise." Lucius escorts Josephine from the beach and says, "We'll see y'all later." He embraces Josephine and asks her, "You ready?"

Josephine tightens her arms around him. "I am ready for your love."

Lucius carries his wife toward their marriage chambers and lies with her.

Twenty-Three

Family Friend

After making love, Josephine lies with her ear to Lucius's chest. "I love hearing your heart beating."

He caresses her long hair beside her shoulder and makes small shapes with his fingertips on her back. His caressing sends goosebumps across her bare skin. "I love this part. I love our peaceful moments after making love, when we hold each other, and you talk to me in all honesty. I feel your love. I'm holding my most treasured blessing. In these moments, I'm filled with complete and utter joy. You're my comfort given by the Lord."

"I love your words," she says resting her chin buried in chest hair. She plays with a few strands and meets his gaze. "You speak so sweetly to me. I love this part as well, just you and me." She lays her head back down. "I wanna hold you longer," she says and pauses with a raise of her head. "I am so thirsty right now. I don't know where I got all that energy."

He smiles. "You draw your energy from me. You grow stronger the more I open-up to you here."

"I feel how tired my body is. I've gotta get something to drink."

"I know what that means," he says patting her lower back. "It's time for a bath. We need to get ready for our visitors. I'll get you some water or something."

"Sounds good." She looks up with an excited smile. "But we're gonna have a baby now, so no wine."

He shakes his head. "No, you're not pregnant yet."

"What do you mean?"

He explains, "Conception takes up to three days after making love. I gave you my seed when I poured my love into you, but your seed and my seed haven't converged yet. Instantly, I'll know when he's here."

She slumps back over his chest with a clap of her cheek over his skin. "That's just great," she says and huffs.

He chuckles and asks, "Because I'll know first?"

"Yeah," she says gazing at him. "I wanna be able to tell you at least once. Every woman practices how she'll tell her husband, and I haven't been able to do that. I wanna see your response."

"Baby, I'll be surprised. I will most likely be standing next to you. You'll most likely see my reaction. Believe me, I'll be excited, and probably start crying. We'll both be happy."

"But I even rehearsed my announcement in my head a few times. Sometimes, it's just not fair. You know everything before me."

He kisses her forehead. "I can taste salty hair. We need to get into a bath. We can talk about first dibs while we're in there."

In the Gamerin bath, Josephine sits between Lucius's legs and, like a hot tub, they take in aromatic vapors. "It's marvelous in here," she says. "This is much better than our garden tub in Texas."

"When we're done, we'll kiss Claire. She's already asleep, and the Bengaldoes are getting everything ready for glamming you up."

Josephine exhales. "I don't know how I'm gonna get used to this. Everybody is treating you and me like royalty."

"We are royalty. And you always have been, but never realized your royal roots."

"You know what I mean," she says. "You know things I've never thought of before." She raises her wet and shriveled fingers. "Like my wedding band for instance. I don't know how to use this thing. Everyone is gonna expect things of me. I don't know how to do this stuff."

He caresses her hand with his palm and kisses her ear. He says, "Then, let me show you." Lucius turns her wedding band for her to see Gamerilaye's stone. "This is the stone of your world now. You have a psychic ability and can open a portal."

She gasps excitedly. "We can go through one together?"

He shakes his head as he reminds her, "No, baby. I couldn't fit through, but you could slide through if one opened-up underneath you."

"Sounds scary," she says glancing back at him. "You broke my fall when we escaped. I could fall and hurt myself."

"Not really," he says redirecting her eyes toward her ring. "It depends on where you open the portal." He interlocks his fingers, resting their wedding bands against each other. "My ring is bigger, so the metals can open a slightly bigger portal. I might be able to fit," he says and raises his portal necklace from his chest. "But I have this one."

"How would I open one without hurting myself?"

He explains, "First, you shouldn't open one without thinking of what you're doing." He gestures back toward where the bed is beyond the bathing lounge. "You could open one above our bed, and land safely. Or over water. Sometimes, I could open one up, step through onto soil, and move the portal up and over me like a hula hoop."

She jokes. "I can beat you to the bed this way, like a race."

"That's what I'm talking about," he says and chuckles in her ear.

She says, "Sounds easy enough. I think of where I'm going, and rub the stone."

He says, "Yes, but you're forgetting one thing, the cornerstone. You must know the cornerstone to open a portal."

"How do I do that?" she asks.

"Who did I say is the cornerstone here?"

"You are," she answers.

He nods. "That's right. You can imagine me opening a portal, and me meeting you on the other side. When you close the hole, imagine me closing the opening with you. This method should work until your mind has mastered your ability to govern over the stones. You can go anywhere on Gamerilaye, but you must see the place in your mind."

She says, "But there's so many places I've never been."

"I'll show you. The more powerful you become, the more you can feel the soil. You will have a relationship with this world. Nothing will be hidden from you. Someday, you will even sense the atmosphere on the five moons, and so on, and so forth."

She admires the precious stones gleaming across her ring until, one humble stone catches her eye. "Is this sand?"

"It's limestone," he answers.

"Where does it go?" she asks.

"Earth," he says and quickly gulps. "*Um...don't—*"

"Jesus is the cornerstone there. I could imagine him opening—"

"Don't use that one. Please. I'll have to take that stone off."

She rips her hand away from his, and looks back with a stare toward him. She says, "I'm not gonna open one, Yuleshua Lucius Gamerin. You don't trust me? Why would you split up my wedding band? You gave this ring to me."

"I did." His stunned face melts away, and he exhales. "I sure did, and my word is law." He holds onto her. "Please, my love, it's dangerous, and I didn't know us leaving Earth would happen."

She rests her head on his collarbone and says, "You already told me it would place all my friends' lives in danger. I love them, and therefore, I will not go to see them without my Father's permission. I promise this."

He exhales over her and says, "Thank you. I know you keep your promises, and it means a lot to me."

She kisses under his chin. "Don't worry about such things." She sits up and stares at her pruning fingers. "I will tell you one thing though. The last time we were in a bath my fingers were like this, our water was getting cold. Remember? We were petting…" she freezes.

Immediately, they both remember someone who was left behind.

Josephine shrills with a deathly scream from her realization. "Leo!"

Lucius is stunned, finally discovering what's been missing the last couple of days.

She cries out to him, saying, "Lucius, he'll starve. He has no way out," and immediately sobs against him.

He tries comforting her, but he's speechless.

Josephine's words run into each other, "He was my parents' cat, and all I had. He trusts us and is probably wondering why you haven't taken care of him. He's gonna starve to death and wonder why we left him to die."

The past catches up to Lucius, and he feels powerless. He embraces her, saying, "I'm sorry I failed you. I'm sorry I failed him." They weep softly for a few moments before Lucius says, "We barely got out. There was nothing I could do." He strokes her cheek. "Baby, there was nothing I could do."

Twenty-Four

Gifts

Josephine sits in front of her vanity. Charony and Thimbette complete the finishing touches of Gamerin tattoos. The queen's skin glows above her gloved area. They carefully move her corkscrewed hair from the ink as it dries. Josephine's face appears downcast most of the time, and she manages only a small pseudo-smile when her helpers look at her reflection.

She says, "Thank you, Charony and Thimbette," and her expression once again is downcast, as she dabs subtle tears with the material of her glove from her pinky.

Lucius watches Josephine as he leans against the doorway of his terrace. He tries to push the heaviness that he carries away from his facial expressions. He copes by asking, "Are you okay?"

She nods, but says nothing.

He closes his eyes and experiences his heart as if it's ripped from his chest. "Be honest with me, yulee. I can sense you."

Josephine signals with her eyes, says, "Not in front of company," and looks at him. "There's nothing we can do. I promised."

Charony and Thimbette gaze at each other but keep their thoughts to themselves.

Lucius gasps when he reads their thoughts. "We're not quarreling. It's something else." He steps toward them and clarifies, "We remember that there was someone who was left behind during our attack."

Charony gulps and asks, "A royal was left?"

Lucius blurts, "No! Nothing like that. A servant of ours in a way, a pet. Leo was special to us, and we just now realized he's trapped inside a barrier. He can't fend for himself."

At this, Josephine breaks down sobbing. She hunches over, barely able to gasp for air. "He doesn't know he's gonna die. He probably thinks he's gonna be saved."

Lucius embraces her and falls to his knees, begging, "Please. Please don't cry. My love, I can't bear to watch you sad."

Charony and Thimbette cover their faces. Lucius's glossy eyes meet their gaze, and he asks, "Could you please excuse us? That will be all for this evening. Thank you."

They gather their supplies, and exit.

Lucius caresses Josephine with fumbling fingers. He says, "My yoshawn, let me make it up to you. I could give you anything, anything you desire. Do you want those blue jeans?"

She pulls away from him as she stands. Her shoulders nearly drag, like her cloak behind her as she steps toward the bed. "What could you give me? Nothing could replace him." She climbs into bed without looking at him so he can't see her tears dripping from her chin. She says, "I don't want jeans anymore. I don't want anything. Just let me sleep." She pulls the blankets over her and quietly whimpers to herself.

Lucius clenches his chest and says, "I'm so sorry." He swallows his tears and looks around. "They'll be here soon." He stands beside the bed, hoping she'll withdraw the blankets, but she doesn't. He says, "I'll place you into a sleep, a light one, so you can wake when you hear my voice after they show. You can greet them with me." He lays his hand over where her cheek is and whispers, "Sleep softly, my eternal love."

Lucius leaves his marriage quarters. He drags his feet while he does a swift perimeter watch like he would do on Earth. He passes by Claire's room and witnesses Artie sitting beside Claire's bed with his wings covering her for added protection.

Artie gazes back and asks, "My lord, are we to have a Gamerin prince soon?"

Lucius nods his head and says, "Within three days from now, she will conceive. I've given my seed, and the atmosphere agrees with her body. She'll be pregnant soon because I can feel the blessing making its way in her. I'll let you know."

Artie smiles and says, "We should throw feasts. Every world should celebrate."

But the king's face does not match Artie's enthusiasm. Artie asks, "What's wrong? You said she'd be pregnant soon. Why do you have an expression that is down?"

Lucius climbs his eyes across flooring, finally matching Artie's gaze. "She's sad, and so am I."

"How come? This is great news about to be upon us in this realm."

Lucius says, "It is, but we forgot someone. We all got out safely; however, we left Leo. Josephine and I know he'll starve to death. He had a platter of eggs and bacon." His eyes swim around the room. "You and I know that he has probably already eaten it."

"How awful. I wish there was something we could do," Artie says.

Lucius says, "I asked her if I could give her a gift, and even offered the blue jeans she wanted." His eyes sink again. "She declined. There's nothing I could give her to make up for what I can't do."

"If only there was a way you could get him back," Artie says and offers a quirky smile. "That would be a great gift." Artie looks over at Lucius. "You don't think...she'll try and—"

Lucius straightens. "She wouldn't."

"Isn't Earth's stone on her ring?"

"I...I spoke with her," he stutters, "she—"

"I'm sure it's fine if you spoke with her," Artie says. "I guess through time, we'll get through this. The attack was hard on everyone. She'll be safe here with the baby. Hopefully, she doesn't wear the stress of losing Leo."

Lucius gasps quietly. "I'll have to give her something to ease her stress. You're right, this is more serious than I thought. She can't be sad while carrying our son. We could lose him."

Artie says, "You could get her a koophoes from the harvester planet. They're kind of like a cat."

"Koophoes are wild and would never love to be treated like Leo lived. Leo's bloodline was tamed through generations of similar treatment to a dog." Lucius shakes his head. "Leo wanted her attention, and slept with Claire at night, comforting them both. A koophoes would run perimeter watch, constantly stressing itself out while guarding my family. It would be a terrible match. Josephine would know what I was doing, reminding her of what she's lost."

"I guess you're right," Artie says. "I'm only trying to help. What is my queen doing now?"

Lucius rubs his eyes. He says, "She's upset," and wipes his nose. "I can't give her everything, and she wouldn't even look at me. I placed her into a light sleep, so she'll wake in the next couple hours or with my psychic voice connection." Covering his face, he hunches forward. "She's sad because of me, and I can't fix this."

"My lord," Artie says and retracts his wings. He takes a step closer. "Please, send me on a mission. I can find a pet-like animal for her, for you. Don't let the troops see you like this, not after getting everything back."

Lucius makes eye contact with Artie and says, "I'm not sending you to Earth."

"I didn't say Earth," Artie replies.

"I just can't..." Lucius pauses, blocking his thoughts from an idea he just came up with. "Never mind. I know what I'll get her." He quickly wipes his eyes and smiles at Artie. "Everything's fine. It'll be okay." He takes a step from Claire's room, almost a hop in his step. "Continue guarding Claire. I'll get you after I meet with my new army."

Artie covers Claire with his wings and answers, "Yes, my lord. I'm glad to see you smiling."

Lucius enters his room. "She will too." He smiles toward his resting wife, and says, "I'll make this up to you. I can give you everything here." He raises his portal key, says, "Because I love you," and opens a doorway to Earth.

Several hundred feet above the Texan cabin, Lucius inspects the landscape for any enemy troops. He closes his eyes and listens to the atmosphere. He smells the recent rain and there is nothing for miles. "The retrieval will be quick," he says recognizing only animal life forms in the vicinity. "I'll make it like it never happened." He closes the portal from high in the air and opens a new doorway directly in the cabin's living room. Lucius steps through and glances back at Josephine with a subtle grin. "I love you, my yoshawn."

Lucius enters the cabin. Old food from two days earlier sends his nose curling with an exhale. The house is dark. The grandfather clock is shattered and leaning to one side, but manages to ding nine times as his eyes scan the area for Leo's vitals.

Then, he sees Leo asleep on his pillow in the master bedroom.

Lucius says, "He's just waiting on us, poor little guy," and jets upstairs. As he treads fast across the loft, he glances down at the open portal. "A couple more seconds."

Lucius presses the master bedroom door open completely, and Leo raises his fatigued body with heavy eyes.

Meow.

Lucius cradles him and answers, "I know they did," rubbing the side of his cheek against Leo's cheek. "Let's get you home."

Click.

The sound came from across the loft, followed by energy charging.

Lucius immediately recalls the tune. "No!" he pivots over to meet another person's gaze.

Blast. A dense surge of green and purple energy rips throughout Lucius's body causing Leo to fly from his hands. The burst throws Lucius back with a powerful impulse like balled-lightning into his chest. The back wall of the master bedroom with bookshelves, windows, and an old safe explode from the impact of his body. Lucius falls from the second story over a willow tree lining the house. The entire upper wall of the master room litters the wet ground outside, and Lucius's body lies on top of mud and debris.

Twenty-Five

Instincts

Lucius grimaces and tries peeling himself from the wreckage. The shooter jumps down from the second story and recharges his weapon. "I don't think so," the shooter says and aims for Lucius's back, hitting him again.

Lucius is thrown ten yards forward, landing face first with the wind knocked out of him. Dazed, Lucius hears the footsteps hiking across rubble to where he is.

"You know, uncle," the shooter says as he closes in. "My father told me you were stupid at times, but I didn't think you were this dumb." He clears his throat and says, "I'm Apollyon, the Gemini twin of Abaddon. You might have heard of me." Apollyon presses his foot onto Lucius's temple and pushes him into the mud. Apollyon says, "I'm your new lord. Bow to me."

Lucius tries moving his limbs with no success. "Augh." He draws whatever energy he can from the opened Gamerilaye doorway. "You," Lucius says as he struggles with speaking through a paralyzed tongue, "little bastard."

"Oh, my servant. Look, he speaks." Glinting silver catches Apollyon's attention from around Lucius's neck. "There it is. We finally got the missing piece we've been looking for." Apollyon rips the key from Lucius's neck. "I'll take that, if you don't mind, peasant." Apollyon places the amulet on and glances back toward the second story. He hollers up, "He's gaining power from the open doorway, Sam! Tell them to hurry up. Rueshta said it would take days to drain him with that gate open after regaining his full power."

Through the demolished opening of the master bedroom, Samstarsey nods. "Got it. I'm getting Devon, Cryline, and Hersone now." He flies from the loft toward the open portal in the living area. As he does, he escorts a small group of Nephilim through the other side. "Devon, Cryline, and

Hersone," Sam says and places his index finger over his lips. He transfers, *"Keep your mouths shut. I can't see through the walls here. We'll have to be quiet while that bedroom door is open. He might have an army nearby. Hurry because our prisoner regains strength from this open portal. Gamerilaye gives him strength during his draining phase."* Sam pauses and looks directly at the oval bed. *"Oh, wow. Hersone, grab her. The master will want Josephine as his prize. Be gentle with her though."*

Hersone wastes no time and activates a transportation device beside the bed. Hersone whispers, "That freak placed her into a sleep, and then opened a doorway?" Hersone levitates Josephine's body over the device. He touches her thighs as she floats onto the transportation stretcher. Hersone raises his voice excitedly. "This couldn't get any easier. Look at this gown. I bet she's not wearing underwear," and lifts her material some.

"Shut up," Sam says. He speaks psychically, *"We can only speak out loud to Apollyon through the portal doorways. If that harvester's here, he'll be listening to the air. Make yourself small. We still need to find his daughter before celebrating."*

Hersone straps Josephine to the levitating transporter, and glances over. *"I thought you said he can't see through walls here. He just burns things."*

Sam replies, *"That Gamerin wanna-be picks up heat signatures, moron. He was trained by a principality, and can sense how many people are in a room without entering."* Sam signals toward under the door. *"Artie can hear the source of heat leaving through cracks. He sees it and hears the atmosphere calling to him like a bird."* Sam eyes signal Devon and Cryline toward the door. He tells them, *"Keep an eye out, Artie might be guarding the girl, or doing surveillance. Do what you want with him, but get the Nephilim female."*

Devon winks. He pulls out a trident and activates the paralyzing electrical current. His vision is activated, and the two Nephilim sneak through the corridor on light feet. They leave the master chamber's door open.

Flutter escapes the room and flies through the crack of the doorway as quickly as he can.

⚜

On the other side of the portal, Apollyon leans over Lucius and says, "You killed my brother, Abaddon. I'm gonna enjoy you working for me, Gamerin traitor. You can call me master for now on."

Lucius grumbles, "I'll never work with you. I'm gonna kill you like your brother, so you'll have to shoot me again."

"Oh, I don't have to shoot you right now." Apollyon raises his brow. "And you will work for me. I'll be your son-in-law when she comes of age."

"You, bastard!" Lucius manages to pull his arm back. "Don't touch my baby!" He grunts.

"Nope," Apollyon says and hits Lucius's neck from behind, knocking him out. Apollyon speaks to Sam from Earth, saying, "I can't speak psychically from here, and my weapon is useless. Hurry up, Sam. He's gaining power from the open door…and he's pissed. This weapon is drained already."

Samstarsey stares between an open bedroom door and portal. "Shut up, Apollyon. The door is open," Sam says.

Artie shifts his eyes over as he rises from a chair beside Claire's bed. "Who's yelling out there?" He stands still and activates his heat sensors, making golden brown eyes flicker yellow. "Lucius?" he asks.

An odd feeling strikes him. The atmosphere isn't right and feels heavy all the sudden. Artie reads the signatures dispersing through the air in the hall. "Is that you, my lord?" he asks, but no answer follows what's getting closer. Flutter flies into the room and hovers nearly on Artie's face. "What is it, little guy?"

Flutter warns him psychically, and Artie realizes the intruders being described to him by the bird.

Artie tenses up. "Who's who?" he asks, pulling his wings from over Claire. "We're not doing this again." Artie activates a portal to the harvester planet. He scoops Claire up, and glances back in time to see two sets of eyes. Artie has never seen these two beings before, but they are definitely not angels.

Artie immediately flings Claire through the harvester portal into someone's arms. "Powtray, catch her!" he says, and she lands in the house servant's arms with Flutter barely escaping behind her.

Devon fires his weapon.

Boom, crack. Artie is shot, and the force of the weapon plants him into a wall. Driven like a trident through his shoulder and chest, the device sends a paralyzing shock through his body. Artie's wings are still displayed, and he's held hostage by three blades. "Augh," Artie moans. The device sends shockwaves, and each pulse paralyzes him more. He gazes toward the open portal. "No."

Devon and Cryline charge toward the opening. "Get her!" Devon yells out.

Artie releases his remaining psychic ability. As Cryline dives, the doorway disappears while he is still in the air. Cryline lands on Claire's bed. "I didn't get her."

As he draws a sword, Devon yells at Artie, "You piece of lushaine," and pierces Artie's other shoulder and wing.

"God," Artie hollers out, "help me." He soon loses consciousness with the final pulses of the weapon stripping his abilities completely.

"Quickly!" Devon screams, "The matchstick just called an alarm! That stupid bird warned him. Move, move!"

"Lushaine! Who set up that little bird as a warning?" Sam hollers out, "They're coming! Apollyon, transport our prisoners now. They sounded an alarm."

Apollyon grabs Lucius's neck, rips his limp body from the Texas soil, says, "I guess you're going with me now, pet," and transports both of them to the vessel.

In Claire's room on Gamerilaye, Cryline jumps from the bed and retreats hastily before the troops arrive. "Let's go, Devon. We don't know where the guardian sent her."

"The guardian does." Devon pulls Artie from the wall and blood gushes from his wounds. Devon says, "If I can't bring the little prize as ordered, I guess you'll do," and drags Artie's paralyzed body, leaving trails of blood on the tiles.

Metal scratches the flooring from Artie's weapons as they enter the chambers.

Signaling Devon and Cryline to move faster, Samstarsey rolls his arms, and says, "Hurry. They'll waste no time in responding. You get caught, Devon, you die. What are you bringing him for? Leave this piece of trash."

"I didn't get the girl, Sam. Some stupid bird ratted us out," Devon says. "This guardian will know where he sent her. I got his portal key, and we can probe his mind when he wakes."

Immediately, angels, hundreds of them with swords drawn, appear throughout the Gamerin palace.

Artie is swiftly dragged through the portal to Earth. There, Devon says, "Lushaine. We gotta go, Sam." in Josephine's old cabin, Devon latches onto Artie.

Deasja runs into the master chambers and glances into the portal. He sees Josephine's living room as Artie and Devon transport before his eyes. "Artie, no!"

Samstarsey winks back at Deasja and flips his middle finger. Then, he closes the gateway behind him.

"The Nephilim transporters have them." Deasja hollers, "Prepare for battle on Earth!"

Twenty-Six

Commander Albercase

Hundreds of portal doorways open. Soldiers spill through onto the vacant land with glinting blades ready for a fight. Deasja and Dextorus take aim for anything that moves with a mad search around them, but there's no movement.

Dextorus runs from room to room. "They demolished the master bedroom. Lock onto the ship, Deasja. Go out there and shoot them down!"

Deasja flies through the walls as he exits. He lands hard on his feet in the driveway and quickly takes aim toward the sky with an electromagnetic pulse device. Fixating his eyes toward a cloudy sky, he's panting and says, "It's activated. It's cloudy." Deasja shakes the device. "Come on, scan for Papa. Find that ship," he says scoping the air in several locations above him.

Running out the back door, Dextorus calls out, "Did you get them?"

Deasja answers, "It's picking up planes, but…" and finally reality dawns on Deasja. "They're not here," he whispers. "It's not registering a craft anywhere, Dex." Deasja lowers his weapon and says, "They're not in the atmosphere."

"They must be. Scan for satellites, anything." Dextorus is breathless. He runs toward several angels coming out of the barn. "Soldiers, report."

A soldier exits the cedar shed, saying, "Not here, Dex. There's nothing."

"They couldn't have gotten far." Dextorus commands, "Check the perimeter for Nephilim holes. They—"

"They're gone, Commander," Deasja interrupts. His eyes never leave the sky. "They got away. They never entered the atmosphere. This device has picked up three planes, and sixty-two satellites. It's working. They're just not here."

Dextorus screams, "They couldn't have got away! It's the clouds. Keep scanning. Increase the ultraviolet sensors, maybe they're cloaked."

"The device is set to sensitive, Commander. They're not here." Deasja walks around the house from the driveway. "We should call the northern commander. You must see what information he has."

"We can't miss this window." Grinding his teeth, Dextorus takes several steps and says, "Deasja, transporters must have gold and quartz in the ground to transport from space." He glances up and says, "Aim your weapon and shoot them down."

Deasja speaks psychically, *They're not there, Dex. I scanned the area. It picked up birds, planes, and satellites, but no unregistered vessels.*

"That doesn't make sense." Dextorus replies. "How can Nephilim transporters move if they're not even in the atmosphere. They need gold and quartz, and this land was specifically chosen because of the lack of those elements." He activates a band on his arm, saying, "Orlando, report. Is there anyone left behind at the palace?" He forgets to use a calm voice, and bellows, "Report, soldier, hurry up!"

Deasja tells him, "Calm down, Commander. We're all in shock. They can't think clearly if you're yelling at them."

A transmission echoes through from Orlando. "Yes, sir. I'm checking the rooms now."

"Is Anyone left behind, Orlando?" Dextorus asks. "Somebody has to know what's going on."

Several soldiers crowd around, but keep a measured distance from a steaming Jett commander who is still biting his lip.

Orlando answers, "Affirmative, Dex. Two females were still sleeping. I just woke them."

Hearty exhales respond to the report.

"Silence," Dextorus says and elevates a palm. "Shush." He asks, "What are their names, Orlando?" and holds his breath.

A five second radio silence follows, feeling like it lasts an eternity from the growing tension.

"Their names are Charony and Thimbette, sir," Orlando answered. "They're called Bengaldoes, maidservants to the royal family. They don't know what's happened, and they're checking the rooms with me."

There's a pause.

"Aw man," Orlando responds with the Bengaldoe's wailing as background noise. "You guys, we found where the trail leads. There's blood everywhere in the princess's room. I don't know if you can hear these creatures screaming or not, but it's very high-pitched."

Dextorus closes his eyes. "I know them, Orlando. Escort Charony and her sister out of the room. Counsel them. Give them peace. Have Wheatley perform a DNA sample on the blood. We're still locking their location. The ship wasn't here. Nobody's here."

Orlando asks, "Wait, you didn't find them over there? That was the cabin's living room Deasja and I saw before that bastard closed the door. Did they set up another area...a look-alike to throw us off?"

"That's not helping, Orlando. We need to know who all that blood belongs to." Dextorus gulps tears of anger before saying, "Please standby," and ends the transmission.

Deasja and Dextorus stare at each other, and silence engulfs the thickness of the humidity.

"What if it's another area?" Dextorus asks.

Deasja shakes his head. "There's blood on that living room floor. I saw Artie, Commander. It's his blood. The abduction was here. They were here."

Another angel walks up and says, "Jackson has confirmed, Commander. Jackson is scanning the living room. They were here. There's a fresh scent in the air of pheromone residue pumped full of adrenaline."

All transmitters go silent after the news.

Deasja says, "It's your call, Dex."

Dex sneers, and says, "Commander Albercase from the north, answer me. We're in need of your assistance. Make haste."

Moments later, a large portal opens with another massive army greeting them. Commander Albercase walks through. He's as tall as Dextorus and has dreadlocks nearly two feet long. He nods and says, "Commander Dex," and glances over, "Commander Deasja." He looks at Dex before saying, "Ironically, I was on my way here. It's why I gathered my army. I'm surprised by your call."

Deasja asks, "What do you mean? The attack just happened. You knew of this and didn't tell us?"

"Attack? I'm not speaking of an attack." Commander Albercase's brow wrinkles. "That explains a lot. My army and I have been monitoring elements in the soil. Besides the mining of human children there, large amounts of gold and quartz have gone missing in Alaska."

Dextorus takes a step back. "No."

Albercase points toward an angel who is actively using a device over the soil. Albercase says, "Reggie's scanning now."

Dextorus glances over, monitoring Reggie using an elemental sweeper. "Do you think they—"

"Affirmative," Reggie interrupts. "Sorry, Commanders, but the influx is here. It's picking up positive increases of gold and quartz under the sod, a massive amount." He presses his foot down and says, "The sod has been recently disturbed. This is it."

Commander Albercase says, "I was going to inform you of the results when I had them," and points toward a time band, "which would have been right now. When we noticed the exchange, we placed transmitters over satellites out of camera view, trying to keep an eye on the Gamerin vessel when it gets close to the atmosphere. There's been no movement for two days besides a few blips over northern scanners. We figured it was transporters removing the elements from soil rich areas."

"You didn't think to tell me of your suspicions?" Dextorus snaps. "I have personal investments in this kid."

"If you're speaking of Lucius, he's hardly a kid." Commander Albercase stands his ground. "Remember your place when speaking in front of my army."

Dextorus says, "I have commanded over the Gamerin principality as my soldier. Your silence might have cost me everything. You're supposed to report to me."

Commander Albercase lifts a brow and asks, "Is that so?"

"Dex," Deasja yaps out, placing a hand on his commander's shoulder to calm him. "This isn't helping. Peace, brother. Let him finish his report." Deasja signals toward Albercase and says, "Sorry, we're all a little rattled from the shock. We just lost a soldier, and can't find the Gamerin. There's been another attack. We might've lost a window."

Commander Albercase nods and says, "It's okay, Deasja, let Jett Commander Dextorus get it out. He has a right to be angry based solely on that understanding." He stares at Dextorus. "But in my defense, I didn't think to tell you personally over a hunch, sending you into dangerous territory after losing two hundred and forty-five of your own soldiers two days ago while we were meeting." He speaks with his hands and continues. "There was no one here after the last surprise attack. Lucius was safe on his planet. I didn't think it necessary to lose anyone else here before you were done gathering your new army for a safe zone on Gamerilaye."

"That's not for you to decide," Dextorus says. "That information could have saved more people than you know."

Albercase straightens his back. "Commander, in front of my army let me give my defense openly, since you openly expressed yours, forgetting we're on the same team. I know what it's like to lose soldiers, and constantly fail missions. In case you have forgotten, you're not over my command up north, Dex," he says and points at his exhausted army before saying, "We deal with multiple, tortured deaths of my own every few months. They're chained up, and watch those women violated in front of them. My soldiers are like family to me too, so excuse me for not getting the word out to over one hundred forty-two million commanders from Jett currently guarding billions of children. You're not the only one that's special. We're all affected personally by the Gamerin curse."

Dex answers, "You have to report your suspicions and findings, Commander Albercase."

"Dex, I informed the General of what my suspicions were, and what I was doing about it. I know how to command my army. Maybe, if He didn't speak with you about my suspicions, you should perhaps speak with Him concerning where your level of command ends, and mine begins." He exhales. "I am truly sorry you lost your window. I told you I was going to inform you."

Dextorus rolls his lips inward and inhales slowly. Making eye contact, he says "Please excuse my previous words. I forgot myself, Commander Albercase." He continues to look forward without blinking. "I apologize for coming off as rude. We are on the same team."

"It's all right." Albercase nudges his chin forward. "I've never known you to lose your cool. This behavior is out of character for you."

"I'm not finished," Dextorus says. "I apologize to all. Let me introduce myself fully, and give my full report of who I really am, but first..." Dex says and gazes around to gather attention. He raises his voice and says, "I was informed that this occurrence was already foreseen. We had a small doorway to act. I didn't expect to lose all of them."

"All of whom?" Albercase asks. "His wife too? Those Nephilim and Gamerin aboard that ship are barren. I personally poisoned them genetically."

"No," Deasja interrupts. "There's more to what's been going on here for the past six years. Lucius was sent here to guard Josephine. This, you know. The past six years was a set up in order to make it to our window that Dex is telling you about. We need to get on that ship."

"What are you talking about?" Albercase asks. "What set up? What window?"

Deasja says, "Firstly, If Baàl has managed to capture a Gamerin daughter, they can breed."

"A daughter?" Albercase's eyes open wide. "Lucius has a child here on Earth?"

"Yes," Deasja replies. "A Gamerin female."

Several soldiers gasp.

"Oh, heck no," Reggie mutters. "That would've been some great information to have."

Deasja continues telling them, "If Baàl managed to capture Josephine, an innocent woman who might be pregnant with Lucius's second-in-command—"

Moans from the crowd escalate, making it difficult for Deasja to speak.

Now, Deasja raises his voice. "Baàlsarideem will destroy that child before he draws his first breath, therefore, maintaining his abilities. Lucius was supposed to have a son, and strip Baàl's power upon that boy's first breath. He will no doubt abort that child from her the moment he finds out."

"For the love of God." Albercase falls to his knees. "God help us. We could've overthrown him."

Deasja says, "Our enemy will become stronger, and increase their numbers, as soon as Claire comes of age. She's the daughter of a principality. Her children will be full-blooded Nephilim, and harbor grand abilities."

Commander Albercase stands upright and says, "I had no idea Lucius had family. I thought he was barren."

Dextorus nods. "His fertility was a secret. Everything about him is. Like you said, your soldiers die often, and that information would have leaked out a long time ago." He takes in a deep breath, fully exhaling before saying, "Now, for my introductory," he says. "You all know me as a Jett commander, but I am Dextorus, a secret servant to the high Council…and the throne. I answer strictly to the General, and have been placed in special care regarding the Gamerin king for thousands of years. My mission is so secret that even I have no idea what it all entails, but this news is tragic. If the females are lost to us, then we've lost our window to take down that army, and release his faithful brothers from captivity."

"A secret servant to the high Council? I'm sorry for my delay." Albercase says, "You're right, I should've spoken to you. If I would've known—"

"Worse would've happened if you had known anything of my mission. I couldn't divulge that information with this threat, and you should block your minds from this knowledge. Although, I don't know how it would fix, or hinder anything at this point." Dextorus says, "It's not your fault, and I'm sorry I forgot myself when greeting you for report." Dextorus walks several steps away to take a deep breath.

Deasja speaks up. "Somebody must have found out." His eyes scan Albercase's army. "Is anyone here, someone who recently guarded this household?"

Albercase's expression melts away as he answers, "Yes."

Dextorus turns back. "Where is he?"

Albercase answers, "He died. He was tortured for days aboard that vessel, and sent home without a body a few days ago. His spirit now rests on Oobadoave. It was right before the first attack. I thought you knew this."

"I don't know all things," Dextorus replies.

"What about our informant," Albercase asks. "Vincentine is able to give us messages all the time. He'll inform us of a way."

Staring off into nothing, Dextorus says, "He's a slave aboard that vessel. He has no power. They've shot all the Nephilim slaves with that weapon, draining every last resource we had. Slaves are nothing but lab rats up there. You and I know, Commander, our informant needs time to work any miracle in those conditions."

Commander Albercase nods. "I understand. I'm sorry we missed our window. We'll have to make plans for destroying all of them. We'll have to wipe them out. A total recall—women and children too."

"No, they're innocent," Deasja interrupts. "It's not over yet. I haven't received those orders. We're to protect them, not kill them because of our failure."

Albercase says, "This can't continue, Commander, and if all is lost…"

"No!" Deasja raises his hands and says, "I'm not giving up. Lucius wouldn't give up."

Dextorus says, "Deasja's right. I need Yuleshua Gamerin alive. I've been ordered to keep him and any captives alive, and if he's aboard that vessel and still breathing, then everyone aboard that vessel lives."

Deasja faces his army and says, "Everybody ordained for Gamerilaye, leave this land, and wait for orders at the palace. We're still fighting, and we can do nothing moping here. Secure your keys, and stand guard in your stations as ordered by the General."

Commander Albercase says, "You're right, Commander Deasja, we're still fighting. The war isn't over yet."

"I don't want to hear the words total recall ever again, Commander," Deasja says. "Thank you for your report, and send any messages our way immediately. Do not hold any information back, especially, from our informant, Vincentine, aboard that vessel. He might be a slave, but he's an ally, and our General uses those most unlikely to do impossible things."

"Amen," Jackson hollers.

"Of course," Commander Albercase says. "I'll inform you of any news. This isn't over."

"Not until the trumpet sounds," Deasja says. "It's not a total recall like the flood."

⸻ ❧ ⸻

One by one, soldiers give report and exit to where their stations are on Gamerilaye. Still on Earth, Deasja calls out to Dextorus, "It's too late here, Commander. They got what they wanted, and we were assigned to Gamerilaye. We should leave now. All our soldiers are waiting on the other side."

"What were they doing?" Dex glances over the landscape. "Why was a portal opened from Gamerilaye?"

Deasja gestures toward Leo climbing down from a Willow tree. "I think I know why."

Watching a cream-colored tabby running down a forested trail, Dextorus's shoulders plummet as he says, "Of course, the cat. There's not one thing us guys wouldn't do for the girl we adore." He pivots back. "We're all fools in love, I guess." Dex presses down any feeling, causing his face to go flat. "I hate this war. It takes everything."

"Not everything. Come on, Commander, we can talk about love and war later." Deasja opens a portal. "Let's stand our posts in case we get word. We need to have clear minds. We know one of our soldiers is hurt, two females are missing, and I have no idea what's going on with Lucius."

Dextorus points toward the broken wall and says, "Isn't it obvious. They shot him with that weapon. He's powerless again, making us have no access to a cornerstone on that ship."

Deasja grunts while walking through the portal, saying, "All of this is premature negativity I keep hearing. You're starting to bum me out. Lucius is right. You need a sense of humor."

"What I need…" Dex pauses before saying, "I need Lucius to survive, Deasja. Only a principality can get back what I've lost."

Deasja signals for Dextorus to follow and says, "Come on, Commander. We knew this was going to happen sooner or later. Maybe this wasn't the window for us to move, and there's another chance. It doesn't matter which one it was because the war is always inconvenient, and definitely complicates things."

Dextorus shakes his head and says, "He has plans within plans. Perhaps, not all is lost in this. Surely He knew." He raises his shoulders back and exhales. "Who can understand the ways of the Almighty?"

Twenty-Seven

Waking Amongst Enemies

Searing pain shoots through Lucius's chest and back as he slowly awakens to yelping screams beside him. His blurry eyes gaze upward toward one of the two lights of the room. The light is dim overhead, for it is deep within a cylindrical hole. He sees the chains of strong metals staring back at him. His hands are bound by them above his head, keeping him hanging by his wrists with his toes barely brushing the flooring beneath. Lucius stretches his toes and touches the cool, wet floor. He's barefoot, and he feels water dripping off him and onto the floor. He's still dazed from his concussion. Screaming, followed by laughter, wakes him a little more.

Lucius turns his double vision over, and he witnesses sparks, followed by more screaming.

Devon yanks a few feathers out of his victim and says, "I've never seen this before. It's like matchsticks," ripping out a few more feathers for his enjoyment.

Artie yelps.

"Stop it!" Lucius kicks at Devon, saying, "Leave him alone!" Devon steps away and is barely brushed by Lucius's foot. Lucius squeezes his eyes closed for several blinks and tries to wipe away the blurriness by rubbing his head against his upper arm. "Stop touching him."

"You call that a kick?" Cryline asks. "He's our prisoner." Cryline points with his nose toward chains that hold Lucius in place, "and so are you."

"Come closer, so I can see your faces," Lucius says. "I'll show you what a real kick feels like, bastard."

"Lots of words coming from you when you're all chained up with nothing but threats," Devon replies. "You're draining faster with each movement. By all means, keep trying."

Cryline slaps Devon's arm. "Don't tell him that. Just let him suffer and find out on his own. It's more fun this way. Let him watch his slave die with no way to save him."

Devon sneers and says, "I was getting bored anyway waiting for you to wake up. It's been five minutes since pouring that water on you in the first place." He grabs the handle sticking out from Artie's injured side, and twists.

Artie yells.

Lucius hollers, "Stop, I'm awake. I'm awake. What do you want? Stop hurting him."

"Nothing." Devon smirks. "I was told to fetch the master when you awaken," he says and kicks Artie into a swing from his chains.

Artie whimpers as his body swings in and out of faded light.

"Go get your master," Lucius says.

"Oh, you don't like that?" Cryline asks, grabbing a handful of brown and red feathers.

Lucius screams, "Stop touching him!"

Cryline pulls the feathers out, sending a line of sparks that follow the air as he drops them to the floor.

Artie groans.

Lucius shouts, "You're killing him! He hasn't done anything."

Cryline walks into the light where Lucius can see him. "He's done plenty. You think we don't get punished for failure?" Cryline takes a step back and says, "I'll fetch my master."

Devon follows behind Cryline and says to Lucius, "You can just watch him die. He's worthless to us anyway."

As they leave, Lucius sees a slim crack in the door close behind them. Realizing that they're gone, Lucius quickly raises his feet and stops Artie from swinging. He twists Artie around, and his breath falls from what he sees. "Oh no, Artie."

Blades and nails have been driven through his skin, feathers ripped out, causing bald spots, and Artie's too weak to open his swollen eyes.

"Artie, answer me." Lucius catches himself from crying and asks, "What about Claire?"

"Pow-Powtray. Safe."

"I'm so sorry, Artie." He stretches his feet out and tries healing Artie. He feels what power he has draining extremely fast. "I won't be able to heal you like this," and he cries as his feet fall back down to dangle once again from exhaustion.

Artie's head swings back, and his jaw hangs loose. "It's okay. My time…" he says struggling for breath. "I know it. Save your power. I'm not worth it."

"Yes, you are." Lucius feels something over his left ring finger, his wedding band. "My friend," Lucius says and opens a small portal over the healing waters in Artie's bathing lounge on the harvester planet. "This is not your time." Starting from under Artie's feet, Lucius's power drains quickly, as he psychically raises the portal over Artie like a tight shirt. As soon as Artie's hands are through, Lucius closes the portal, snapping the chains that bounded him. Lucius stares at the empty chains and knows that Artie is safely on his world with Claire.

Lucius exhales. "Thank you, God."

Clap…clap…clap.

Slow, applauding sounds ring out from the blackness of the room. He couldn't hear anyone or feel anyone, but someone is there. Lucius has a sinking feeling and says, "Lushaine." He swallows hard.

"Wow," a voice like a gong in Lucius's ears breaks through the clapping as Baàlsarideem enters the light where Lucius hangs. Baàlsarideem is very similar in appearance, except his hair is nearly black from hiding in the dark for so long. Baàlsarideem stops his slow claps and says, "Yuleshua, has it been ten thousand years, and you still make mistakes for unworthy people? How many times have I told you that he's just a slave?"

"Baàl," Lucius says as his eyes seal shut, "it was a set up."

"Of course. My servants know what to say. Apparently, you think I'm stupid to leave you alone in a room with your favorite servant, no matter how close to death he is." Baàlsarideem steps closer. "I had to see one last time how you treated him over your family. I knew you wouldn't be able to help yourself if you had any energy left. A Gamerin always has a way, and if you had one, you'd waste it on that harvester servant you always favored over everyone else."

When Lucius says nothing, Baàlsarideem cocks his face sideways.

"Stop," Lucius says. "Quit probing, Baàl, I know what you're doing. I can feel it."

"I'm reading your mind, and you can't stop me this time. I'm the lord on this vessel, the cornerstone." Sighing, Baàlsarideem sarcastically says, "Aw, you're sad you have no more energy to save yourself with that little portal you had stashed away." Baàlsarideem opens his palm out in front of him and psychically pulls the Gamerin metal from Lucius's finger.

"Augh." Lucius squirms. "It won't work. Whatever you're doing won't work."

Baàlsarideem takes a few steps back and stares down at his palm, saying, "This is a pretty nifty device you came up with. I'm surprised Artorus could fit in it with it all warped like this. Now, let's see what—"

"Quit reading my mind," Lucius snaps.

"Oh, you don't order me around, Yuleshua. Not anymore. I'm no second best here." Baàlsarideem chuckles. "You're trying to block your mind, but it's not going to save where you sent Artorus." He clenches a firm grip over Lucius's neck. "I see everything here. Nothing is hidden."

Lucius grunts, finding it hard to breathe with Baàlsarideem squeezing his neck and trying to search for the location of Artie's planet.

"Now, where did you send him?" Baàlsarideem asks and concentrates. "You can't block this from me. I'm going to find your daughter."

"You won't find them." Lucius grimaces. "It's Trinitarian country. I have no name for the world, and I can't interpret the knowledge to others. It's my Father's language."

"Maybe not," Baàlsarideem says and let's go with a yank of Lucius's head forward. "Are you hiding any other keys, a matching belt perhaps?" His palm opens and uses telekinesis for gathering any loose Gamerin metal. Nothing moves. Baàlsarideem says, "I might not have access to your interdimensional spaces, but I have my ways. I'll find out where your daughter is when you start cooperating."

"I'm not opening anything or cooperating with you, bastard," Lucius says.

Baàlsarideem clicks his tongue against his pallet. He shakes his head and says, "Oh dear, what a potty mouth we've developed. Is that any way to speak with your little brother?"

"You're a fatherless bastard, and no brother of mine."

Baàlsarideem frowns as he asks, "Were we not friends for fifty-eight thousand years? Did you not used to call me Baàl, your dearest friend? Was I not charged over your entire army and governed to protect our people?"

"Don't make me puke." Lucius rolls his eyes. "I only knew the Baàl who served the Trinity. I don't know any damned bastards. I never charged any fallen with any power."

Baàlsarideem smiles, acting offended with a hand to his chest, saying, "Don't make me cry by your mean words." He chuckles. "I've been controlling the whole Gamerin army for ten thousand years. I've been their king."

"Not all of them answer to you. I know that they are in captivity and hate you."

Baàlsarideem replies, "The ones that matter answer to me. My faithful brothers, the smart ones."

"Where did you put them, Baàl? Where are my brothers? Give me my brothers back."

"I imprisoned them, like you said. That's all you need to know. They're safe." He points at Lucius and says, "They're safe because someday they'll bow down to me. You will too, the way it should've been."

Lucius says, "I'll never bow to you, coward."

"Blah, blah, blah," Baàlsarideem says. "Just words from a prisoner right now. You have no idea what plans I have."

Lucius says, "You're just gonna have to kill me."

"Wow." Baàlsarideem again claps sarcastically. "You're very dramatic. I don't think so," he says and his expression flattens before saying, "You're going to wish for death like all the others that have been held in those chains above you. I'm not letting you out that easy. I had to suffer, Yuleshua, while you left us to rot."

"Blah, blah." Lucius chuckles. "Blah. You're so getting judged for this. I've probably thought of six different ways I'm gonna kill you."

Baàlsarideem huffs with a slight chuckle of his own. "And how do you think that's going to happen? You'll never be strong again. I feel your powers draining throughout your body, wiped from your DNA, and so do you. The weapon would've worked the first time if the Mangoram wouldn't have betrayed me." He scratches his chin and says, "I thought you died."

"I did. In front of my wife, thanks very much, inconsiderate jerk."

"How did you come back?" Baàlsarideem asks.

"I died in my brother's arms."

"Who? That stupid harvester? What did he do? He has no power."

Lucius shakes his head and answers, "Yeshua himself rescued me. Don't forget who you are talking to. I was resurrected, but Artie's my brother as well. He has skills."

Baàlsarideem rolls his eyes and says, "Shut up about that stupid harvester." He pretends to gag. Baàlsarideem stops and thinks quietly to himself. He nibbles on his bottom lip for a moment. A moment later, says, "That's some plan that they had. They threw me off for a while, but I have my ways."

"Your way sucks."

"I have to tell you," Baàlsarideem answers as he shakes his head before saying, "you speak differently. Before, I would've had you crying by now from how sensitive you were. Are you sure you're not willing to work with me? I never used to hear you speak with sarcasm." Baàlsarideem wiggles his fingers like tiny wings. "You always lived in a la la land. You lived your life thinking everything would be given to you, and you didn't have to pay for your crimes."

"What crimes!" Lucius shouts. "I never did anything to you. You turned your back, not me. You abandoned me!"

Baàlsarideem walks forward and screams into Lucius's face. "What about my son! Have you forgotten you killed my boy, Abaddon?"

Lucius pulls on the chains, screaming, "Get out of my face!" and spits.

Baàl punches Lucius, bloodying his lip and nose. "One time," Baàlsarideem says. He pauses as he raises his index finger and presses it into Lucius's face. "That's the last time you disrespect me."

Lucius shakes a dizzying head and tries focusing through disorientation. He grunts with an overwhelming headache that pulls at his gut, making him want to puke. Not only does his stomach churn, but also his ears are ringing from the punch to his skull. His nose pours blood, and he tastes the iron as it runs off his lips and chin. "I'm gonna throw up," Lucius says and tries swallowing down his saliva.

"Yeah," Baàlsarideem says. "The injuries will get a lot worse the more tired you get. I'm basically a principality aboard this vessel. You'd better join me before your strength is completely gone from your DNA. Once the power is gone, your genetic structure will continue to replicate, but the ability to process power will be eliminated, like a blind man trying to read a flat road map. Only I will be able to wield your DNA. I can still pull you out of this deterioration. I have that power to save you if you would only give me permission."

"You have nothing. You're nothing, just lies, Baàl. You have no authority over me and no permission. Again, you have nothing from me."

"Nothing?" Baàlsarideem walks around the room and turns on the lights. "I have every motivation for you to join me," he says and continues to walk toward the center of the room.

"What's that?" Lucius asks.

Baàlsarideem stands beside a stone altar that is fitted with a dark satin sheet on a mattress. The stone alter sits soundless in the center of the room. Baàlsarideem stands in front of it, and leans back as if resting as he flashes a crooked smile.

"What are you doing?" Lucius asks. "What are you planning?" He yanks at his chains.

Baàlsarideem gestures up and says, "You can't break those bonds. They don't answer to you." Baàlsarideem pretends to yawn and says, "I grow tired of these games, Yuleshua. I'm offering you to work alongside me. I'm willing to forgive you for the murder of my son. Join me. Let's be brothers again."

Lucius fights hyperventilation as he stares at the alter and replies, "I don't follow you. I don't follow any damned."

"You're not listening, Yuleshua, as always. We can open a portal for this entire ship to pass through safely. We can be together again. I can release our brothers when we are home."

"You need the cornerstone's permission to create a large enough portal like that for you to enter through. I'm not giving that permission to you. My permission will never be given to a fallen so that a curse will carry into my realm."

Baàlsarideem shakes his head and says, "I knew you'd fight." He pauses for a moment and nods. "I can find where the special chromosome is hidden in your blood for my plan. I can make it like the way Dugand and Moarscii exchanged inheritance. I can replicate that arrangement without your word. I found a way." Baàlsarideem stands up and holds a hand out, begging, "Work with me. Make it easy on yourself. I—"

"What are you talking about Baàl? I'll never help you out of this place. You're gonna rot here, and if you kill me, I'm coming back to destroy you with an entire Oobadoave army."

"Only threats," Baàl says and sidesteps. "Here I am, offering you suns and moons, and you're still resisting."

Lucius says, "It is written, Baàl, that Heaven and Earth will pass away, but the word of God will never pass away. You offer nothing. You own nothing. You are the one with only words."

Baàlsarideem stares at Lucius and says, "Is that fact? Well, I'm not going to kill you. I'm going to imprison you for eternity since you won't join me, just like your worthless brothers. If you join me, they will too. You can free them all. I'll let you live freely among your people."

"You're a worthless liar. I'll never turn my back on my Father like you did. He gave me authority to rule over that realm. I'm the first, and you must submit to—"

"Blah...blah..." Baàlsarideem says slowly. His eyes glance up sluggishly as if he's bored. He says, "Blah. You bore me to tears, Yuleshua. This obviously isn't working. Time to bring something in that will."

"Torture me, Baàl, and I still won't work with you. I will not suffer the lives of billions in my realm."

Baàlsarideem flicks a brow and says, "Sure." He hollers toward the door, "Bring in my new bride."

"The master calls for his bride!" a voice yells down the hall.

Baàlsarideem meets Lucius's gaze when the order is called. He says, "You'll wish you would've reconsidered."

Twenty-Eight

Stolen Bride

Voices from out in the hall call out, "Get the Master's bride."

Lucius tenses up and asks, "Baàl, what are you doing? What bride?"

Baàlsarideem folds his fingers together. He rests his hands over his thighs and leans his back against the altar. "I know your weaknesses, Yuleshua. Don't forget where you released me, causing me to do what you call, 'falling.'"

"Baàl, please." Lucius gulps. "Don't."

"I know what you've gone through. I know what you're willing to go through." Baàlsarideem's voice plays like a gentle tune of a violin as he says, "I fell in love almost instantly when I saw a woman for the first time. A new race, I thought…"

"Please, don't do this."

"…a race almost identical to mine, but weaker, much weaker. I felt how fragile she was in my arms, gentle, soft, and how much she needed me. I had to take care of her." He slaps at his chest. "Was I wrong to give in to what felt natural for me? Did I have to have permission when she's what my body screamed for?"

Lucius starts hyperventilating, panting, and pulling on his chains. "You can't do this."

"Oh, Yuleshua," Baàlsarideem continues. "I know what it's like to have your heart ripped out of your chest, to love a woman doomed to wither in front of you. I was willing to endure the pain alongside her…knowing I still had a key to get back home. When the time came for you to call us back, my plan was to place her in healing waters every day in the palace on Gamerilaye." He pounds on his chest and screams, "But what I wasn't willing to do was to be punished from ever going home for taking her as my wife. I watched our sons living their lives as mules because they couldn't procreate. Our sons were powerful, nearly worshiped by those people."

Lucius hollers back, "You should've never had wives or sons!"

"You sound like them, the guardians to the people of Earth." He lowers his voice, "Humans adored us, but they were weak."

Lucius gasps and asks, "What are you talking about?"

Baàlsarideem says, "Humans weren't worth saving anymore."

"Baàl," Lucius says. "If you recant, there might still be a chance for you. My blood was spilled as a sacrifice. You might still be able to go home. You're not judged yet."

"No," Baàlsarideem says. "I don't answer to you or the Trinity anymore. Half of who I was, was ripped from my arms."

Lucius is stone faced as he asks, "What happened to you?"

"I came up with a plan."

Lucius asks, "What plan?"

"It's simple. I was one of the strongest second-in-commands in existence. After my key was taken, I realized I could get home another way. I only had to wait, but the entire world turned. With only a small amount of technology, a baby race of instant followers and takers, fell apart within a couple thousand years. I had nothing to do with it."

"Do you tell yourself lying lullabies to go to sleep at night?" Lucius chuckles. "There are holes in your story, big gaping ones."

"Holes?"

"You're hiding something and not doing it very well."

Baàlsarideem folds his arms. "The truth, Yuleshua, is that no matter how hard I tried, all our wives would've died. My followers, all our sons—"

"Your followers? You weren't a king on that world. I tasked you to serve." Lucius licks the blood from his bottom lip and says, "This is starting to make sense. I can see what you were really planning and why you were so terrified of judgement."

Baàlsarideem ignores Lucius's comment with a wince. "All I had worked for was wiped away. I wasn't told about the flood. Imagine my surprise when everything I had built was gone, and all I had left was what was on this ship. I was stuck. I needed you to rescue us, but you never showed."

Lucius says, "You should've trusted God. You wouldn't have been alone if you trusted in Him. What could I have done outside of my jurisdiction? You were supposed to help them, not rule over them."

Baàl raises a hand. "What was I to do, Yuleshua? He wasn't listening to the humans anymore. I had to save my wife and children. My wife became frail. She was sick beyond what I could fix." He exhales with his arms opening as he says, "It wasn't just my wife, Sonja-Cain, but all our wives were dying. My brothers were lining up for me to save the mothers of their children. We were running out of resources aboard this vessel. We didn't expect everything to die off on that planet. There were no planets nearby with any resources for us. The entire planetary system was desolated when the waters of Earth hit the top soil. The only ones set to live in the entire solar system was a family of primitive humans floating on a wooden raft. We barely had enough soil with the seeds we had, so we could grow food. But the need was too high, and we had become too tired."

"You deserved what you got for turning your back on Him."

Baàlsarideem points and says, "And there, the judgement of who you really are shows its face. I realized something that you didn't understand at the time. I realized that my way was better, and you wouldn't have understood without seeing my vision."

Lucius asks, "What way was that, to fly your craft over the Earth's orbit until Jesus comes back?"

"You mock me?"

"I haven't heard a good argument since you started talking," Lucius says. "I don't work alongside evildoers."

Baàl nods. "Moarscii had the right of ruling figured out is what I learned. He knew he could save his people with more inheritance. I could do that very thing. I could move within the systems of the law. You would have us all back lawfully."

Lucius rolls his eyes. "Please, somebody wake me up from hearing this nightmare. You make no sense, Baàl. I would have to give up my…"

Baàlsarideem stands up, nodding. "Now, you're figuring it out. I told my Gamerin brothers of what I was planning, a way of saving everyone if we could get back home with this ship." Baàl stares off as he finishes saying, "and they turned on me."

"You can't be serious? I never would've handed over my birthright to you."

"You would have, and I knew they would reconsider. However, I couldn't save their wives after the flood," Baàlsarideem says glancing over before casting his eyes into another direction. "I didn't have enough power to rescue all of the wives."

"Now, it's starting to make perfect sense," Lucius says. "You never cared for humans."

"Don't be so forgiving of worthless servants." Baàlsarideem says. "The Gamerin were my people. I was their rightful leader, a true savior aboard this ark. Surely once you understood what needed to be done, you'd join me, and they would join in recognizing me as a king over them. We'd all be together again like it was in the beginning, like it should've been."

"You're crazy," Lucius says. "You really went crazy. You're no greater than Dugand or Moarscii's tainted mind." Lucius's jaw drops before asking, "You killed their wives, didn't you? They were worthless to you."

"I didn't need to waste my abilities healing useless people anymore, but I kept them alive as long as I could. I did that for my brothers."

"You were keeping them alive for the sole purpose of waiting, hoping for something to happen. You made this vessel, holding your hostages ransom like cargo."

"I had no choice," Baàlsarideem admits.

"Why did you really kill them?"

"I told you, I had no choice. I had to protect the cargo that mattered on this ship."

"No," Lucius says. "You found out I no longer had a stone. That's what you were waiting for. You got angry when your plan fell apart, so you destroyed the only bargaining chip you thought would've worked on me."

Baàlsarideem snaps, "Those women would've died anyway! I was being merciful. I kept them alive as long as I could because I saw how you treated that worthless harvester, and I knew you would have a bleeding heart for them too."

Lucius screams, "You're not God! You're not the author of life and death. You can't judge who's punished and who isn't. I go to the Father when I'm in need, but you didn't, just like Moarscii and Dugand. You would've lied to me, tried tricking me into giving up my inheritance for you, knowing I didn't want it already. Now, stop lying."

"I saw you throw your celestial robe into the sea. Is that a lie?" Baàlsarideem leans forward and says, "And that's why you don't deserve to be a king. You never deserved an inheritance because you can't think beyond the rules. You never punished anyone for their crimes. You would cry for traitors to come back," he says and shoves a finger in the air as he continues, "even after they tried to destroy you. You would beg for their return, trying to find a way for their forgiveness." His lip curls, and he lowers his voice with outstretched arms. "Let me take the burden off your hands. Give me that permission, so we can all go home. I'll give you a neighboring galaxy."

"I already told you, I spilled my blood as a sacrifice. You won't accept it." Lucius chuckles. "You're just a coward, thinking you're entitled to something you never deserved. All those lies you just told me, all those lies you're starting to believe, and all the lies you've been feeding the Nephilim and Gamerin so they'd buy into what you lust for. Tell them the truth. You're using them to take over an inheritance that's not even yours, one that will eventually pass away. I see the greed for power clearly on you. You wanted power from the very beginning."

Baàlsarideem silently gazes over, staring at Lucius for a moment. He says, "I wanted what was mine. Gamerin are superior."

Lucius says, "You and I know that the Gamerin were servants from the beginning. We always will be. You were sent to help the human children, and that is all you were ordained to do."

"He didn't want those people anyway. My followers turned on me as well. They're nothing but cattle out here."

Lucius says, "You're a liar. You wanted them to worship you, but your plan backfired."

"I have a plan. I still do, and I was smart enough to come up with it before the flood. No one reads my mind aboard this vessel. I know how to work the system, the laws, and bring about order amid chaos. I only need to get this ship through a big enough portal for my plan to work."

"I'll never give you permission to bind a key big enough. You'd have to have hundreds of keys to form one. You're nothing but a liar, even unto yourself," Lucius whispers. "You've forgotten who you were."

Baàlsarideem smirks. "I tell you the truth. I never tried killing you for a reason." He gazes off and says, "But you will beg for death for slaughtering my son. Taking my son changed things between you and me." He bites his bottom lip. "It never should've been you to govern over those realms, and you didn't want your inheritance." Baàlsarideem takes a step toward the door. "You're too weak, and I'm about to show you why."

Voices from out in the hall chatter louder and louder.

Baàlsarideem says, "But you will change your mind, Yuleshua. You will give me the inheritance you never deserved or wanted. You'll join me. Sooner or later, you'll join me. You'll be my second-in-command, or you'll scream for mercy."

The door opens.

Baàlsarideem continues. "By the way, I never lost my wife. But you're about to lose yours."

A levitating stretcher carries Josephine's slumbering body into the room.

"Oh, God, no," Lucius says, as a moan escapes his bleeding lips.

"Call out to Him all you want, but He can't hear you in here," Baàl answers. "I'm the cornerstone of this vessel, and He won't go where it's forsaken. We all know this."

Lucius jingles the metal above him, pulling with all his strength. He says, "You can't do this, Baàl. What's wrong with you?"

Shortening the distance between him and Lucius, Baàlsarideem examines him closely as Lucius begs.

"Please." Lucius pants with tears streaming down his cheeks. "Baàl, please have mercy," Lucius rests his forehead against Baàlsarideem. "You can't do this to me."

"How sad." Baàlsarideem pulls away and huffs. "You think I'm going to change my mind when you rejected my offer. You left me to die, thereby condemning my wife, and I was willing to forgive you. I tried doing this the easy way, offering mercy. I would've allowed you to reign alongside me, which is more than you had done for me." He walks away and stands beside Josephine. "You've left me no choice but to make my reign right through her."

"Stop what you're doing!" Lucius yells. "Or judgement's coming for you. I promise."

"With her as the current queen, when I claim her, I will rightfully be a king."

"Don't touch her, Baàl!" Lucius tugs on the bonds, spitting as he screams. "I don't give you permission! She'll never give you permission!"

Baàlsarideem places an index over his lips. "*Shhh*. Don't wake her. Make this moment easier on her, so she can enjoy our union." He nods. "To tell you the truth," Baàlsarideem pauses and stares at Josephine's jawline and strokes her shoulder straps. "I've been waiting a long time for a young and ageless wife that can heal on her own. We're perfect for each other."

Twenty-Nine

Harvester

Artie falls from the portal window. His body splashes down into the healing waters of his bathing lounge that Lucius had blessed him with on the harvester planet. Unconscious, with barely any life in his body, Artie sinks down and hits the bottom.

Moments after the splash, gentle hands reach in and pull him up. "Artie!" Powtray cries out. "Breathe, my friend."

Artie gasps and opens his bloodied eyes. "Pull them out. The knives," he says grimacing. "I can't heal properly."

Powtray glances down and tries pulling out six-inch nails and several large knives. "Who did this to you? Why are these bonds on you?"

"Just yank them out and quit talking!" Artie snaps. "Hurry, they're poisoned."

Powtray pulls on the last nails that are curled like quills and stuck in Artie's flesh. Artie yelps with every pull. "I'm sorry," Powtray says.

Artie concentrates and tries to keep his screams to a minimum. "Take the bonds off and I'll help," Artie says.

Powtray pulls the chains and tries to unlock the shackles around Artie's wrists. The metal makes no sounds of giving. Powtray grabs a rod-like tool to pry open the latch and says, "I've never seen this metal before." He then uses a small enough pin from an interdimensional space. "I use this for the chicken house. It might work to unlock the mechanism."

"Just hurry and don't explain why." Artie wheezes.

Click.

"Got it," Powtray says with shaky hands and releases the shackles. Powtray tosses the chains into the corner of the room. He gasps, and points with his chin. "There's a dagger in your back, and…" he jerks out a different sized nail from Artie's shoulder and arms. "The weapon back there is next to your lungs."

"I know," Artie braces. "Just yank it out. I'll get the one in front."

Powtray breathes in and pulls. *Swish.* Blood spreads quickly, darkening the water.

"*Ahhh!*" Distended veins cover Artie's flushed face, and he holds his breath instead of screaming.

Powtray embraces him. "You can let it out."

Artie shakes his head and lets out a slow mumble. "Where's the princess."

"She's—"

"Artie," a tiny voice enters from around the corner. Claire pokes her head through the doorway and asks, "Where's Momma and Daddy?"

Artie grunts and says, "Not here, princess." He gestures toward Powtray with his bloodshot cornea, and tells him, "Tend to her while I get this last one. Don't let her see me like this. Recovery takes longer in harvester water. I need to stay in here for a while."

"I'm coming, princess," Powtray says. Helping him to the safety of the guard rail, he floats Artie over so he can hold on. "You got it?"

Artie nods. "Yeah." He grimaces. "Hurry, I'm trying not to scream in front of her, and it's a poisonous dagger that's left."

"Do you need anything else?"

Artie exhales slowly. "Yeah, fetch me his majesty's Gamerin shawshea battle attire, will you? It's hanging in the guestroom."

"You sure?"

Artie nods. "Hurry, Powtray."

"Indeed," Powtray says. "Let me get her settled." Powtray climbs out of the water, occasionally glancing back as each step he takes splashes crimson water from his legs.

Artie braces himself and looks up. "This fight isn't over, Powtray. I need to prepare." He gestures with his nose and says, "See if she's hungry or something."

Powtray takes a deep breath and attempts a smile toward the doorway. "You want me to get you something to eat, Claire?"

"What happened to Artie?" she asks as she is escorted from the area. "Why he so dirty? Is that blood?"

"He'll join us soon, your majesty," Powtray says and closes the door behind him. "Let him get washed off. We can give you something fun to do."

Claire snuggles her doll and asks, "Why did Artie throw me to you? Where's Momma?" She yawns. "I'm tired."

"They're not here, princess. Let's wait for Artie before asking questions, okay? Would you like to sleep? You look tired."

In the bathing lounge, Artie grunts. He rests his fingers over a dagger handle, and tenses. "*Ahhh*, stings." His head sinks below the waterline, freely letting himself scream under the water while pulling out the last poisoned weapon.

The water deepens in a rich red color, and tastes of blood. The water is sticky with his blood before he floats up. Panting, he latches onto a guard rail and gazes at his mutilated wings. As his wings begin to heal, the poison exits his body. Tiny feathers press through his skin, like blades of grass with quick growth. His teeth clench, and he says, "I knew they were prejudiced against me."

Letting relief remind him of how tired his body is, his head rests against the stones. He floats momentarily and stares up at the ceiling before sobbing. "I didn't deserve to be spared over you."

A little later, Artie walks up the far steps from the pool. Powtray enters with a stack of clothing and examines Artie's eyes and body are healed. "What happened?" Powtray asks.

Artie shakes his head and says, "I'm not sure. Everything was safe. I was guarding over the princess. The palace was quiet. We were waiting for the army to arrive."

"Where was our lord?"

Artie answers, "He went into the master's quarters. I had just spoken to the king about something, and next thing I knew—"

"What about?"

Artie starts to say, "The queen was upset because of her…" He gasps. Artie rubs his fingers through his wet hair and says, "The cat."

"What's a cat?"

"It's like a tamed koophoes. We were talking about the royal cat from Earth. His name is Leo, and he was left behind on accident." Artie looks at Powtray. "It's a pet. He must have gone back to get Leo. That had to be what happened." His expression falls. "Our king wanted to give her a gift for carrying his son. He told me that Josephine wanted nothing when finding out that Leo was left behind. He offered whatever he could, but she declined. She was sad because she knew that Leo would starve to death while waiting on them to come home."

"They attacked you while your wings were out?" Powtray points and says, "They pulled your feathers out."

"Yes. I saw two Nephilim when Flutter tried to warn me. I grabbed the princess, but I didn't have time to place my wings back when they shot me with something," Artie says.

"What was it?"

"Some hellish pitchfork thing." Artie slams down a wet bloody towel. "The thing kept shocking me until I was knocked out. I almost didn't get the door shut in time to protect you and the princess."

"Thanks for saving us."

"With my last breath. At least she's safe. I trained on Jett Commdearadea. Some good that did. They have our king chained up. No doubt he'll be tortured, and I don't know where our queen is. All for some little cat. He knew it was too dangerous. Why?"

Powtray asks, "You saw our king? Are you sure it was him?"

"The room was dark where they had us chained up." Artie nods. "But he's the one who opened the portal for me. He was hanging beside me."

"Maybe, he'll open a portal for himself."

Artie slowly gazes up and says, "If that were true, he'd be here by now. I don't know how I'm going to tell Claire about her father, her mother," Artie pauses and rubs his eyes closed, "or even the silly cat."

"I'd wait on telling her. Maybe, if we band together in prayer, as a community, Yeshua will show up and help her understand."

"I can't. It's not wise to alert the innocent people of this realm. Lucius never invited his people into worrying about the war for a reason. I need to find out where the queen is. I can't report anything without knowing. I'll check in somehow. I don't know how to get a hold of anybody from here because this is a hidden world. They took my only key."

"This is definitely some troubling news." Powtray places a pile of clothing down. "I'm even sorry to hear about the a…a…"

"Cat."

Powtray nods. "Yes, the cat." Powtray takes a step out of the lounge and says, "She's eating cheese and crackers and yawning. She might take a short nap. Flutter is staying close to her now. She's sharing her juice with him."

"I'm jumping into the shower. I must get this blood off. I'll be out in a minute, don't let her sleep. I'll have to wake her up for what I need to do."

Powtray pauses from shutting the door completely. "Artie."

"Yes."

"Why are you going to put on his majesty's clothing? What you said earlier scares me."

"Powtray…my friend, the war just came home to Gamerilaye with this attack." He glances up and says, "I have no way off this planet. They took my key, but I have a plan. I know how to get their attention without raising awareness of our people. Hold your tongue and block your mind. It would be better if you stayed here."

"Consider my mind blocked." Powtray shuts the door.

⁓⚬⁓

Fifteen minutes later, Artie enters the kitchen area and asks, "Are you awake, princess?"

She smiles up at him and says, "You're dressed like Daddy."

"I sure am," Artie says and gestures toward Powtray. "I need you to take this." Artie hands him a moment filer. "Take several shots. I must send a message to Oobadoave."

"How are you going to do that?" Powtray asks. He examines the device in wonderment. "Is this one of those guardian devices? What is it?"

"Yes, it's something soldiers use. It's called a moment filer. We had an army that was scheduled to be there. If no one's there when they arrive, they'll know we were captured or something is wrong. They'll be keeping a close eye on communications. This device instantly sends a picture into the eternal file on Oobadoave. It records everything, including what I am thinking and feeling at the time." He winks. "They always have an eye on

Yuleshua's kingdom, and because I'm a servant of the throne, they'll have their eye on me as well. Our lives are secret enough that only the Father will get this message and understand."

Powtray nods. "You're letting them know you're okay, but you're stuck?"

"Yes." Artie smiles. "And that's exactly what I'll be thinking."

Powtray studies the device. "This thing is a miracle."

Artie says, "It's our only way out." Artie poses with Claire while Powtray takes a handful of pictures.

"What do we do now?" Powtray asks.

Artie raises one side of a smiling lip. "Now we wait for a messenger." He takes his moment filer and places it into an interdimensional space. Artie soon opens the massive bay doors.

"Why are you opening those?"

Artie smiles and slowly turns back. "It's so the archangels can get in."

Powtray's mouth drops. "Archangels?"

"Yeah. Few people know this planet exists, and this is a war situation. He'll be sending archangels." Artie points at Flutter and says, "You're staying here, little guy. Powtray will take care of you."

Flutter fusses.

Artie answers, "I know you helped, but that doesn't mean you're going into battle. You're staying here until otherwise. I'm not losing any other family members."

"Artie," Powtray says. "I've never seen an archangel. Are they dangerous?"

"No," Artie answers with a shake of his chin. "Just be you. Any visitor won't be here to talk to you, but they won't be rude either. They're stricter than Jett commanders. Don't expect conversation."

Flutter climbs in Claire's flaxen locks. She giggles.

Artie shoulders drop and he says, "Okay, Flutter, come out of there. War isn't a place for a little hummingbird."

Flutter sinks low while trying to blend in with Claire's hair.

"Is he gonna bite me?" Claire asks with a tiny squeal.

"Not this guy," Artie says. "He's nice, but you don't need to touch him. He's delicate," he says and gazes at Flutter. "Okay, if she goes, so can you."

Flutter immediately flies loops around Claire.

Artie shakes his head and says, "Already spoiled, just like the cat."

Thirty

Mustard Seed

Baàlsarideem brushes his fingers over his new prize. Lucius yells, "She's my wife, you filthy bastard! Get your hands off her."

Baàlsarideem mocks Lucius with flailing hands. "Get your hands off," he says. "I deserve more because of what you've done."

Lucius screams, "Wake up!"

"Shush, she'll hear you. You don't want to watch her scream, do you?"

"Please." Lucius gasps. "Don't do this terrible thing."

Baàlsarideem gazes down at Josephine's body and glides his finger from the top of her breast all the way to her drooping gown at her ankles. "I do." He touches her toes and gazes up without moving his face. "Is that what you told her? I do?"

Lucius says nothing.

Baàl slightly squats and looks under her hanging material. "She's beautiful. I can see why you chose her."

"Stop looking at her!" Lucius snaps. "You don't get to look at her."

Baàl smiles and says, "I'm doing a lot more than looking at her right now." Baàlsarideem strokes her arms that are folded over her chest. "I've never seen Gamerin tattoos on a woman before. She's stunning."

"You're not doing anything. Stop touching her." Lucius yanks on his chains.

Baàlsarideem glances up, says, "Stop me then," and chuckles. Several in the room snicker with Baàlsarideem, and he grins at them. "I'm the king, and he can do nothing but watch me."

A Nephilim touches her glowing designs and says, "These are the tattoos you told us about."

Baàlsarideem snatches the Nephilim's hand.

Crack, pop. He breaks several fingers.

Baàlsarideem says, "Don't touch her. She's mine. She's your queen."

The Nephilim falls to his knees. "Yes, my lord. Forgive me."

Lucius pulls on his chains, yanking as hard as he can. The jingle of metal fills the room. Baàlsarideem glances over and says, "Try if you must, but they won't obey you here." Baàlsarideem raises his hand, and the chains levitate Lucius higher in the air. "They answer to me. I told you, I'm the cornerstone on this vessel, and I know how to make Gamerilaye obey me…with or without your permission." Baàlsarideem touches Josephine's bare shoulder.

Josephine sighs in her sleep. "Baby."

"Ooh." Baàl winks. "She called me, baby."

"Josephine," Lucius says. "It's not me," his voice sticks like a lump in his throat. "Please, baby, it's not me."

Baàlsarideem puckers a bottom lip out to mock Lucius. He says, "You have no more strength, at least, not enough to wake her from a deep sleep that you obviously placed her in." He gestures toward the door. "Everyone leave me. This is between my new wife and my newest servant."

The chains drop Lucius down and snap the bones of his wrist from his body weight. "Augh."

"How weak you are, Yuleshua," Baàlsarideem says. The doors close, and Baàlsarideem carries Josephine's body from the levitation device. He places her over the altar. "Sonya-Cain won't mind. She never does. I always tell her what I'm doing, and she understands I have needs."

"All of you are sick," Lucius says. "Get off of her."

Baàlsarideem pulls the silky material of her nightgown up over her thighs. He listens to her breathing sounds. "She never tells you no. She knows that she is being touched, but says nothing. She must trust you." He gazes back at Lucius. "She won't anymore."

Lucius yells, "Wake up, Josephine, it's not me!"

"Shush," Baàlsarideem says. "You can't stop what is happening." He rips her right glove off and climbs up on top of her. "I'm fairly gentle," he says and yanks her thigh toward him while kissing on her neck.

"*Mmmm*, easy," she mumbles.

"Don't touch her like that. Josephine, wake up. It's not me, baby."

Her brows frown, subconsciously recognizing a different set of hands rubbing over her body. Her spirit screams deep within, *It's not him. It's not Lucius. Wake up, child.*

Baàlsarideem grabs her exposed skin with rough movements and pulls her against him. He raises himself up and undoes his clothes. He sneers at Lucius. "I'm halfway there. This'll be quick."

Lucius is red in the face, saying, "Wake up. You'll hurt her. Get your hands off my wife, you evil demon. I'm gonna kill you!"

Josephine senses something is wrong. She immediately hears Lucius from across the room, but someone is directly on top of her. She's scared to open her eyes as she hears a voice she's never heard before. She speaks psychically, *"Lucius?"*

"Oh, baby. Thank you for talking to me. I can't enter your mind. I'm weak. Listen to me. Don't open your eyes. You have to get out of here."

She asks, *"Who's touching me? Is this you?"*

Lucius sobs in his chains. *"No, my love. You must fight."*

"What do I do?" she asks.

Baàlsarideem throws his shirt off and loosens the tie over her breasts.

She thinks. *"He's molesting me."*

Baàlsarideem says, "I feel like she's waking up," and looks toward Lucius. "You might get a show after all."

Lucius tells her, *"Close your mind. You must close your mind. Do it now. He's gonna read your thoughts."*

She does, and is no longer connected.

"Is she waking?" He gropes her. "Let us see?"

Josephine squeezes her thighs closer together, pretending she pushes Lucius away in her sleep. "Not now, Lucius. I'm sleeee…" her voice trails off.

"She's a deep sleeper," Baàlsarideem says. "You must've put her into a deep sleep for your stupid mistake."

Lucius tries to get Baàlsarideem from her and says, "Hey, Baàl. I remember your son. He was a worthless pansy like you."

Baàlsarideem looks over. "Don't talk about my boy."

"I gutted him. Your son kneeled before me with his dying breath, which is what you'll probably do. Judgment's coming."

Baàlsarideem bites his lip while climbing down. "I'll never bow to you."

"I might not be the true son of God, but I'm the cornerstone of Gamerilaye." Lucius raises his voice and says again, "I'm the cornerstone. The rocks of my world answer to me, and I'm the cornerstone."

"You're nothing, and you'll never have your strength back," Baàlsarideem says.

Lucius fires back, saying, "I bet your wife never loved you, and you kept her as a hostage. I bet that's all you ever did, keeping her only as a hostage."

Baàlsarideem steps closer to Lucius and says, "You know nothing about my wife. And you have no right to talk about my son." He stands in front of Lucius. "It's you who will bow to me."

"I should've known it was your son." Lucius tries to laugh with tears streaming over his cheeks. "He was the ugliest bastard I'd ever seen."

Baàlsarideem throws a fist forward. As he does, Lucius wraps his legs around Baàlsarideem and holds him in place. He screams, "Baby, do it now. I'm the cornerstone. Imagine me opening it over the bed. Do it now!"

Josephine stands to her feet. She wheezes as she gazes upon her bloodied husband dangling in bonds. "Lucius."

Lucius cries out, "Open it!"

Baàl drives a sword through Lucius's stomach. Lucius sucks in air and says, "Spirit, help her."

Clear minded, Josephine rubs over her gloved left finger. She imagines Lucius opening a portal to their bed. Within a twinkle of an eye, she falls through the tiny hole. An oval mattress breaks her fall. She looks up and envisions Lucius's teary blue eyes gazing at her.

"Noooo!" Baàl hollers as he breaks away.

"I love you," Lucius's spirit silently mutters before closing the gate.

After the portal disappears, an empty ceiling stands above her. The last thing she saw is the only thing she can say. "Lucius," she whispers as tears drip down her face. She hunches forward into a ball on the bed.

Dextorus and Deasja run over to her as an army follows behind them. Dextorus says, "Your majesty. Josephine, where were you child?" He holds onto her and helps her to stand.

Deasja grabs a robe for her. "Turn away," he instructs the army in her room. Seeing her loosened garments and ripped sleeve, Deasja covers her. "Give her privacy."

Dextorus asks her, "Did they hurt you?" He nods with his nostrils flaring. "They did this?"

Josephine wants to answer but can only nod her head. Tears swell making streams flow down her cheeks, but no words pass her lips for fear of wailing. Deasja sits beside her and strokes her back. "You can speak psychically," Deasja says with a whisper over her cheek. "I'm listening, sister. I'm listening."

Sobbing bitterly, she finally gasps. Her mind tumbles through her thoughts, but Deasja and Dextorus gather all the information they need through her testimony.

Dextorus gestures quietly to his army. "She's in shock," he tells them, "but she is untouched by our enemy. The Holy Spirit was summoned and found awake in her. She was able to open a portal through His guidance." He pauses, as more eyes grow wider from waiting for the rest of the report.

Deasja speaks up, "They have Lucius. They have him as…a prisoner. He'll not kneel to Baàlsarideem. His spirit cries to the Father, but as you know, there is no holy cornerstone for that vessel." Deasja makes a notion with his eyes, and psychically finishes, *"He's on his own in the dark."*

Orlando speaks up, "What of—"

"No," Deasja raises a hand to interrupt Orlando from speaking. "We will finish report in private."

"He saved me," Josephine whimpers. "Where's my baby?" she asks, answering Orlando's unspoken question. She speaks up again, "Where's Claire?"

Deasja closes his eyes and is hesitant to turn back toward her. The room grows silent.

Deasja and Dextorus look at each other.

Dextorus lowers his eyes as he turns back toward her silently. With his appearance, Josephine loses strength in her legs. Dextorus catches her from falling to the floor.

Aboard the vessel, Baàlsarideem turns from the empty altar. "You just cost yourself more suffering. You'll wish for death every day aboard this vessel. I'll give you nothing to ease your pain." Baàlsarideem rips his blade from Lucius's stomach. His lips hover over Lucius's cheekbone as he says, "I'll send somebody to fix that for you, lord of the failures, so you don't die. I'll never give you that pleasure."

Baàlsarideem exits the room with a slam of the door. He enters the hall and grabs Samstarsey's neck. "I want you to pull the sword out of him and heal him only enough to keep him alive. Go now." Baàlsarideem hurls Sam to the floor and says, "Now, fool."

Sam runs into the torture room, and Baàlsarideem remains in the hall. He lashes a backhand at Devon and Cryline. He says, "What moron forgot to disarm the queen?" He signals at his ring finger and says, "She had a portal key on and slipped away before I could claim her."

Hersone says, "I didn't see anything. She was asleep." Baàl stomps closer, and Hersone guards his face, saying, "I was told not to undress her, lord." He shrinks down. "Women have no power to open portals."

"She's no ordinary woman!" Baàlsarideem kicks Hersone's side. "She has Gamerin principality DNA in her veins from bearing his daughter." Baàl paces while spouting a legion of cuss words. "Have Rueshta bring me your woman. I want her prepared in my chambers within the next shift cycle. For this failure, you will be celibate like one of my slaves."

Thirty-One

Fenn

Baàlsarideem walks a long, old metallic corridor. A walled-opening folds back, disappearing like liquid as he walks through. He enters another enormous doorway and passes along the amber pebbles embedded through the wall framing until finally arriving in a warehouse within the bowels of the ship.

The engine's hum echoes across the walls like whistles of wind in a deep cavern. He stops and grips the railing overlooking thousands of amber stone sarcophagi surrounding an inner tomb.

Inside each amber enclosed sarcophagus lies a Gamerin brother of Yuleshua, completely cognizant of mental transference and held defenseless within their prison.

Baàl whispers, "Wake up." He walks down the steps through the crypt. "Your minds are open to me, you worthless Gamerin traitors." He sneers beside an amber coffin and says, "Fenn, why do you block your mind?"

Yaztarifenn lies frozen in place with his eyes shut.

Baàlsarideem says, "You have no good plans. You can never leave this prison without a principality's permission. You've been my prisoner, and you always will be my prisoner." He kicks the amber, letting it swing from barbed chains. "Your son serves me now. You'll never have a way out," he says closing distance between Yaztarifenn's face and his. "He's my boy now. He's my Rueshta, and he'll always be my best servant. It's his devices that make me succeed."

Baàlsarideem raises up. "If I don't need you with what I plan," he says with a pause and uses fingers to stop the amber from swinging, "you will be among the first to die." He stares quietly for a moment and then says, "My mind is opened to hear you, yet you don't speak to me."

"You don't govern me," Yaztarifenn psychically tells him.

Baàlsarideem chuckles and enters the thoughts of Yaztarifenn.

Immediately, Baàlsarideem stands in a fern filled forest that is vividly identical to that of Gamerilaye. He grips the bark of a redwood tree and looks around. Baàlsarideem asks, "Where do you hide when I visit you, Fenn? I'm in your mind. Come out. I have good news."

"Leave this sanctuary, you unholy being, murderer of my wife, and failure of the Gamerin race. You're not welcome in my mind."

Baàl opens a palm and smiles before saying, "It's not even real. You made all of this up." He half turns and gestures toward fake trees. "It's because of me, you'll be one with the land someday. Because of me, you'll go back home, if you cooperate." He gazes at a stream and walks along a lagoon. "Come on out. Talk to me."

"I have nothing to speak to you about. I do not consort with evil spirits. I seek no counsel in your lies," Fenn's voice echoes through the wilderness, "Leave me."

Baàlsarideem squats down and scoops water from the lagoon with his hands. "I remember this place." He studies the memory and says, "Copper Island. You must speak telepathically with Sheriffson often to remember it so vividly. I'll arrange him to reside alongside you on Gamerilaye if you'd like...only...speak with me."

Silence follows. Even the birds of Yaztarifenn's mind stop singing.

Baàlsarideem's expression melts into anger. His lips crinkle. "Or," he says raising his voice, "I'll kill you and him for your ongoing defiance and retaliation against me."

Wearing Gamerin warrior clothes, Fenn walks up behind Baàlsarideem and says, "So you let your truth slip out with your anger." Fenn strokes his goatee. "My brothers are true to the Father and will never obey a fallen creature like yourself."

Baàl turns back to face him. "There's that goatee I've missed so much," he says pleasantly. "You do speak with me."

"Why do you speak to me like we're brothers?" Fenn sidesteps, rolls his eyes and walks off. "You're not welcome here. I wait for my lord's return."

"What do you hide in your blocked mind? Hosh does it too, along with Sheriffson and many others," Baàlsarideem says and looks around to hear the thoughts that are watching. "In fact, many of them do." He shouts toward the emptiness of the trees. "Do you hear me? I know he speaks to all of you. Why do you hide from me?"

Yaztarifenn stops, pivots, and raises a fist. "You've taken everything from us. We've paid for our crimes against the Father. You told us our king was slaughtered by the Mangoram."

"I am the king."

"You are nothing."

"It should've always been me!" Baàlsarideem answers with a snap of his voice. He quickly squints and covers his lips with knuckles. He breathes deeply to control his anger. "The one you speak of is my servant aboard this craft."

"Yuleshua lives?" Fenn asks.

Baàlsarideem steps closely and says, "He'll serve as my second-in-command. He's already agreed. I'm making plans for my new inheritance even now with your son by my side."

Yaztarifenn's jaw loosens as he says, "You lie," his words fell as he pauses. "Yuleshua's blood was a sacrifice. Why would he betray that? He'd never turn his back on us."

Baàlsarideem huffs and says, "I just thought I'd tell you that everyone you loved serves me now." Baàlsarideem opens his arms and turns a complete circle for those listening and says, "You can spread the news to the other traitors before they're forced to bow to me as their new celestial lord." He chuckles and presses a transferring thought through a segment of memory of him over Josephine. "Did you like that recollection? I just experienced it."

"Stop." Fenn covers his temples, screaming, "Get out of my head! This is a holy place," and he binds any invading impressions from Baàlsarideem. "Don't taint me with your fallen ways."

"I'm not. Did you notice the Gamerin attire she's wearing?"

Yaztarifenn stiffens his back.

Baàlsarideem grins sideways and says, "That was me taking Yuleshua's wife as my new queen. He stood by and watched, for he knows she'll be safe. He wants to be a family again and understands joining together is the only way. I told you he would fall like the rest of you."

"We didn't." Yaztarifenn shudders in place as he tries to rid his mind of the tainted thoughts that Baàlsarideem tries placing into it. "You lie," Fenn murmurs.

"Weren't her tattoos stunning? Did you notice the royal crescent over her nightgown?" He glances back with a wink. "I can't lie about that when

I've never seen those on a woman before." Baàlsarideem walks off and says, "It's only a matter of time, and nothing you think will be hidden from me. To any of you who might be listening, you'll have no power. You hear me? Even the deepest places of your souls will be revealed. Even you, Hoshtravay, who curses me every time I walk by."

"Leave them alone," Yaztarifenn says.

Baàlsarideem lifts a brow back toward Fenn. "So they do listen." He points. "You shield your mind very well, so I can't hear them or see them."

"I might not be as powerful as you, Baàl, but I was among the first. They follow behind me." He nods. "Leave." Fenn walks off, saying, "you're not welcome here. Take your lies with you."

Baàlsarideem leaves Yaztarifenn's mind.

Baàlsarideem stares down at Yaztarifenn inside the amber encasement. "I have been nothing but merciful to you, Fenn." His eyes slowly look over the eight thousand sarcophagi spiraling up toward the entrance of the enormous crypt. "I made you all an offer, and I'm the savior of the Gamerin. You had an opportunity, yet you still turn your backs."

Baàlsarideem walks the ramps winding upward that encase a center chamber that is ornately decorated by precious stones to be a shrine.

Baàlsarideem passes by his brothers' sarcophagi that are carefully set in a forced bowing position to honor the one guarded within the shrine. Before entering, Baàlsarideem glances back at his silent prisoners. "Some of you are so weak," he says pointing at his temple. "I hear your thoughts when you're emotional. Even now." He raises his voice, "I know you speak to each other when awakened, but soon all your thoughts will be revealed. Yaztarifenn cannot block all your minds, no matter how hard he tries. As for you Hoshtravay," he says glaring down toward the bottom row. "I'll be placing your son through a special series of tests for my new weapon because of that name you just called me as I passed by." His eyes scan around as he says, "You will honor the one I have designed to be over you. There will be no blasphemy." He snarls. "Sleep, you insolent fools." And they're forced into a deep slumber.

Thirty-Two

Sonya-Cain

Baàlsarideem enters the sanctuary of the shrine and faces an illuminated amber stone in the center of the room. "My love," he whispers, walking toward the rubbed down areas over her hands and face where he visits daily. "Sonya-Cain, daughter of Cain, my wife. I'm here."

Inside the amber encasement lies a woman with delicate features, a beautiful complexion, and pure white hair. Sonya-Cain reposes frozen in time.

Baàlsarideem lays his head down and rubs his cheek inches above her face. "If I could touch you one more time. I could heal you of the slow aging process." He presses his face forward and stares down. "What I wouldn't give to hold you again as it was." His eyes seal shut. "How are you today?" he asks and enters her mind.

Sonya-Cain stands in a wheat field that rests fifty yards outside of a cottage. She picks brightly speckled weeds and wildflowers between the stalks outlining a glen and binds them into a bouquet. Relaxed by her surroundings, she hums a simple tune. Baàlsarideem walks a few feet behind her, pleasantly smiling and simply watching her.

Sonya-Cain takes a ribbon from her hair to use as a tie around the stems of her wildflowers. Her long flowing hair shines like snow in the evening of a mid-summer's day. Baàlsarideem says softly, "Those are beautiful."

Shocked, Sonya-Cain turns around with a gasp and drops her wild arrangement. Bending down, Baàlsarideem gathers them for her. "I didn't mean to startle you," he says.

Smiling, "I wasn't expecting visitors," she says. Skipping a glance over several foothills in the distance, her eyes search for something across the land.

He asks, "Who are you looking for if you weren't expecting visitors?"

"Umm," she says holding her bouquet to her abdomen and tapping a few fingers to her bottom lip. "Somebody…" she says with a pause and sighs, "I'm…" and she shrugs. She gazes back at Baàlsarideem, "Someone is taking me away, but I can't remember who."

Baàl stares into her deep, brown eyes and asks, "Does your husband know of this person?"

Her smile grows, and she tilts her head while lowering her bouquet. "Maybe that's who it is." Turning from him, she steps away a few feet. She calls out, "Abaddon. Apollyon, where are you boys?"

Baàlsarideem squeezes his eyes closed.

"Have you seen my boys?" she asks and faces him. "I have twin boys." She speaks through her smiling teeth to hide her embarrassment of losing them. She says, "I never know where they run off to." Her head sinks between her shoulders. "Have you seen them?"

Baàl nods quietly, and pretends to be looking off behind her. "I saw them earlier," his voice cracks. "I'll tell them to visit their mother."

"Oh, would you?" She hides behind her bouquet and says, "You're so sweet."

He takes a step forward and asks, "Are you flirting with me?"

She places the arrangement behind her back, slightly swinging her hips with a hidden smile. "My husband would have a jealous fit for such a thing."

He strokes her upper arm and says, "I don't think your husband would mind so much with me talking to you. I'm a nice guy."

She blushes, says, "I'm not that kind of a woman," and turns away from him. "A savior's coming soon. He's taking me to a new place. My Father, His Spirit told me."

"What's his name?" he asks.

She takes two steps toward the stalks of flowers in front of her and kneels to pick a few more pink flowers and adds them to her arrangement. The wind blows through her thoughts, sending shiny white strands of hair across the blossoms.

Baàlsarideem stands still and watches her. Within moments, she starts humming her simple tune again. Baàlsarideem says, "What beautiful singing," his voice cracks. "Almost as beautiful as you."

She turns swiftly with shock in her eyes and stands to her feet. "I didn't see you there," she says. She looks around and searches in several areas.

"Who are you looking for?" he asks.

"Umm, someone's coming." She gazes at him before saying, "He's supposed to be here soon. I was promised."

He asks, "What does he look like?" He raises a few fingers to be even with his height and teases as he speaks gently to her. "Is he this tall and ruggedly handsome?"

Embarrassed, her hands plop in front of her as she says, "I can't remember." She shrugs. "Oh, well. He'll show. He always keeps His promises."

Baàlsarideem walks in a circle around her until he's standing in front of her. "I tried to get married today. She got away from me. She was pretty, but not as pretty as my first wife."

She picks a couple wheat grains and asks, "What happened to your first wife? Did she die?"

"Sometimes…" he says and takes a moment before continuing. "Sometimes she talks to me," he says locking her gaze, "and other times…" His eyes fall as he stops speaking for another moment. He shakes his head and says, "I want her back, and I want to feel her touch again. She speaks of saviors, and I think she's confused. She's forgotten who I am and lost to me."

She tilts her head and says, "How sad. You must be lonely."

He answers, "I sometimes get married to fill in the empty spot of missing her, but they will never be the same as her. I'm going to save her someday. I think she knows that I am. I think she's waiting for me."

"Is she someone I might know?"

He glances around and answers, "She visits here…occasionally."

"She might meet the savior who's coming here soon." She shrugs. "I hope you find your wife someday." Sonya-Cain turns from him to glean a few more sprigs of wheat stalks to add to her bouquet. Moments later, she begins humming again.

Baàlsarideem follows a few steps behind her and mimics her song.

Wide eyed, she springs back. "I didn't see you there."

"I didn't mean to startle you," Baàlsarideem says. He points at her flowers and asks, "What are you making?"

"My youngest twin boy, my son, Abaddon…he…" she stops speaking and scans the perimeter frantically.

"Who are you looking for? Abaddon?"

"No. Someone is supposed to be here," she says. "He's important."

"Who? Who is it you keep looking for?"

Shaking her head and staring off with teary eyes, she touches her lips and says, "I don't know. I can't remember." Terrified, she looks at Baàl-sarideem and starts crying. "I don't remember, but he's saving me. I must be ready, but I can't remember."

Baàlsarideem races over to her, shushing her tears with an embrace. He says, "It's okay. Don't cry, my darling. I'm here. It's me, Baàl, your husband."

"Baàl?" She looks up at him. "Is it you?"

His eyes close as he strokes her hair. "I'm always here with you." He kisses her. "I love you, Sonya-Cain. I must be the one you always speak of."

She tightly embraces him and asks, "Baàl, where have you been? The storm's coming. I can feel it. It's coming."

"Shhh, there's no more storm. I've been here all along. I'm working to get you out. I'll hold you soon."

Sonya-Cain says, "That's not the storm I'm talking about. It's worse," she whimpers. "A lot worse. We must be ready when the savior shows. It's coming."

"Shhh, it's me. You're okay," he says stroking her cheek. "We'll be together again."

Her brows come together, and she says, "You're here now. I don't understand. We must get ready."

"I've told you before," Baàlsarideem says as he kneels. He rests his cheek against her pelvis for comfort and holds her thighs. He tries to remember what her touch feels like. He says, "I'm taking you home, Sonya-Cain. I'm going to heal you there, and I'll feel your touch again. I'm the savior. We'll be together very soon on Gamerilaye."

Suddenly, the wind stops blowing, and the sky grows dark. "No," she whispers. Her hands drop away from him as she stands in silence. A thunderous boom shouts across the sky.

Baàlsarideem squeezes her closely and closes his eyes. "Please don't be mad at me. I hate when you become angry. Don't ruin what moments I have when you remember who I am." He looks up and says, "Sonya, I've had no choice but to lock you in this memory."

She stares forward with glossy eyes and digs her fingers into his shoulders.

He says, "I couldn't heal you beyond this."

But Sonya says nothing, gripping her nails deeper until she tries pushing him away with all her strength.

"No, stop." Baàlsarideem pulls her tighter to him. "You can't fight me in here."

"Get off me!" she screams. "You're not him. You're no savior."

She swings her hands, and Baàlsarideem catches the slaps midair. "Sonya," he says tangling her arms into a lock behind her. He speaks against her neck, "Hold your temper for a minute, little woman." He breathes deeply and says, "Give it a moment. You'll forget. We can start over with this greeting. Don't ruin my time with you."

Sonya screams louder, her voice echoing like thunder throughout her mind. "I won't forget. I hate you for what you've done to me. Judgment's coming for you."

"Don't say that." Baàlsarideem presses his face deep into her neck and keeps her from struggling. He says, "Please, hold your tongue. You don't mean what you say. You love me forever. Let this moment pass."

She says, "You keep me here against my will. Let me die, so I can go home. I don't love you."

"That's not what you say to me every day."

"I want to go home."

He stills her wiggling body in a tighter embrace and says, "There's no home. I already told you. It was destroyed by water. I'm saving you. You're only confused at the moment."

"I want to see the Father," she says slightly nudging her hand toward freedom. "Have Him tell me there's no savior."

"You can speak to Him when we're finished, remember? You're bound to me. It must be this way, and I am the savior."

Sonya slaps Baàlsarideem's cheek and breaks free. "Monster, why don't you understand? You're not my savior. This body is too old, cursed. I've lived my life. Let me pass on. I'm not one of your slaves."

Baàlsarideem rubs his cheek and fights tearing up. "Why do you hurt me so? I've made plans for you."

"I'm not confused right now." Sonya steps forward and places her palms on each of his cheeks. Baàlsarideem melts in her arms. She whispers, "I'm not one of your prisoners. Let me speak to my Father, so I can ask for forgiveness. You should do the same. There's still a chance."

Baàlsarideem answers, "I won't do that."

"Then you've already fallen." She drops her hands. "And He can't help you."

He glares into her eyes and says, "I have a plan. We can be together." Pulling onto her, Baàlsarideem says, "I've seen Yuleshua, and he married a woman. Now I can repair this damage between us. You'll be the cornerstone by the time I'm done. This will give us trillions of years before judgment."

She says, "I don't want what isn't mine. I never did. I'm not a fallen daughter. I follow the ways of Enoch, and you keep me prisoner. We've had our time."

"Our time doesn't have to end. I'm almost done with my plans. You'll change your mind when you can think clearly. I know how to beat our curse."

"I'm thinking clearly right now. I won't change my mind, and it's already ended between us when you turned your back on my Father. Please, help our boys, so they don't fall." She gasps and asks, "Can't you feel the storm?" She strokes his cheeks, telling him, "I feel the storm. Oh no. I'm already forgetting." Tears drip down her chin as she says, "Please. Please, you're prolonging my curse by keeping me here against my will. You're ruining our children by this rebellion. Our lives were never supposed to be this way." While staring deeply in his eyes, she begs, "Let me go. Hurry, and let me go while I still have my wits. Obey my wishes and let me die." She cries and says, "Please, release me. I never wanted…"

After a moment of crying, she becomes quiet. The storm in her mind subsides, and once again, a gentle breeze blows through the wheat grains.

Baàlsarideem strokes her shoulders as he holds her. He says, "There, there, now. Everything's better. How are we doing today, my sweet wife?"

She looks up with tears she has forgotten about and says, "Baàl?"

"Yes, my eternal love."

"Where have you been?"

He smiles and uses his nose to point towards bountiful stacks of wheat lining a storehouse. "I've been with the boys. We've been harvesting all day. I had to see you before rounding up the stags. We're all going home soon, and we can be together."

She pats his cheek and says, "How sweet you are to me. I love you." She takes a quick look around and asks, "Where are my boys now? I don't see them. Is Apollyon teasing his brother Abaddon again?"

"No." He says. "I'll tell them you're looking for them, so they can say hello to their mother."

She embraces Baàlsarideem and says, "Will you tell Abaddon I made him something? He loves flowers."

Baàlsarideem holds her tighter and says, "I will."

She soon releases her embrace and smiles before turning and facing the cottage. Taking several steps, she gathers a basket from a pile of wheat and begins humming once again.

Baàlsarideem stands, quietly watching her a few minutes.

<hr />

As he exits her mind and is standing beside her sarcophagus, he stares down through the illuminated amber. "You will remember, and you'll not fight me." He strokes over the area above her hand. "I'll be able to heal you of your confusion, and it will be as it was. You'll see."

Footsteps close in behind Baàlsarideem. "Is she having a good day?" Apollyon asks.

"Still getting me confused with someone else. She keeps looking for a—"

"A savior." Apollyon nods. "I know."

"It's just her confusion talking." Baàlsarideem wipes his eyes, turns toward his son, and sniffs. "She wants to see Abaddon. When you visit and pretend that you're him, I want you to accept her gift as if you are him." Baàlsarideem turns back and strokes the amber stone. "Part of her knows he's missing. She's trying to cope with his loss." He gazes at Apollyon. "Allow her to believe she's there in the field. Just let her talk. Don't remind her of anything."

"I take it you've spoken through a moment of clarity. Those moments are rare." Apollyon leans against the Amber. "Mom's still angry, huh?"

"She'll change her mind when we're on Gamerilaye. She'll have to change her mind when she's connected to Gamerilaye."

"How will she be connected?" Apollyon breathes in deeply and asks, "Why haven't you told me what you're doing? Come on, I know you've already told her, and she can't remember."

"That's between her and me. I know the laws." He points at Apollyon. "Quit trying to probe her mind. It always ends badly, and the name-calling starts flaring up. She tried hitting me a moment ago."

"We can't feel her slapping us without physical connection. It's not like it hurts."

Baàlsarideem rubs his chest momentarily and says, "It still hurts when she thinks about it. She never would've done that before."

Apollyon snickers and says, "Well, she called me a bastard last week for keeping her here, as if I have a choice. She thinks I can get her out. She has no idea she's stuck in this casing until a principality releases her." He looks down at her and says, "She can get nasty angry sometimes."

"There are no principalities I trust to open this casing. I'll have to release her the hard way with Yuleshua. Fallen principalities only care about themselves. They would kill her."

Apollyon says, "I heard about Yuleshua's wife a moment ago." He rubs the bridge of his nose and asks, "Is this going to cost us more time?"

"Not really." Baàlsarideem shrugs and says, "The threat was worth a shot, mainly mind games." Baàlsarideem turns back toward the door and says, "Try not to piss your mother off, will you? She subconsciously remembers every squabble. I think all women have that superpower."

"Hey," Apollyon says and steps forward. "I can block my mind, father. I'm more powerful than Abaddon was, and they didn't find out with him. You can trust me with your plans."

"I've come so far. I can tell you that Abaddon was still questioned before his judgment. The fact that he didn't know protected my plans. I can't let anyone know, especially some other random principality that is chained in Hell or wandering around Earth wanting a key back to his own jurisdiction. I was the second-in-command of the army that placed those fallen principalities there. I know what I'm doing," Baàlsarideem says and takes a few steps toward leaving. "I have plans within plans, and your mother will be a shining star among them. She won't abandon us when she thinks clearly. Her anger is a fleeting emotion. It'll pass."

"Sure, pops." Apollyon stares down at his mother. "How long do I have?"

Baàlsarideem pauses in the doorway. "She's doing good today. A few minutes, maybe. She just needs to see you."

"You mean Abaddon?"

"Both of you." Baàlsarideem smiles. "Wait until she turns around and is singing the lullaby that she used to sing to you, and then you can be you," he says and leaves.

Thirty-Three

Rafael

On the harvester planet, Artie paces a long line on the rug in his living area. The sun rises slowly in the east over snow-covered mountains. Powtray stands beside Claire as the toddler starts wiping her eyes. Distracting her from falling asleep, Powtray points at the village in the distance beyond the landing bay. Artie's steps catch his attention for a moment, and Powtray glances back toward the town, saying, "Calm down."

"How can I? They know that I can't communicate from here. Somebody must know that we were attacked."

Powtray has no way of answering, as his eyes skim the room, watching a dying fire in the fireplace crackle. The moment strikes him with a surreal feeling. "I'm not a soldier, Artie. I'm a simple farmer. I don't know. War is only something I've heard about but never experienced myself. The only experience I have, is my king was greatly hurt by it."

Blowing out a deep breath, Artie nods. "I'm sorry. I shouldn't have brought you into this."

Powtray shrugs and says, "You didn't. It's the war. The war is unfair, all of it."

"It's not your war." Artie gazes at Powtray and says, "This war belongs to the Father. Don't trouble yourself. He takes care of His children."

Powtray caresses Claire's hair, as she snuggles a handsewn doll against her. He stares at the button-eyes and says, "Then why are you fighting in it, Artorus?"

Artie shoulders slump, and he answers, "Good question. The Father never asks for more than what we can handle, and He equips his children for battle when He calls them. He doesn't set us up for failure, and He has a plan behind everything."

Powtray looks at him like an orphan when he asks, "Then is our king coming home?"

"I don't know," Artie says as his vision lowers. "I don't know that, Powtray."

"I think," a tiny voice breaks the silence between them, as her blue eyes stare up at Powtray, "my daddy and momma are okay."

Powtray stiffens, and Artie shuts his eyes. Artie says, "We shouldn't talk about such things in front of her. Especially, while we're waiting for someone to tell us what's going on. Everything's subjective at this moment." Artie gathers a few logs and sets the fireplace ablaze once again.

Powtray studies Artie's nervousness and glances down as Claire's eyes becoming heavy with sleepiness. He says, "I need to make Artie breakfast."

Claire perks up.

"You want to help me?" Powtray asks.

"I can't cook," she says raising a palm. "I'm only free years old."

"It's better than you falling asleep sitting upward." Powtray signals toward Artie and says, "You said you didn't want her to sleep yet."

Artie nods. "Do what you feel is right, but I'm not hungry."

Powtray laughs. "You? You're always hungry."

Artie nods again. "You got me. Maybe a little something."

Lifting her to sit on the countertop, Powtray directs Claire. Artie's footsteps pick up again, and Powtray shakes his head because of the constant anxiety weighing on Artie's shoulders.

A bright flash of light silently flickers from out on the frozen terrace. Powtray races over and covers Claire's eyes. Artie yelps out, "She'll be okay. It's just his skin, not Oobadoave. They know she's here."

Powtray lowers his hand and asks, "Who is it?"

Artie smiles and says, "It's Rafael. Thank God." He strides to the bay opening to let in his guest.

Powtray and Claire slowly enter the living area and behold a beautiful, yet terrifying sight. Rafael stands twelve feet tall. Powtray glances over just in time to see his large wings folding back into an interdimensional space. Awestruck, Powtray is speechless. Rafael looks over, and Powtray's knees knock.

Rafael says, "Peace be upon you, child. I mean you no harm."

Claire takes a couple steps, but Powtray's legs can't move to stop her.

Artie greets Rafael, saying, "I was hoping you would get my message."

Rafael nods and says, "We were waiting for you to contact us."

"What do you mean, Rafael? This just happened."

Rafael kneels on one knee. His face is even with Artie's. "Soldier, this was foretold. There are many things that happen for a reason."

"My principality was kidnapped." Artie slaps his forehead and asks, "Are you telling me that that was planned?"

"No one knows the ways of the Father," Rafael says and looks down for a moment, watching tiny fingers playing with his glowing pants pocket. He meets Artie's gaze once again and says, "I'm here to bring you a new portal cross, so you can get the princess back home. She'll be safe there with an entire army waiting for her. You can't stay here. This planet isn't for refugees. It was prophesied that this world would be safe during the war. There is no war on Gamerilaye; therefore, she must go home at this time."

Claire touches Rafael's gigantic boots and says, "You look like my daddy when he looked like a Christmas tree. You're pretty."

"Claire," Artie says. "Please."

Rafael raises a couple fingers. "She's okay." He smiles down at her. "I know your daddy. I saw him two days ago. I hope I'll see him again soon; however, I'm not pretty." He smiles down at her, saying, "I'm an archangel. I'm cool."

She smiles with one dimple. "Just like my daddy's an angel?"

"We fight in the same war and sometimes in the same battles."

"But he's just my daddy," she says as her eyes drift toward Artie. "Where's my daddy?"

Rafael wraps his finger that is half the size of her face under her chin. He redirects her to look up at him as he says, "I don't know where your daddy is. I'm here to give Artie his new key, so he can take you home. Somebody's there for you now."

"Who?" Artie asks.

Rafael stands to his feet. "I'm not sure. The commanders are there, but a small portal was opened, and it was a difficult reading. There were two lives that made it through simultaneously. They both have Gamerin principality DNA, but that's all we know. The commanders are to report once you're there. We keep communications at a minimum during times like these."

"I knew he'd be okay." Artie exhales. "I don't know how he got back to Gamerilaye, but he can always figure it out. Nobody can keep a good principality down."

Rafael steps through the bay doors and says, "I told you we're not sure. Don't celebrate before the report is given. Some things may be deceiving from aboard that ship."

Artie says, "Yuleshua has a portal ring for a wedding band. If two lives made it through, it was probably him and the queen."

"I'll wait for report from the commanders before speaking to the Almighty about your testimony. Get her home." And Rafael leaves.

Artie sweeps Claire up in his arms. He says to Powtray, "Never mind breakfast. It's only four in the morning there."

Powtray asks, "You really think they are okay?"

Artie guards his tongue while governing a smile. "You heard him. I shouldn't say anything until we know for certain. I'm to get her home. I'll let you know when I can. Keep us in your prayers."

"Goodbye, old friend." Powtray waves.

Artie exits through a portal with Claire and Flutter.

Thirty-Four

Reunion

On Gamerilaye, Josephine paces an imaginary rut over the marble stone lining the terrace outside the master's quarters. As she circles around for one of her loops. Dex raises an arm to console her, but she turns to make her imaginary rut deeper. Dex lowers his hand and waits for the next time she comes around. Deasja watches her circle around three more times as Dextorus lowers his hand each time.

Stepping forward, Deasja stops Josephine in place. "All of this isn't helping, your majesty."

Josephine snaps her arms out, and Dextorus holds his breath as she says, "My husband could be dead."

Deasja shakes his head. "Not true. We would've had word from the spirit world on Oobadoave. Not hearing means he's still alive."

"You didn't see what I saw." Her eyes immediately flood as she stares through the tiles. Her mind plays the memory again. "He was bloody and hanging by chains," she says and gazes up at Deasja. "They were killing him."

"Looks might be deceiving," Dextorus says. She turns to look at him, and he continues. "Mind games. Our enemy is brilliant with mind games."

"I know what I saw."

"All we know is this…" Dextorus presses his shoulders back and says, "He was beaten, you were molested, and Lucius gave all he had to free you."

"That's what I said," she reiterates.

Deasja says, "Commander, this probably isn't the time."

"It's important," Dex says and meets her gaze before continuing. "From the beginning of his mission with you, there was always a possibility of him being trapped aboard that ship. They will stop at nothing to recruit him, warp his mind, and destroy who he is."

"He wouldn't do that to me," Josephine says.

Dextorus nods. "Correct. That's why you were given permission to be with him. Together, you're stronger. Together, he has something to fight for, something he had lost and thought he'd never have again. With you, he has a family."

"This was all planned?" Josephine asks. "From the beginning?"

Deasja uses a soothing voice and says, "It's not without heart." Josephine turns to look at Deasja. "This battle between Yuleshua and Baàlsarideem began a long time ago, and before the temptation could take place, your husband needed the right weapons to guard his heart." Deasja lifts a brow, moonlight glistens across his eyes, and he exhales. "You. You and the Father are the strongest weapons Lucius has to guard his heart from the temptation of turning away."

Josephine whimpers into her hands, and Deasja wraps his arm around her, bringing her close to his shoulder. Dextorus holds a palm out and mutters quietly toward Deasja and says, "Natural for you."

She says, "Y'all thought he was gonna fall. You're scared even now."

Silence blankets the terrace, and several angels bow their heads in prayer. Dextorus speaks calmly, "I know I speak bluntly, but my heart has been through a lot in this war." Every eye looks at Dextorus. He knows that he's being watched and buries his thoughts as he continues. "I'm not the only one who has seen the unthinkable rip the foundation from our existence. No one has suffered as much as the Father, but that doesn't mean He doesn't care." Dextorus clears his throat and wipes under an eye. "Our suffering doesn't mean He doesn't care, but nobody understands the things He goes through in order to grant His children success."

Josephine points at Dex and says, "But you believe my husband could become a fallen?"

Dextorus grows silent, and he stares off as if thinking about the question. "If you're asking, I never make promises. A promise was made to me once, and it hasn't been fulfilled." Dex meets her gaze. "If you're asking for my opinion—"

"Yes," she whispers. "Please, anything Dex."

Dextorus nods. "If I know Lucius, and I believe I do, he will fight with his dying breath to get home to you. He will rip the heads from his enemies," he pauses for a rare smile as he continues, "build stairs with them, and climb up from the pits of Hell in order to hold you again. That is Yuleshua Lucius

Gamerin. He does not ask his enemy for permission, and he does not give up in battle."

Her eyes shut, and her shoulders drop. "Thank you. I know it's not a promise, but thank you."

But moments later, she whimpers again.

"You think of your daughter and Artie," Deasja says and rubs her shoulders.

She looks up at him. "Where are they? If that devil has them…If he has my baby, oh, Lucius…" she starts to say before falling to her knees. "What's to become of us?" She wails, "My baby. Why would she have to be aboard that vessel? Why would He put my family at risk? She's done nothing wrong."

Dextorus says, "Lucius has to free them."

She looks up at Dex and asks, "Who?"

"Those aboard who secretly serve the Almighty. They've waited a long time for their king. Lucius is the only one to bear this burden because he is their savior."

"What about my daughter? I don't mean to sound selfish. She's just a baby."

"There is one that we have been in communication with," Dextorus says. "He's been working to free the women who are captured aboard that vessel. He promised he would gather Claire, even if it costed him his life if she were to be captured."

"Who is it?"

"Vincentine," Deasja says. "With us, he goes by Vincentine. They call him something else in the dark. We don't know his real name. He's a double agent." Deasja places his hand upon her head. "I'm blocking your mind. This information cannot get out, or many lives will be lost."

She exhales. "Thank you." She stands up, and Deasja escorts her to sit on a low branch etched into the shape of a bench. She says, "Has Vincentine said anything about what's happened?"

Dextorus says, "We've lost communication with him. No doubt because of the high alert of what's happened aboard that vessel, but we figured as much. Communications on both sides are at a minimum for safety. Vincentine will let us know when it's safe enough."

Suddenly, a portal doorway opens from inside the master's chambers. Artie holds tightly to Claire as he walks through. He quickly closes the gate behind him. Glancing over at Josephine, he says, "My queen," and places Claire down.

"Mommy." Claire runs over to her mother.

Josephine pops up from the bench and starts crying. "My baby," she says holding onto Claire.

Several angels rush to Artie. Deasja asks, "How did you get out? How did this happen? How do you have Claire?"

"I sent her to my world when the attack started. I was captured, but my king saved me from death." Artie's eyes race across a sea of faces. He stops searching when he sees Josephine. "Where's Lucius?"

Soon, a soundless choir fills the atmosphere when their questions are answered by Artie's statement.

"No," Artie says and falls to his knees. "Where is he? Rafael said two lives made it out through a small portal." He holds up two fingers. "He said two lives were safe."

Gasp. Josephine touches three fingers to her abdomen, and gazes up. "Because I'm carrying his unborn son." She glances down. "I feel him now. Our son is safe."

Artie trembles and hides his expression from his royal family. Deasja and Dextorus help to stand between her and Artie. They shield him so he can have a moment to compose himself.

Dextorus says, "This is true. This means the odds are in our favor for battle, and Yuleshua is victorious once again."

Deasja says, "We will defeat Baàlsarideem." His eyes look around as his words raise the hearts of many watching. "When the prince is born, he will strip Baàlsarideem of his power, and even our odds during battle."

The angels hoot.

Dextorus says, "Even now, in the midst of darkness, the glory of God prevails. He has triumphant plans within plans and smites our enemies."

A roar of cheers follows.

Meeting the queen's gaze, Deasja interrupts, "Have empathy." The crowd quiets down. Deasja rubs Artie's shoulder before saying, "Although this is joyous news in the light of eternity," he lowers his voice, "for now, it is grievous. A celestial principality is held as a prisoner, and his only hope of escape is in someone he doesn't know."

Artie raises up and asks, "Who?"

Deasja says, "I'll let the queen discuss that with you, but block your mind afterward."

Dextorus stands in the center of the large crowd and says, "Deasja and I have to give report." He meets Josephine's gaze and continues. "You may grieve, but only for a moment. You must guard yourself by allowing the Holy Spirit to rest his peace upon you. Do not give into temptation of mourning the loss of your husband. He is not lost to us, but serves the Almighty even now." He points toward her womb and says, "His son must be born to become his second-in-command. You mustn't trouble yourself. We need him to be healthy."

She steps forward as several tears journey to her chin. "I make no promises, but I'll do my best." Her shoulders slouch as she says, "He promised me he'd be here to deliver our son."

Finally, Dextorus places a hand upon her shoulder and speaks kindly, like a dear friend. Peace flows through Dex in a way that lets her know how rare the moment is for him. He says, "Sweet child, there are times that the enemy interrupts our promises. But I trained alongside your husband. I can deliver a child as gently as he would."

She gazes up at him.

Dextorus continues. "I owe it to Lucius. I consider you as my family, and Lucius's children are precious to me."

"Stop. You owe me no explanation. Quit trying so hard." Josephine's eyes soften. "You don't scare me, Dex. You never have. I see you." She swallows tears and says, "I see tenderness in your eyes like I saw in my Lucius."

He nods silently.

She says, "I trust you. There's more to you than a harsh commander, and I trust you because my Father trusts you."

After speaking with the commanders, Josephine steps through the open doorway to lay Claire down. Artie follows her, and she raises Claire up to be held by him. "Can you help me lay her down, Artie? I need you to place her into a deep sleep, and then—"

"I'll place you in one," Artie speaks softly, "your majesty."

"Yes," she says. "Thank you. You're good to us."

"I wish I were better. I could've stopped this."

She pauses outside Claire's door. "Artie?" She turns back and asks, "What happened?"

Artie frowns.

"You know, don't you?" she asks.

He nods, barely uttering, "An idea…something I…."

Josephine brushes Claire's hair against his shoulder as she says, "We'll talk after she's asleep."

"Yes, your majesty," Artie says and tucks the princess into her bed.

Deasja and Dextorus close the doorways of the palace. Deasja gestures toward several angels and says, "I want you three in the western wing and the rest of you break off in threes throughout every corridor, garden, and grand hall." Deasja nods toward Dextorus as he finishes saying, "The commander and I will give report on Oobadoave and we will be back shortly to stay close to her majesty as she sleeps." Then, the commanders leave.

Thirty-Five

Gentlemen

Dextorus closes the portal after giving report on Oobadoave and gains a position beside Deasja on the large landing bay. "Did you hear what he said?"

Deasja answers by asking, "Which part?"

Meeting Deasja's gaze, Dextorus says, "It's not what Rafael said, more of how he acted. There was doubt in his eyes, and Rafael was trying to shield it."

Deasja breathes deeply. "We see from different angles sometimes, you and me."

"How so?"

"This is closer to what you've experienced, and I think it's bleeding into your judgment of the situation a little. When we spoke to Rafael, I saw hope, patience, and a warrior waiting for battle. I didn't sense any doubt."

Dextorus nods and then says, "That is not exactly the same as what I've experienced."

"Maybe not, but you've lost those closest to you before."

"I'd rather not speak of what I've lost. Not speaking of her helps to keep the pain away," Dex says and closes his eyes. Dextorus clears his throat. "Every few months, Baàlsarideem's vessel goes back to Earth to retrieve women."

Deasja looks over and asks, "What?"

Dextorus continues. "When I can speak to my contact, I'll tell you everything I know about Lucius's return."

"Oh," Deasja says. "You're changing the subject."

"I am."

"I know Josephine is grieving right now."

Dextorus groans and says, "I know what you're about to say."

"She'll lose that baby if she stays like this, Dex. She almost starved to death last time." He glances over. "She gives up without him."

"Lucius does the same. And she knows he's being tortured." He exhales. "No tongues may slip to make mention of such things around her. We must make our conversations sound like Lucius is in a prison cell like they do on Earth. Maybe her mind will make his torture more peaceful. It's one thing to die, but it's entirely different to be tortured, healed, and tortured again." His eyes study the soft waves that are illuminated by moonlight sprinkles in the distance. "It's lovely here."

Deasja points up toward the moon. "I've never been here before. Is that a mountain orbiting around this world?"

Dextorus places his foot up on the balcony railing and says, "He and his brother Yaztarifenn placed that moon there."

"A complete race of builders, people who made civilizations and delighted in the ways of our Father…only sadness remains. Who would've thought, one of them would become a false god and lead two worlds astray?"

Dextorus says, "It seems Lucius has experienced many of the same things the Shadow Cluster has been through."

"Nothing but thieves and gangsters out there."

"Not all." Dextorus's eyes glaze as he says, "Hopefully, not all."

"Sorry." Deasja pats Dex's back. "I forgot my tongue." He lifts his foot to rest it on the balcony railing beside Dex's foot. Deasja leans over his knee and looks down the cliffside. "This world is impressive."

"Few people outside this realm know about this place," Dextorus says and looks toward the beach before saying, "I'd like to keep it that way."

"You're changing the subject again," Deasja says. "For someone who's been through what you've been through, you do a great job of hiding it."

Dextorus says, "If it wasn't for work, I would've fallen apart after losing her. I'm a servant of the Almighty God, and I'm honored by His love. I know He keeps His promises."

"That's what you were saying to Josephine earlier. Is that what you believe? You think that the enemy changes the promises that are originally given to you? He would move the heavens to keep His promises to one of His children."

"I try believing that." Dextorus pulls out a cigar from a hidden pocket and slowly examines it. He sniffs the tobacco before placing the cigar between his lips. "Amazing how something so small and insignificant could be all that you have left and become so priceless to you because of the memory it carries."

Mimicking Dextorus, Deasja pulls out a cigar with a purple hue to it.

Dextorus continues. "When she handed these to me…" he pauses, his smokey eyes glisten with pale light, "I thought we'd smoke them later that day together." He sniffs and clears his throat. "That was thirteen thousand years ago. They finally got so old, I blended hers with my own from Jett, so they'd last longer." He pulls the cigar inches from his vision and says, "There's barely a fragment of what she gave me in each one, but it's all I have." He flicks his fingers, makes a flame from a finger lighter, and burns an orange fire at the end of his tobacco.

"He's like you, Dex. There are times when I see why Lucius was chosen."

Dextorus shakes his head and thinks for a moment. He says, "Yuleshua has got so many messes over here. I don't know if he'll ever be ready for that place."

Deasja exhales. "I've never heard you talk like this." Dextorus's eyes cloud over as Deasja continues. "I like it. I think it's good for you to finally talk about your feelings."

Dextorus rolls his eyes. "Forget I said anything and quit counseling me. I forgot who I was talking to."

"Fellowship is good for the soul."

Dextorus huffs. "All you Oobadoave commanders are the same, smooth talkers."

Deasja chuckles. "All you Jett commanders are the same. You're too tough to have feelings." Dextorus cracks a small smile, and Deasja points at him. "A smile. I knew one existed in there."

"Don't let it get to your head, Deasja. These are trying times."

Deasja puffs his cigar and makes rather large smoke rings in front of him.

Dex studies the strange purple colored tobacco in Deasja's fingers. "Where do you make yours?"

"I can't tell you, but I'll say that they're better than anything you get from Jett or anything V made you."

Dextorus says, "I don't know about that. She was talented in making cigars. Why are yours purple?" Dextorus asks.

"Because…" Deasja pauses and smiles before saying, "they're perfect."

Dextorus squints and says, "I don't think so, Deasja. I've been making cigars for over two hundred thousand years, and I don't even know how old you are."

"Just because you're from Jazee Su Thrace," Deasja says as he winks, "doesn't make you the oldest. I'm over forty-seven trillion years old. I know how to make a cigar." He raises his tobacco and says, "And I didn't need a girl to show me how either."

"She didn't." Dextorus curls his lips inward, offering a mild weakness with his eyes. "Do you ever share those?"

Deasja chuckles. "I knew you'd ask me when you found out how old I was." They trade cigars and Deasja says, "Anytime." He breathes in the savory aroma of Dextorus's cigar and says, "This is pretty good. I'm honored to experience one of your coveted cigars. I know how special they are to you." He winks. "But I know you're probably bribing me to keep my mouth shut from you spilling your heart earlier."

"Partially," Dex says as a smile slips from his lips again.

"Wow, that's two smiles I got."

"Calm down, Deasja." Dextorus investigates the cigar and says, "There's not a truth serum in this, is there?"

Deasja says, "While you finish that, I have to stand guard." Deasja takes his foot off the balcony and steps away.

"Deasja? What's in this?"

Deasja ignores answering him, saying, "She's already asleep. I'll meet you in there."

"Deasja? Deasja, what did you just give me?"

Deasja snickers as he stands his post beside the sleeping queen.

Dextorus exhales with a slight shake of his jawline. "Oobadoave commanders." He looks back where Deasja had walked off and says, "Quit teasing me." Dex sniffs the cigar and studies it. "Surely, there's nothing in this."

Thirty-Six

A Dark Place

Several Months Later

In a dimly lit cell, aboard an ancient craft hovering on the dark side of the moon, a tortured king lies on a dirty metallic floor. Lucius's arms are bound in a way that his binding keeps his upper body hanging a couple of feet off the ground while everything below his waistline places weight over pressure wounds. He grimaces as he tries to angle his waist with a pull of his arms. His body tremors with every movement of open sores over soiled coverings. "*Augh*," he yelps.

Lucius rests his cheek over his shoulder, trying not to lick his parched lips. The humming sound of magnetic engines helps to lull his mind away from the random screams that break the silence in between painful movements.

Step, step, step.

Lucius tenses.

A woman screams, "Let me go!"

Immediately, Lucius squeezes his swollen eyes shut from hearing again what's happened all before. "Let her go," his voice crackles through a weakened wheeze of dehydration.

Snap.

Just like before, another woman's neck is snapped outside his door. The airlock sounds its usual sequence of buzzes, and he listens to a body flung against the wall in the room beside him. The airlock safety door closes, and a sinister chuckle introduces a body into space with the remaining sequences of beeps, letting him know the woman's body is no longer on board and he's about to receive a visitor.

Lucius thinks, *I hate you, murderous turd.*

"I can hear your thoughts," the visitor enters the room and flips a light on.

Lucius clears his scratchy throat and says, "I've been beaten six times today, if you'd like to make an appointment," he coughs, "my schedule's clear tomorrow."

"This isn't a game, Yuleshua, Lucius, or whatever you want to call yourself. I lost my wife because of you. I don't feel sorry for you."

Lucius peels his lids apart and squints through the mangled skin and dried blood. "Oh wow, a light. Honestly, I didn't think that thing worked. How nice for you to drop by, Samstarsey," Lucius says while shutting his eyes again. "Excuse me if I can't greet you properly...I'm kinda tied up at the moment." Lucius's head falls back. "You were saying? Something about lies your fake king told you."

"He is a king, and they're not lies," Sam says.

"Is that what he told you, Sam? Baàl always had a thing for the theatrical. His name means he who speaks like a sweet serenade in Gamerin. Baàlsarideem speaks with a silvery tongue, even with his lies. I hate to break it to you, Sam, but you've been lied to."

Slam. Sam kicks Lucius against the wall. "Shut up."

Only catching snippets of what Samstarsey says, Lucius is dazed momentarily. Thick blood drizzles slowly from his bottom lip, and he feels the cold of the metal wall against his cheek, reminding him he's still alive. He mutters through Samstarsey's rant, saying, "I can't breathe."

"Lushaine," Samstarsey says, placing angry hands over Lucius's caved in ribs. "You deserve this. If it wasn't for my master, I would've killed you already."

Lucius's breathing normalizes, but the searing pain from his lungs remain.

Samstarsey says, "You smell like a sewer. You're repulsive to look at." He slaps Lucius's cheek, and says, "I always knew you'd wind up like this," and leaves.

Several minutes pass, and Lucius breaks down, sobbing against the wall. His body falls deeper into dehydration, and hallucinations become his friend.

"Daddy." His mind plays tricks.

"Pumpkin?" he asks while turning over, momentarily believing he's at the cabin. "Claire?" He soon drifts into vivid dreams, watching Josephine holding onto Claire in front of a snowman. He reaches out for Josephine with his hands bound above him. Josephine smiles at him.

He says, "You're beautiful to me. I need your comfort, baby."

She says, "Be strong." Josephine's eyes sadden as she starts to vanish. "Stay strong for me."

Lucius wakes up and is staring at a notch in the wall. "Quit crying." He gulps. "Crying makes the dehydration worse."

After finding a position that hurts the least, he says, "Well, I'm gonna die in here. I love you, Josephine. I tried being strong, but I feel death." He bows his head a little toward the wall and prays, "Father, my body's dying. I wanted to do more for you. Thank you for giving me Josephine, for letting me experience being a father. As my spirit leaves this body, please know that I served you with all that I was."

Step, step, step.

He's too weak to tense up anymore. He whispers, "Can I have a break? I'm dying here."

The cell door opens.

"Seriously," Lucius says as he groans, "a few more moments of peace."

Rueshta closes the door and swiftly locks the mechanism. "I don't have much time," Rueshta says and squats down beside Lucius. "I'm not your enemy."

"Who are you?" Lucius asks.

Rueshta places his hand over Lucius's head and says, "I'm blocking your mind from this meeting. They started watching us closely. Many of us are beaten for even walking this direction."

"Who's us?" Lucius asks.

"There are three hundred and twelve who do not follow Baàlsarideem. We secretly serve our king and worship the Almighty," Rueshta says as he opens an interdimensional space. "I'm your servant, sire, and I'm going to get you home." He places a water bucket down and dips a sponge so Lucius can drink. Lucius slurps up the water as Rueshta continues. "We've been waiting a long time for you to come and save us."

Lucius gulps. "I don't know if you've noticed," he says gesturing down with his nose. "I'm paralyzed, and I have no energy to save anyone."

Rueshta says, "I can help you regain some of your strength, but we'll have to finish your healing when we get you home."

"Who are you?"

Rueshta says, "I can't give you my real name, but my soldier's name is Vincentine. That's what the commanders know me as."

"If you are who you say you are, then why have you only now come to see me?"

Rueshta, known to Lucius as Vincentine says, "I must wait for orders before entering this section. Samstarsey just left and was fearful of what he'd done. He doesn't want to be punished for being the last one in here, so he ordered me to tend to you. He believes I don't have the ability to heal, so he ordered me to give you nourishment and to clean you a little. I've been putting in requests so that I can tend to you in such a way, but they would figure my loyalty to you out if I pressed too hard. I must make my service sound like I'm trying to keep you as a prisoner longer, so we can perform tests on you." His hands shake as he dips more of the bloody sponge in the water. "I'm so sorry for this." He presses the nourishment against Lucius's lips, allowing him to slurp once again.

Vincentine continues. "They've been trying to make a large portal for the entire ship, and they're very close. They're still trying to find where your principality DNA is hidden."

"How do you mean? It flows through my veins."

"That's true, but they're trying to find where the enzymes are produced, so he can transplant the enzyme making organ into his own body," Vincentine says.

"What are you talking about?"

"He needs more than a simple blood transfusion because your blood's enzymes, the one that sets you apart as a principality, immediately dies and vaporizes without the organ's natural factors. He needs to transplant your entire organ into himself. Your spleen, kidneys, and heart don't carry the enzyme he's looking for. He's checked all your bones, and none of them have the gland that produces the enzymes for creating your principality power."

Lucius says, "That's why they've been sticking those needles in me? I never thought much of where to find where my principality DNA is produced. It's kinda who I am."

"They know that the information has been blocked from you by the Trinity, and that's good. The search has been buying us time for the next festival." Vincentine nods and says, "They're going to kidnap more wives soon. That's when our opportunity will be the greatest for escape. I've been in contact with a commander. His name is Dextorus. He and I have been planning together, but it's difficult to get a message out to him."

"Dex?"

"*Shush.*" Vincentine glances back and whispers, "You can't say anything. They don't know I can block minds, and my life would be forfeit, along with many if they found out. My father would die. I need you to stay strong, you're almost home. Don't give up."

"You've gotta be kidding me. We have someone on the inside?" Lucius bows his head. "Oh Lord, I thought my fight was over, and then you bring him in here. A lot has happened in the last thirty seconds. Forgive me for almost releasing my spirit."

Vincentine squeezes bloody water from the sponge and wipes his king's eyes.

"Can you heal me? My body's dying," Lucius says and is barely able to shake his head. "I won't make it through another beating."

"A little," Vincentine says and sniffles. "I'm not as powerful as the Gamerin. I've been healing many women recently. Healing others drains me. Often my powers run out because the women are moments from death by the time that I get to them."

Lucius asks, "What do you mean?"

"I'm the one they order to discard of the bodies when they don't do it themselves. I often hide them in my quarters and heal them there by placing them in a deep sleep before dropping them off to a commander named Albercase. I tie letters to them, or I stuff the letter into pockets of their clothes."

Lucius says, "Wait. You're the Nephilim double agent, the one they hinted about, but wouldn't tell me? I thought you were a figment of my imagination."

He says, "I'm Vincentine, and if you would've known for sure, they would've found out when probing your mind before I could get to you." He places a hand over Lucius's thigh and says, "I'll have to heal some of your wounds. They're infected. You have a couple of open pressure wounds over your sacral area. You're septic and have a fever."

Lucius moans with his healing and says, "Don't heal my paralysis. They'll find out."

"How do you mean?" Vincentine asks.

Lucius answers, "Because I would beat them with their own heads if I could move. Besides, the paralysis below my hips helps to cut the pain when I can't feel anything down there."

Vincentine chuckles to himself and says, "I'd love to see you fight, but you're right. I'll heal you just enough until I can get my orders to come down here next. I'll bring more nourishment next time. You need protein for your flesh to rebind anyway."

"You can stop healing me," Lucius says. "I'm good enough."

"I have more."

"No, save your power for the women. They're the Father's children. His daughters. Our Father will reward you for helping them. I have no doubt in my mind that's why I'm here now. I'll survive. Thank you for pushing the infection out of my body. The chill from the fever is leaving me." Lucius glances up with swollen eyes and asks, "Can you lower my chains, so I can sleep on the floor. I have constant muscle spasms from hanging like this."

Vincentine lowers his eyes and says, "I'm sorry, lord. The chains are as low as they can go. Even if I could, they'd think I was being merciful. I must often pretend I have no heart. Forgive me. I must pretend laughing about your condition in front of them."

Lucius nods. He grunts a little as he moves into another position and says, "I feel much better with what you've given me and this will be added on to you. I forgive you." Lucius gestures with a nod of his nose. "Will you help me?" he asks and grunts again with his movement of trying to be upright. "I want to sit against the wall now that you've closed my wounds on my back side."

Vincentine helps Lucius to sit up because the paralysis has taken the ability away from him.

After Lucius feels a little more normal from sitting with decency, he asks, "How long have I been here? The days have started blending. Why do they keep shooting me with that awful weapon? I have no power, and I'm moments from death every time the pulse goes through my body. My heart has stopped a couple of times. They race to heal me. Why do they keep shooting me?"

Vincentine explains, "They're scared of you. They never want you to regain your abilities, even when you get home. It'll take years for you to heal."

"I'd like to get my hands on the guy who made that stupid thing," Lucius says.

"I'm sorry, sire," Vincentine says. "It was me."

"Oh," Lucius says as his eyes expand. "Well, it works. Good job, kid."

"I can read your mind," Vincentine says. "How come you don't want to kill me for what I've done?"

"I figure you were ordered."

"I was."

Lucius half smiles and says, "If it wasn't for your design, I wouldn't be here," he pauses before finishing sarcastically, "in all my glory…and smelling of urine and feces."

"Don't cast yourself down. You have no choice. Very few are treated like royalty here. You should see some of the rooms I have to clean up." Vincentine reaches in the water bucket and takes out a few hidden fruit pieces. He pulls apart an orange and feeds a small slice to Lucius before saying, "I'm not sure how long you've been here. We're not, I mean, your servants are not allowed to live normally. We must maintain our orders, but when we do go down to Earth, we find out what year it is. I know you've been here at least six months. But I don't know truly how long."

Lucius swallows his bite nearly whole.

"Be careful. Take your time." Vincentine says. "I have a few minutes to feed you."

"You said you had a father. Who is he? Which one of my brothers is he?"

"I can't tell you," Vincentine says and places another orange slice to Lucius's lips. "Sire, you have eight thousand brothers who are trapped in something called amber stone. It was once sap from gopher trees, mixed with the extract taken from the Tree of Life in the garden of Eden. The sap hardened into amber stone and was turned into sarcophagi, which allow their bodies to exist by anabolic conditions."

Lucius immediately sobs. "They live. They're here with me?"

Vincentine embraces him and says, "They await you to release them. Because of the extract that was used, only a principality is powerful enough to release them."

Lucius asks, "What happened to them? I want to see them."

"I can't arrange that. They're in the crypt. Baàlsarideem tricked my uncles into the stone."

Lucius asks, "How did he trick them?"

"We were short on food. Baàlsarideem said that only the Gamerin were the ones strong enough to withstand the process of stasis; otherwise, we would all die of starvation. Baàlsarideem promised that the Gamerin who went into the stone would be sparing their wives. There was an agreement made. Only a few Gamerin would remain awake as workers to tend to the gardens and protect the women and children. To spare their families, one by one, the Gamerin gave themselves as a sacrifice and were imprisoned." Vincentine pauses for a moment and then says, "Baàlsarideem never told them how many workers would stay awake or that he had already spoken to his army about a different plan that he had made.

"What happened to the women and children?"

"They were slaughtered, and their bodies were made into compost for the gardens. Only the strongest Nephilim were spared and sent to toil the earth for crops aboard this vessel."

Lucius closes his eyes and mourns for a moment. He thinks of the pain that his brothers must have suffered and asks, "Do they know of what happened to their wives?"

"Yes. A psychic connection can be made with them. But it's rare for someone like myself."

Lucius takes in a deep breath and asks, "What are the numbers of this ship? I need to know our chances."

Vincentine says, "There are four thousand fallen Gamerin, and sixteen thousand Nephilim bred for Baàlsarideem's army. It's why it's difficult for me to sneak in here. There are only three hundred and twelve who serve you secretly, and we have very little power compared to the Gamerin army. We must constantly block our minds. They believe I have no power, and I continue pursuing that falsity because of them." He dips more water for Lucius.

After Lucius drinks, he asks, "Is there any way you can send a message to my brothers? Do you have a psychic ability to speak with them?"

"From time to time, I can sneak in and speak with my father. He knows you're onboard this ship. He speaks with the others for me. He shields their hearts and minds so the information stays guarded."

"He must be one of the older Gamerin if he can do that," Lucius says.

"I've said too much…here." Vincentine stops talking and places another orange slice into Lucius's mouth. "You need more nourishment. They're going to be taking more blood soon. I must hydrate you."

Lucius asks, "More tests? When you plan on getting me out, can you get the women out too? How many have been added to their army because of those women?"

"My lord, they've been sterile a long time because of Commander Albercase. I'm sorry, but the only way I can get you out is during the festival of wives," Vincentine says.

"Festival of what? That sounds dreadful given the context. What is the festival?"

Vincentine explains, "They kidnap more women, and a selected few of us are left preparing those women as brides in their chambers."

"This sounds sick," Lucius says. "That must be what is happening when there is a massive disappearance of women from Earth. They told me that the Nephilim were responsible for the death of thousands of women each year. That the women just go missing."

Vincentine nods and continues. "My plan is that during the preparation of the women, the Gamerin will continue to have their festival. When they do, they always drink too much. When they're preoccupied with taking their new wives after becoming drunk at the feast, that's when our small army is going to be able to get you out."

Lucius gasps and asks, "Wait. The women will be assaulted during this time?"

"I have no better plan, my lord. Baàlsarideem takes his key off only when he's about to take a new bride. I will swap out the portal key while I'm preparing his new bride and they're celebrating in the weapons barracks. When they go back to their chambers, after having drunk a lot, we can get you out of here."

Lucius shakes his head. "I can't be a part of this…Freed during the suffering of the innocent."

"My lord, if you ever want to save these women, then we must get you out of here first. I can't save the women this time."

Lucius nods. "There should be two keys. My daughter's guardian angel was kidnapped too."

"Artorus?"

"Yes," Lucius says. "What about Artie's key?"

Vincentine wipes the clotted blood from Lucius's eyes with a wet rag. "I hate to tell you, but that key is already being used to create a huge one."

"You can't bind portal materials together without a celestial principality's…" he pauses while saying. Lucius leans his head back and says, "Now it's starting to make more sense. Where did he get the material to produce such a key? He'd have to have hundreds of ordained metals."

Vincentine says, "He's been torturing guardians a long time. He has quite a collection, although he hasn't used all of them. I don't know what he's planning with the ones that he hasn't used. My guess is as a bargaining chip for anyone in any army he chooses. Baàlsarideem knows that because you're a Gamerin principality, he has complete access to any gate because you were the builder of the keys. He needs your principality permission somehow and has been trying to capture your ability to give that power. He knows that the ability to give permission is found in an enzyme that is replicated by an organ that sets you apart from the rest of the Gamerin." Vincentine gives him another sip of water and says, "Once he has that organ, he will bind the metals together like you can, to make a massive gate."

"That way he can get the entire ship across for some reason," Lucius says. "Why not just enter two Gamerin at a time? I'm not complaining. I like him delaying his invasion of my inheritance and all, but why the whole ship?"

Vincentine answers, "The amber stones. He's planning something with them, but I can't figure his plans out. I've tried to sabotage the process of binding the gate for as long as I could. With all my fallbacks and obstacles that I have been putting in place, they're figuring out your DNA trail. They only need your blood producing enzyme that is specific to you currently, the organ."

Vincentine washes Lucius's exposed skin with soapy water.

Lucius groans and says, "If they need my hidden organ, then they still need my permission. I've almost died several times already, pretty much daily. They're doing a poor job of trying to keep me alive, if that's what they're trying to do."

"Baàlsarideem is trying to break you. After he breaks you, he'll play his mind games. He allows some to come in here to torture you as long as you don't die."

Lucius looks at Vincentine and says, "Well, they're terrible at following orders." Lucius clears his throat from his mouth becoming moistened by the nourishment he has been given. "You say Baàl's wife still lives. What's wrong with her? Why does she allow him to do whatever evil he wants? She must be a dreadful Jezebel."

Vincentine shakes his head and says, "It's not what you think. A human mind was never made to endure such gravity of an imprisonment. She doesn't remember."

Lucius asks, "What does she not remember?"

"I heard that she suffers from her mind withering from dementia. Baàlsarideem doesn't care who he destroys in order to release her and heal her. He believes his plans are perfect. He thinks he can heal her once he has it."

"Has what? What is the 'it' you just said? The organ that makes my principality enzymes? Is he gonna poke me for another biopsy or something?" Lucius opens his swollen eyes up at Vincentine. "What's that face you're making? What are you not telling me?"

Vincentine exhales a deep breath and apologetically says, "I tried to get them to think of something else, but they wouldn't change their minds."

"Change their minds on what?" Lucius asks.

"They're making a new device for you." Vincentine closes his eyes and stays silent.

A brief pause passes, and Lucius asks, "What device? An MRI maybe?"

Vincentine lowers the rag in his soap bucket. "They're making a device that'll open up the dimensional fields around you, granting them access to what is hidden."

Lucius slightly chuckles and says, "I don't have the energy to get any swords or knives. They're wasting their time."

Vincentine comforts Lucius by holding the underside of his forearm that is held by chains in the air. He strokes his arm and says, "We're going to get you out of here. We're going to put you in healing waters as soon as it happens."

Lucius was smiling for a moment until he sees the seriousness in Vincentine's expression. Lucius asks, "As soon as what happens? There's only knives and swords tucked away. I have nothing of any value to them in those pockets. Maybe a couple of batteries."

Vincentine continues. "I've already made plans with the commander. They keep the waters ready at your palace for healing. It'll stop the bleeding."

"What are you talking about...bleeding? Why are you making it sound..."

Vincentine shakes his head and says, "They're not making the device for your swords and knives."

"Oh, no, no, no." Lucius sobs. "They can't take them."

"I've tried to talk him out of it, but they know your wings are the largest because you're the Gamerin king and principality. Only the mighty sons of God have wings that big. I'm doing all that I can, but they're planning on amputating soon."

Lucius hyperventilates.

Vincentine rubs his neck. "Please calm yourself."

"Please! Can you lock the door? Weld the door shut for me."

"I can't keep them out of here, and I'm sorry for that. I'll bring you food and drink later. I must hide the good stuff in your bathwater." Vincentine shakes some sodium bicarbonate mixed with charcoal powder down along the wall to rid the room of such a strong ammonia smell. "This'll help to deodorize the air for you. It's dark due to the charcoal so they won't see the mixture." He glances back. "I feel someone coming. I must go." He places his hand over Lucius's head, whispers, "Your memory of this meeting is blocked," and swiftly leaves.

Thirty-Seven

Predicament

On the breathtaking world of Gamerilaye, a lonely wife mourns the loss of her husband while she watches her young four-year-old playing in the royal garden. The light of early afternoon shines over the top terrace of the palace, as the wind blows the sweet fragrance of spring flowers in the gardenia garden. Soldiers stand watch at every corner of the top-tier garden. Two guardians protect the snake path leading down the mountain from the garden to keep the princess from venturing off.

Josephine sits on the padded chair in the center of the garden. She stretches her back to find a comfortable position. "He's kicking my bladder," she says to herself. "Why is it always my bladder?" Josephine leans back a little more to support her pregnancy waistline. The queen is in her third trimester with the king's heir.

After hearing her whisper beneath her breath, Deasja looks over at Josephine and sees her trying not to grimace. He scans her vitals and says, "Your blood pressure is up again." He walks over to her.

She says, "I'll be fine. It's only been an hour since the last time that you healed me. I'm just uncomfortable. Let me get in a good position."

He smiles and speaks with a voice of soothing rain. "You aren't bothering me. This is why I am here. I was chosen to heal you in Lucius's absence because the king trusts me. Dextorus and I are your guardians."

Deasja touches her shoulder and heals her. As her body relaxes from the healing, Josephine tries to smile at her innocent daughter. Claire walks around and looks over at her mother. She smiles and shows her mother what she can do. Claire runs to a large gardenia that droops near the white roses. She places her tiny hand upon the pedal and looks at her mother again. Claire gives the gardenia strength to stand on its own and heals the flower.

Josephine smiles when she sees how well her daughter is becoming a Gamerin builder. She says, "Daddy said that growing things is among the first gifts that a Gamerin receives, Claire. Daddy would've loved to see that. He always loved to heal flowers. You're just as wonderful as him."

Claire plucks a rose and runs to her mother. "This is for you," she says while handing her mother the rose.

Josephine holds the rose and sniffs.

Claire says, "I want you to have it because I love you, Momma. I'll give my baby bubba one when he's born."

Josephine holds the white rose to her face and says, "I love you, Claire. You're wonderful and as loving as your daddy. I'll always keep it, and when it dies you can heal it for me like your daddy used to do. Does that sound like a good idea, sweetheart?"

Claire innocently nods and says, "I can heal it every day until daddy gets home."

Artie stands beside Claire as he studies how Deasja and Dextorus guards his queen closely, knowing that her condition is teetering on the verge of seizures because of her stress. He then smiles at Claire and says, "I think that's a great idea. You can heal the rose every day for your daddy, and when he returns, he'll have a fresh new rose waiting from his daughter."

Because she is so mournful waiting for her husband to return, Josephine feels that she is exhausted and needs to excuse herself before her blood pressure rises again. As she tries to stand, Deasja races to her side and gingerly helps her rise from her position. Deasja says, "Take your time."

While he helps her, Josephine watches the angels gathered around her every move. She says, "I need help on the stairs…" and pauses to make eye contact with several of them before saying, "but leave me alone in my quarters. I must lie down for a nap."

Deasja and Dextorus read her mind and know she is not only taking a nap, but she is going to grieve.

While escorting her on the stairs, Deasja counsels her, saying, "It's not good if you cry. You're eight weeks from birthing the prince and he should not come early because it would take much power to heal him. We need him to be strong like his father. Don't be upset. We know Lucius will not fall now, and he could be here soon."

As they get to the bottom step, Josephine tells him, "As an Oobadoave inhabitant, I know you visit often with the spirit world, but I don't. Without my husband, one day is unbearable to me. With Lucius absent, a part of me is missing, and I don't know what they're doing with him. Whatever they're doing, he doesn't deserve it. So, excuse me while I have a heart for things that I have no power over." Josephine covers her face with one of her gloved hands.

As she tries covering her tears while walking the corridor that leads to her room, angels stand guard by lining the great halls of the Gamerin palace. A couple angels notice her behavior and take steps from their posts so that they may console her. Before they reach her, she walks into her room and closes the door behind her.

With the door closed, Deasja stops outside her room and redirects the concerned angels to regain their posts.

Josephine draws the decorated bed curtain to fully close and lies in the dark of her solitude. As she whimpers in want for her husband to return, she whispers, "Lucius, come back to me, my love."

Outside the quarters, Deasja and Dex stand with dozens of assigned guards in the hall. They all hear her as she weeps.

Although Dextorus is the number one commander over the angelic forces within the Gamerin household, Deasja is second-in-command over the troops.

Because Deasja wants none to hear the weakness of the queen, he tells them, "Please give her privacy. I need you all to protect the perimeter outside. Keep an eye open for the return of the king."

Every soldier except for Dextorus and Deasja exit the stronghold and fly around the perimeter and forests to maintain the security.

Artie and Claire are still in the garden when Artie watches the exiting horde of security leaving the queen's side. He knows why they were asked to leave, for he can also read the queen's mind. Bending to one knee, he says to Claire, "I have an idea. Why don't we go down to the beach and collect flowers and seashells for your momma?"

Claire smiles and answers, "And we can make sandcastles with our buckets also."

Artie nods. "Great idea. We can collect shells to decorate your brother's bassinet."

Artie lifts Claire into his arms and tells her, "Hold on, princess. We're gonna take the long way down." He carries her down to the beach to keep her from hearing her mother cry, so that she may continue with her faith in her father's return.

When Josephine wakes from napping, she calls Thimbette and Charony because she is too far along in her pregnancy to make the bed herself. She says, "Sleep is difficult and makes me tired. I can't get proper rest." Josephine sits at her vanity mirror of polished silver. Feeling faint, she can't raise her head to look at her reflection.

While Thimbette is making the bed, Charony does the queen's hair so that she may leave her quarters in dignity.

Outside the door, Dex and Deasja sense a change in the air coming from Josephine's quarters.

A sharp pain shoots across Josephine's abdomen causing her to grimace and clutch the area with her forearms. She gasps and leans forward from pain.

Deasja and Dex both look at each other. "Preeclampsia," Dex says before running into her room. Deasja and Dex witness the queen trying to stand while hunched over. They run to her aid. Deasja picks her up and Dex yells, "Get her into the water!"

Running as fast as he can to the healing waters, Deasja releases some of his healing power and says, "I told you it's not good to cry, your majesty. We want Lucius to be here for the birth of his son."

In pain, she becomes short-tempered and snaps at him, "I don't need your lip. I'm the one in pain, remember?" She grunts with every jostle of his steps. "Stop shaking me."

Deasja takes a few steps into the healing waters and floats the queen in the middle. He tells her, "I wasn't shaking you. I think you're going to have to stay in here until evening. You can cry all you want in here. Next time you want to cry, instead of taking a nap, go swimming in the king's healing waters and save yourself the trouble."

Deasja says such stern things to the queen to toughen her spirit. He knows when Lucius arrives through a portal, his appearance will be difficult for her to look upon. He sets her on a built-in chair to the side of the healing pool and excuses himself. "I'm leaving you in here for a while. I must speak with Dex and have your maidservants tend to you when you get out. I'll make sure no angels will look upon you because that's what Lucius wants."

Dex enters the healing water chamber.

Exiting the pool, Deasja stares at Dex. Rarely has Dex ever witnessed fear in Deasja's eyes, but there is fear in them, nonetheless. Deasja shakes his head in disbelief to how close they came to a disaster. After psychically expressing his annoyance about his situation, Deasja places his hands over his chest and lowers his hands toward his feet, psychokinetically drying himself off. When he's completely dry, he gazes down at the queen and tries not to look bothered. He takes in a deep breath and exhales his anxiety, saying, "Josephine, are you feeling better?"

Cross, she says, "I feel better. Thank you for helping me, but that doesn't mean I want your lip."

"I understand that you are embarress—"

"No, Deasja. I have the right to have feelings and cry. You ask of me the impossible. Of course, I mourn."

Deasja says nothing because there is nothing he can say. She speaks the truth, and she does have every right to miss her husband and worry for him.

When Deasja says nothing, Josephine tells him, "Don't forget that I need Charony and Thimbette because not all of us can dry off by our minds. I'm sopping wet and can barely dress myself because of my preeclampsia episodes."

Deasja silently nods like he is listening to her, but his mind is somewhere else. With like-mindedness, Deasja and Dex walk out of the healing lounge thinking the same dreadful thought. Upon their exit, Dex says, "I know what you're going to say. I was thinking the same thing."

As they walk the corridor back to the king's chambers, Deasja tries to remain calm and answers, "Commander Dex, I have healed her nearly a dozen times today, and it is barely afternoon. Whatever we do, we can't let her see Lucius when he comes through that portal. She will go into preterm labor. That water is to be ready for Lucius, not her. Vincentine told me what they were doing, and if Lucius is still alive when he comes through, the queen will give birth. I will not have enough energy to heal her body from seizures and a principality's son. If Lucius comes soon, all our concentration and healing will be upon the grim condition of the king to keep him alive. We must try and protect his son, Dex. Lucius wouldn't want her to see him as a broken being anyway. I know Lucius is humble, but he's still a royal principality. He just wouldn't want her to witness him like that."

The two commanding angels stop in the middle of the hall.

Dex looks at Deasja and says, "I can heal her of the seizures, but I won't be able to stop her from going into labor if her water breaks. She stays near the lounge during the day hoping for the return of Yuleshua. Nobody can force her away because she's a stubborn queen. When we do get her to go elsewhere, she worries that she will miss him. I can try to keep her away from the bathhouse.

Deasja says, "No, Dex. If she keeps crying, then she's going to need the healing waters as well."

Dex asks, "Are you saying that she needs to be near the healing waters?"

Deasja shakes his head. He answers, "We are in a predicament. We don't have the power to make another pool without the king. Healing waters can be made only by a principality with our General's permission. Also, we must keep our tongues mute about this realm's situation. It's a God-given gift to make a pool of healing water. That's how Lucius was able to save Artie, but we're in a mess because we have only one at our disposal. Artie's healing waters were drained because it was tainted with poisoned blood, making it unholy. I know we can heal the newborn with our abilities when he is birthed, but I want to save whatever energy I have for the Gamerin celestial that we know will be crossing that portal. Vincentine said that Lucius will need much healing. The waters might heal Lucius's body, but they can't heal his spirit and his power within. His mind will be weak from the torture and will most likely need counseling. I must heal his mind too."

Dex nods. "Vincentine said that the healing process could be months or even years. The water will only keep him from dying. Lucius is going to need time, and with the threat of Baàlsarideem invading, I don't know how much time for healing we have. At least, his mind will be working well for planning a battle. He's a builder and has a great way of thinking about such things."

They walk as Deasja says, "I must get Thimbette and Charony before I get in trouble with Josephine. I wouldn't want the queen to tell everybody I dunked her in water, and left her to fend for herself. Even with no power in Lucius's body, I wouldn't want to face him after that. He has his ways of getting even without breaking the rules."

"You're right. You wouldn't want Lucius mad at you."

Deasja walks into the queen's chambers and looks at the maidservants. He says, "I need you two to grab robes, a change of clothes, and whatever else you do to aid the queen when she gets out of the healing waters." He points at what they are doing and corrects them, "She's not having her baby right now, so you can put the birthing stool back. The queen is waiting for you in the healing chambers."

Dex and Deasja watch the Bengaldoes gather their supplies. When done, the commanders follow behind them as they all make their way to the queen.

As they walk the halls, Dex psychically says, *"I think it's time to call the troops back. Let them know she's in the healing waters. Lucius doesn't want anyone to see her the way he sees her. He struggles with jealousy. Baàlsarideem molested her in front of him. I don't think he'll ever get over that. He's going to enjoy killing Baàlsarideem."*

Deasja nods his head in respect and places his fingers to his temple as he softly speaks, "Okay, guardians. It's time to come back in. Don't enter the healing chamber. The royal queen is in that room, and she is not decent for any to look upon her while her body heals."

Artie is on the beach collecting shells and flowers with Claire when he observes the angels returning. He smiles at Claire, and asks, "Do you want to go back in? Or would you like to stay out here longer?"

"I wanna give these flowers to Momma."

Artie and Claire make their way through the main entrance. Looking at the Gamerin tree, Artie says, "The fruits are blooming. I see cherries."

She points up and asks, "Artie, can you get me some of those cherries for my momma?"

"Good idea." He flies up, walks a branch, and grabs a handful of the sweet fruit. He gazes down below and says, "There are about twenty on this branch here. Do you think that's enough?"

"Yes," she hollers up.

With a pocket full of flowers, cherries, and seashells, Artie and the princess are passing by the healing lounge on the way to Claire's quarters to prepare the gift for her mother. As they pass the healing lounge, Artie is shocked to see the door open. Thimbette exits the healing chamber to grab a hairbrush for her queen.

When Artie sees the queen in the healing waters, he is troubled. He sprints to the door as it closes. Careful of the queen's privacy, he looks at Dex and asks, "Why's my queen in the healing waters? What's wrong?"

Deasja answers, "Not in front of Claire. I'll take her to her room and finish the project you're thinking of until you can return to her. I think a mobile will be nice over the bassinet. Good idea. Dex will explain everything to help you with what needs to be done."

Lovingly, Deasja holds Claire's tiny hand and leads her away from the concern.

After they walk off, Artie stands closer to Dex and asks, "Why is she in the waters, Commander? What's happening?"

Dex explains, "We had to act fast. Her stress was causing her to go into preterm labor with seizures. Her water almost broke. Her preeclampsia leaves when she is healed, but not for long. Her stress always returns when she thinks of Lucius. She's fine for the moment, but we're faced with a new problem.

"What problem?" Artie asks.

Dex says, "When the king returns through the portal gate, we know he won't be easy for Josephine to witness. With her body extra sensitive from mourning her husband, we're afraid we'll be forced to use our healing powers to heal the prince if he comes early. His lungs won't be mature enough."

"Aren't you two here for that, anyway? Deasja has enough ability to heal her body and the prince."

Dex answers, "We are, but we've become limited due to how much healing she has been requiring. We need to save our power for Lucius because of the weapon they've been using on him. That's where the predicament comes in because of Lucius."

Artie asks, "How are you planning on fixing the predicament?"

Dex answers, "We are trying to come up with a plan to keep her away from the portal for when Lucius arrives. One of us needs to have enough power to keep Lucius's spirit from leaving his body before he can get into the water. There won't be enough power between us if she keeps going into preeclampsia. Only Deasja and I have been trained to deliver children. And Lucius doesn't want everyone in the room when she delivers the prince either. Lucius won't be in any condition to aid his wife to deliver the boy. If she has already drained us from healing her all day, she can't be near when Lucius's broken body is pulled through."

Artie nods until staring off. Deep in thought, he says, "I don't know how we're going to fix that."

"Any ideas?"

Shaking his head, Artie says, "She waits for him right here. Nobody can force her away, not without telling her why. We can't tell her how gruesome the enemy is without causing her to go into labor." Artie lowers his head.

"Do we have any idea of when he'll be coming through, or when they're going to try and break him out?"

Dex says, "I've spoken to Commander Albercase, and he told me soon they'll be abducting new wives. While they're doing their evil deeds, Vincentine is planning on saving the king. It'll be soon, but it'll be too soon for her to have the baby. If the king's son is born while Lucius is still in captivity, Baàlsarideem will lose his power."

"Isn't that good?" Artie asks.

"No," Dex answers. "Baàlsarideem will feel the power leaving his body. He might slay Lucius out of anger. Lucius needs to be here before the boy is born, and that is why we must keep her from delivering too early. When Lucius arrives, he will require much healing. There's not enough power between Deasja, you, and me to heal a principality. Soon after Lucius and the Nephilim escape, we will have to plan for an invasion. We have a staggering issue because Lucius will be no stronger than an ordinary man."

Artie places both of his hands over his face. He lowers his fingers and pulls his cheeks down while emitting flames on his head. He takes in a few breaths to calm himself, and the flames turn into dissipating sparks. Artie shakes his head and says, "I don't think you can have her stay away from the healing waters if she might accidentally go into labor."

"Deasja said the same thing," Dex replies.

Artie continues. "Because this area calms her spirit, she should stay nearby. The prince can't be born before Lucius is back. We can't risk Lucius or his son dying. This entire realm...We'd lose everyone."

"That's what I was saying."

Shaking his head, Artie includes, "No, you don't understand. Josephine could die if she isn't healed."

Finally realizing what Artie is saying, Dex stares at the ceiling and lets out a deep breath. "All three of them will need healing," he says.

Artie says, "Let her stay calm so that your healing is not used. Stop having her go to the garden or talking her into taking a nap. Let her decide. Prepare for all three to need healing."

Dex says, "You're right. We'll have to keep her close until right before Lucius comes through. I don't think anyone can get her away from that area when the time comes. I know Lucius doesn't want her to see the condition he'll be in, but its unavoidable."

Artie walks toward Claire's room and says, "Yep, we have a problem."

Thirty-Eight

Yaztarifenn's Son

Aboard Baàlsarideem's ship, Vincentine uses the guise of merely keeping his test subject alive. With his strict orders, Vincentine secretly nurses Lucius back to some health to better the king's chances for survival when escaping.

His visits are few and for short amounts of time. After one of his meetings with Lucius, Vincentine goes to the slave quarter's greenhouse located in the floating city section. The floating city is considered the slums of the ship because the housing is made of scraps.

At one of the outer filtration systems that feed into the orchard, Vincentine cleans out the king's bloody bucket after visiting with Lucius. He hangs the newly cleansed bucket beside the filtering stream. Vincentine glances up and sees several of the secret followers of Lucius staring over at the blood as it runs into the filtration stream.

The Nephilim slaves bow their heads in grief as they hide their emotions. At the same time, there are fallen Gamerin picking produce within the gardens because of their preparations for the soon coming festival.

One of the fallen Gamerin, known as Shelah, walks toward a slave named Akhtar in the garden. Akhtar isn't looking and is busy because he wipes his tears after watching Vincentine clean the bucket.

"Move!" Shelah violently pushes Akhtar into a metallic beam that holds up some of the hanging gardens. Shelah grabs an orange from the tree beside him and mocks Akhtar, saying, "You're not a real Nephilim, Akhtar. You're not a Gamerin at all because you would've known I was going to do that if you truly read minds. We should've killed you with the rest of the whining brats that had no abilities and were eating all our food. You're weak. You're as worthless as your stupid sleeping father, Hoshtravay."

Akhtar stands slowly to his feet and picks up his torn, woven hat from the ground. He tries not to look at his superior in the eyes to provoke him. Akhtar nods his head in respect, but Shelah kicks him into the post again and says, "Don't get up in front of me, slave. I didn't give you permission to stand. Stay there on the ground like the worthless slave that you are. Baàlsarideem only spared you because he has a soft spot for Hosh." Shelah points toward two other Nephilim slaves within the garden and yells, "Akhtar, you're more worthless than Nicholson and Hatrueshian over there. At least, we can do tests on them. You would die. You're nothing but a worthless gardener."

As soon as Shelah walks off with his back turned, Akhtar stands to his feet and flips his middle finger at him. When he feels vindicated some, Akhtar places his hands to his hips and is left shaking his head while whispering to himself, "I hate that turd. He does that every time to me."

Vincentine and Hatrueshian walk over to Akhtar. Nicholson coughs in the distance to cover the sound of Akhtar rebelling while Shelah is close enough to hear. After Shelah walks out of the area, Nicholson knows that the sounds of the pylons will mask anymore outbursts. Nicholson joins his irritated cousin for support a few minutes later.

Pretending that they are all picking fruit, Vincentine speaks with his mind, *"You can't let any of them hear you say that, especially, Shelah. They're watching us closely. We won't be here soon. I blocked your mind so they can't read it. I know that's why they get angry, like Shelah does, because they think that's some kind of power you have. It angers the ones like Shelah because they can't read your thoughts."*

"I hate them. Maybe someone should tell him that he has a girl's name," Akhtar says.

Hatrueshian coughs while saying, "Shut up," and masks the comment well.

Vincentine enters Akhtar's mind, saying, *"Hatrueshian is right. Be quiet. We have come too far to get caught with careless actions. I can hear your thoughts if you want to speak."*

Akhtar fights tears of anger and bites his lip for a moment. He thinks, *"There is nothing left of me. That device you made took every power I had. It's been five years. I can barely grow things. I'm worthless."*

Nicholson pretends to be gathering fruit for wine and speaks into the conversation, transferring, *"That's just your captivity talking. Believe me, you don't want to have abilities because they would come in here and take you to the lab. Because you don't have abilities, we can usually persuade them to spare you. This won't always be home."*

Vincentine continues. *"When we get to Gamerilaye, if the king receives his power, then he will heal yours. He doesn't know that they had used the pulse weapon on many of us before using it on him. He suffers too much to grieve him with that information. Stay strong, my cousin. We'll be at our true home soon."*

Akhtar lowers his head as he grabs his gardening tools and replies, *"I can hardly wait. I wanna stick a spike through Shelah's head."* Akhtar walks by Nicholson and Hatrueshian as they load their fruit into a bushel cart.

Two Gamerin with purple and silver eyes enter the garden. They look around. Samstarsey follows in shortly after they do. Samstarsey points at Nicholson and says, "He's the biggest in the garden." He tells one of the Gamerin, "Grab him."

"Wait." Nicholson holds his hands up and begs, "I was just tested. My wounds haven't healed." Nicholson glances over at Akhtar and immediately remembers how fragile Akhtar is. Because Akhtar is close enough to be chosen, he is at risk of being tested on. Nicholson falls to his knees and says, "Here I am. I'll go," and he is forced to follow the Gamerin to the lab.

Samstarsey smiles and moves his finger to choose another slave. Akhtar can't make any sudden movements. If he were to run, he would surely be chosen. Hatrueshian runs in between Akhtar and where Sam points. Hatrueshian falls to his knees and says, "I haven't done anything."

"That's interesting," Sam says as he drops his hand from curiousness. "What do you mean?"

Although the statement worked to keep Akhtar from being pointed at, the arising question weighs heavy over the remaining slaves on that side of the grove.

"He hasn't finished his bushels today," a voice calls out.

The second Gamerin standing beside Samstarsey walks over toward the owner of the voice as Vincentine turns his eyes to see Akhtar speak out again, saying, "He was almost done with his bushels. We must make the festival wine." Vincentine notices how Akhtar's knees are beginning to buckle as the Gamerin comes closer.

Vincentine then speaks as the lead scientist, Rueshta, and says, "I only need one. The master only wants one at a time for this experiment. Weaker slaves could die."

The Gamerin stops moving just before he could grab Akhtar. Samstarsey says, "Rueshta, he didn't tell me to gather only one. Baàl said that the device needs to work before the festival."

"Let's not waste our resources on the slaves we are unsure of if they have wings or not," Vincentine says.

"Very well, slave," Sam says and leaves.

The Gamerin in front of Akhtar, pushes Akhtar back and says, "Nobody gave you permission to speak, slave," and he leaves as well.

Akhtar squats on the ground, wobbly, and hyperventilating. When he is able, he gets up and crawls toward the cart and hides behind a wheel so he can catch his breath.

Hatrueshian is still on his knees and bends forward in relief of Akhtar being spared. As Vincentine takes two steps toward his exit, Samstarsey enters back into the grove. He glances over at Hatrueshian and says, "I'll grab him. I know he has wings."

"I only need one for this experiment," Vincentine says.

But Vincentine's words are in vain as Samstarsey uses blunt force to backhand Hatrueshian into a large fruit tree for arguing. With all the air knocked out of him, Hatrueshian struggles to get up from the ground this time. Samstarsey yanks Hatrueshian by his hair, and says, "Better safe than sorry, Rueshta." Samstarsey glares back at Vincentine and says, "Just like the rest of these weak Nephilim around you, you're just a worthless slave, no matter how much the master protects you. You're nothing to me like your father before you. The time is short where you will soon be put in your true place." He looks around at a sea of terrified eyes. "All of you!" Sam yells out to the Nephilim. "You will bow to me as a god before you."

Trying to act emotionless, Vincentine watches as Hatrueshian is dragged off. Several slaves within the garden silently bow their heads. Akhtar covers his eyes as his weakness has once again placed him in a position of hurting others. Beneath his breath, "I'm sick of this," Akhtar breathes out.

All the nearby Nephilim heard him. *"Be mindful of even the slightest hate in your heart, Akhtar. Hate is fuel for them,"* Vincentine transfers the thought.

Pretending that he is doing his daily duties, Vincentine speedily goes to the lab for testing on Nicholson and Hatrueshian. As he enters the lab, Vincentine witnesses three Nephilim being forced into a shielded cell. Nicholson and Hatrueshian are being tied up with Hersone in the lead embossed, containment area. "Why is Hersone here?"

"Punishment," Baàlsarideem says.

"Don't punish me again with these slaves, my lord," Hersone cries out before they close the seal of the containment area.

A Gamerin scientist telepathically inserts codes into the network of computers and starts the relays for the negative air flow. "They are about to be shot at by the new device that opens the trans-dimensional spaces of the king. Half of the Gamerin offspring have inherited the DNA of wings. These three Nephilim have inherited the trait of wings." He turns on the shields to reinforce the barriers and says, "This should protect us from any backfire of the ions, my lord."

Vincentine tries to maintain a strong face. As he watches, Baàlsarideem stands behind Vincentine and stretches his back with a small grunt. He says, "Rueshta. You almost missed all your work's success. We're almost done with the device if this is successful. Pretty soon, I'll have the king's wings and his permission in my blood."

Vincentine answers, "I wouldn't want to miss the show. I've worked years on this."

Baàlsarideem looks at Vincentine and says, "I looked at your request for twisting his mind, Rueshta. You're very crafty and wise. I want you to start washing him as we had discussed. Start giving him some fruit and act like you're his friend. I want you to report to me everything he does. I want him to be my second-in-command because he's a wise builder. I believe he could be a general in my army when he comes around."

Vincentine nods and says, "After I'm done enjoying this, I'll go and wash off that trash for you."

Baàlsarideem pats him on the back and says, "Go easy on him, Rueshta. We're supposed to make him like us now, remember? But if we get this device to work, and he hasn't turned to serve me, then I don't care what that traitor thinks."

Vincentine bows his head and continues to watch the results of the trans-dimensional device that will be used to help to amputate Lucius's wings. He watches as Nicholson is shot with thousands of joules of electricity from the device.

Nicholson's wings become visible for only a moment. He moans in pain as his skin is burned.

Baàlsarideem rejoices, and shouts, "Eureka! We're close. We need to infuse dampeners to slow the organic response, but it works."

Vincentine looks over at Baàlsarideem, and tries to manipulate him to spare Hatrueshian from the torture. He says, "I think we need to leave the other two for the later trials after I infuse the dampeners. They appear to have been beaten into exhaustion. I want all of them to be strong, so we can be sure that it works well on the Gamerin trash down in the cell."

Baàlsarideem shakes his head, and says, "No. Hersone is being punished as a regular slave now. Besides, I like to watch them scream. It's funny to watch them shake when they're electrocuted." Baàlsarideem sticks his finger into the air, and signals the Gamerin scientist working in the lab to continue firing at the other two Nephilim slaves.

Hatrueshian is shot next. His body violently shakes while hung up against the wall. He screams, "Please!" After the shot has been fired, Hatrueshian falls limp while hanging in chains. Soon, Hatrueshian becomes silent and is left drooling from pain.

Vincentine strains to hide his facial expressions. His anger wells in him and battles within himself to sneer while wincing as he smiles. Vincentine looks over at Baàlsarideem, says, "You're right. It's always fun to watch them," and pretends to laugh.

Baàlsarideem continues to pat Vincentine on the shoulder as Vincentine's stomach churns from the disgust of every time Baàlsarideem touches him as a friend. Maintaining his façade, Vincentine chuckles when Baàlsarideem does.

After he finishes the lab trials of the new weapon, Vincentine prepares himself to visit with Lucius. Throwing some fruit, he had gathered earlier into a bucket with water, he makes his way down to the dark chambers beneath the bowels of the floating city. He enters the dark chamber of the king.

Upon entering the prison cell, Vincentine witnesses two fallen Nephilim, Devon and Morgafa, beating Lucius. Vincentine runs over to Devon and pushes him away. Morgafa steps back and hits Vincentine in the back, knocking him toward a wall. Vincentine catches himself against the wall and says, "I've spoken to the master, and he says to quit beating him." He turns toward them both as he continues. "Now heal the prisoner, or I'll tell Baàlsarideem myself that you've turned against his orders."

Morgafa leans down and begins to slightly heal Lucius. But Morgafa forces Lucius's head against the wall, holding his neck to strangle him during the healing of his chest cavity. Vincentine places down the bucket and kicks Morgafa in the back. Morgafa falls to the side and lands in urine. He jumps to his feet, and says, "I'll kill you for that, Rueshta."

Vincentine says, "Morgafa, next time you disobey Baàlsarideem, I'm going to have them run trials on you like the other slaves in the lab. I'm sure that Hersone would love the company."

Morgafa snaps at Vincentine, "Rueshta, you think you are so strong because you work with Baàlsarideem in his lab. But when we all get home to Gamerilaye, you'll be worthless again. He won't need you anymore. Watch your back on that day!"

Vincentine stands straight up and puffs out his chest, as he says, "I can't wait for that day. I have a special device just for you, Morgafa."

Devon says, "We were done anyway. He's no fun to beat anymore. He doesn't even whine. Let's go Morgafa, so the little lab rat can do his chores."

As soon as Morgafa and Devon leave the presence of Lucius and Vincentine, Lucius starts to cough up the blood within his chest cavity. He's nearly chocking and wheezing to catch a breath.

Vincentine squats down and places his hands upon Lucius's body. "I'm healing you," Vincentine says.

Lucius feels the air in his lungs become less painful to inhale and exhale. He asks, "Are threats the way to make friends around here? If they are, everybody must love me by now." Lucius spits the blood that is caking his mouth on the floor."

Vincentine shakes his head and grabs the bucket of water with fruit in it. He feeds Lucius and is careful to give him small bites.

"I'm starving," Lucius says.

"Your body aches because of the malnourishment. You need protein and vitamin D. At least, you don't have scurvy anymore." Vincentine pulls out a strawberry.

Lucius asks, "Strawberries? Now I know you're on my side. Those are my favorite food." As Lucius chews on the fruit, he says, "My daughter loves these. She's just like me, but she's as beautiful as her mother." He becomes quiet, and Vincentine reads Lucius's thoughts as Lucius continues, saying, "I miss my family. My wife's gonna have our baby boy. I don't think I'm gonna be there for her to deliver our son. I told her I was gonna be there to deliver him with her. I made that promise to her, and I don't know if I can keep it."

Vincentine lowers his head and whispers, "Don't let anyone know that you're going to have an heir."

"They already know. They read my thoughts and know that I opened my wife's womb and laid with her right before my abduction. Baàlsarideem already told me that he was gonna kill my son aboard the ship if I didn't turn. He's a monstrous demon. He said he wants to kill my boy in front of me because I killed his worthless son." He pauses a second, and then clarifies. "Well, Baàl didn't call Abaddon worthless, but I do."

Vincentine gives Lucius a drink, and says, "That explains why Baàlsarideem has been hurrying to get every device working. He knows he'll lose his power when your second-in-command is truly born. He knows he has a limited amount of time. I was wondering why he's become so cruel against even his closest Gamerin brothers. However, he's always been cruel to the Nephilim slaves."

"What do you mean, 'Nephilim slaves?' I don't understand the ship's layout," Lucius asks.

Vincentine continues to explain what he has tried to keep from Lucius, saying, "The sons of the Gamerin who are in captivity aboard the ship are considered slaves, my lord. I'm one of them; however, I hide everything, and I have great manipulation skills against Baàlsarideem. He doesn't know my name is Vincentine. He still calls me by the Nephilim name because he doesn't know my soldier's name." Turning his head away from Lucius, Vincentine tries not to get emotional. "I watched him kill my mother, and my two brothers after the captivity of the Gamerin."

"How old?"

"I don't remember. I was a young boy. And to show my allegiance to the Gamerin, I was forced to place my father into the amber. To save my family, my father was among the first to choose to go into the amber. He leaned down and looked me straight in the eyes. I remember his goatee and smile. He wiped my tears and said it would be okay and to do what I was told, that the savior would help me someday. He said that patience would be my ally. As I placed my father into the sarcophagus, I did it in such a way that even without my abilities as a young boy, I could touch the skin of my father's hand and speak to him psychically because he was strong in his abilities and would know that I was there. Now, that I've matured, I keep my gifts secret because I've been waiting to destroy all of them. I knew the Almighty would send you someday. My father has never lost hope."

Lucius asks, "He had no idea that their families would die?"

"I remember running down to the crypt, hyperventilating and nearly blind with tears," Vincentine says. "I touched my father's hand through the small opening. I told him that it was a trap and that mother was murdered while suckling my youngest brother. As they forced my older brother to bury their bodies, they stabbed him in the back and kicked him into the pit on top of them. I ran to join them in death, but Baàlsarideem grabbed me in midair. He said, 'One must remain from that line.' As I spoke to my father, he said that he worried that some would die from the starvation of our punishment, but he had no idea that they would be murdered by their own, that his own brother would murder him by slaughtering his wife."

Lucius asks, "Why do you think Baàl chose for you to live?"

Vincentine answers, "There was one chosen from every line. I was old enough to feed myself and gather what I was ordered to fetch, but too young to wield a blade. My guess is that we were bargaining chips to entice the Gamerin to serve Baàlsarideem, and still young enough to be brainwashed. Some Nephilim fell, others died, but we were all slaves because of our fathers not submitting to Baàlsarideem's rule." Vincentine pulls apart an orange and says, "I want to kill him so much that my stomach turns inside of me."

Lucius leans back his head as the juice from the orange drips from his beard. While he rests his head against the metal wall, Lucius says, "You'll have to get in line because only the king of the Gamerin can kill Baàlsarideem, and I wanna kill his crappy son, Apollyon, as well. Baàlsarideem is stronger than a principality because of my inheritance."

"He has bragged of such. The only reason he remains in the dark is because he is the cornerstone of this vessel, and he can shroud his secrets by hiding in the dark." Vincentine nods and says, "I brought something to shave your beard. I was told your wife is sensitive."

"Right now?" Lucius starts to pant. "Have you heard back from the Commander? Is she okay? She becomes tired when pregnant."

"They say she is well, but that she waits for you. Two commanders have been sent to protect over her. But they didn't tell me that she was pregnant with your son."

Lucius says, "She almost miscarried my daughter because she believed I had died. She goes into depression when she loses the ones she loves. She isn't strong enough yet, and she can't see me like this."

Vincentine says, "Let me clean you then. I wouldn't want my queen to see the king of Gamerilaye as weak as a broken man."

Lucius looks up at Vincentine as he starts to wipe his king's face with the rag. Vincentine uses scissors and snips the long thick beard away so he can clearly see the wounds underneath. Lucius's face is grossly disfigured from scars and wounds, so that not much of the beard grows normal. Vincentine dollops lavender and charcoal soap to Lucius's beard for shaving the remainder hair off.

Lucius says, "My wife was not raised to be a soldier. She's young. She's only twenty-six years old. She watched me die in our home the first day we were married. She is fragile, but when I was near her, I would heal her often. Healing her was my joy because she was my all, my comfort." Lucius's eyes tear up. "I wanna hold my wife again, deliver my son, hold my children. I don't want her to see me like this. I don't want her to know how weak I am or that I'm disfigured like this."

Vincentine says, "I've heard about the healing waters. I know once we get you into the healing pool, the waters will repair your flesh and the disfigurement. You won't always be this feeble. Over time, you can gain your strength back because of your inheritance."

"I hope," Lucius says.

When Vincentine is done washing Lucius, he discusses what he has learned in the lab. He finishes by saying, "They only need a few moments to amputate your wing. I don't think they're going to take both, but I'm not sure."

Lucius asks, "When did you say you can get me out of here?"

Vincentine shakes his head and answers, "I'm reading your thoughts, sire. I'm sorry. We can only get you out of here during the festival. There's nothing I can do to keep them from using the device on you."

Lucius asks, "I thought you said they're gonna try and twist my mind. I'm not gonna like them very much if they start taking my body parts."

Vincentine says, "Because I talked him into the idea of manipulating you. That wasn't his original plan. Baàlsarideem will often have several plans running to hide what he is truly doing."

Lucius nods. "I see. At least, I won't be beaten again by random visitors. In exchange for Adam's rib, he got a wife. I guess the going rate for a principality's wing is a lot less. I wonder if I can get a refund."

Vincentine says, "I wish I could help you more. I've read their minds. Baàlsarideem will most likely take your wing before the festival. Apollyon, especially, wants to hurt you. They know that they're close to manipulating your power. When Baàlsarideem figures out how to open a large portal, they won't care what happens to you."

Lucius says, "I still want a refund."

Vincentine shakes his head and chuckles inwardly. Before leaving the room, he says, "I must speak to my father. He wanted to know how you were."

Lucius looks over to Vincentine, and asks, "I know every one of my brothers. Who's your father? Please tell me."

Vincentine replies, "I can't tell you. I can't let them read your mind. I'll tell you when we get home. I keep secrets to keep everyone safe. Without me, many of the Nephilim slaves would be dead, and there would be nobody to help me save the women." Vincentine is quiet for a moment before saying, "I look like him, and that is the only thing I can say."

"I can't see you because my eyes have become weak in the dark. Can you turn the light on and let me see you?"

"I forgot that you can't see in the dark because of your loss of power. I'm sorry, my lord. I've said too much."

Before Vincentine can open the door, Lucius says, "Wait. You must block my mind before you leave."

Vincentine walks back over to Lucius and lays his hand upon his freshly cut hair. He blocks his mind while giving a small healing, and says, "I must leave, sire. It's always a pleasure to see you."

⤙⚬⤚

After cleaning out the bathing bucket, Vincentine makes his way to the Amber crypt. While in the crypt, he goes to the place of his father on the bottommost layer, the last stone.

Hidden from any eyes that might enter the crypt, Vincentine crawls behind the stone and into the corner. He places his index finger into a small hole of the stone and touches the skin of his father's hand.

Instantaneously, Vincentine becomes psychically linked to his frozen father and says, *"Father, I've come to see you."*

Within an evergreen forest, Yaztarifenn answers, "My beloved child. How is our king today?" Yaztarifenn walks to his son and greets him with a strong hug. "I've been praying for your safety."

Vincentine says, "I have both good and bad news, Father."

Fenn answers, "I hope that Yuleshua is well. Please tell me that he is okay."

Nodding, Vincentine says, "I just visited with the king, and he's still very weak, but he's keeping his spirits up. Baàlsarideem will not stop torturing him. I've managed for a short pause, but it won't be long until they start beating him again."

"What do you mean for only a short time?"

"Father, they figured out the device. I did all that I could do to stop them. Pretty soon, they'll be able to use the dampener on him. I'm afraid that his wings are going to be all that they need. When Baàlsarideem becomes a principality by force, he will destroy our king. I must wait for the festival to escape with Yuleshua. If Baàl amputates before the festival, then I might be too late. I would have to get the king out to safety, but no one else. Yuleshua will surely bleed to death when his wing's wounded area goes back into hiding. I will have almost no time. I can't get my entire army out if the amputation is rushed.

"I don't know what to do, Father. Baàlsarideem always has secret plans and keeps me questioning what he will truly do next. What do I do?"

Yaztarifenn says, "I believe you are wise, my son. Speak with Baàlsarideem. If they want to use the dampener before the festival, then save the king's life by persuading him to introduce the amputation as part of the festival, and to take place at the same time. It would be the only way to save his life, and they would believe that you are true to Baàlsarideem by your actions."

Vincentine nods and says, "You're wise, Father. I get sick to my stomach every time I pretend with that wretched demon. It makes my heart break to think they believe I am one of them. I want to destroy every one of them."

Fenn hugs him. "I believe in you. I know your heart because you are Gamerin. You are not Rueshta the Nephilim, but you are Vincentine the Gamerin warrior. You never had a wife, and you never destroy life. You understand what things are sacred and what things are not. I know you will be rewarded for your service to the Almighty. This too shall pass, so stay strong, my son."

Vincentine walks along a forested trail with his father. Other Gamerin brothers who stay safe in Yaztarifenn's mind, wave from a distance. Vincentine waves, but he does so with a heavy heart.

Fenn says, "My son, your uncles are aware of your worries. They read your mind here with me. They have faith and so should you."

"I can't stay long." Vincentine gives his farewell, saying, "Father," he pauses and the sky of Yaztarifenn's mind becomes cloudy as Vincentine's thoughts are easily shared among the eight thousand Gamerin brothers. Vincentine holds tightly to his father and keeps from weeping as he continues. "I don't know if I'll ever see you again. When the truth is revealed after the festival, they will set a course to enter a portal to Gamerilaye. I don't know if Baàlsarideem is going to kill you before that happens. When he finds out that I'm the one who rescued the king, he might take his anger out on you." Vincentine can no longer retain his tears and begins to sob.

Hoshtravay and Sheriffson walk up to him. Hosh says, "Don't be troubled. We are one here, and our hope lies within a mighty God. Do what is right."

Yaztarifenn says, "Hosh is right. Stay strong and do what is right. Not to complete your destiny is the same as never having one."

Vincentine nods. "True. I miss my brothers and my mother. Baàlsari-deem has become more hateful these last few months. He's even imprisoned some of the other Nephilim who were never slaves. If he has nobody to punish for my actions, then he might send his son, Apollyon, to kill you. I know that he doesn't have the heart to kill you himself. Father, I love you."

Yaztarifenn answers, "I serve the Almighty. Forever is a long time. Death is not forever for us. I'm imprisoned as my punishment for taking your mother without permission and giving technology to a fallen people; however, my soul is not lost because I believe that my king has set me free. If my body dies, I will see you after the war. Stay true and serve who is true."

Vincentine nods and looks at the crowd of Gamerin brothers surround-ding him and his father. "I will miss all of you."

Sheriffson answers, "Don't say that. Say, 'until next we meet.' You are going into battle, and a proper farewell for a Gamerin is always positive. We are an undefeated army. Remember that we are victorious no matter what because we stay together as one."

"You're right. I guess this is what it feels like to go into battle then. I'm ready. Thank you, uncles," Vincentine says.

When the meeting is finished, Vincentine disconnects his psychic link. He removes his finger from the hidden opening of the amber stone and stares at his frozen father. "Let this not be the last of my farewells."

Thirty-Nine

Burns Going Down

Aboard the Gamerin vessel, Vincentine is summoned to Baàlsarideem's quarters. Upon entering the quarters of Baàlsarideem, Vincentine sees a woman almost completely dead.

Baàlsarideem looks over toward Vincentine and says, "Rueshta, my boy. I need you to finish her off and throw her out. There's nothing left of her. I'm tired of healing her worn-out body anyway."

Vincentine walks over to the woman and places his hand upon her carotid artery and says, "I think she's dead already, sir. I'll get rid of her for you."

Baàlsarideem stops him before he walks out the door and says, "Even though you're a son of a worthless Gamerin, I've always appreciated you. Too bad you never had any powers to heal anybody or read minds. But you're one of the best scientists we have. I'm proud of you, Rueshta." Baàlsarideem brushes Vincentine's face and says, "You look like him. Too bad he won't join me like you have. Your father never loved you, not like I do."

Vincentine nods and says, "Thank you, my king." While leaving, he pauses for a minute, and asks, "Are we going to get more wives soon, lord?"

Baàlsarideem raises his brows and becomes almost ecstatic as he asks, "Are you interested in having a wife, Rueshta? I can make arrangements this time for you."

Vincentine shakes his head and chuckles. "No, I don't want to clean up the mess. I only wanted to know because of the device."

Baàlsarideem sits at the end of his bed and asks, "Why do you ask? Why would it matter about the device and the festival of wives? I thought you wanted to lose your virginity."

Vincentine starts to walk out of the room because the woman is becoming healed by his touch, so he answers Baàlsarideem quickly, saying, "I thought it would be good during the festival if we waited to amputate his wing while we were feasting. The festival will probably be the last one, and the opportunity would be a great way to end our weddings on Earth. Everyone would love the wing held up for all to see. Like a trophy."

"A key to go back home," Baàlsarideem says. "That is an intriguing point. The moment would boost morale and add to the festivities."

"That would be better than a wife for me, my lord."

As Vincentine starts to walk off, Baàlsarideem says, "Rueshta, I'm always surprised on how wonderful your mind thinks. In fact, I'll even let them beat him a little more. Maybe I'll have them take out his eyes."

Vincentine says, "I always like to see the fear in the prisoner's eyes. I don't want him to have to lose those. It would be too easy for him to hide away in a different world within himself. I think we should just break his fingers." Vincentine takes a few steps to start walking off before the woman can moan.

Baàlsarideem says, "Rueshta, again you surprise me with your wisdom. I'll have them break his fingers and toes, but leave his eyes and tongue. I like to listen to him beg for mercy. I too like to see the fear in his eyes." He stands and continues. "We should do that. We should save the amputation for the festival since the device will be ready by then. Now go and have them take the ship back to Earth. I want to celebrate our victory with a new woman."

Vincentine hurries down the hall and goes to his small slave quarters with the sick woman. He lays her within a hollow bench in his quarters and places her into a deep sleep. He whispers to her, "I'm going to block your mind from the abuse you received. I'm sorry for what happened to you. Soon, you'll be home."

After securing the woman in a hidden spot, he sits down to prepare a letter to the northern Commander. Vincentine's note reads:

Commander Albercase, this is the last batch of human abductees we can bring back. They have figured out the device, and it will be operational during the gathering of women. They are going to amputate one of the king's wings. They will have the festival of wives at the same time of the amputation. During the consecration of the women, when they are all preoccupied and have celebrated much with heavy drink, I'll gather my army and the king. We'll be in Gamerilaye soon. Prepare the healing waters for the king, as promised. They're going to break much on him, and he will surely bleed to death shortly after. I hope God gives us strength during this rescue.

The Almighty's servant, Vincentine

Once Vincentine is done with the note, he hides his message upon the woman with a special seal that has his warrior's name upon it.

After a couple of days of Vincentine protecting and rounding up the battered women who are hidden in several secret servant's chambers, he arranges for the gathering of the women during the festival. Vincentine speaks psychically with Nicholson, *"Get all the Nephilim that can teleport and tell them to bring the women hidden in our quarters directly to Commander Albercase. You know the rendezvous point. Don't worry. Our cousins that will be left up here will cover for your absence if anyone asks. This is a request of our true king. Yuleshua has repeatedly asked that the women be brought back home. Have them leave in sequence as soon as we are close enough to the atmosphere of Earth."*

Nicholson answers psychically, *"It shall be done."*

Baàlsarideem's vessel enters the Earth's orbit, and Vincentine goes to visit Lucius. As Vincentine enters the cell, he sees that Lucius has been left alone with whatever small protection he provides. He squats and says, "The device is working. I'm sorry, but I talked Baàlsarideem into waiting to amputate your wing."

"What of the women? Please say you rescued them."

"We're in the Earth's orbit to pick up the new women. We have been rescuing women recently. Almost a thousand of them still live."

Lucius asks, "Why do you sound so down all of the sudden?"

"I…" Vincentine pauses and says, "I can't keep the fallen out of here much longer. Baàlsarideem wants to have you tortured. He even wanted to take your eyes, but I talked him into breaking your fingers instead. I'm sorry."

"How long before those bastards come here?" Lucius asks.

"Maybe a few days."

Lucius exhales with a mild moan and says, "At least, I know I have some time to sit against the wall before they start to torture me again. It's a good thing too, I was starting to get lonely."

Vincentine smiles. "I can see you have a strong spirit. You're a true king and fear nothing in battle. It'll be my honor to serve with you, my lord."

Lucius tries to look up, but his neck has healed in a disfigured position from being broken several times. He strains for a moment until saying, "Sit down next to me, Vincentine. My bones won't allow me to face your voice anymore."

"It would be my honor to sit beside you." Vincentine sits down and leans against the wall like Lucius.

Lucius says. "I have one weakness, my family. They're safe. Dex will protect them. Knowing my wife is safe keeps me strong. Josephine brought me back from falling into true death. Torture is nothing when a spirit is alive, and I won't lose my spirit because she completes me and gives me a purpose because she is my yoshawn."

"What caused you to be captured?" Vincentine asks.

"Our pet cat," he answers. "I was captured because I wanted to please the queen and going back and rescuing her cat. A woman is a different being. A man or Gamerin is completely defenseless from what a woman does to his heart. Have you ever been married or in love?"

Vincentine says, "No. Slaves don't get married." Vincentine pulls a small metal bottle out of his jacket while speaking. "I've never thought about a woman that way because I've been trying to save them for a long time." He serves the bottle to Lucius by placing it on his lips. "Here. It's like bourbon. This will aid in your pains. The only love I ever knew about a woman came from my mother. I miss my comforting mother."

Lucius gasps for a moment after taking a swig. "It's an extremely strong bourbon." He coughs.

Vincentine says, "The Gamerin won't drink it because it's made with honey. I drink it to help me sleep when I feel turmoil in my spirit."

"Honey?"

"Yes. The alcohol should help you with that cough that you developed."

Lucius feels the warmth flow through his veins and immediately becomes relaxed. "I don't touch honey."

Vincentine asks, "Why?"

Lucius says, "It's made from bee spit. Because I am a celestial, we don't touch honey because it is filthy. Honey has been made only for His special children to represent the sweetness of who they are to the Father."

Vincentine says, "Right now you probably could use it."

Lucius smells the cell and hears the engines of the ship and he can barely see. Nodding slightly, he says, "You're probably right." Vincentine gives him his third gulp of bourbon. As the burn slides down a little smoother than the first swig, he asks, "Besides making good drink, what abilities do you have?"

Vincentine says, "Not all Nephilim have the same number of abilities. I can't tell you all of them, but I can say that when I touch the back of my father's hand, the link feels like I'm holding him. I visit with all the faithful Gamerin during our meetings. I hope they don't kill my father when they find out what I'm doing."

Lucius grunts from the burn of his fourth large swig, says, "I never realized how strong this stuff was when you don't have strength to drink. I'm starting to feel warm. Everything is wonderful right now. I've never had the effects happen this fast before. How about, before they come in here to beat me, you give me a few pints of that."

Vincentine chuckles and says, "If I gave you a couple of pints of this stuff, I would wind up killing you myself. This is too strong to drink in large amounts. I'll come in here and give you plenty before we pick up the women though. I hope the tranquility of the drink doesn't wear off before they come in here to take your wing."

Lucius angles over toward Vincentine with a slight lean. His chains grind between the links. With a woozy giddiness, he says, "I think this is the beginning of a good relationship between us." Lucius nudges his shoulder onto Vincentine's and signals for more of the strong drink. "Honey isn't that bad. Don't tell nobody."

"I won't. Who would I tell?"

Lucius says, "My wife. She loves honey, but I tease her about it. Josephine has been through much turmoil because of who I am. Still, she loves me unconditionally."

Vincentine says, "Sounds like you truly love her. You talk a lot about her."

"I do love her. I need her."

Vincentine says, "We can change the subject to keep you from getting down."

But Lucius continues. "She deserves so much more. She's perfect. I love her *sooo* much." Lucius looks over at Vincentine and signals for another swallow by puckering his lips.

Vincentine says, "You might have had enough."

"I'm grood, I mean, I'm good and great."

Vincentine gives a very small swig this time. Lucius continues blabbing on, saying, "Someday you'll find a woman that completes you."

"Okay, we're done drinking right now, sire." Vincentine places the cap back onto the bottle.

Lucius says, "I hate to say this, but it might be one of my daughters someday. There's not a lot of women on Gamerilaye."

"You've definitely met your quota with my recipe," Vincentine says.

Lucius raises his heavy brows and says, "Someday. A very, very, very, very, very, long time from now. I might let someone marry my daughter. Maybe. She's only four, and she's my little princess, and nobody's ever gonna be good enough for her."

Vincentine shakes his head and says, "I think you've had a little too much of this. I wouldn't want you talking to anybody because you're not about your wits."

As Vincentine gets up from his seat, Lucius says with a serious tone, "I'm not kidding. No one's gonna date my daughter until I say it's okay."

"Don't worry, sire. I'll make sure nobody gets near your daughter. I'll serve you until the end."

Because his head is heavy from his buzzed state, Lucius leans his head to rest on his arms. He relaxes and says, "Yep, this is gonna be the beginning of a good relationship. I like you. I think you're really, really, really grood."

"I hope that means that I am great and good."

"Yep," Lucius says as he starts to drift off to sleep.

Vincentine says, "I need to get you something to drink and eat. I'll be back soon. I think you might be too weak for this stuff right now," and hurries to fetch some food and water for him.

Vincentine hurries back. Upon his return, Akhtar is outside the door of the cell.

Vincentine asks, "What are you doing here, Akhtar?"

Before he can answer, Akhtar and Vincentine are surprised when they both hear singing coming from the king's cell.

Vincentine says, "Oh, *nooo!*"

Vincentine opens the door of the cell and Akhtar asks, "You got him drunk? Are you insane?"

"I didn't know that…" and Vincentine huffs instead of finishing his defense. Akhtar shuts the door and locks it while Vincentine tries to calm down his king. Vincentine says, "Sire. I brought you some food and water. I need you to be quiet, or they're going to be able to hear your thoughts. We can't let them find out what we're doing, or we can't get you home. We'll all die."

Lucius slurs loudly, saying, "I want my home. I don't want them in here anymore. There're very bad, terrible, not nice guys."

Akhtar stands guarding the door. He hears a sound and looks back, saying, "I think somebody's coming. He's going to get us all killed."

Vincentine tries to heal Lucius, and whispers in his ear, "Sire. Please pretend you're sleeping so they don't come in here. I can't free you if they can read your mind because you're drunk. Sire please, be quiet, sire. My lord, please shut up."

Lucius becomes a little quiet for a moment but soon starts to sing again.

Both Akhtar and Vincentine look at each other. The footsteps get closer as Lucius sings, "This little light of mine, I'm gonna let it shine…"

Vincentine stands in shock with his only way to cover the blunder. As the door opens, Vincentine has no other option, he punches Lucius and knocks him unconscious.

Baàlsarideem and Apollyon enter the room and see Vincentine hitting Lucius. Baàlsarideem sprints over and tries to stop him. He says, "No, Rueshta. You don't have the ability to heal him. You and Akhtar both can't heal him. I want you to be his friends now, remember? I was coming in here to apologize to him like we agreed. I see he's out cold."

Apollyon squats down toward Lucius. "He completely unconscious." Apollyon asks, "Do you want me to heal him, Father?"

Baàlsarideem nods. "Yes." He studies Lucius's face and says, "He doesn't look the same."

Apollyon places his hand to heal Lucius and sniffs him. He says, "He smells like alcohol." Apollyon turns to face Baàlsarideem, and says, "Rueshta got him drunk. He knew he could get away with hitting him. When he wakes up, this traitor won't know what happened." Apollyon looks at Vincentine, and says, "You're smarter than I thought."

Baàlsarideem says, "Rueshta, I know it's hard, but you must twist his mind for him to trust us. Whether he's drunk or not. I know it's his fault that your mother died and the reason why your father had been imprisoned. When I'm king, you'll be with your father again. I want you to treat Yuleshua physically well for the next few days. No more alcohol."

"Yes, my lord," Vincentine answers.

Baàlsarideem points at Apollyon. "Let's not waste our time with Yuleshua right now. Everyone leave." He turns back to Akhtar and says, "I don't want you to touch him either. I know your powers haven't returned. Slaves aren't allowed to have alcohol. In fact, I don't want any powerless slaves in here except to dump the bodies. Only Rueshta is trusted enough to be in here before the festival."

Apollyon grabs Akhtar by the shoulder and escorts him out of the cell by pushing him out into the hallway. Akhtar falls on his side and shields his face from being beat. Apollyon says, "You're not worth my time, slave," and walks off.

Baàlsarideem looks back toward Vincentine and says, "He's about to wake up. You might want to wash off the blood from his face and pretend like nothing happened. Don't let the slaves beat him."

Vincentine answers, "Yes, my lord," and watches Baàlsarideem walk away behind Apollyon.

Akhtar walks off with an expression that nearly punches Vincentine in the face. He asks, "What were you thinking?" He leaves to go back to the orchard.

Vincentine enters the prison cell as Lucius wakes up. He washes his face and says, "I'm sorry, sire."

Lucius grunts and grimaces. "What hit me? I have a horrible headache."

Vincentine tries to clean him off and explains, "I gave you too much alcohol, and you were drunk. You started to sing, and it was attracting attention. I had to hit you and knock you out, so they wouldn't read your mind. I did it to rescue you, sire. I'm sorry. I understand if you want to kill me when we get home."

Lucius shakes his head and says, "No. I'm not gonna kill you. I might, however, take you to a bar sometime. I know this really great place on Constantinople that has the best banana rum. Once I give you much of that, well, I think I'll leave the rest for a surprise."

Vincentine slants his head as he says, "All right. I understand revenge. I deserve it. I just hope it doesn't hurt or leave long-term scars."

Lucius smiles, saying, "Not any more than what I'm getting here."

Vincentine says, "How kind of you, sire."

Forty

Festival of Wives

The vessel of Baàlsarideem enters into the atmosphere of Earth for the wife gathering. Nephilim transporters ready themselves for battle. They will not be taking guardian hostages this time. Because Vincentine has been genetically altered to transport down to the surface, he has waited to place his rescued women to the surface and deliver his message personally. He goes to his chambers and grabs the woman for Commander Albercase. As always, Vincentine alerts the troops below before too much damage can be done.

The specialized troops of Baàlsarideem gather into their groups for retrieving women from areas that they have scouted earlier. Successfully, many women are abducted before the guardian forces on the ground take notice. For the guardians that weren't prepared, they were slaughtered on the field or left to die.

In all, Vincentine transports down twelve women that have been hidden in his chambers. Because Baàlsarideem's ship is swift during abduction, Vincentine never stays to converse with any commanders or angels.

At their normal rendezvous, Commander Albercase checks the tattered clothes of the women for hidden messages. Upon one of the first bodies that have been dropped off, the commander finds Vincentine's note regarding Lucius.

Commander Albercase opens a crypted relay message to those working alongside Dextorus through an unregistered transmitter, secretly channeling the message through the Oobadoave network. After his message is sent, Commander Albercase tells his troops, "Look for survivors. Vincentine said that soldiers were left to die before he teleported out. This will be the last time the enemy will invade this atmosphere."

Within minutes of receiving the message on Oobadoave, an archangel opens a portal gate from Jett Commdearadea to Gamerilaye.

The archangel, Michael, stands at sixteen feet and enters the Gamerin home through a large bay terrace. Trying not to alert the sensitive queen, he silently steps through from outside the kitchen area.

Dextorus senses the change in the atmosphere and looks at the side entrance near the kitchens.

Michael nods as soon as Dextorus makes eye contact. Deasja, Dex, and Michael immediately block their minds from being read by Josephine. Michael psychically informs Dex, *"Be ready. Lucius will be beaten badly. He'll be on the verge of death. The waters must be ready for the king of Gamerilaye, for there will be much blood loss from the amputation of his wing. Many Nephilim slaves will be with him during the exodus."* Michael quietly leaves.

Dex looks at Deasja, and psychically tells him, *"It's time. His arrival is going to be bad. Keep the healing lounge doors wide open and ready with standby angels in place. Expect a multitude of visitors with him."*

Deasja answers, *"I will be at the location Vincentine was given for his entry, right outside the lounge doors. I will guide Lucius and Vincentine into the water. I hope that I can keep Lucius alive."*

"Let me. You've healed her seven times today. I will give Lucius healing until he's in the water. Save your healing until called," Dex answers.

Deasja nods in agreement.

Waiting outside the lounge where the healing waters are located, Josephine sits on a bench. When she notices movement from the corner of her eye, she stands while holding her abdomen as soon as Deasja nods. With her ability to read minds, she realizes that Deasja's mind has been blocked. Josephine quickly tries to investigate Dex's mind, but his mind has been blocked as well.

Deasja looks over and observes her expression. Knowing she has caught on, Deasja hears her ask, "What are you two talking about?" Josephine walks over to Deasja. "What is it? Is he coming home? Please, don't tell me he's dead. I can feel that there is something wrong."

Deasja cannot lie or mislead her with such straight forward questions. He tries to encourage her to stay in her room while Lucius heals. "That was Michael the archangel," Deasja says. "He said Lucius is close to being here. You should wait in your chambers for him. He wants to clean up before he sees you."

Shaking her head, Josephine tells Deasja, "No. I'm gonna wait for my husband here. I wanna see him when he arrives."

Dextorus speak up, "There will be a multitude with him. We can't overload this area. You could be pushed. I think it would be wise if you waited for Lucius safely in your chambers. He'll come and see you after he's cleaned off and changed into his clothes."

With moderate irritation, Josephine answers, "I'm not gonna do that."

"Calm yourself," Deasja says placing his hand upon her shoulder to heal her rising blood pressure. "You're causing harm to yourself for no reason right now. I am healing you even now. Please be calm."

"I'm trying, Deasja. Why do y'all try to get rid of me? I won't be able to rest, and you know I can't do that. I haven't been sleeping because of his return. I wanna see my husband." Josephine puts her fists to her cheeks and smiles about his return.

Deasja and Dex look at each other when they notice her body relaxes with the joy of his coming home.

Dextorus says, "As you wish, Josephine."

Deasja swiftly swings his gaze between Josephine and Dextorus from the answer that Dex has just given. *"Why?"* Deasja psychically asks. *"Why would you give into her request?"*

Dextorus answers him, *"Because letting her stay here, spares your healing abilities. Look at her. She hasn't smiled like that in months. We can't be far from her if she is in another room. Let her have her way. We won't be able to persuade her."*

Deasja nods slightly. He replies, *"I think females are your true weakness, Dex. You have no heart to tell them no."*

Passing through the healing lounge's resting area, Artie holds Claire on his hip. Claire says, "My dolls are lonely in my room. You can be the daddy doll."

Shaking his head, Artie says, "I can't wait until you grow up and stop making me play with dolls."

Deasja and Dex watch Artie passing through the main living area with Claire. Artie steps through the resting level of the palace and makes eye contact with Deasja.

Deasja instantly forms a link with Artie and transfers, *"I think we have a problem."*

Artie blocks his mind when he senses the gravity of the message coming from Deasja. Artie places Claire down and says, "Okay, princess. Go play in your room for a bit. I must speak to Deasja. I'll be in there shortly."

Claire nods and says, "Don't keep me waiting long. I wanna play, and you have to be the daddy."

Artie replies, "I won't keep you waiting, princess. I just have to talk to Deasja for a quick minute."

Deasja and Artie walk down the hallway towards Claire's room, and Deasja speaks psychically, *"The king will be here today, but he won't look like himself."*

Artie stops walking and strains to keep from wailing. "He's coming home?" Artie barely asks before his eyes tear up.

Deasja places a hand on Artie's back and motions for him to keep walking away from the queen. He continues. *"I can't get the queen to leave the healing lounge area. I don't know what to do. She can't see Lucius like this, or she will surely give birth this day. Michael said the wounds of Lucius are severe. Dex has given Josephine permission to stay because she is calmed by the lounge. I won't force her to leave, but maybe you can help persuade her."*

"I am already guarding someone," Artie transfers and shakes his head in disbelief. *"I don't know what to say about helping to remove Josephine. I certainly can't make my queen, whom I bow to, do anything against her will. We just have to hope that she won't go into labor. You're not going to be able to move her. Even Dex knows that that's not going to happen. Maybe, if you catch her soon enough, you can put her in the water as well."*

Deasja replies, *"I guess that's our only option if we can't get her to leave."*

Artie walks off toward Claire's room, and Deasja walks to the lobby and over to Dextorus.

Deasja shakes his head, letting Dextorus know that there is nothing they can do about the queen leaving her husband's side.

To aid in Deasja's concern, Dextorus looks at Josephine and says, "Maybe, you can make Lucius a meal. I'm sure they don't feed him well. You have plenty of time before he arrives. You can rest here for a while and then make him something so it's warm when he arrives. There's plenty of fresh produce in the garden. Lucius adores your cooking. Maybe some of your potato soup since it's his favorite?"

Josephine is so excited that she is barely able to say, "I know he's coming today. I can't stand long enough to make him a meal. I'll just wait for him here. I will have Artie make something for him. We could have a banquet then."

Deasja answers, "Sounds lovely," and tries not to clamp his teeth together too hard with his sarcasm.

Dex tries asking, "Is there anything else you can do before he shows? I know he'll want to look nice for you. Maybe you can get dressed in his favorite outfit before he shows. He hasn't seen his queen in months. I can call Thimbette and Charony to help you get ready."

Josephine says, "No. I'm gonna wait right here."

Deasja scans her vitals and says, "You're right," so her blood pressure will stop rising. "You're absolutely right. Wait here for him. I will get Thimbette to bring you pillows to rest your back against." Having enough of trying to coax her into leaving, Deasja walks off aggravated and mumbles underneath his breath. "She's so stubborn."

Aboard Baàlsarideem's vessel, the new women are placed into bridal sleepwear by the Nephilim slaves, as they remain in a deep sleep to keep them from fighting with the slaves or hurting themselves.

As the feast is prepared in the large weapons barracks of the vessel, Baàlsarideem gives his speech. "Brothers and my closest family," He says. "I should've always been the king over Gamerilaye. I will be a principality and we will finally be happy. This is the last time we'll have women brought to us because we'll make them live forever as our wives on Gamerilaye. Never again will you watch a wife die. I will heal all your bodies there, and we will procreate a new race of people on our home world. Be gentle to your wives this festival, for they will be the mothers of your offspring and provide our army for our new battles to protect my realm."

Many of those eating at the table of the Feast of Wives begin to holler, "A true king brings abundance! Baàlsarideem is the true king!"

When the crowd quiets from chanting, Baàlsarideem continues, saying, "We have constructed a device that opens the dimensional field around the failed Gamerin king. We're going to take one of his wings from him. After transplanting the organ into my body, I will have the permission I need to open a portal a few days after the transplant. We'll no longer be outcasts, no longer must we bury our wives in the expanse. I'll see my Sonya. Many of you will have wives again to grow our army as some of the strongest beings in creation."

He reaches to the middle of the table and raises his carafe of strong whiskey. They all raise their goblets and follow his lead as he drinks the entire carafe before he continues his blasphemy. "I'm going to go down to the traitor's cell and make him suffer because of my son's death. You know he killed my son, Abaddon." He drinks another goblet of Whisky. Apollyon drinks alongside him as Baàlsarideem's goblet and carafe are refilled. Baàl says, "I'm going to bring his wing back and show you my trophy, and what it is like to fall against me, the true king of Gamerilaye. I'm the true savior of the Gamerin. Someday, Yuleshua will kneel to me." Baàlsarideem looks over at Apollyon and says, "Let us go retrieve our victory."

Vincentine steps away from the wall from behind Baàlsarideem. He tries to follow them both when he sees them stumble with each step. *They are too drunk and might kill him,* he thinks. Vincentine says, "My lord, let me help you."

Baàlsarideem looks back with heavy eyes, says, "No. I want you to prepare my chambers for my new wife. I only trust you because you've never touched a woman. I know you won't take her virginity away or molest her before I get to her."

Vincentine nods in submission. "Yes, my king. I'll prepare her for you." Vincentine goes to Baàlsarideem's quarters as commanded and prepares for his own plans quicker than usual.

In the quarters, he sadly walks by the young woman he cannot save from her torture. As he looks over at her, he changes her clothes and says, "I'm sorry. This too shall pass my poor human female. Please don't hate me. It's a means for an end." He looks at the bedside table and sees the portal cross lying down as it always is when Baàlsarideem expects to have a new bride.

Underneath his shirt, Vincentine pulls out a replica of the portal key and swaps them out. As he prepares the room, he hears the screaming out from Lucius in the bowels of the ship.

Because he knows he cannot enter the cell while Lucius is being tortured, Vincentine must wait in the outer areas, hiding while he gathers his troops to prepare them for a quick escape. Vincentine will have a short window to escape with Lucius and the true servants of the king. He telepathically tells Hatrueshian, *"They're drunk. They might kill him because they aren't thinking straight."*

"What do you want me to do?" Hatrueshian asks with his transfer.

"I don't have enough power to heal him when we enter the cell. I only have enough to open a portal. I need you to heal him." Vincentine transfers.

"I don't either," Hatrueshian answers.

They both look around and transfer to the others, *"Does anyone have healing ability?"* But none answer, only shaking their heads.

Vincentine nearly hyperventilates, listening to the deathly hollers of Lucius in the cell. Hatrueshian places his hands on Vincentine's shoulder and reminds him, *"The waters are ready. Have faith."*

Within the dark cell, Apollyon breaks every finger of the king's body. Apollyon says, "You're paralyzed. I've broken three toes, and you didn't wince."

Lucius gasps and stares into the dim light above him. "Bastard," he says as he drools.

Baàlsarideem gloats as he stands over Lucius's body and says, "I tried to get you to be my second-in-command. I tried to be nice to you. After all that I've done for you, you continue to be defiant of me. I've suffered for thousands of years, and you even took one of my son's lives."

Apollyon breaks another finger. He laughs and says, "I love to hear you scream, traitor." He glances at Baàl and nearly stumbles back. "Father, listen to him whine. He's actually crying," he says and kicks Lucius kneecap into a different direction.

Lucius smells the alcohol and says, "Go ahead, jackass. I can't feel that leg anyway." Lucius becomes quiet when Apollyon heals his left side from paralysis. "Stop!" Lucius screams.

Apollyon opens his own hidden sheathes and grabs a jagged dagger. He slices across Lucius's left thigh.

Lucius yells, "I'm gonna kill you, you drunk bastards! I'm gonna kill Apollyon after I kill you, Baàlsarideem. I hate you. All of you are gonna go to Hell because you are damned bastards. You're gonna burn. Judgement's coming for you."

Baàlsarideem says, "So many threats when you're chained up like a dog, brother."

"I'm not your brother!" Lucius screams.

Baàlsarideem laughs as he pulls out his own weapon, and says, "I think you underestimate my plans, Yuleshua. I should've always been the king. I've already taken your power, and now, I'm going to take your principality permission. I'm going to rule over Gamerilaye, and I'm going to be the principality over the Gamerin galaxies from my plans. I'm an ageless being. I'm going to have much power when I get back home to my kingdom."

"Your kingdom sucks," Lucius says with a grimace. He grinds his teeth and says, "You'll never rule over my realm."

Apollyon stops torturing him for a moment so Baàlsarideem can show Lucius the new device. Baàlsarideem holds up a band and wraps it around his arm. "Stop dry heaving for a moment so I can show you something. I made this for you, Yuleshua. Do you want to know what it does?"

Lucius tries to gather his breath and replies, "Go to Hell, bastard." His head falls back from his weakness. Apollyon pulls Lucius's hair and keeps him straight and forces him to watch.

Baàlsarideem shakes his head, and makes clicking noises with his tongue. He says, "Now, now, now. That's no way for a principality to talk, is it? I've noticed the way you speak. You sound like a redneck country bumpkin. You hardly sound sophisticated with that Texan accent."

"Go to Hell, Baàl."

Baàlsarideem glances at Apollyon and says, "Raise his chains higher. I need a clear shot. My eyes are blurry right now, and I might miss."

Apollyon raises his chains.

"Wait," Lucius begs. "Please wait until tomorrow when you're not drunk."

"I've waited long enough," Baàlsarideem says. "This is a new weapon I made especially for you. I'm going to shoot you with it, and then I'm going to take something from you." He pauses for just a moment before saying, "I'm going to take your wing."

Lucius replies, "You're sick, Baàl."

Before Lucius has a chance to beg again, Baàlsarideem shoots him with the trans-dimensional device without warning. In one swift move, Apollyon grabs his longsword from his holster, and amputates Lucius's wing.

Still in its trifold position, a perfect white wing falls to the dirty floor.

Lucius hollers so loud, that the entire ship hears his cries.

Apollyon laughs over the screams as he picks up the folded wing, saying, "It has piss on it." Blood begins to trickle and then pour from Lucius's back.

Baàlsarideem and Apollyon leave the cell and return to the feasting hall to show off their new trophy.

Moments after they leave, a secret army races through the shadows of the bowels of the ship toward the screams that are becoming more and more weak. Vincentine tells his troops to stop by holding a fist to his nose. They stop. He says, "I must go up there or they will know what we are doing. Wait until you hear them celebrating in the weapons barracks. We must cover the noises that will be coming from the other side of the portal. I will be right back."

Baàlsarideem finishes another goblet as Vincentine enters the barracks hall. Baàlsarideem turns and sees Vincentine. He says, "Take my prize and begin working on it right away, Rueshta."

Vincentine nods his head. "Yes, my lord," he says and holds Lucius's folded wing. With all his effort, he guards his eyes from welling up with tears when he sees the blood over white feathers.

Baàlsarideem sees his face is down and asks, "Why do you make this face, Rueshta? Aren't you happy we're almost home? That's the key to get all of us home."

Vincentine answers, "I've had a lot of drink. I couldn't be happier my king. I just don't want to mess my work up tonight. I'm going to put this in the stasis lab and work on the transplant tomorrow. I'm only sad because I can't work on it tonight. I should sleep."

Baàlsarideem raises his newly filled glass and says to everyone, "This is a good servant. I'm proud of Rueshta. He's like my lost son, Abaddon. Yaztarifenn should have been like him. He is Fenn and Abaddon to me from this day on. He's going to get all of us home." Baàlsarideem pats him on the back and excuses him.

Vincentine is followed to the lab by Apollyon who says, "Don't let it get to your head. You're a slave. He'll forget his words by the morning." Apollyon points at the stasis table and says, "Careful. Don't forget to turn the stasis table on so it won't rot by the time your lazy body gets out of bed."

"Yes, sir," Vincentine says. After setting the wing in the special place to maintain it, Vincentine excuses himself, saying, "I can't hold my alcohol like you. I feel that I will vomit."

"You make me sick," Apollyon says. "Leave before you dirty up the lab." Apollyon walks back to the weapons barracks for the remainder of the festival.

After he excuses himself, Vincentine runs down to the cell. Above the bowels of the ship, a mighty ruckus of celebration reverberates across the walls. With the loud celebration, all the 312 Nephilim race to the cell behind Vincentine.

As they enter the cell, Vincentine almost slips from the blood on the floor. "Release his chains," Vincentine says as he grabs onto Lucius's limp body. "Cut him down." As Nicholson snaps the chains with a clamp, Lucius drops into Vincentine's arms. One of Lucius's wings remains, unfolded, and is soaking up the blood from the floor.

"Hurry. He's dying," Nicholson says.

Vincentine swiftly opens the portal to Gamerilaye and looks back, saying, "We're going home."

Forty-One

Hurry

A large portal opens into the waiting area outside the healing water's lounge. Josephine stands as a frantic group runs through. She sees somebody with a bloody wing dragging the floor as he is carried in someone's arms. "He's dying!" she hears someone scream. Nephilim race through the opening and quickly force their way through, entering the mighty corridor. As the room fills with screaming and worried Nephilim, Josephine searches through the crowd to see if she can spot Lucius.

"He isn't breathing," Dex says and rushes over to try healing Lucius. "Into the water."

As soon as Josephine sees the terror in Dextorus's eyes she realizes that the mangled flesh of the one being carried is Lucius. "Lucius!" she cries and tries to push her way through the crowd that rushes toward the healing pool.

"Where?" Vincentine asks. "In here?" As soon as he sees the waters, Vincentine runs, nearly slipping on the blood trail that follows behind him. "Which of you is Dex?" he asks.

"I am. I'm trying to heal him, but he's not breathing. Go into the water with him. Hurry!"

Vincentine slips with Lucius down the steps of the pool, and they both fall into the water. Quickly regaining his footing, Vincentine holds Lucius's face above the water. "Breathe, sire!"

Nephilim shove through with their limited time. Josephine is accidently pushed against a wall but manages to enter the lounge. An entire army of guardians help to guide the Nephilim through to make room for the other Nephilim trying to escape. Deasja runs through the crowd to stand at Josephine's side. He asks her, "Are you all right?" and places healing over her body while helping her to stand off to the side, protecting her from those piling into the lounge to aid the king. "Stay here," he says and turns to face Lucius in the water. Deasja walks closer and asks, "Is he breathing yet?"

"No," Vincentine says shaking his head. He knows that at any moment, Lucius's spirit could release from his broken body. "Wake up, lord."

Josephine begins to shake and cries, "What's happening?"

Deasja glances back for a moment, saying, "Josephine, stay there."

Vincentine keeps Lucius's neck and body below the waterline. "Oh, God. It's not working!" Vincentine cries out.

As soon as the small Nephilim army finishes traveling through the portal, an angel asks the last one through, "Is that all of you?"

Akhtar answers, "Yes. I was the last one."

The angel waves his hand and closes the portal gate for good.

Many of the Nephilim gather into the large healing quarters. Dex stands, and says, "Stay back. Pray that he lives. Give him your prayers." Dex soon turns and sees Josephine, white as snow, leaning against a rock bench and holding her stomach. He stands beside her. "Deasja, she's about to faint."

"I must heal Lucius when he wakes, Dex. I've done all that I can do with the queen." Deasja reaches into the water and feels Lucius's neck for a pulse. "He isn't responding to the water."

When Dex sees that Josephine is still standing on her own, he steps toward the pool and asks, "How long has he been like this, Vincentine?"

"I'm not sure. Five minutes, maybe?" Vincentine answers.

Akhtar speaks from the other side of the room, saying, "He stopped screaming four minutes ago and has been silent since then."

Hearing their words, Josephine becomes faint and holds onto Dex's arm for support. Dextorus turns and wraps his arm beneath hers to keep her from falling. "I've got you, child," he says.

"My lord. Wake up, please!" Vincentine calls out.

Josephine says, "Lucius, baby, come back to me. God, help us."

As soon as she calls out to him, a calm breeze blows through the open bay terrace of the healing lounge.

The smell of gardenias enters Lucius's nostrils. He takes in a deep breath of Gamerilaye and immediately screams from the pain of his disfigured body finally healing itself. With no energy to open his eyes, the screaming drains him more, for the healing is slow and excruciating.

Many angels cry with joy, but the screaming is felt deep inside of Josephine. A pain pierces across her abdomen and causes her to hunch forward. Water soon splashes onto Dex's boots. Both Deasja and Dextorus turn to look at the floor beneath the queen. Her water has just broken.

Charony and Thimbette enter the lounge of the healing waters. Deasja looks over at Charony and cautiously commands her, "Get her into the birthing room. She's in labor."

While Lucius is still screaming with the strength he has in his lungs, Charony hands a bowl of Bengaldoe medicine to Deasja. "I made this for him. It heals my lord from the inside out. Give it to him as Yeshua has commanded," she says as she turns to guide her queen to the birthing room.

"Lucius," Josephine barely says with a weakened voice.

Charony says, "Come on, your majesty. Let us get you somewhere private."

Dextorus sees how Josephine struggles to walk with her contractions. He says, "Let me help you, Josephine," and picks her up in his arms. "We can't have the prince born in front of all these people, your majesty."

Artie runs by Josephine and Dextorus toward the screaming. After Dextorus looks back one more time into the lounge, he says, "Lucius will be okay."

Josephine tenses up and screams, "Don't jostle me like Deasja does!"

Dextorus grins, saying, "Never." He walks into the master's chamber and tells Charony, "Get the stool ready for her. She will have him soon." He looks at Thimbette and says, "Grab the supplies and a warm blanket."

Josephine can hear her husband screaming, and his bellowing can be heard throughout the entire palace. She weeps in Dextorus's arms and asks, "He's in so much pain. How do you know he'll be okay, Dex?"

Dextorus answers her, "He's breathing. The healing water is doing its job when you hear him. Because he is being healed, it hurts him. But when it's all over, he'll have no more pain. I know he wants to join you, so don't worry for him right now. We need to concentrate on you and the little prince." Dextorus gently places Josephine onto the stool as Charony changes the queen's robes for giving birth.

While Lucius lies in the bloody healing waters, many Nephilim hold him up in place to keep him from drowning.

While his wing is growing back, Artie watches as the new wing begins to form beneath the red waters. Artie says, "I know it hurts, sire."

When Lucius hears Artie's voice, Lucius reaches his hand out toward him. "Brother," Lucius says while grunting and grimacing.

Artie grabs onto Lucius's hand, and Lucius squeezes his healing fingers over Artie's fingers. Lucius opens his teary eyes. Artie's eyes are drowning in tears as well. "Brother," Artie says. "You're home."

After a while, the pain begins to die down a little. When Lucius can speak, he says, "Vincent, place me under the water because my face needs to be healed."

Vincentine realizes that Lucius has just changed his name as he reads his thoughts. "Yes, sire," Vincent answers.

Akhtar says, "I want a new name."

Hatrueshian laughs and pats Akhtar's shoulder. The room becomes light with joy.

Lucius takes in a deep breath, and Vincent baptizes the king beneath the waterline for his complete healing. After Lucius is fully baptized within the water, hundreds of angels stand around the room to watch the Gamerin king come back up healed.

When bubbles start to arise from the surface of the red waterline, Vincent lifts his king to break the surface of the bloody waters. Lucius takes in a deep breath of the Gamerin air into his lungs and looks like himself once again.

As angels rejoice, Deasja grabs a change of clothes for Lucius. He speaks loud enough over the crowds for Lucius to hear, saying, "I'm supposed to heal you after you've used up all the healing from the pool. Charony made some soup for you." Deasja stands on the top step of the pool and watches Lucius still needing help to float above the water.

"It isn't soup. Don't drop it. My body still needs healing. I'm weak," Lucius says. He leans against the side of his healing pool with his neck back, resting over the side stones to keep him above the filthy water. He opens his eyes and looks at Deasja shaking his head. Lucius says, "What? I can't read your mind, brother."

"You," Deasja says. "You always surprise me."

"Me?" Lucius rhetorically asks. "And miss all the fun? Are you kidding?" Lucius coughs from infection clearing from his lungs. "I'm only getting started."

Deasja says, "You had me worried. Dextorus never lost faith in you. I guess you can't destroy the humble Gamerin son of God."

"To be honest…" Lucius stops speaking for a moment as Vincent helps him balance to his feet, "I uh…" Lucius grimaces as his bones in his legs and hips pop back into place. He grabs onto Vincent's arm and tries to stand still.

"You okay?" Vincent asks.

"In a second," Lucius doesn't move. "The healing is slow because the water is tainted by Apollyon's blade." Lucius looks up at Deasja on the top step before finishing what he was saying. "To be honest, I almost died some weeks ago." He looks at Vincent before saying, "And then I met him, my brother here."

"Brother?" Vincent asks.

"Of course," Lucius answers. "We are brothers." Lucius hugs Vincent and says, "I have no slaves here, Vincent. You will be known as Vincent, brave warrior of the king." He looks at Vincent. "Help me get to Deasja, okay?"

The Nephilim in the water help Lucius up the steps. Midway up, Lucius stops and rests because his muscles are tired. Deasja steps into the water some and says, "I'll help you the rest of the way."

"Thank you, Deasja," Lucius says while taking his last heavy and wobbly steps up. "I haven't walked in months."

Deasja stares at Lucius's tattered clothes, dripping wet, and reeking of all that is foul to the nostrils. Deasja blows the air away from him and psycho-kinetically dries Lucius off. Once he is dry, Deasja hands him a bowl of Charony's healing remedy and a pair of clothes, saying, "I think you want to wear something a little more modest and cleaner than that attire you're barely wearing." Deasja coughs because of the overpowering smell. "Your clothes reek, Lucius."

"Shut up," Lucius says with a raspy voice. "Their room service was atrocious." Lucius swallows the bowl of 'soup' with a mild face of disgust and says, "This tastes better than what they were feeding me. Believe me."

"Don't change into those clean clothes yet. You need a shower," Deasja says while he helps Lucius to the showers within the healing lounge and beyond the indoor waterfalls. "I'll put these new threads to the side for you. I'm going to get rid these other ones by burning them." Deasja stands guard outside of the stone wall blocking the showers for the king's privacy.

In the shower, Lucius leans against the stones under the warm waterfall. He allows the therapeutic waters to soothe him for the first time in eight months. "This makes me feel alive." Lucius scrubs his body with his finest Gamerin soaps and erases any remnant of Baàlsarideem's ship from his body. Scarred skin that has healed and stuck to his hair and body sloughs off and into the drain. Lucius asks Deasja, "How long was I gone?"

"About eight months," Deasja replies.

Lucius has trouble hearing his reply and asks again, "How long? I can't hear your thoughts, and there's too much noise right now. Everyone is talking and this room echoes when the water is flowing." He hears Deasja answer again but the sounds of his voice are muffled. "Deasja, there is a waterfall in my ears. You're gonna have to speak up, brother."

Deasja raises his voice, says, "Eight months!"

Lucius gasps and asks, "How's Josephine? I wanna see her. She can come in here if she wants. Will you get her?" Lucius asks louder, saying, "Deasja, can you get Josephine for me, please?"

Deasja holds his breath for a moment and tenses because of the question. What could he say? He pretends he can't hear.

Lucius scrubs the shampoo through his hair and waits for Deasja's answer. "Deasja?" Lucius asks.

Reading Lucius's thoughts, Deasja is slightly scared to answer. He tries to remain quiet to buy more time for Lucius to recover. "Finish your shower, brother," Deasja whispers beneath his breath.

Because he cannot hear Deasja, Lucius asks again, "Deasja, did you hear me? Tell Josephine to come to me. I want my little momma."

By this time, the sounds of the room hush to a moderate level as the eyes of the lounge start to face the river stone walls surrounding the shower area. Deasja disconnects his mind from Lucius and answers with a misleading honest answer, "It's very loud in here with everyone talking and the waterfall. There's a wall between us and I'm not connected to your mind right now. We'll talk when you get out of the shower and everyone is quiet. I hope you can hear me."

After his shower, Lucius stands behind the changing shade. Lightheaded, he balances against the wall as he finishes getting dressed. Lucius says, "My muscles are still atrophied and wobbly. I need to eat protein for my body to properly heal. The device retards my healing and makes my body ache." When Lucius loses balance and falls against a wall, Deasja steps behind the changing area to hold Lucius's pant legs for him, helping him to get dressed.

Many angels quiet down when they see Lucius emerge from his changing area with the help of Deasja. "You already look better, Lucius. Your color has come back," Orlando says. He looks at Lucius's wobbly legs and says, "You'll be okay."

"Thank you," Lucius says. He's nearly out of breath from the walk across the room and needs to rest. As he rests against Deasja, he looks around the room. "Where's—" the scream of a woman paralyzes him.

"Lucius," Deasja says. "Loosen up."

"He's scared," Vincent says. "Who is screaming?"

Lucius shakes and is overcome with dread. He stares at the door as if someone is going to turn off the light and beat him. The screaming continues, and he grabs on to Deasja's arm. "Save me."

"I've got you," Deasja says reading Lucius's mind. "You're safe, Lucius. It's Josephine."

Lucius swiftly looks at Deasja. "Josephine?" he asks. "What's happening to her, Deasja? What's wrong with my wife?"

Shaking his head, Deasja answers, "We tried to stop her, Lucius, but your wife is stubborn. She went into labor when she saw you come through the portal gate. She's been weak these last few months. You need to rest. You are in no shape to deliver a baby." Lucius fights Deasja who is trying to keep him from walking toward the delivery room. Deasja says, "Dextorus and Charony are in there with her. She'll be fine. We need to get you taken care of while your muscles strengthen. Lucius, you're dizzy and in shock with traumatic stress. It's not safe for you to be near her."

"I wouldn't hurt my wife, Deasja. I promised her. I want to see my son."

Without a second thought Lucius tries to run. He nearly trips from his weak legs, but Deasja catches him and keeps him from falling. "You're just as stubborn as her."

Lucius orders Deasja, saying, "I need you to help me to my wife. Hurry. We must save my son. He's premature. I gotta be there with her."

"Give it another hour. I must rest, Lucius. I don't have enough energy to heal your mental health and heal the prince's lungs too."

Lucius shakes his head and commands, "No. I want you to heal my son. I know you've been ordered to do that. Don't worry about me."

Deasja answers, "I'm going to save your son. Okay, you win. Let's go."

Lucius struggles with his steps down the hallway as he races toward the screaming. "Baby, I'm coming," Lucius says.

"You Gamerin always cut everything so close," Deasja says.

Lucius says, "I want you to heal my wife with the power that you have left, Deasja."

"But that will take everything that I have to heal her uterus, Lucius."

Lucius smiles and says, "It's fine. We're gonna have many children, and I can't have her scarred inside of her body. I need all my children to be healthy. I'm ordering you to heal my wife to her original state like she was before bearing my son. Heal her instead of me. I want nothing more than to be beside her. I'm a father and a husband first."

Forty-Two

Push

The moment that Lucius is finished speaking, he enters into the room where Josephine is. Dextorus is helping her to sit upright, and Lucius's heart rejoices as he watches her on a birthing stool and trying to deliver their baby boy without him. "You're so strong, Momma," Lucius says. With an extremely large grin emerging across his face, his eyes well up with tears of joy.

Lucius walks over to Josephine and kneels beside her. "Baby, I'm here." He tenderly places his hand upon her back and leans his face against hers.

Josephine cries, "I've missed you."

"I know." Lucius strokes her cheeks.

"I can't do this. I'm so tired," she says.

"Yes, you can, little momma." They both weep against each other. He says, "You can."

Josephine says, "Because you're here now."

Lucius says, "I told you I'd be here, Josephine. I knew I'd be here beside you for this. I wanna be near you and deliver our boy."

Josephine has another contraction, and her body tenses up. She screams, "I can't!"

"I can't take away the pain this time, baby." Lucius places his hands upon Josephine's abdomen and calmly says, "Hold on. Don't push yet. I have to make sure your dilated first." He spreads her legs further apart and gently tells her, "I'm gonna touch you and see how dilated you are. I just need to make sure you can open and push, Momma."

Josephine breathes out slowly, saying, "Okay."

Only Dextorus, Charony, Lucius, and Josephine are in the birthing chamber of the master's quarters. Deasja remains at his post in the hall, guarding the event as ordered.

Lucius examines his wife. With shock in his eyes, he glances at Dextorus. "How long has she been in labor, Dex? She's completely dilated." he asks and immediately starts to cry when he feels the head of his baby boy.

"She's been in and out of labor for weeks. We've been healing her," Dextorus answers.

Lucius says, "I can feel his head, my yoshawn. I can feel our baby."

Lucius looks up at Dextorus and says, "I need you to get me some towels for my son. I need something to tie off the cord and cut it when he's out. His lungs aren't mature yet. How much ability do you have after healing her?"

Josephine whimpers from the pain. Lucius looks at her and says, "I can't take away your pain this time." He looks at Dex and asks, "How much ability do you have?"

"Lucius, I gave almost all of what I had to you when you came through that gate to keep you alive. What's left is for helping the boy until Deasja comes in here when he's delivered."

Lucius holds Josephine and apologizes, "I'm still healing, sorry. I can't do anything about the labor pains right now. I'm gonna need all the healing I can from Dextorus and Deasja to help our son's lungs."

Josephine lowers her head from a hard contraction. "*Ah!* I'm just glad that you're here, Lucius. I'll manage."

Excited, Lucius raises his voice over her screaming, says, "I need you to breathe in deeply and hold it. Then, I need you to push. Ready. Breathe in."

She takes in a deep breath as she is instructed.

"Push, Josephine." Lucius directs her as he feels the tensing on her abdomen and her body continues to contract harder to ease their baby through the birthing canal. He yells out, "Push! Push! Keep pushing, Momma! Keep pushing."

Josephine bears down while pushing with all her strength.

Lucius says, "You're doing a great job. Keep pushing for me. I can feel his head coming." When her body releases the tension of the contraction, Lucius says, "Okay, Momma. Wait a minute. I want you to breathe in deeply and relax. Give our son air by breathing for him."

Josephine releases her breath and sighs while resting. She leans against Lucius, and Dextorus helps her to sit up when Lucius becomes weak in the knees. "I've got her, Lucius," Dex says.

Lucius readjusts himself to rest on his knees and says, "Just rest for me a moment. I need you to keep breathing for our son. This is when he gets the oxygen he needs during labor." Lucius looks up at how tired she is. He knows that she is giving every ounce of her energy to birth their son. "Deasja will heal you when our son is out, okay?"

She nods as beads of sweat pour down her neck.

Lucius smiles and says, "I'm so proud of you."

Shaking her head, she says, "I'm so tired, Lucius. I've missed you so much."

Lucius kisses her, embracing her in between the heavy contractions, and says, "You're gonna do an amazing job for our son. I'm here now, Josephine. I'm not going anywhere. I might be tired, but I'm not gonna leave your side during this time. I've been dreaming about delivering our son every day. I'm here now."

As soon as another contraction builds up, she begins to scream.

Lucius instructs her, "I need you to take another deep breath for the baby. Stop screaming, Momma. Take a deep breath and hold it in for me. You can do this."

Sweat beads slide down her face and drips off her nose and chin. Josephine takes in a deep breath.

Lucius guides her as he gently places his fingers on the crown of his baby's head, and says, "Hold that breath. Push! Push! I can feel him coming!"

With his encouragement, Josephine pushes.

While Lucius is investigating the careful movement of his son through the birthing canal, he sees Josephine struggling with her failing strength. Realizes her body has not had time to build up the natural energy before labor, Lucius becomes worried about losing them both.

Dextorus reads Lucius mind and says, "We won't lose them. We will call all the angels in here if we must to heal her and the prince."

Lucius nods, saying, "Thank you." He kisses her cheeks and says, "Push. I know you're tired, but I need you to push harder, Josephine." Feeling his son nearly through the birthing canal, Lucius screams, "Push! He's coming, Momma. Our baby's coming!"

Josephine concentrates on her last push. Lucius looks over at Charony and says, "Charony, I need you to get the bowl. You're gonna have to help me with that part while I'm tending to my son."

After directing Charony, Lucius looks up at Dextorus and orders him, "Grab me two more towels from the rack in the lounge behind you so I can wrap them around my son. Hurry, Dex, he's almost out." Lucius looks at Josephine as she stops pushing and begins to cry. "No, baby, don't cry. Save your energy for me. He needs you."

Dextorus rushes to lay out the towels and utensils needed to suction the prince's premature nostrils and throat. Then he lays out the ties and the cutting utensils for when the time comes to cut the prince's cord. "I'm ready, Lucius." Dextorus rubs Josephine's arms and says, "You're too stubborn to quit now. Stop crying and get ready for your last push." He speaks gently, saying, "You can do this, Josephine. You're nearly holding him in your arms."

Charony gets the bowl ready for the placenta. She says, "Ready, your majesty."

Lucius quickly gets everything set up for pulling his son out, and he rests both his arms beneath Josephine to pull his fragile son out safely. Lucius is hunched over his wife's thigh, and Josephine leans across his back, resting during the short minute she has before her last contraction.

"I love you, yoshawn," Lucius says. "Okay, breathe in deeply for me one last time." As soon as she does, Lucius hollers, "Push!"

With her final push, Lucius grabs onto his son's head and shoulder. He carefully eases the baby through the birthing canal and pulls him out to rest upon the clean towels on the floor between her thighs.

Because his son isn't breathing, he yells out to Dextorus, "Heal his lungs so he can breathe! Dex, hurry and help him."

Resting on Lucius's back, Josephine is limp with exhaustion. Lucius siphons the surfactant fluid from his baby boy's airway.

Dextorus leans down and places his hand upon the new prince's chest. His hands are nearly twice the size of the boy.

Josephine doesn't hear anything. "Why can't I hear him?"

Lucius looks at Charony, and says, "I need you to hold her up, Charony, so I can tend to my son better."

Charony helps Josephine to sit up, and Lucius hurries to his son.

While Charony is keeping her held up, Josephine asks, "Why's he so purple?"

Lucius doesn't answer, and his hands shake as he rapidly wipes the surfactant away from his baby's face after suctioning it. Dextorus pushes everything he has into the boy with little response. "Lucius, there's nothing left in me," Dex says.

"Deasja, get in here and help me!" Lucius screams.

Deasja swiftly runs in and places his hand upon the tiny newborn. Moments later, the baby finally gives a positive response and starts to cry with his first breath. Everybody in the room cries with him, and they laugh together as he gets louder with every breath.

Lucius's voice quivers as he announces, "My new second-in-command is born! My son's born!" Lucius carefully wraps the prince in a warm, dry towel and holds him.

As he turns toward Josephine to hand him to her. Lucius sees that Josephine is too tired to lift her hands. His smile fades. He turns toward Deasja. "Heal my wife, Deasja. She needs your healing."

Lucius watches Deasja healing her with every bit of his restoring power as the king had commanded him to do. "With whatever is left in me, Lucius. I am stopping the bleeding and shrinking her uterus back to what it was before bearing your son. She will be completely healed."

As Lucius watches Josephine regain her strength, he says, "That's all I ask."

Deasja nods his head and says, "I'm not going to have any more healing power after this for several days. I won't be able to heal you of anything."

Lucius smiles at his wife and says, "I have an idea for getting my strength back, Deasja. Don't worry about me." Lucius rubs his wife's back while holding his newborn in his other arm. He leans into his wife, and says, "I always need to make sure she's taking care of." Lucius kisses his baby's head and says, "I'm so proud of you, Momma. You're such a good momma."

While Dextorus handles the tying of the umbilical cord, Lucius watches his wife gain power and hold her son for the first time in her arms. When she cradles her baby boy, Lucius holds them both and kisses them.

Dex smiles and asks, "Did you want to cut the cord, Daddy?"

Lucius turns and says, "Yes."

Once they are finished cleaning the room after the birth of the prince, Deasja is the last to leave the master's room. Lucius tells him, "Let everybody know that my son is born. Tell them that Baàlsarideem has no more strength of a second-in-command in his body."

"They'll love to hear the news," Deasja says as he looks down the hall and sees that Dextorus has already started spreading the word. "Never mind, Dex beat me to it."

"Lucius," Josephine signals Lucius to enter the bathing chambers with her. "I need to bathe him and myself."

"I'm coming," Lucius says. He waves at Deasja as the master's chamber door is closed for privacy. Lucius and Josephine take a bath together with their son to heal his body in the Gamerin oils and to bond with him.

Forty-Three

Gamerin Song of Victory

After the birth of Lucius's new second-in-command, an ordained supernatural shift of power occurs.

Aboard Baàlsarideem's Gamerin vessel, Baàlsarideem is asleep in his quarters with the new woman. Power immediately drains from Baàlsarideem and wakes him. With his power draining from his body, he opens his eyes.

Baàlsarideem yells, "Rueshta!" but there is no answer. Because he has the wing in stasis, Baàlsarideem says, "I'll kill Yuleshua to keep my power." He grabs a sword and heads down to the prisoner's cell.

Noticing subtle changes during his walk, the halls are much quieter. Baàlsarideem looks around. None of his normal slaves and servants are at their usual posts. None are maintaining the pylons, tending the fields, or even answering him. "Rueshta!" he yells again.

But no answer.

When Baàlsarideem arrives to the prisoner's quarters and opens the cell, Lucius is no longer chained up. Blood covers the floor, and the chains have been cut in half. Baàlsarideem squats down and sees footprints left behind by the slaves' leather soles. "*Rueshtaaaa!*" he yells louder than before.

Every Nephilim and Gamerin left behind immediately awakens with the cry of outrage emitting throughout the ship. Many of Baàlsarideem's army exit their quarters.

"Rueshta has left me!" Baàl screams. "They've escaped!"

Back in the king's palace, Lucius is soothed inside a Gamerin bath with Josephine and their new son. He takes great joy in watching his wife holding their son and is completely comforted by her presence.

While Josephine holds her newborn son, Lucius cannot force himself to stop caressing and kissing his wife and his son as he allows the tears of joy to fall.

After one hour of bonding after childbearing, they are completely washed and rejuvenated of muscle pain. Lucius exits the bath, saying, "You and he should lie down so you can feed him again. I want to hold you both in the bed."

Dressed in her nightgown, Josephine carries her newborn to the bed. Lucius covers Josephine and his son in warm blankets and lies beside them.

As Josephine feeds her baby from her breast, Lucius smiles. "I think that's amazing how you can feed him nutrients like that. He feels warm and comfortable next to his mother."

Lucius leans over and kisses his baby's head. The moment reminds him of when he would kiss Claire as a baby. He says, "I love the smell of Gamerilaye on him. I haven't seen my baby girl in a long time. Now I want to see my princess."

Josephine says, "I can fix that. Your daughter can hear me whenever I talk to her. I can speak to anyone psychically." She speaks with her mind while she openly says, "Claire, your daddy wants to see you. It's time for you to meet your new baby brother. Come to Momma."

As Lucius hears the long-awaited sounds of his daughter's feet running down the hall to greet him, he gets up from his spot and stands to welcome her. He opens his arms wide and Claire runs full speed to him. "Daddy," she says.

"You've gotten so big," he says. "How's my princess doing? I love you, Claire." He grunts while holding her. "Daddy loves his little princess. I've missed you so much." He takes in her fragrance with a deep breath. "My baby smells of Gamerilaye."

Claire says, "I missed you, Daddy. I knew you were gonna be here."

"Your voice is so precious to me, pumpkin." Lucius becomes emotional hearing her and squeezes her tighter.

When Josephine sees that the prince is sleeping, she places her index finger in the corner of his mouth to stop the suction. She covers herself modestly and looks up at Claire, saying, "When you're done with your daddy, I have your baby brother here."

Lucius turns around with Claire in his embrace and presents his son to his daughter. "He's little and fragile right now, but he'll be as big and strong as your daddy someday," he says.

⚜

For a short time, the Gamerin family spends time alone together for the first time in eight months. Lucius caresses his daughter's head with his right hand and holds his son's tiny fingers with his left. "This is heaven for me," he says and watches as Claire falls asleep in his arms. Lucius lets go of his son's fingers and asks Josephine, "Do you want to introduce the new prince of Gamerilaye with me? Many angels are anticipating seeing my new second-in-command. I'd be honored if you would present him with me to my army."

"I'd love to show our family to everyone with you," Josephine says.

"We also have nephews," he says as he carefully moves from his position on the bed. "I'm trying not to wake her. It's nearly nine o'clock. She'll be up all night."

Josephine says, "Artie can put her to sleep, baby."

He makes his way around the bed and reaches over his wife to take his son in his arms. "I forgot," he says. "I've been out of energy for a while, and the commanders being weak threw me off."

As Lucius helps Josephine stand, she asks, "What are you planning with your energy, Lucius?"

Lucius hands Josephine the baby, and she cradles him in her embrace. He picks up Claire and says, "Let's not worry about tomorrow. Let tomorrow worry about itself. Put your robe on. Let me help you."

They perform almost a ballet with maneuvering children as she dresses in her evening robe so she can leave the room. When she is finished with her royal attire, Lucius and Josephine lay Claire down in her bedroom down the hall.

Afterward, Lucius and Josephine enter the main chamber of the living area of the palace. Dex and Deasja nudge Artie, and Artie nudges the other angels, Wheatley and Orlando, and down the line they nudge each other. Not long after, everyone is looking at the royal couple with a baby.

Lucius's lips quiver as he raises his hands and shouts to the group, "I have a son! He's the Prince of Gamerilaye!"

Everyone roars in celebration, and the baby flares his arms out from the abrupt noises.

Josephine places her finger over her mouth. "Shush. Celebrate quietly," she says.

Because Deasja was the loudest, he says, "Sorry."

Dextorus stands to his feet and says, "I'll give a speech in honor to you Gamerin Warrior." Dex pauses for a moment before he says, "I've known Lucius for thousands of years. He always surprises me and is still one of the humblest principalities I've ever known. Other than Yeshua, he is the only principality that will openly call you brother. The one that will share his table with a stranger." He looks at Artie and says, "He would sacrifice himself for a friend." Dextorus gazes at Lucius and Josephine and says, "I had all faith in you. I knew your heart wouldn't mislead you. I've never known a more fearless warrior in battle. I've only known one other wonderful father. My heart is overjoyed with this new child, the firstborn son on Gamerilaye. This is the heir of Yuleshua Lucius Gamerin, a mighty warrior and a mighty principality. Yuleshua is my friend because he is a servant of the Almighty God, and he's a true principality. I am honored to work alongside you in battle."

"Well said, my friend," Deasja says.

As the angels continue cheering, a voice lifts above the crowd. Lucius recognizes the song as the crowd hushes. Soon, the guardians back away from the one singing, and Lucius smiles. Josephine says, "I've never heard him sing before," as all eyes stare at Artie, singing an ancient Gamerin song of praise.

Lucius whispers to Josephine, "We usually sing this song for the Trinity, but today, he sings it to me."

Artie sings:
The war may take many lives,
The war might threaten his soul.
The war can't take a true king,
Into the bowels of Sheol.
I've seen it before and I've seen it again,
My heart cries out for my dearest friend.
The one that's willing to die for his own,
Is a true king that sits on a humble throne.
From humble roots it shall always be,

Of the royal bloodline
From the royal family.
One of the Almighty's sons,
May for a time stand alone,
But in his fight we shall see,
He will sit on a humble throne,
And shout the victory!
I've seen it before and I've seen it again,
My heart cries out for my dearest friend.
One that's willing to die for his own,
Is a true King that sits on a humble throne.
The Lord is true until the end,
My heart cries out for my dearest friend.
One that's risen from the dead,
And life comes from the blood he shed.
I've seen it before and I've seen it again,
My heart cries out for my dearest friend.
One that's willing to die for his own,
Is a true King that sits on a humble throne.
One of the Almighty's sons,
May for a time stand alone,
But in his fight we shall see,
The loving Lord and principality!

"You changed the words in honor of me. I love you, brother," Lucius says.

Artie never stops singing, and others join in. Soon, Josephine sings the Gamerin Song of Victory. Lucius sings with his friends, and the house is filled with song and unity.

Although war will be at their door soon, the present moment is a victory.

Lucius becomes tired during the celebration. He excuses himself as they continue the music and celebration. "Continue celebrating with my new nephews. Allow them to celebrate their freedom here," he says. Lucius and Josephine walk back to their chambers to rest.

Once in the room, Lucius's body nearly aches again from the simple chore of walking down the hallway and standing for an hour. He crawls into bed with a grimace. "Why am I the one that feels like turd? You're the one that just had a baby."

"I'm healed, that's why," Josephine says and lays their son in his bassinet next to her. "He's asleep. That will give me another hour before feeding him."

"Good," Lucius snuggles her in bed, saying, "I wanna sleep next to my comforting wife tonight."

"Should I check on Claire?" Josephine asks. "They were loud earlier. I can still hear them a little over the pond flowing."

Lucius gets back up and says, "I wanna check on her." As Lucius opens the door, Artie is already standing out in the hallway.

"I heard your thoughts," Artie says. "I just checked on her. She's safe. You should rest."

Lucius hugs Artie and says, "I wasn't doubting you."

"No, you just forgot that I was there." Artie looks Lucius in the face and nearly tears up. "You're home. I wish I were powerful enough to heal you of your mental trauma. I sense your pain, but there is no need to suffer tonight. I only ask that you still trust me as you say that you love me." Artie pauses for a moment and then stares at the floor. "I feel your thoughts, Lucius. Nobody is going to come through that door and hurt her. I would rather die. Rest. You need rest."

Lucius steps from the room once as Artie walks off. Before he closes the door, he sees many angels in the hall guarding the corridor. He says, "On Earth, we had sort of a deal with the angels."

Artie stops and finishes what Lucius was saying, "If you hear him crying out in the morning, please don't answer without the queen's permission." Artie turns back to Lucius and asks, "Was that what you were going to say?"

"Pretty much. I might be weak, but I'm not dead. I miss my wife's comforting love over me." Lucius closes his chamber doors and leans against the frame for a moment out of weakness.

"Come to bed," Josephine says. "You look exhausted."

Almost dragging his feet, Lucius takes off his Gamerin warrior shirt and climbs in the bed next to his wife. "I feel like I've moved and entire house."

Josephine is fast asleep.

Lucius cradles her like a baby and says, "You might be healed, but you're exhausted as well." He starts to fall asleep as he prays, "Lord, help me take care of my family. I can't do anything without you. You know all things, and I can't do anything without you. I love you, Father. Amen." He kisses his wife on her shoulder and falls asleep.

❧

While they lie in the warmth of the blankets, Lucius experiences post traumatic nightmares. The soldiers make their rounds, and when Lucius hears the footsteps, they sound as if his torturers are coming to beat him again. The baby becomes hungry and cries in his crib, and Lucius's mind hears the screams of women. His body tenses up and grits his teeth in his sleep.

Josephine bumps the mobile with her hand and it plays a tune.

Thinking he hears the sequence of buzzes from the airlock, Lucius jumps from his bed screaming. He hides in the corner and leans against the wall with his hands out to guard himself from his routine beating. "Get your hands off me, you bastards. Leave them alone."

Josephine holds the baby against her and calls out, "Deasja, Dextorus help me! Lucius needs help!"

"I'll kill you," Lucius says.

Several guardians run into the room and try to comfort him, but Lucius fights them by throwing punches and curses at them. "Get your hands off of me, you son of a bastard." Abruptly, Lucius punches Deasja in the face a few times while biting his lips and yelling, "Stop hurting me you bastards! Don't touch me anymore."

Angels are wrestling with Lucius to restrain him from hurting anybody else, Deasja gets socked in the jaw a few more times. He rattles his head before climbing on top of Lucius who is face down against his will. Deasja yells, "Wake up, Lucius! It's just us." Lucius kicks his legs back and knocks Deasja forward. Like a ninja, Lucius twists around and locks Deasja in a head lock. "Stop," Deasja punches Lucius in the rib before his neck is broke. "Lucius, I'm trying to help."

Dextorus stands between Josephine and the wrestling angels trying to restrain Lucius.

Josephine cries out, "Lucius, what's wrong? What's wrong with him, Dex?"

Dextorus answers, "He's dreaming, defending himself."

Standing to face each other, Deasja takes a few more punches to the face. "He punches hard too," Deasja says. Lucius kicks Deasja and knocks him into a wall. "That hurt."

Dextorus says out loud, "Leave him alone. Let him sit in the corner while he wakes up. He doesn't think you're helping him. He's a warrior, remember?"

With a grimace on his face and a grip to a cracked rib, "Okay everybody, just walk away," Deasja says. As soon as they stop coming toward Lucius, Lucius backs toward the wall and is panting.

Deasja grabs at his chest and wipes his face. He looks at Dextorus, and mutters beneath his breath, "Man, I told you I needed to heal him."

Dextorus studies Lucius's next moves. "It's okay, soldier. You're okay."

Lucius holds his hand out, saying, "Don't touch me. Don't. Don't touch." He cowers down into the corner. His body quakes from the experience. Lucius nearly urinates himself until he realizes that he can feel the sensation and clinches the muscles before wetting his clothes. He feels his legs. The wall is warm behind him, and the rug is soft beneath him. His arms are in front of him and he can see his hands. "Where have you taken me? I don't serve you Baàl…" but the smell is familiar in the room.

"Lucius," Dextorus says. "Wake up."

Lucius looks around the room and becomes aware that he was asleep. He glances at the bed and sees it's empty. He quickly jumps up. "Josephine! Where is she?"

A voice from behind Dex answers, "I'm right here, baby. I'm holding our son and feeding him, remember?"

Lucius exhales in relief and leans against the wall. Recognizing the faces in the room, he says their names as he looks at each of them. When he looks over at Deasja, he explains what they are reading in his mind, "They killed them," and he starts weeping. "Hundreds of them." Lucius squats back down on the ground. "Baàlsarideem is torturing them even now. I couldn't save them. They raped and beat them until there was nothing left, and then they discarded them like trash into the expanse. They never loved them, and many of them were wives and mothers. All of them were someone's daughter, and they killed them like they were nothing."

Josephine carefully lays her son back in his bassinet. She joins beside her husband on the floor and holds him.

Lucius looks at her and says, "I can't let this continue, baby. They're evil. I'm going to free my people, and kill every one of those evil monsters for hurting my sisters."

Deasja looks at the guards and says, "He's fine. You are excused for now, but stay close."

Dextorus walks around and helps Lucius to stand to his feet. Lucius then helps Josephine up from the floor.

Lucius says, "Go ahead and lie down, baby. I'll be in here shortly. I must speak to the commanders."

Because they can read Lucius's mind, Dextorus and Deasja wait for him on the bay landing outside of his chambers.

Lucius watches as Josephine lies back down in the bed, and he says, "I'm sorry about scaring you, my love."

Lucius walks over to his son's bassinet and kisses him. After loving on his son, Lucius walks over and kisses his wife on the cheek. He tells her, "I'll be here in a little bit." He grabs the curtain and says, "If you're scared that I might do that again, I can have Artie put me into a deep sleep. Do you want me to have him do that?"

Josephine says, "No. The guardians are nearby and we're safe."

"I want you to be able to trust me."

"I do trust in you. It wasn't your fault."

"Thank you," Lucius says as he sighs in relief. He closes the curtain and walks outside.

Forty-Four

Scared of Who

O nce Lucius is outside on the bay landing, he stands next to the guardrail that overlooks his ocean. Although it's night, Lucius looks up and sees his two large mountainous moons above the atmosphere.

"It's springtime here," he says toward the night sky. Deasja and Dextorus watch him closely. "I know you're reading my thoughts. I have no ability to stop you. Because you care about me, please ask instead of plucking the information from my head."

"I don't need to read your thoughts, Lucius," Dextorus says. "I see that you are troubled about Baàlsarideem."

Lucius says, "I have no power. They shot me with a weapon that has broken me. Vincent told me that over time I'll have my power back, but I'm powerless right now." He looks down to the ocean as he continues, "I don't know when Baàlsarideem will figure out how to use his portal device. I know it's gonna happen. He's going to invade, and I can't let his filthy hands touch my family."

Dextorus pulls out a purple cigar, and Lucius takes a step back to watch him. Dextorus lights the large cigar with his finger lighter and says, "A smoke helps me think."

Staring at the cigar that Dex holds, "Have y'all been sharing cigars?" Lucius asks.

From behind Lucius, another lighter flicks; this time from Deasja. "Yeah. Mine are better." Deasja rubs his tender jaw and wipes a little more blood from his face.

"That's because mine are old," Dex says. "When fresh, mine are better."

"Only because you don't know what's in mine." Deasja smiles.

Lucius notices the blood on Deasja's face, and says, "I'm sorry for hitting you. I didn't know what I was doing."

"I know," Deasja says as he rubs his bloody nose. "From your pinpoint accuracy, you could've fooled me. You have one heck of a left hook, and a mean right uppercut, Lucius." Deasja shakes his head and sniffles the blood back up. "I wish I had enough ability to heal myself," he says while rubbing his chest. "Your roundhouse kick is phenomenal, by the way."

Dextorus chuckles inwardly. "I'm glad I was on the other side of the room."

Lucius snickers. "Don't make me laugh, Dex. I feel bad about hitting Deasja," he says and stares at the beach in the distance until he's no longer smiling.

Reaching into his pocket, Deasja pulls out a cigar, hands it over to Lucius, and says, "Congratulations, Daddy. I think you deserve this."

Lucius cautiously looks around. "I don't know if I should. My wife doesn't like to kiss me when I smell of cigars."

Dextorus asks, "What did she do when I gave you that other one?"

Lucius confesses, "I smoked a little bit of the cigar before she got me to give it away. I opened a portal and gave it to Artie."

"I bet Artie liked that. That brimstone angel has wanted one of my cigars for a long time," Dextorus replies.

Lucius holds the cigar in his mouth. "He did, but…" he begins to say as he looks at Deasja and Dextorus. He holds his hands up and says, "Okay guys. I can't light the cigar on my own."

Dextorus uses his vision and sees Artie doing his rounds below. Dex looks back at Lucius, says, "Why don't you have Artie light your cigar for you?"

Deasja and Dextorus both laugh.

Lucius says, "I'm glad that you guys are good friends now, and that Dex finally has found a lame humor, but I still can't light this without help."

Starting the flame of his Gamerin, customized, finger lighter on his hand, Deasja walks over and lights the purple cigar for Lucius.

Lucius takes a couple drags and decides to tease Dextorus back, saying, "Deasja, I haven't had one of these in a long time. I'm glad you told me where you make them."

Quickly offended, Dextorus looks over at Deasja and replies, "Hey, I thought you said you couldn't tell me where you make those."

After his comment, Lucius chuckles.

"I didn't, Dex. He's only teasing you."

Dextorus says, "Well, the young principality's got jokes. I bet you think you're real funny."

Lucius continues to smoke his cigar, and nods his head, says, "Yeah. I know I'm funny. I never lost my humor. It's too bad you never really found yours."

Deasja laughs. "Don't start, guys."

Dex flicks the ash of his cigar, looks over at Lucius, and says, "You think you're funny? I wonder how funny you'll be when I tell your wife you're smoking out here with us."

Lucius pulls the cigar out of his mouth and says, "Dex, you wouldn't dare."

"I wouldn't what? What wouldn't I do?" Dextorus calmly looks the other way as he stares in the distance to watch the glistening of the ocean with the night sky.

Lucius lifts the cigar up. "You wouldn't tell my wife I'm smoking." He places the cigar back into his mouth. "Stop teasing."

Dextorus turns back toward Lucius, and then looks behind him before saying, "No, I wouldn't tell your wife you were smoking, but you would."

In a flash, Lucius takes the cigar out of his mouth and tosses it over the cliffside balcony. Slowly, he turns around to see what Dextorus is looking at.

Nobody is there.

Both Deasja and Dex laugh until nearly coughing from their exhaustion.

Dex says, "I have jokes too, Gamerin."

Lucius raises his hands up, and says, "That's so mean, Dex. I just lost a perfectly good cigar. I can't fly down there and get it either. It's not like I have those lying around on this planet, guys."

Flying up from the cliffside, Artie puffs a purple cigar in his mouth. He takes a couple drags, and says, "I heard everybody outside. Thanks guys. Somebody nice gave this wonderful cigar to me. I don't mind hand-me-downs."

Lucius walks over to Artie and takes the cigar from his mouth. "Give me that."

Artie slumps his shoulders. "I can never get a full cigar. Why doesn't anyone ever give me a cigar? Are y'all prejudiced against me?"

Lucius puffs circles of smoke above him. He smiles as the commanders continue to snicker.

A few moments later, Dextorus turns back and stops smoking. His cigar nosedives from the corner of his mouth. The cigar rattles with his words as he asks, "What about your wife, Lucius?"

Lucius puffs a large cloud of smoke above his head. "I'm not falling for that again."

Immediately after Lucius answers Dextorus, he hears, "Lucius? Are you smoking out here?" Josephine asks.

With one quick nonchalant movement, Lucius hands Artie the smoking cigar. He turns and stares several feet in front of him. "Not anymore, my love," Lucius answers her.

Josephine looks around at everyone on the porch. The atmosphere feels heavier for some reason, causing Dextorus, Artie, and Deasja to look the other way, trying to escape the eyeballing from Josephine. Lucius, however, doesn't turn away and faces her.

Josephine lowers her hands. "You look so tired, baby." She rubs his arm and says, "Be careful and wash off when you're done. Our baby's lungs are fragile. I don't want him to get third hand smoke from your clothes and hair."

After Josephine walks back into the room, Lucius turns and starts to grumble. "Thanks for the heads-up, guys."

Deasja, Artie, and Dextorus all raise their hands, and fill the air with their defenses of how they had no idea.

Shaking his head, Lucius takes two steps and yanks the cigar from Artie's mouth. "I was beaten in captivity for eight months. I just had a son. I almost died today. I think I deserve a cigar this time."

Artie says, "You do," and he turns toward the commanders, holds his hand out for either Dextorus or Deasja to give him a cigar.

Pulling out a new fresh cigar, Dextorus gives the brimstone angel one of his own cigars for the first time.

Artie feels as though the world has gone into slow-motion as he holds the cigar from one of the staunchest commanders in existence. He says, "Thanks commander, Dex. I like your cigars." Artie puts the cigar in his mouth and lights a ball of fire within the palm of his hand.

Deasja says, "Must be nice to light whatever, whenever."

"That's a handy fireball, for sure," Dex says.

Lucius asks, "What do you think gave me the idea for your finger lighters I gave you?"

Artie nods. "I helped make them."

"I never knew that you helped to make my lighter, Artie," Dextorus says.

Deasja pulls out another cigar and hands it to Artie. "I had no idea. Just let me know if you need more."

Artie smiles and says, "Finally."

Cigars are halfway smoked. One moon remains above them and is midway across the sky. Not a word is spoken until Lucius says, "I was supposed to be captured," speaking out loud what they were hearing his thoughts wrestle with. He continues. "There was no other way to see how badly Baàlsarideem was treating them."

Artie crosses his arms and rubs his own shoulders, seeing Lucius's thoughts.

"Cry not for me," Lucius says. "Mourn for those still hurting. Eight-thousand of my brothers are in captivity."

"What are the numbers, Lucius?" Dextorus asks.

Lucius answers, "Four thousand Gamerin warriors, along with their sons, are leading an army against me."

"Who are the Nephilim guys that came through?" Artie asks.

Dextorus says, "Vincentine…I mean Vincent." He smiles at Lucius before continuing. "Vincent said they were slaves aboard the vessel because their fathers served Lucius and the Trinity. They would not turn."

"Only 312 of them. A small army, barely stronger than I am right now," Lucius says. "We are up against an army of twenty thousand of the strongest warriors known in existence. Are you all going to stand with me still?"

Artie says, "Until death is crying from my blade, I follow you."

Deasja puffs his cigar. "You don't need to ask. I signed up for this, Lucius."

Turning to face Dextorus, Lucius awaits his answer.

With the tiniest hint of a grin on his face, Dex says, "Someday, you will understand me completely. You will know why I fought every victorious battle with you. Someday…" he pauses as his smile increases, "you will smile when you realize that we are exactly the same. I will always fight alongside you because I owe you my life…because of someday. Never doubt me, soldier. Someday, you will know who I truly am."

Relieved, Lucius stares down at the tiles of the terrace. He says, "I'm going to need prayer. I could fight nearly all of them on my own, if I had my strength."

Artie asks, "What about their weapons, Lucius? I thought they had weapons that cause us to be weaker too. I know I was almost paralyzed by one that looked like the devil's trident. That weapon wasn't the same as the pulse device I saw in your mind."

Lucius shakes his head. "I don't know. Vincent helped to develop those weapons. Maybe we can pull his plans together and find a weakness." He places his leg back up on the guardrail, and says, "I'm worn out right now. Apparently, I need a shower before I can lay down or hold my son."

Deasja places his leg up on the guardrail like Lucius. Standing almost side-by-side, Lucius, Deasja, Artie, and Dex rest one foot on the banister, staring out toward the ocean and finishing their cigars.

Deasja says, "Your wife is stubborn, Lucius. I don't know how you can handle being married. You two are a lot alike."

Lucius chuckles and says, "I love that she's stubborn. She listens, learns, and when pushed into a corner, her stubbornness makes her a strong leader. Josephine was born to be a leader." Lucius lowers his leg and says, "I have to take a shower and lie down."

While Lucius walks off, Deasja turns and asks, "Why do you call her 'baby'?"

Lucius stops and looks back. "The name was chosen for me by the Spirit. He showed me how precious she would be to me." He stands for a moment and then says, "There was a time that I had almost lost her love because of attacks. When she was freed, she blessed me with the privilege of calling her baby. I will never stop calling her that. Night, y'all."

—⋆⋅☙⋅⋆—

Lucius showers and enters his room. He sees his wife nursing their son and carefully crawls into bed. "Is he hungry, or did you just wanna hold him."

Watching her baby suckling, Josephine smiles. "A little bit of both. He's so tiny."

Lucius leans down. He gives his boy a kiss and smells the top of his head for several moments. "He's perfect."

"I'm glad you washed off for him. I wasn't trying to be bossy, only protective." With her free hand, she massages Lucius's shoulder and neck while he is still kissing his baby boy. As she presses harder into his tight muscles, she says, "You're very tense, baby."

He moans. "Feels so good."

Josephine smiles and presses into his neck and rubs down his spine.

"*Aaahhh*," Lucius moans out, nearly melting from the relief. "You have no idea how good that feels."

"Actually," she says, "I read your thoughts and feel all your body senses as my own, just like you could with me. My ability has grown. I'm bio-empathic now."

Lucius looks up at her. "Can you say that again?"

"You told me not to tell anyone about my abilities to protect me." She smiles and says, "I'm glad you like that I'm stubborn. I also think you deserved a cigar."

"Well, you dirty dog. You didn't tell me that before I went out there. You knew everything I was thinking and saying to the guys while I was outside having a private conversation. That's hardly fair in my condition."

Josephine stops massaging his back, and says, "I think it's fair. When you were assigned to me for nearly two years, you read every dirty thought and every yearning sensation that I had in me. You didn't even tell me until the week we were married. You knew everything about me. I only kept my secret from you for this one conversation, hardly unfair."

"You're a good actress. That's scary," he says. He becomes a little confused after a moment and asks, "How come the other angels don't know you're reading their minds?"

Josephine starts massaging his back again and explains, "I've been working with Artie. He taught me how to block my mind. I decided to work on that before anything else."

"Do you mean to tell me that my best friend knew about your ability and kept it a secret from me?"

Josephine places her hand upon his head. "I'm blocking your mind right now. Nobody in our palace will enter your thoughts."

Lucius asks, "Can you message my right shoulder?" He points a little back. "Just under my shoulder blade there."

As she digs into the tense tissue, Lucius moans and groans. As he carries on, a few angels become scared and run into the room. "Lucius, wake up," they say.

Lucius pops his head up and turns back, saying, "I am awake. I thought I told y'all not to enter without my wife's permission."

Deasja also enters moments after hearing the angels rush in and call out. As soon as he sees Josephine's hand over Lucius's shoulder, he says. "Just a back massage. He's fine." Deasja nods at Lucius and says, "We'll be outside until the queen calls for us."

After they leave, Lucius looks at Josephine. He says, "I'm glad we weren't doing anything private. The intrusion would've put a damper on us making love."

Josephine slowly gets out of bed and carries the baby to his bassinet. Lucius smiles as he studies the bassinet. "Who made that for him?"

"Artie and Claire. They added the seashells and flowers to it on the bottom. Deasja helped a little too." Josephine snuggles back in the bed with Lucius and entangles her leg in Lucius's.

Her body feels warm to Lucius so he grabs onto her, bringing her closer to him. He lets no air between them, and says, "Holding you will keep me calm."

"If I were any closer, we would be making love."

"I'm too tired, but I'm leaving my options open for in the morning," he answers.

"You're right," she says. "I can feel your body. You're in no shape to make love."

"Excuse me?" he asks.

"I was just saying that you can't perform right now. You are tired."

Lucius lifts her gown up from under the blankets.

Josephine giggles, and says, "You don't have to prove anything, baby. I was just saying you're too tired."

Lucius unzips his pants and rubs against her. "No. I'm not going to have you think that of me, never ever," he says and kisses her on the neck.

Josephine touches his cheek and says, "I want you to feel what I feel."

As soon as she does, Lucius feels her power enter him. He looks her in the eyes, and says, "Have I ever told you how much I love you."

Josephine smiles. "For all time, you will."

Out in the hall, angels hear Lucius softly moaning at an increasingly gentle frequency. The angels look at each other, but Deasja waves his hands calmly, saying, "Calm down. He's just getting a massage."

Soon after, they all hear Josephine make a small amount of moaning mingled with breathy sighs.

Dextorus asks, "Do you think he's massaging her back now?"

Deasja shrugs, and soon after, Josephine and Lucius both become slightly louder, but none of the angels can peer into their blocked minds.

Deasja stands into the middle of the hallway, "What do I do?" he asks and looks at Dextorus.

Dex suddenly smiles and asks, "Deasja, what exactly are in those cigars?"

Deasja says, "I mix some additives to keep warriors energized." Immediately after thinking of the additives, he places his thumb and middle finger to his nose and supports his elbow. "The cigars have stimulants and energy metabolizers in them. They're for longevity during battle." Slightly embarrassed, Deasja decides to walk off. "They're fine. I'm going outside for a while."

Soon after he leaves, all the angels follow him and walk away from the hall outside of the master's quarters while Lucius and Josephine are counseling each other.

<hr />

On the landing bay outside of the kitchen preparation area, the commanders discuss options and plan for the approaching battle for Gamerilaye.

Dextorus says, "In a little bit, I'll stand guard outside the door. Tomorrow, Lucius wants to have a meeting. Artie told me that he was going to discuss what he wants for his army against Baàlsarideem in battle."

Deasja says, "We have a large group, but not all of them are soldiers. Although Vincent's smart, he's no warrior. He's a scientist, and I bet he couldn't wield a sword."

Dex says, "You heard Lucius. We have very few numbers. We can't fight an army that is almost twenty thousand strong. We have only a few hundred soldiers, and a few hundred Nephilim slaves. I know Lucius has a lot of faith in his people, but the Nephilim slaves aren't trained on the field."

Vincent walks outside to join the gathered group. "I can hear you speaking of me. I understand your worries, for I hear your thoughts. I'm no warrior on the battlefield, but I'm good in preparing for battle. I know that Lucius is the high commander now because he's my king in this realm. Never underestimate the craftiness of the Gamerin principality. Lucius will save us."

Deasja says, "I'm sorry. I didn't mean to offend. I know he's your king. I'm only trying to calculate our projections for battle. I might be forty-seven trillion years old, but I'm not done fighting in this war. I've never fought on this side of the universe, and I don't want to die on this side of the universe either."

Vincent says, "My father used to tell me of the amazing creatures that Yuleshua governed over. I heard that after he inherited many of the galaxies from the fallen principalities, he had some of the oldest and most difficult creatures known in existence from the Creator. Some of them are undefeated in battle, and he's always found a way to protect them from invasion. Many of them are a living miracle because of their existence. I have no doubt in my mind that my king will provide for us while we fight Baàlsarideem in the same way."

Dextorus answers, "I have a lot of trust and faith in Lucius. He's a genius warrior, and he never gives up. He will find a way like he always does."

Deasja raises his hand to halt the conversation. "Dex and Vincent, it's true that Lucius is very cunning in battle. But don't forget that we're fighting against a powerful Gamerin army that has been waging war against God's true Son for ten thousand years. Even if Baàlsarideem has personally lost his own power, he is almost twenty thousand strong against us. With those numbers, Lucius is going to have to pull every Gamerin trick out of his hat to save us. Right now, he can't even light a cigar. So, excuse me while I go and pray." Deasja walks into the palace and stands guard outside of Lucius and Josephine's room. Remembering all the soldiers who have been captured, tortured, and destroyed by the hands of Baàlsarideem, he stands in silence. "That guy is a devil," he whispers to himself.

Standing outside, Vincent lowers his head and continues to believe in his king.

Dextorus looks at Vincent and says, "I too trust in Lucius. I have fought alongside him in many battles. I've never known anyone to find a way through a tough situation like him. The Almighty will not abandon us, and Lucius will guide us to victory with the Creator we all serve."

As soon as Dextorus is finished speaking, Deasja whispers, "I hope they're right."

Preview

RECKONING
OF THE KING

~ WEAPON OF WAR ~

BOOK FIVE

ALETHEA STAURON

One

Coffee

Lucius and Josephine are snuggled tightly in the bed against each other. Hours before the light of day rises, their newborn baby boy lies sound asleep from his first hours of being born.

Josephine wakes up thinking, *I wanna check on the baby*, but an arm is wrapped tightly around her like a rope. She knows why her husband holds her in such a way, but comforting Lucius is not the only protection she is thinking about. *I can't wake Lucius, but the baby hasn't cried for a feeding in a while*, she worries.

Josephine lies still until her worrying becomes unbearable to her. She makes the smallest movement and Lucius folds his fingers slightly inward. To move from Lucius's grasp would wake him or make him hold her tighter. She exhales as she realizes there is no other way around her worry, and says, "Lucius, I need to get up and check on the baby. He hasn't cried, and I'm worried for him."

Without opening his eyes, Lucius calms his wife down. He speaks with an exhale. "After delivery, babies are tired. It's a lot of work for them too. You might be healed, but after using all your energy, you also need rest. All three of us are exhausted, Momma. If you want, we can have someone come in here and watch him so we can rest, and you can continue calming my spirit so I can sleep."

Trying to relax, Josephine smiles as she strokes Lucius's warmth of his forearm. "You're really warm." She tries to rest but the maternal instincts become too strong and makes her uncomfortable.

"Baby," he whispers while rearranging his arm around her tighter, "quit wiggling, little momma."

"I can't. I have to check on him."

"Call someone you feel most comfortable around in here."

To Lucius's surprise, she quietly calls out to the one she trusts the most with her son's safety. "Dex, I need you to watch over my son as he sleeps. The baby is being very quiet and making it difficult for me to rest."

Dextorus walks into the chambers, and Lucius opens his eyes and looks at his wife. He says, "I'm surprised that you called for Dex because he's so big. Not many people know he's gentle with children. He's downright terrifying to everyone else."

"Depends on what side you're on," Dex replies.

Josephine lays her head back down on her husband's biceps, and says, "Dex has been nothing but kind to me. He's very gentle, fierce, but gentle."

Lucius can barely keep his eyes open in Josephine's arms.

Dex checks over the baby in the bassinet. He runs a vitals scanner and knows that the boy is well and then scans Lucius's vitals as well. Realizing Lucius is already fast asleep, Dex says, "You bring Lucius peace."

"Thank you." Josephine asks, "How is the baby?"

Dextorus says, "He's perfect. He's just sleeping."

Josephine says, "Thank you again." Comforted by the reassurance, her eyes immediately become heavy.

Only moments pass, and Josephine hears, "I'm sorry to bother you both, but what's your son's name?"

Lucius and Josephine open their eyes to look at each other.

Lucius speaks with a raspy voice when he says, "We haven't had time to think of a name. We'll do that later. I have a lot of work to do today." He starts to drift off and mumbles, "In a…bit."

Lucius doesn't finish speaking another phrase as his body forces him to rest.

With not another word from the royal couple, Dextorus stands guard over the baby's bassinet. As he stands and studies the little Gamerin boy, he hears a grumbling noise. The grumbling increases and decreases until he realizes that the sounds are coming from somebody breathing. Slowly turning his head to the royal bed, Dextorus grins. He says, "I can't believe it," hearing Lucius snoring so loud that it rumbles the furniture. "That's intriguing," Dextorus whispers. "I've never heard an angel snore before."

Josephine rubs her fingers through Lucius's soft hair behind his ear. "Is he really snoring?"

Dextorus says, "The weakness might be there for quite some time. He truly needs your comfort."

She whispers, "Bless his heart. He's so tired."

As Lucius is completely unaware of the conversation, Dextorus answers her, "Because he is safe in your arms now, I will give a report to you, knowing that the news won't affect our outcome for success, but give you an understanding in your heart. Vincent told me that they kept him chained up in such a way that he could never lie down. Lucius had a beard and they barely kept him alive on purpose. He was also left paralyzed from the beatings." Dextorus assesses the baby again, and continues to speak, "I'm telling you this not to upset you but to express how good it is that he has you during his healing stages and why he suffered the post-trauma episode last night. He needs to rest, and he needs your love as well. The fact that he sleeps so peacefully with you is a good sign that you are his equal. He needs your balance, Josephine."

Josephine tries not to cry, but allows silent tears to run sideways down her face.

"Don't allow yourself to remain troubled from what is no more," Dex says. "We are facing a different time with new trials soon. Prepare your heart for future things. Lucius will be stronger from the experience, but over time."

Josephine continues to caress Lucius's ear, listening to him snore inches from her nose. She whispers, "I know he suffered and that he's going to save all his people. He wants a large family. I know he saved them as well. Lucius loves with a genuine heart, doesn't he? He's the good principality."

Dextorus agrees quietly. "That…he is."

She says, "You seem to know a lot about love, Dex."

"His suffering is worth something, that's all. Nothing planned by the Father is in vain." Dextorus looks down and smiles at the tiny Gamerin stretching while he sleeps, seeing so many resemblances, imagining what Lucius would look like as a baby. He laughs inwardly with the thought. Dextorus says, "I'm going to let you sleep, your majesty. You need rest. It's still early, and Claire won't be up for another hour or two." Dextorus stands guard over Lucius's heir quietly.

After several hours, the baby fidgets from being wet. Dextorus gives the newborn the pacifier and changes him. As soon as the Gamerin prince is dry, he falls back to sleep and suckling on the pacifier.

Josephine wakes with a stretch. Before her son wakes up as well, she decides to slide out from her husband's grasp and feed her little boy.

As she carefully moves, Lucius holds on tighter to her. He moans in his sleep. "Why does time have to keep moving? Can't I just hold you?"

Because she is not tired anymore, Josephine decides to find a gentler way for Lucius to release her. She rubs her fingernails across his back.

The comfort she gives him causes Lucius to loosen his grip with his goosebumps rolling over his upper body. She slowly starts to get out of the bed and lets go.

When he realizes she tricked him, Lucius speaks with a whisper, "*Aww.* You tricked me. I thought you were gonna love on my back. I wanna hold you longer."

Josephine shakes her head while looking at Dextorus. She stands over the bassinet with a quiet reply, "I wanna hold the baby and feed him. I'm gonna lie next to you, but with our son also."

Lucius stretches in the bed. He speaks with his mouth wide open during an enormous yawn, saying, "That's okay. I'm awake. I must find some coffee and eat something." He smacks his gums a few times and immediately yawns again while saying, "I haven't eaten in two days, and you don't wanna know what they feed prisoners." He finishes yawning a third time and drags himself to sit on the side of the bed. "I have a lot to do today."

While Lucius wipes the sleep from his eyes, he looks over at Dextorus and yawns for the fourth time while asking, "Do we have coffee here?"

"I think I heard you say coffee, but with your mouth open, it's hard to tell," Dex says.

Lucius half chuckles.

"You know what he said. Don't be mean to him because he's tired," Josephine says.

Lucius explains, "Oh, no. He never teases. He doesn't know what a joke is. He's being completely serious right now."

Dextorus says, "I could joke if I wanted. I just choose not to."

"Okay, you can leave now, Mr. Serious. I need to feed my son." Josephine says. "And thank you for changing him earlier."

"You're welcome." Looking at Lucius, Dextorus walks around the bed, says, "Artie made sure that we had the best coffee from his planet. Josephine has wanted some for a while, but she couldn't have any while she was pregnant or breast-feeding."

While holding her baby in her hands, Josephine lays herself on the bed and comments, "I know. It smells so good. I do savor the fresh orange juice that he brings me instead."

"At least, that's something you can have," Lucius says. He stretches with arms far in the air as if reaching behind himself. When done stretching, his recoil appears more like a flop with a slap to his thigh. "That's okay, baby," he says, and turns his head back while smiling. "I'll drink your portion today."

She says, "You two are so facetious."

"Maybe a little," Lucius teases.

She says, "I don't mind if you drink it. I think you deserve a good cup of coffee. Just give me a kiss afterwards, so at least I can have a small taste."

Lucius chuckles. "I'll be happy to oblige you with the request."

Dextorus rolls his eyes. "*Ugh.* I don't like to hear about what goes on between couples. It just sounds gross to me. Kind of like how you were massaging each other's backs last night."

Lucius laughs inwardly and says, "Oh yeah, that was a good back massage last night. I feel much better."

Josephine and Lucius both begin to laugh quietly from what they think is an inside joke between them.

Dextorus walks off. "Yuck. Kissing again and with morning breath too."

When he hears Dextorus's response, Lucius says, "I might have got carried away with the therapy of my wife last night." He turns around, whispers over his baby while Josephine is breast-feeding, says, "I think they heard me enjoying my beautiful wife last night. Oh well, Daddy loves Momma. All is fair within closed doors between a husband and a wife."

Josephine says, "If they're gonna be right outside the door every night, we're gonna have to work something out with them like we did on Earth."

Lucius says, "I'll talk to them. We'll have our privacy." Lucius walks over to the other side of the bed and gives Josephine an open mouth kiss. "I don't care about morning breath."

When he is done kissing her, she says, "I want you to do that again, but with a coffee taste on your tongue next time."

"Yes, Ma'am." He says, "When I'm healed, I can make it where you can have coffee while breastfeeding."

Josephine smiles, "Really? Lucius you're awesome."

Lucius kisses her again, and says, "I know." He stands and begins to exit the room. "I'll see you in a minute. I'll ask Charony to come in here if she's finished eating, so you can join me for breakfast when you're done, Momma."

"Okay," she answers.

Artie's Pita Bread

Set Aside Ingredients
4 1/4 cup All-purpose flour
2 tsp   Salt

Main Ingredients Mixture
1 cup   Lukewarm water
1 cup   Lukewarm milk
2 tsp   Dry yeast
1 tbsp   All-purpose flour
2 tsp   Sugar

Extra Ingredients
2 tbsp   Olive oil

Combine the, Set Aside Ingredients, together with a whisk, and then set aside.

In a mixing bowl, add and mix the, Main Ingredients Mixture, and then set aside for 10-15 minutes to let yeast activate. Wet dough should become fluffy on top, yeast is activated. Add the olive oil along with all the, Set Aside Ingredients, and knead for about 12-15 minutes.

In a lightly greased large bowl, place the kneaded dough inside and cover. Set aside for 1 hour.

After setting for 1 hour, cut dough into 8-10 equal amounts.

On a lightly floured work space, roll each portioned section into 6-8 inch circles.

Place rolled dough to the side and cover, allow dough to rise for another 30 minutes.

In a lightly greased or grease sprayed skillet, cook each pita on medium-high heat for 20-30 seconds on each side, continually flip until completely puffed and cooked. If pita does not puff, increase heat slightly.

Enjoy!

Lucius's Cheesy Cream Eggs

8	Eggs
1/4 c	Heavy whipping cream
1/2 c	Shredded cheese
1/4 c	Sweet onion
3	Cloves of garlic
1 tsp	Favorite steak seasoning
1 tsp	Salt
1/2 tsp	Dill weed
1 tbsp	Olive oil

Mince the garlic well and dice the sweet onions into small squares. In a skillet, add oil, diced onions, and minced garlic. Cook on medium-high heat until golden in color. In a bowl, add the seasonings and add the eggs. Partially mix the eggs to break the yolks. Add the partially blended, seasoned eggs to the skillet with the cooked onions and garlic. When the eggs begin to cook, add the heavy whipping cream and mix well.

Just before the eggs are completely done, add the cheese and fold into the eggs.

Quickly remove from the heat to prevent overcooking the eggs. Makes 4 servings.

Enjoy!

Alethea Stauron has moved mountains since her time as a registered nurse. Diving into different cultures during her studies and with a passion for community, she's traveled around the world and lived along the east coast and mid-west of the United States. Four countries and forty states were either hiked or called home (including San Antonio, Texas!) before she became a full-time designer of worlds as a novelist. In fact, the Weapon of War series was completely written as one whole story before the prologue was added. Each book in the series stays true to the story, engulfing readers into a fully developed realm on a mind-bending experience that never releases tension…until the end. When Alethea isn't writing, she's cooking up signature dishes, forging new relationships, or taking in the adventure of life where it blossoms.

ALETHEA STAURON

IGNITING THE
PHOENIX

WEAPON OF WAR • BOOK ONE

ALETHEA STAURON

ASHES
REMAIN

WEAPON OF WAR • BOOK TWO

ALETHEA STAURON

RED DAWN
RISING

WEAPON OF WAR • BOOK THREE

ALETHEA STAURON

ABDUCTED

WEAPON OF WAR • BOOK FOUR

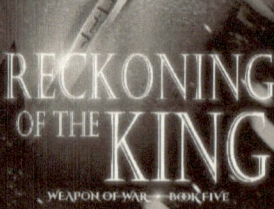

ALETHEA STAURON

RECKONING
OF THE KING

WEAPON OF WAR • BOOK FIVE

ALETHEA STAURON

PRINCIPALITY
WARS

WEAPON OF WAR • BOOK SIX

ALETHEA STAURON

SHADOW
CLUSTER

WEAPON OF WAR • BOOK SEVEN

www.ingramcontent.com/pod-product-compliance
Lightning Source LLC
Chambersburg PA
CBHW060415030726
47495CB00003B/586